SOMEDAY, SOMEWHERE

Holly sat back on her heels and looked at the painting. How beautiful he was, how wicked his smile. It could not be, of course.

She pulled herself up as if she were an old woman and climbed the stairs to the attic. The paintings were still there; they had not been dream or a nightmare. She turned a second, a third and she gasped. They were, for the most part, large canvasses, and yes, the child Holly was in several of them.

But she did not dominate the paintings. Each and every one of the paintings featured one man. In turns he was thoughtful, joyful, desolate, mischievous and he was Blaise Fougère, indubitably the greatest tenor France had ever produced and possibly the greatest French singer of all time.

About the author

Eileen Ramsay was born in Scotland and has lived and
worked in both Washington DC and California. Several
of her historical novels were published before she wrote
Someday, Somewhere. She and her husband, a scientist,
now live in an old house in Angus, Scotland.

Someday, Somewhere

Eileen Ramsay

coronet

CORONET BOOKS
Hodder & Stoughton

First published in Great Britain in 2003 by Hodder and Stoughton
A Division of Hodder Headline
First published in paperback in Great Britain in 2003
by Hodder and Stoughton
A Coronet paperback

5 7 9 10 8 6

A CIP catalogue record for this title
is available from the British Library

ISBN 0 340 82573 1

Typeset in Linotype Plantin Light by
Hewer Text Ltd, Edinburgh
Printed and bound in Great Britain by
Mackays of Chatham Ltd, Chatham, Kent

Hodder & Stoughton
A division of Hodder Headline
338 Euston Road
London NW1 3BH

For my favourite tenor, my husband, Ian

ACKNOWLEDGEMENTS

This book could not have been written without the help of very many people, most of whom I do not know. Some of them wrote books that I have read over the years: among these are *Canaletto* by J.G. Link, *Caravaggio* by Helen Langton, *David Donaldson* by W. Gordon Smith, *Veronese* by Clare Robertson, *Constable, the Man and his Art* by Ronald Parkinson, the excellent Doris Kindersley book on *Titian*, and *Drawing and Painting the Portrait* by John Divan. The art teacher in this novel uses a phrase that belongs to the great painter and teacher David Donaldson. It was told to me by former students and is in the wonderful book by W. Gordon Smith and I hope they will all forgive me for using it.

I have to thank, too, The Friends of Scottish Opera for study days and all the companies here and elsewhere who have shared their art with me.

My thanks to my friends Sister Meeda Inglis who tried to teach me about light, Alison Prince who answered questions about the Slade and Bill Littlejohn, RSA, RGI, RSW.

Very special thanks to my friend Catriona Campbell who made me believe I could write about a painter and who tried to teach me the importance of seemingly empty spaces! Have I got that wrong again?

Dr James Inglis, as always, answers all my questions about medicine.

G. Fraser Ritchie kindly researched and helped with questions relating to the law. Any error here is mine.

Grateful thanks too to Pascal Iovanovitch, and very special thanks to Chantal Underwood for sharing memories of her childhood in Paris and for the crash course in French! Any mistakes here are mine.

Thanks to Brian Osborne, Arbroath librarians as always, and very special thanks to Yvonne Monks of Dundee City Library Reference Room, the Imperial War Museum, the National Library of Scotland, and the London Academy of Music. Ian Kirkby of the Edinburgh Reference Library was unfailingly helpful.

Thanks to David Spink of Zigzac Computers who saved my sanity at great risk to his own.

And to my agent, Teresa Chris – *merci mille fois*.

1

<Ornamental divider>

Torry Bay, 1998

Everything, darling Holly, that you find in the cottage is yours to do with as you think best. I made a pact – but no one is alive now who cares one way or the other.

Holly looked up at the cottage that she had once considered her second home. Aunt Tony was dead – the awful news was beginning to sink in – and now this cottage, where she had had so many wonderful holidays, was hers, but it would never be the same, not without Tony, her ghastly cigarettes, her far from fashionable clothes and her boyish haircut.

The building was as it had always been, a small squat structure that looked as if it had been set down in the bay and then patted firmly on the head by a kind but giant hand, so that the base seemed to have spread out slightly farther than the edges of the roof. It was, it seemed to say, there to stay and would withstand the storms that raged around it during the winter months and would bask in the heat of the sun that played on its white walls in the summer. The petunias in the window boxes suffered no matter the weather, but on the few days when everything was perfect they rewarded the careless gardener with an almost embarrassing exuberance of colour.

A scrabbling sound on the roof distracted her and she looked up. A young seagull had landed on the incongruity of the large window that Tony had had inserted into the roof so that there was some light in her studio. Holly half laughed, half sobbed as the young bird scrambled wildly to keep his balance as he slid inexorably down the sheet of glass. Just before he reached the base he obviously remembered that he could fly and took off into the air with an angry squawk. Young birds had been doing that almost as long as Holly could remember.

She sighed and took the keys out of her handbag. Keeping the cottage was out of the question, no matter how it called to her. Glasgow was where she worked and she did not earn enough to keep two places going. The cottage would have to go, but first she would take away one or two of the things she had loved as a child. The old armchair where Tony had died would be first on the list. A thousand happy memories were in that chair. It would go in her bedroom in her thoroughly modern apartment. One day soon it would be a feature in her home, hers and John's.

Holly turned the key in the lock and, pushing back a sob, opened the door and stood in the doorway waiting just as she had always waited, looking, listening, smelling, assessing. The past, with all its happy memories, drifted out with the dust sprites to meet her. To the left was the main room, the living room which doubled as a dining room, ahead of her the almost perpendicular staircase to the bedrooms and the bathroom that huddled together under the roof and, to the right, the tiny kitchen. Some time in the last twenty years Tony had had a wall knocked through to the old washhouse so that she would no longer have to challenge the elements to do her washing.

All mod cons, darling girl.

But no, there was no time to wallow. The school had been so kind about giving her a few days to go off to Argyll to arrange the funeral but it would not be too happy if this second visit to close the cottage extended into another week. She would be ruthlessly efficient. Her flat was too small to take many of the loved items; after all, some of John's things would be coming soon too. John loathed what he called 'old tat'. She would look round and, no matter how forcibly her heart told her to keep and cherish some valueless treasures, she would dispose of them; silly to keep junk for memory's sake. John, however, would understand that she had to have some souvenirs; he loved her, didn't he, and would want her to be happy. She would make quick decisions; pack the items she just must keep before going back to the city. That's where her life was, no matter how unsatisfactory.

We write our own scripts, darling girl.

The voice was so clear that she started: Tony might

3

have been standing at her elbow, just as she had been so many times for over thirty years. Holly smiled and closed the door behind her. The living room of the cottage was just as it had always been: two huge shabby armchairs in front of the fire, another in the window looking not at the fire but out to the beach, a table with two chairs . . . Two? One for Tony and one for Holly. As far back as she could remember there had only ever been two people in the cottage, herself and Tony.

Don't be childish, Holly, she scolded herself. Tony must have had friends from the village.

Of course. Mrs Fraser from the shop. She would have to go up to the village to see her, to ask her if she would like some memento. Who else? The canon? How real he was and yet Holly had never met him and he was dead now, had been dead a long time, although he would live for ever in the magnificent portraits that Tony had painted of him.

Tony had learned to drive some time in the sixties and had always met her waif of a niece at the station in Glasgow. For me, Holly had thought with childish satisfaction, she learned to drive for me.

'I know there are closer stations, darling girl, but we are so privileged to be able to drive through Argyll.'

Holly had loved those drives in that ancient car. What kept it going? Prayers probably, more than science, but what joy those drives had been, what fun they had had, talking and singing and stopping abruptly to drink in a view.

'Holly, look at the light on the sea.'

'So blue, isn't it?'

'No, it's not, see – it's lilac . . . and pink. Look with all your senses, Holly, not just your eyes.'

Sometimes, if the weather was right, they would stop for a picnic on a bank of purple heather. How that heather scratched, but views like those were worth a little discomfort; Tony never remembered clever things like blankets.

Holly went back to her inventory. There, against the wall, was the settee that was never used, the bookcase with its eclectic collection of books under the window, the ornaments, the vases and the oil lamps. For the first time she realised that the lamps had Tiffany shades. That would please John. She sighed. John: John who was the major part of her unsatisfactory life. She would not think about him now. There was too much to do and too little time in which to do it.

Instinctively she looked at the mantelpiece and smiled with relief. The clock was still there, the beautiful gilded girl holding up her pendulum, as she had held it all through Holly's childhood. The pendulum was motionless but Holly remembered a time when she had eaten something that disagreed with her and Tony had carried the clock upstairs to the little room under the eaves where the young Holly had gone to sleep, lulled by the swinging pendulum and the soft tick-tock. The adult Holly looked at the clock with John's eyes and saw that it was valuable, but she would not sell, she would keep it. Perhaps one day, if they didn't wait too long, there would be a little John to soothe to sleep.

She picked up her overnight bag and went upstairs. Her room was just as she had left it. Damn, damn, damn. When had she last spent more than an afternoon in this cottage? John did not want to 'waste time in the wilds of Scotland', and so for almost five years she had made little effort to see the person who meant more to her than anyone else in the world. She lay down on the bed under the window and wept, as copiously as the child Holly had wept but with a woman's damaged heart. Had she known Tony was failing she would have come: John would have come. He was not so selfish. But Tony had never complained, never fussed.

'Young people in love, darling girl. I know all about that. Don't worry about me. Come when you can. This is your home, you know.'

She had meant to make the journey but she never had. Tony, who knew nothing whatsoever about being madly in love with the most unsatisfactory person, who knew nothing about love at all, had absolved her niece of all guilt.

Holly slept and when she woke in the dark room she did not for a moment remember where she was. She turned and lay on her back and looked at the night outside her window as she had done so often growing up. She heard her own voice from the past.

'Don't draw the curtains, Aunt Tony. I want to see the stars moving.'

No stars this evening but time itself seemed to be rushing past the window. John expected her to be away for only one night and now, stupidly and childishly, she had slept hours away. She would get something to eat and then continue her inventory. He missed her when she was not there, he said. She refused to question how John could miss her if he was often too busy to see her when she was there.

He is working hard so that we can marry soon, she told herself.

Downstairs she lit the oil lamps because they were so much friendlier than the electric light that Tony had installed in the seventies and then went into the kitchen and fought with the cooker until eventually she found which button went with which plate. She made instant coffee and ate bread and cheese and fruit sitting at the table looking out onto the beach. The moon was high and it played on the soft surface of the sea. Sometimes its rays darted in the window and doused the stones and shells on the window ledge with soft pale light. The stones. The shells. Every holiday they had collected them and one had been selected to sit on the window ledge.

Holly 1966 . . . Holly 1970.

The dates went on. None had been thrown away as soon as the child Holly had been taken back to Glasgow and put on the train or the plane that would take her to be deposited once again in her boarding school or with her rather overwhelmed parents.

Holly piled her dishes into the sink – she would wash all the dishes at one time – and went back upstairs. She would choose some things from the bedrooms. If she kept the chair and the Tiffany lamp, the clock, some books, an ornament or two, things that whispered, 'Tony', perhaps her flat would remind her of Achaho-ish and Torry Bay.

The main bedroom was as it had always been. It held the large comfortable bed with its pile of pillows, the chair, the wardrobe with Tony's clothes, and her dressing-table. Holly stared at the dressing-table that was so neat when Tony had been so unbelievably untidy. What was it that was so different about this dressing-table? That was it. Every other dressing-table she had ever seen had at least one photograph on it but Tony had no framed photographs.

'The people I love are in my heart, Holly. I don't need photographs.'

'People? But there aren't people, Tony. There's only me.'

She heard again her jealous childish voice and she saw again Tony's smile.

'Of course there's you, darling girl,' Tony had said, lighting a cigarette. 'Now don't tell Iron Girder that I'm still smoking like an old chimney.'

The young Holly had laughed guiltily because, really, Aunt Tony must not call Mummy Iron Girder. Her name was Gilda. She had forgotten that Tony had not agreed that there were no other people in her heart. But they were all dead now: Daddy, who had never quite lived up to his own expectations of himself, Mummy, and Tony herself.

One by one she opened the drawers. There would be nothing that she would want to keep here. Tony had been small and dainty – beside her, Holly had some-times felt large and ungainly although she was barely five foot five herself – all Tony had ever worn were her oversized shirts and paint-marked jeans and occasion-ally a flamboyant flowing skirt. Holly would take every-thing to a charity shop, perhaps in Glasgow – she no longer knew anyone here in Achahoish. Tony's old friends, whom she had met from time to time, were all dead, except for the doctor who had retired to Spain and had felt too old and too sad to come to the service. Maybe one day she would write to him or go to see him, but what would she say? 'Do you remember me? I used to visit my aunt. You took a fishing hook out of my ear once.'

No, he would not care. Why should he?

She was faintly surprised to find a lovely evening stole and she held its soft fabric against her. It smelled slightly of very expensive perfume, Tony's 'special day' perfume. Perhaps she might keep just this one personal possession although she had never seen Tony wear it. In the bottom of a drawer filled with sketchbooks was a large box tied up with string, and on top was a sealed envelope with 'Holly' written on it in Tony's elegant hand. She picked it up, opened it, and a large old-fashioned key fell out.

Darling girl,
Everything in the boxes is for you. Enjoy them.
The key is to the attic and that's where I keep the
work that I never wanted to sell in my lifetime. But,

9

as I stated in my will, do what you like with them now. I hope you will keep one or two to remember.

Yours, with all love,

Tony

Her work. Tony had been a painter: one, moreover, who sold what she painted. Holly's father had never quite come to terms with having a painter for a sister, so Bohemian. But Holly knew that her aunt had trained at a world-famous art school in London and had had several shows until the seventies, when she had stopped exhibiting. Her shows were the only times she left Torry Bay. She put her beautiful landscapes, the odd portrait of a local worthy, into the trunk of her funny old car, drove to London or Glasgow or Edinburgh, handed over the work, and returned as soon as she could get away.

That stole must have been what she wore to openings. Her one bit of glam. I can just hear them: 'Here comes old Tony Noble in her ancient stole, poor old thing.'

But this note, this note that she was holding to her face as if it were Tony herself, was saying that there was other work.

Holly put the large box to one side – she would look at it later – and went out on to the landing. There were four doors at the top of the stairs: Tony's room, Holly's room, the bathroom and the attic.

It was as if the lock had not been turned in some time, for it was difficult to turn the key but eventually the door opened and again Holly was assailed by memories. The air in the dimly lit room was stale; it smelled of disuse but above all it smelled of paint. Memories of a pig-tailed Holly standing in a swimsuit daubing paint on a canvas while Tony stood beside her and made wonderful swirls of blue and pink and grey which somehow metamorphosed into hills and the sea and the village over there across the bay. There was only one easel there now. Tony had long ago agreed that Holly's genius, if it existed at all, did not lie in paint pots.

'But there is something, darling girl, and we'll find it. Don't listen to those teachers. What do they know?'

The teachers had known and Tony had not. There was no genius lurking in Holly Noble. Antonia Noble was the family genius.

Holly smiled as again she saw her aunt in her jeans and her oversized shirt, cigarette (often unlit) hanging from her lip, painting, painting, painting. She looked around at the bare walls and the huge window which Tony had had put into the roof. During the day or on a bright starry night the electric light was hardly necessary and, by the light of the moon, Holly saw bulky sheet-wrapped shapes that had to be the canvasses mentioned in the letter. They were everywhere. She walked over to those directly under the window and knelt beside them for a moment.

'The work that I never wanted to sell in my lifetime.'

They must be of me. But she couldn't have painted – Holly looked around wildly; there were canvasses everywhere – thirty, forty paintings of me? She gave them to Mummy, anyway, didn't she? Holly drew back the sheet that covered the pile beside which she was kneeling. The paintings still mocked her. Their faces were turned modestly away from the prying eyes of their public. She stood up and turned the first one around. For a second she was relieved. It was one of Tony's wonderful seascapes, that was all. What had she expected?

Not this, not this stunning vision of a sea such as she, Holly, had never seen and, in the middle, a boy, a youth, a satyr, difficult to tell. His green eyes gleamed at her from his perch on the back of a whale. The youth's face was vaguely familiar. No, it could not possibly be . . . Holly turned on the light and the harsh modernity of electricity banished the moonlight and Holly blinked.

Damn this light. Damn this room; it was so small. This was a large painting and she had to see it better. Holly manhandled the painting down the stairs and into the living room where she propped it against the dresser. She went round the room turning on every lamp and then she stood back and looked again at the painting. Yes, a seascape, and a mythological story; an old, often told story, 'The Boy on a Dolphin'. The boy's eyes smiled at her out of a tanned face of almost amazing beauty. A working title was written on the back in Tony's flamboyant hand: *Sea Sprite*: London 1937.

Holly sat back on her heels and looked at the painting. How beautiful he was, how wicked his smile. It could not be, of course; not that she had seen too many paintings of him, or photographs. Besides, it was impossible. *Sea Sprite*, 1937. Where was Tony in 1937? At the Slade. And he, the boy, the sea sprite? 'No,' she said loudly this time so that there could be no doubt. But it was.

Tentatively Holly reached out a hand that was shaking but she did not touch the picture.

Oil on your fingers, darling girl.

She pulled herself up as if she were an old woman and climbed the stairs to the attic. The paintings were still there; they had not been a dream or a nightmare. She turned a second, a third, and she gasped. They were, for the most part, large canvasses, and yes, the child Holly was in several of them. But she did not dominate the paintings. Each and every one of the paintings she uncovered featured one man. In turns he was thoughtful, joyful, desolate, mischievous: he was Blaise Fougère, indubitably the greatest tenor France had ever produced and possibly the greatest French singer of all time.

With a cry of pain Holly turned off the lights and, locking and closing the door behind her, ran back downstairs. It was still there, *Sea Sprite*, and the beautiful eyes, mocking, yes, they were mocking, looked straight at her.

. . . as near as I can get to where I want to be.

Holly had almost forgotten that throwaway line. She looked across at the sideboard where she had put the casket that she had carried with her from Glasgow. No, said Holly, and again, no. She loved me and she loved

Torry Bay. This is where she wanted to be buried.

'Tomorrow, Tony, I'll take your ashes up to the little headland and I'll scatter them. That's what you wanted.' She spoke directly to the urn.

Tony, vibrant, wonderful Tony reduced to a few handfuls of dust.

Sea Sprite, 1937.

Just before the war. Did they worry about war? Did he, this sprite? The sea was so real she could almost smell the tang. If she touched the painting the spray would dampen her hand. She looked into the green eyes. They did not mock. They were smiling at the artist. What did they say?

'I know you. I love you.'

For a moment Holly felt like a voyeur, as if she were looking at something private and holy, and she had no right, no right at all.

'There's only me, Tony.'

The painting told her that part of her life was a lie. Tony might have been everything to her but she was not everything to Tony. Antonia Noble, beloved spinster aunt who had lived alone in this cottage, happy to wait for visits from her niece, had had another very different life. How well that secret had been kept. Holly had lived with her on and off all her life because her parents, missionaries, had been overseas. There had never been anyone else there, never, ever, and certainly not this man.

Holly looked at the kneeling figure and he looked back at her.

Hollyberry.

Who spoke, who spoke?

She was my aunt, she was adamant: I would have known. She would have told me. Holly looked at her watch. This was madness. It was after midnight but she had to see them, had to find out. She went back to the attic and one by one she unwrapped as many of the paintings as she could reach easily and, to her, it was obvious that these were not the paintings of a diseased mind. These were not a lonely, frustrated, sex-starved old woman's paintings of the man on whom she had an unhealthy and secret crush.

These were named and dated. *Blaise, Kensington Gardens*, 1938; *Blaise, Paris*, 1954; *Blaise, Torry Bay*, 1969; *Blaise*, 1990. Blaise, Blaise, Blaise.

She knew little of opera singers but he had been so famous – a household name – and so the world knew that 1990 was just before his death.

Holly looked at the paintings in which she featured. In one he was holding her hand and she was dancing into the sea beside him, at ease, content: she had met him, known him, and she did not remember.

With a stifled cry Holly threw the sheets over the brilliant images. She had to get away from them. She locked the door and stood leaning against it for a moment with her heart thumping madly against her ribs. Tony and Blaise Fougère.

'The people I love are in my heart.'

Tony Noble and Blaise Fougère had known each other for over fifty years; the paintings showed an intimacy, knowledge. They were paintings of a man by a woman who loved him and, from the light in his eyes in the paintings, who had been loved by him. A secret life. How could Tony Noble have known Blaise Fougère so intimately for over fifty years and no one had known? No, it was impossible. Fougère was world-famous. For a time so had Tony been. The press would have known, would have ferreted it out, would have emblazoned their love across the tabloids.

But the pictures were not lying. They were too . . . intimate to be fantasy. Holly retreated downstairs. There she curled up in the big armchair – he had been painted relaxing in it – and she looked out over the water to the hills beyond. The moon laid a carpet of silver from the sky to the sea and then across the surface of the sea to the beach.

The fairy's path.

How Tony had loved that view and how she had loved to tease her brother, Holly's father, the arch-bishop in fact, the Reverend Frederick Noble.

'I to the hills will lift mine eyes,' she had managed to quote at least once on each of the few occasions that her brother had visited her. 'From whence will come mine aid.'

'Really, Antonia, how many times must I tell you that it's a question. From whence will come mine aid? The hills are full of bandits.'

'Not these ones,' Tony had retorted.

Now, thinking of them, one whom she had loved so dearly and the other whom she had tried so hard to respect and love, Holly sighed. They were both dead, her father aware too late that he had never really known his own daughter, and Tony whom Holly thought she had known so well and had never known at all.

Blaise Fougère? I knew she liked opera. She introduced me to it. She played records – did she play Fougère's? She went to the opera in London or Glasgow when she was showing, but this . . . ? I knew him when I was small and obviously liked him. But did I? There is no memory. Yes. Tony would never lie.

Her life was a lie.

Was he the reason why, when I was older, my visits had to be rearranged sometimes? He wouldn't want me to see him if they were keeping their relationship a secret, but why? Why didn't they marry? He was French. Was he Catholic? Tony never worried about labels. Perhaps he did. He was married to someone else? But why didn't he get a divorce? The Catholic business, I suppose. This painting is dated 1937. Did people care more about divorce in those days?

Holly got up and made herself another cup of coffee. She could barely assimilate what she had learned. Never ever had she thought of a man in connection with her aunt. Even when her parents had muttered things about wishing Antonia would find someone nice and stop living such an unconventional life, she had reflected complacently that Tony loved her, Holly, and therefore had absolutely no need of anyone else. And all the time Tony had been in love with Blaise Fougère.

No, that could not be. An affair? Tony? Eccentric

Aunt Tony had had a relationship with a world-famous man. Possible? No, they could never have kept it a secret. But those paintings? Even examined by moonlight they showed a man who loved the artist who was painting him. Holly knew enough about art to know that. She took her coffee and went back upstairs. Perhaps the boxes would yield some clues.

She opened them on the bed and was glad that she was sitting; her knees would never have stood up to this new shock. Tiffany's windows were nothing. The boxes contained jewellery, expensive, custom-made jewellery: diamonds, emeralds, sapphires and gold bracelets. There was a note.

He was a very naïve man in many ways, Holly. He could not believe that some women don't like jewellery. He was incredibly generous to everyone – charities, of course, but he loved giving and when he made a great deal of money he spent it on presents. I gave up arguing with him and wore the jewellery when I was with him. The rubies are my favourites: they look fabulous with jeans! No pearls. Pearls are tears. He did not want to give me tears.

Holly picked up the necklace and bracelet made of rubies. The precious stones formed the centres of tiny gold flowers and were surprisingly delicate.

'But not with jeans, Tony,' she said as she held them for a moment close against her heart and incidentally against her one piece of good jewellery: the pearls John had given her on their fifth anniversary.

The rubies, whatever John said, she would keep.

What on earth was she going to do? She had faced the prospect of losing the cottage and had accepted that. Life moved on and one had to leave people and places behind. But now there were the paintings that had to be worth something and the jewellery and even the furniture that her child's eye had not recognised as anything special.

I suppose that I am now a rich woman. John will be pleased.

But thoughts of John's pleasure did not thrill Holly. She almost wished the solicitors had not given her the letter with the will. She did not want Blaise Fougère's jewels and she did not want his paintings.

'Do what you like with them.'

But what do you want me to do with them, Tony? You say that you hope I'll keep a few. I will but I can't house all of them and . . . they're important, aren't they? You were a more than respected painter and he was, well, he was who he was. John will be very practical and say things like, 'This will make a great deal of difference to our plans: we won't have to wait now.' But I wanted to marry him yesterday when we had nothing. By my standards I am now wealthy. What would the Director of Education say if I resigned?

But she could not do that. She loved children. Oh, how much she had grown to love other people's children. But now . . . No, too much to think about. One step at a time. She had to put the cottage on the market and the next step would be John. Again Holly lifted up the glittering rubies, the little drops of blood that sparkled and winked at her.

Shall I keep you? Shall I wear you or will you only speak to me of another side of my beloved Tony and the lies we have all lived?

It was now so late that the only sensible thing to do was to go to bed. The paintings had waited – some of them – for many years. They could wait another night.

Holly woke very early next morning and was aware of a feeling of deep happiness. She stretched her hand out for John but met the edge of the bed and, for a moment, was disappointed. Then she remembered: she was at Torry Bay.

She sat up but it was too dark to see out of the window and so she lay down again and curled herself up into a happy little ball.

'Perfect, perfect.'

No, it was not perfect, for she was here only because Tony was dead. Tony, her wonderful aunt, who had made total joy out of an unsatisfactory childhood, was gone for ever. This house was full of her. She could call, 'Tony', and a voice would answer, 'In the studio, darling girl.' There she would be painting, painting, her cigarette hanging unlit from her lip. Unlit. Of course it was unlit. She loved a singer, a tenor, for God's sake, the most delicate plant in the operatic garden.

And I never guessed. What a self-absorbed little snot I must have been.

Perhaps all children are self-centred. Holly knew lots of children; hundreds had passed through her care. Were they self-absorbed? She uncurled herself and turned over on to her back. She lay and looked at the ceiling and as dawn came up light began to stretch across the room; her lovely perfect room where she had always been so happy. But nothing is perfect. There was a damp patch in the corner. It would be better to get the roof mended before putting the cottage on the market.

Then she remembered that she need not sell the cottage if she did not want to. She could keep it. She and John could come here. She could hear herself selling him the idea.

It will be a perfect place to get away from it all, John.

John wanted to go into local and then national politics. Holly lay and painted a rosy picture of Mr and Mrs Robertson with their daughter, no, their son, their son and daughter. She groaned and turned into the pillow, her whole body aching for John – or was she aching for the baby John could give her? She thought too much in this place, felt too much.

Please, John, there are so few years left for babies.

It was over two years since she had spoken of a marriage date and the prospect of a family because John had been hurt and angry when she had tentatively suggested a legalisation of their position. She had apologised, of course. She had agreed with him that, no, she did not need children to prove that she was worthwhile, that she was a fully functioning woman. No, she did not see him merely as a carrier and then a donor of sperm. She loved him, adored him. She just had this picture of a happy family, father, mother, child, all loving, caring, functioning together and apart, and yes, she was prepared to wait for that until the time was right.

That had been the beginning of the doubts that attacked her in the middle of lonely nights. How long had it taken her to appreciate that she had done nothing for years but work and minister to John's needs? But people liked their politicians married and with children. Everything would be all right, thanks to Tony and her unexpected generosity.

It will be perfect. Holly smiled. And I'll teach the children to swim and sail right here at Achahoish.

The future looked as rosy as the sky. Holly almost jumped out of bed and her bare toes met the cold floor. Carpeting. She began her list. Next chore – no, it was not a chore – was to ring John and bring him up to date.

He sounded as if he were in the next room. 'How are things, Holly? Have you talked to an estate agent yet? I hoped you would be on your way home.'

She wrapped a blanket round her. September in Scotland might look nice but it was cold. She laughed. Surely the jewellery would not be worth that much, but maybe.

'What's funny?'

'Nothing, sweetheart, and no, I haven't seen anyone

yet. I fell asleep.' She waited for the explosion but it did not come.

'Get someone in today, and get the place on the market.' He stopped talking and she could see him, mastering himself, trying hard to be supportive. 'Did you find anything you want to keep? I hope she didn't have a grand piano you just have to have.'

He knew there was no piano.

'I want a chair.'

There was silence while his quick mind surveyed his memories of the cottage furniture. 'You have got to be kidding, a chair; but come home. My bed looks so empty. You could be here with me, waking up together.'

She would not think about beds either.

'John, maybe I won't bring the chair—' she began. She had to tell him she wanted to, intended to keep the cottage.

'Great,' he interrupted. 'I mean the furniture was lovely, but not for our dream flat.'

'You're right, so I'll leave it and we'll enjoy it here.'

Now he did explode. 'Damn it to hell, Holly. I told you a thousand times we have to watch every penny. One day we'll have a beach house but at the right beach.'

Her turn to interrupt. 'John, I can afford the cottage. Tony left some paintings in her studio. Remember the landscape I sold when my parents died.' She did not mean to say it, but out it came. 'The one that I used to help with your down payment; ten thousand pounds.

That was five years ago. There are maybe forty paintings.'

His voice was excited. 'Ten times forty? Four hundred thousand pounds. Christ.' He was quiet, stunned perhaps as he tried to assimilate the news. 'No, they can't be worth that, Holly. Grow up, for God's sake. They're the ones she couldn't sell.'

'I can't hear you. My battery's shot,' said Holly and disconnected.

She had never hung up on him before. In fact she had never hung up on anyone before.

It's the air.

Holly was laughing as she hurried downstairs. By the time she had had two cups of coffee she was ashamed of herself but consoled herself by thinking that she could ring John when he got back from the office. It had not been a great idea to call him early. He was never at his best on a weekday morning. Saturday and Sunday mornings were different. He was definitely at his best then. She smiled reminiscently, rinsed her cup out – how decadent – and went upstairs to shower and dress. No shower.

The list again. Carpet. Shower.

She had to get back to school. Other people's children. There is nothing wrong with wanting children before my biological clock cuts off and no, I do not have to have a child to fulfil myself as a woman.

So there.

She needed to find out about the paintings. She went to Tony's room and opened the drawer again, the one that held the boxes of jewellery and the sketchpads. Tony had made notes on some of her sketches. She did not particularly relish one on a sketch of her and John.

'When will she learn?'

She didn't like it and it made her mad, mad as hell. How dare Tony who knew zilch . . .

But Tony had known.

She leafed through the sketchbooks and laughed and cried as she saw her parents, herself, and Blaise, Blaise, Blaise. The canon who had been Tony's friend and whom she had painted, the doctor, the old woman who used to run the village shop, her swans, horrible birds – swans, lovely to look at but . . .

Faithful unto death.

Was she hearing things? Who had said that? It had to be something she had read somewhere she supposed. She put the books back and closed the drawer. Downstairs again she went through Tony's drawers. She needed the number of an art gallery whom Tony had dealt with. An expert would have to come and value the paintings. Then the jewellery; she would have that valued before she sold it.

Otto von Emler. There was the name in Tony's address book. It rang a bell; possibly she had heard Tony speak about her agent. He, of all people, would know the value of Antonia Noble's paintings. Holly panicked. It was too soon. She could not start to sell them before she had assimilated the fact that they were there. She had to find out something about Fougère. She had to talk, face to face, with John, ask for his

25

advice. He was, she supposed, her lawyer, although Tony's Edinburgh lawyer had been rather sweet.

She would leave the paintings here while she came to terms with their existence. As for the jewellery, the lawyer would have a place to keep it until she arranged for it to be sold. The rubies. She would keep the rubies.

'Perfect with jeans.'

Like hell, Tony. Holly started to laugh, ran upstairs and got out the jewel boxes. The rubies winked and cajoled her. With shaking hands she put them on.

Where could Tony Noble and a world-famous French tenor have met?

Where?

2

London, 1937
SEA SPRITE

May was the most beautiful month of the year. She would paint it so that everyone else would be compelled to agree. London was incomparable among world cities – she said this even although it was the only one she had ever seen – and in May, well, quite simply, it was breathtakingly beautiful. The streets were hazy with a magical light that turned the buildings to pink or blue or lilac or, surely that was the palest, the faintest green. The trees were in full leaf and the tones of green on London's streets dazzled the eye. In Regent's Park and, no doubt, all the other parks, swans and ducks glided majestically over the glass-like water, then lost their dignity when they waddled up on to the grass.

'Oh, silly, silly swan,' Antonia Noble addressed the rather malevolent eye of a great white bird, 'you really must stay in your element if you want to hide your weaknesses from your admiring public. On dry land, my dear, you look like Uncle Thomas's daily. In a

27

minute you will take a cigarette from under your wing and start puffing it defiantly.'

The swan hissed at her and waddled away.

Tony, who had become Tony as soon as her train from the country had arrived in London, laughed. She was eighteen years old, and studying art in London. Her parents had been absolutely astounded that she had wanted to go to art school. Painting was for Bohemians; it was certainly not for the daughter of a village schoolmaster. Their son was destined for the Church and their daughter should become a schoolteacher.

But she did not want to be a schoolteacher. It seemed to her parents that she had never wanted to do anything that they had wanted her to do. They tried to convince her to conform.

'Get a decent degree, become a teacher, and paint little pictures in your free time. Art school, well, really, Antonia, it sounds so racy.'

But they had capitulated because she had refused point-blank to do anything else. Frederick, thank God for Frederick who could hardly wait to get into college to study Divinity. Then he was determined to go off and find some heathens to convert.

'Poor unhappy heathens,' mused Antonia. 'Watch out or he'll get you,' she shouted and the young couple helping their fat baby throw bread for the ducks frowned at her.

Impossible to explain that she was not talking to their baby.

She walked on happily, swinging her satchel. She had a sandwich – cheese – and an apple. She would eat her lunch when she found a quiet seat in the sun.

There was an iron seat on the path but it would be so much nicer to sit on the grass under the trees. She was still too close to her mother's apron strings. She could hear her voice.

'Stay off the wet grass.'

'Make sure the seat is clean before you sit down.'

Automatically Tony dusted the seat and sat down. She opened her satchel and savoured the smell of bread and cheese and apple. Mrs Lumsden, the landlady in the 'Rooms for Ladies' boarding-house that was a mere step from the British Museum, baked her own bread and she was generous with butter and cheese. Tony was just about to bite into her sandwich with her strong teeth when she became aware of the man.

He was lying on his stomach on the grass reading a book as he propped himself up on very tanned slim arms. He was so engrossed in the book that he had not heard her approach across the grass. She saw his face and knew, without a doubt, that it would haunt her for the rest of her life if she did not sketch it immediately. He was beautiful, with deep-set eyes – she wished she could see them; they would be blue – a straight nose, a high forehead on which black curls tumbled as if they had been artistically arranged and a well-shaped and sensuous mouth, spoiled by the grass he was chewing, but she could leave that out.

She took one healthy bite of her sandwich, put it

down, pulled out her charcoal and began, swiftly, to draw. He was a perfect subject because he did not move. She caught the face – she had to see his eyes, she had to – and then sketched the hand that was holding the book flat in front of him. What a wonderful shape, the fingers long and delicate, the nails clean – how refreshing to see clean nails on a young man – and they were well cut. Perhaps he was a pianist: it was a book of music. No, he was only a boy, but she would know better if she could just see those deep blue eyes.

They were green. What a surprise that was, but immediately she knew that green was just right. He was a sea creature, thrown up by the waves. In another life he had ridden on the backs of whales. That's how she would paint him with his sea-green eyes and his black curls: mystical creature.

'You have permission?' he asked suddenly and she jumped because she had not expected him to talk. He had been so still, a still life in Regent's Park.

'Permission?' she asked stupidly.

'To make my portrait?' he asked again. His voice was strongly accented, French, she thought, but the English was good, if a little archaic.

'No,' she said and knew that she sounded even more stupid than she had sounded a moment ago.

'Then I will have to examine and decide.' He got up in one quick, lithe movement, and she realised that he was tall, too. He towered over her as those beautiful hands held themselves out waiting for the surrender of her sketchbook. She looked at them – she would have to sculpt them – and wordlessly handed him the book.

He sat down again, cross-legged on the grass. He really was incredibly fit. Perhaps he was an athlete because the body was a very good shape: broad shoulders, deep chest and slender hips above those long legs. She stifled a sudden and frightening desire to touch him.

He looked through her sketchbook slowly, methodically. She would learn that he always worked that way.

When he was finished he handed the book back to her and he smiled. How powerful that smile was. It was electric.

'*Bien.*' He nodded his consent. 'You may proceed, but first I shall eat the rest of your sandwich for payment.'

She was confused, floundering. He smiled at her again as if she were a child and picked up her lunch.

'You may have the apple,' he said magnanimously, 'but this bread, the smell came to me across the grass. English bread is without taste, you understand, but this?'

'My landlady bakes it herself.'

'Does she take male students?' He pulled the sandwich into two unequal parts and handed her the smaller part out of which she had taken a bite. 'There, I will not be greedy. I will give you back half.'

Tony looked at her share. His mathematics was not so good as his English. 'No. I mean, thank you for the sandwich and no, it's a hostel for females.'

'Me, I am in a small hotel on the Marylebone Road –

he pronounced it Mary Le Bone – and everything I have ever heard about the cooking of England was written in this hotel.' He had demolished her sandwich.

A hotel? He was on holiday and he would go away and she would never see him again. The world was suddenly bleak.

'Go on,' he said. 'I arrange myself.'

She laughed at him. He wanted to be sketched: he was delighted that she had acknowledged his beauty. None of the boys in the village would have reacted the way this young man did. Already he was folding himself back on to the grass with the book. 'Male students.' Could he be a student and live in a hotel? He would have to be very wealthy. She had never met anyone who was wealthy and so she had no idea whether this young man – what was his name? – was typical.

'Why do you laugh?' He did not move, did not turn.

'Your ego.'

He sat up quickly and looked at her, astonishment in his eyes. 'But the ego is necessary. Why do you say it with the disdain? You must have the ego too, or you will never be a great painter.'

'Oh, yes I will. I'm going to be the greatest.'

He nodded seriously. '*Bien*. That is correct. Without the ego you will not struggle. You say, "I am great," *et voilà*, before you know, you are great, and, more important, the world admits too.'

'Lie down again,' she said and blushed at his wicked smile. 'I don't have too much time.'

He arranged himself and she began sketching again.

What could she say to him? How could she keep him here? How could she keep him? She did not understand but with one glance from those wicked eyes he had enslaved her. Was it terribly rude to ask intimate questions such as, 'Who are you, how long are you going to be in London, will you please stay for ever and ever?'

'What is your book?' she asked lamely.

'It is not, strictly speaking, a book. It is a score, *Lohengrin*.'

She had no idea what he was talking about.

'Wagner,' he said impatiently. 'You have heard of Wagner?'

Of course she had heard of Wagner. 'He's awfully German,' she mumbled.

He threw down the book . . . score. '*Mon Dieu*. He is a composer. What does it matter how German he is, whatever that means? You, Mam'selle, are *awfully* English.'

She laughed. '*Touchée*.'

He sat up again and smiled. It was a relief to see him smiling; she thought she had infuriated him, but she could not sketch while he was sitting cross-legged like a very tall gnome.

'You speak French?'

'No, *touchée* is about it.'

'I will teach you. It is a very civilised language. And now I must go or I will be late for my class.' He gestured vaguely towards the Royal Academy of Music.

He was going. Stunned, she sat and watched him

walk with long strides across the grass. He was going. He was . . . turning. 'Tomorrow,' he called. 'Bring more bread.'

She stood watching until he had disappeared and then she pushed her sketchpad back into her bag and made her own way out of the park. He had a class. She too had a class, but if he had stayed in the park she, without thought of the consequences, would have stayed. Now, without really being aware of what she was doing, she made her way to her bus stop and managed to get on the bus that would take her to Gower Street, to the Slade. The day one meets one's fate is not a day for economies.

That morning, being a student at that most prestigious school had been the most important thing in her life. Now, nothing was relevant, nothing but a boy with green eyes and beautiful hands who had eaten her sandwich and whom she would probably never see again.

She smiled, skipping like a little girl, and the two elderly women sitting on a bench watching the world go by looked at her and remembered past days.

When she reached the studio where she was to have a lesson in anatomy she drew a circle of leaping whales around the figure of the boy. If she painted him she would change them and make him ride the whales across the waves.

Too difficult, she decided, because I sketched him lying down. Now I want him kneeling and laughing with glee but I didn't know that when I started.

She tried to sketch the face from memory, to put the imp of mischief into the green eyes, but although she did manage to get close to the colour she merely made him cross-eyed and was in a thoroughly bad temper when the lecturer deigned to put in an appearance.

Next morning she asked Mrs Lumsden if she might have two sandwiches.

Her landlady, who had tried to serve her some filling porridge, smiled. 'Course you can, love, but don't I keep telling you that if you starts the day with a nice plate of porridge, you'll last through till your dinner time.'

Tony sat down and poured herself a cup of tea from the large pot. 'You're right, of course, Mrs Lumsden, but you do see that that is exactly what my mother always says and I am quite determined to do things my way. Besides, I loathe porridge. One understands about the Scots when one sees porridge. It either looks completely dead or as if it's a bubbling volcano.'

The landlady folded her arms across her massive but shapeless bosom. 'Whatever will you say next, Miss Noble? Better not let any of my Scotch ladies hear you.'

'It'll be our little secret, dear Mrs Lumsden. And I may have two sandwiches today, large ones?' She looked winningly up at her landlady who shook her head and went off into the kitchen to make sandwiches. Her young ladies were well fed and if they chose to eat nothing at breakfast and two huge sandwiches for their lunch that was their prerogative. They were ladies all, even if Miss Noble was a little different, and ladies did things their way.

Ten minutes later she handed Tony a large packet. 'And take two pieces of fruit from the sideboard,' she suggested. 'You mustn't get so fired up with lessons that you neglect your health.'

Tony smiled as she obeyed. Later it would occur to her that it was not strictly ethical to have her landlady feed . . . whoever he was, even if she herself skimped on breakfast to make up, but for now all she could think of was getting through the morning.

Her lecturer's magic wove its usual spell though. He was opinionated but Tony was willing to listen and then to study and think and make up her own mind.

'Reason tells me and everyone else with a perfect eye that Turner is the greatest of all British painters. You will find those who copy Constable – and that will teach something – but Constable is for the amateur, Turner for the professional . . . But if you really want to paint, not just make some pretty daubs of oil on a canvas, study Titian. Go to Italy. Go by bus – a few pounds will take you there. Titian manipulated paint as no one else has ever done. His blues and reds sing. Your red, Miss Noble, is crying out in agony. Relieve its pain.'

She would study Titian. She would study Turner, although his ability to paint the sea terrified her with its power, but she would also study Constable. She liked the canvasses of his that she had already seen, and she would make up her own mind. In the meantime she tried to put her red out of its misery but since she could see nothing wrong with it, except that it did not sing, she failed to please the master. She decided not to ask her father for 'a few pounds'. Titian and Italy would have to wait as she waited now for the lunch break.

Today, of course, several other students stopped her in her flight to ask her to join them, to go later to the National, to continue the argument, Turner versus Constable.

'They're two different painters,' she yelled as she sped down the staircase. 'I love them both.'

And then she was out and the sky was overcast. He would not be there. Dejectedly she sat on the park bench and listlessly chewed a sandwich. 'I should have stayed to fight about Turner,' she told a sparrow and threw him a piece of her bread.

'Who is Turner?' He was there. She had expected yesterday's open-necked short-sleeved shirt but he was bundled up in a heavy dark green sweater.

'You look like a fisherman,' she said and she tried to speak calmly although her heart was beating rapidly as if she had just run for a bus. 'Yesterday I thought you resembled a sea sprite.'

He looked down at his legs. 'I am with too long legs for a sprite, I think,' he said judiciously, 'and you have not answer my question.'

'What is *Lohengrin*?' she said. She could not look at him as he sat down on the bench beside her but she was aware of him, more aware than she had ever been of anyone.

'*Touché*,' he said. 'Now I will tell of *Lohengrin* and

you will tell of Turner but first, have you bring some bread?'

Wordlessly she reached into her bag and took out his sandwich.

'Such a waste of good bread,' he scolded as he spread open the sandwich and scraped off the cheese. He produced a package and when it was opened Tony smelled unknown but tantalising delights. 'I have bring sausage and real cheese,' he said. 'Now throw the inside of yours to these hungry little birds and eat. I have wine also.'

'Wine?' Wine, ginger wine, was something Tony's family had every Christmas. This was not the same thing at all. It was red and smooth and slipped down Tony's throat so easily.

'The civilised way to eat,' he said. 'Bread, sausage, cheese and a glass of wine. Fruit we should have also but all I could find was old and wrinkled.'

'I brought an apple and a pear.'

He examined them critically. '*Bien.* And now I think we should be introduce, don't you think? Who will introduce us? This little sparrow? Monsieur, will you introduce Blaise Fougère to this great artist?'

'How do you do, Mr Fougère,' said Tony gravely and held out her hand.

He took it in his and Tony gasped as the distressing tide flooded her face and neck. What was he doing to her? It must be the wine.

'And you, Mam'selle. You will allow Monsieur Sparrow to make the introduction?'

Oh, if only he would release her hand.

'Antonia Noble,' she said.

'Antoinette. How perfect,' he said.

'Actually I have begun to call myself Tony. I think it sounds like an artist, don't you?'

'I think it sounds like a man, but it is your name, Tony, and Tony you will be.'

'And you are Blaise?'

'Yes. The patron saint of the throat, but it is a coincidence, or again, maybe it is not. My parents are not thinking that their child will be a singer; they are thinking he will be a lawyer like his papa.'

'A singer?' She remembered the book, *Lohengrin.* 'An opera singer? Goodness, I have never met an opera singer before. I've actually never heard an opera.' She was babbling and she could not stop; he would think her stupid. 'I know, "Your Tiny Hand is Frozen", and "Oh, My Beloved Father", and "Blow the Wind Southerly" are on the wireless all the time.'

An expression of severe pain crossed his face.

'You have the most incredibly expressive face, Blaise,' she said. Blaise. She had never heard the name before but she liked it. 'That's not opera, is it?'

'We have both much to learn, Tony. I am not an opera singer. I am a student. I study voice and one day, maybe, I will sing.'

'I would love to hear you sing,' she said shyly.

He shrugged. 'One day. Now, Miss Tony, tell me about Antoinette. Why is she a painter?'

'I'm not, and I think my teachers believe I never will

39

be one. My favourite tutor told me today that my reds don't sing. That was rather demoralising.'

'I think I understand him. Reds should shout, "Look at me." You will learn. You must study the masters. We learn from the magnificent dead, Tony. So many great men and you think, It has all been done; there is no need for me, but there is. And you listen to the teacher who breaks your heart but you do not permit him to break the spirit, and one day your red will sing higher than the red of anyone else.'

'And will your voice do that, sing higher?'

He laughed. 'I am not, in case you have not notice, a soprano, and to sing highest is not the goal. To interpret the role with the colours, like your reds, with subtlety, and with sensitivity, to say one day, Maybe Beethoven would be please with how I sing his Florestan—'

He broke off and looked at her. 'You know Beethoven?'

She nodded.

'But not Florestan?'

She shook her head in shame.

He hugged her. No one had ever hugged her like that. How very French of him. She rather thought she might have some French blood somewhere because she wanted to hug him back, but already he was reaching out his hand to pull her up.

'What fun we are going to have, Toinette,' he said, already forgetting that he had promised to call her Tony. 'You will teach me about painting and I will teach you about music. But for now, I have a class and the maestro will say, "Go back to France. You sound like a pig caught in a drain." I do not really understand the pig and the drain but I will hang my head and beg for another chance because I have hear that he says this to everyone. And one day he will say in the Crush Bar at Covent Garden, "Fougère, I taught him all he knows," and you will make my portrait as Lohengrin to hang in Paris.'

She believed him. It would happen. There was nothing they could not do. They were young. They were in London and a dazzling future spread itself out before them.

But first she would learn how to make red hum a little and she would paint him on the back of a whale.

3

Torry Bay, 1998. Glasgow, 1998

Decisions had to be made. The paintings would have to be evaluated and the best person to do that was undoubtedly Tony's agent. Did he even know that she was dead? No one except Holly, John, the lawyer and Mrs Fraser from the shop had been at the funeral. Tony had wanted no fuss, and no publicity.

'I'll worry about him later.'

The ashes. Tony's last wish.

As near as I can get to where I want to be . . .

Holly put her list down on the table. Later she would add phone lawyer, phone agent, but first she would carry out Tony's last instructions. She picked up the casket containing her aunt's ashes. Outside it was cold and clear and the sea around Torry Bay was calm. Several swans floated on the water rising and falling with the tide. That was why Tony had painted swans – they were there. 'God, I can't think of a prayer. Forgive me.' She wondered for a moment if her father knew that his only child could not, at this stressful moment, recall one word of an established prayer.

Lohengrin.

'That was not a prayer. A whisper. Silly Holly, there is no one here to whisper.'

Hollyberry.

She shook her head and wiped tears from her eyes. 'Tony, dearest aunt, dearest friend, here we are together for the last time. No, that's not right. You'll always be with me. Can you see us – your niece and your swans? Where are you now? Here, some ash in a little casket or somewhere with him? If God is just, Tony, and I always thought He was, you're with Blaise. I'm wearing your rubies. I must say they feel a bit odd but they were your favourites and they'll give me courage. I wish you were here so that you could be at the exhibition, for that's what I'm going to do. Next year some time there will be an exhibition of your glorious paintings that will stun the art world. I won't say goodbye.'

She saw that the swans had bobbed round to face her. Another title for an unpainted masterpiece. *Mourners at a Funeral* or *Swans at Torry Bay*. But there was no one there to paint it. She opened the casket and scattered the ashes.

Damn it, damn, she could see nothing because of tears and the September sun on the water. She closed her eyes for a moment and was aware of the powerful smell of the sea.

'I only just decided about the exhibition, Tony. Is that what you want?'

Hollyberry.

Who spoke, who spoke?

'Did you tell me that one hears better with one's eyes closed, Tony? I hear the sea, a kind of slurping sound, and I can smell it and I can smell the funny coconutty smell of gorse, and if I was anywhere else in the world and closed my eyes I think I could conjure up Achahoish and Torry Bay and you, darling Tony. Paint, every time I smell paint I will be here with you in the attic. Remember what fun we had, you with your glorious swirls and me with my splodges. How generous you were to live with such ghastly paintings.'

The child Holly had taken it for granted that her paintings should hang side by side with Tony's. She had been fourteen before she had been able to convince Tony that she knew how worthless her work was and that she would not be traumatised to have them put – where they belonged – in the bin.

She was sobbing now, loud, harsh, uncontrolled sobs that made her nose run. She had no hankie and drew her hand across her nose like a child. A hymn; there should be a hymn. The only words that came in to her head were 'Silent Night, Holy Night' and she almost cursed but remembered in time that this was at least trying to be a religious service.

I should have been better prepared for you, dearest Tony.

She opened her eyes and all that was before her was the softly sighing sea and the swans still rising and

44

falling at the whim of the waves. 'Goodbye.' There, she had said it after all.

She turned and ran back to the cottage. She washed the dishes, took the sheets off the bed and bundled them into her suitcase, and turned off the electricity. The paintings and the jewellery were back where she had found them. They had been there for years. Surely they would be safe until she had spoken to Otto von Emler.

She stood in the doorway for a long moment, aware of how very much she wanted to stay. This is my home, the nearest to a real home that I have ever had. Its magic tugs at me wherever I am. Then she smiled, for, thanks to Tony, it was hers and she could stay for ever if she so chose.

She drove slowly back to Glasgow and was unaware of the distance because her mind was busy. The paintings would have to be sold. Their sheer size meant that they could not be housed in a normal home and, more importantly, they were, taken together, a valuable historical document and should be seen by millions.

How I would love to see them all hanging on walls that are the right size for them. But first I want to look at them quietly by myself, learn their secrets because they have secrets, and then I want the world to acknowledge that Tony Noble was a genius.

Stopped at a light, she closed her eyes and conjured up John's face. A warm glow suffused her . . . It would be all right. Everything was going to be all right. This, not Torry Bay, was home. Of course it was. The past, all of it, had to be allowed to stay in the past: no point in being selective.

She had left flowers on the kitchen table and they were sad.

Had I thrown them out before I left I would not have had to look at sad, dead flowers as soon as I walked in the door.

Holly could never bear to throw flowers away and cut their stems religiously, discarding the droopiest flower and putting the remainder in smaller and smaller vases until there was barely enough to fit in a sherry glass.

'This is a ridiculous economy,' John would say as he threw the wilting flowers in the garbage.

But it had nothing to do with economy and everything to do with beauty and vibrant life. Holly threw these forgotten ones in the waste bin, apologising to them as she did so. Then she checked her answering service but there were no messages that just had to be answered. She had a shower, changed the sheets on her bed, and then looked in the refrigerator. Sadder than the flowers.

'You are wasting time, Holly Noble. Ring John.'

But she wanted to think about her legacy and make her decisions before she talked to him. There was a pizza in the freezer; she put it in the microwave on defrost and dialled his number.

'You have reached John Robertson. I can't take your call just now but if you leave your . . .'

You couldn't really expect him to be in, sitting by the phone, waiting for your call.

Yes, I could. What would be great would be if he was rushing to see me, or even better, if he had been waiting in the flat.

How could he, when he didn't know for sure that you were coming?

Would it have made any difference?

The bell on the microwave answered her. She had forgotten to heat up the oven but she turned it on and sat at the table with a notebook and pencil while she waited for the pizza to cook.

Question: What am I going to do with the paintings, the jewellery and the cottage?

Answer/solutions: Keep them all. Impossible. Sell everything or keep some, sell some; but how do I choose?

What to do with the rest of your life?

Have some pizza, unpack and go to bed. You have to teach tomorrow. That's good enough for now.

It was difficult to get to sleep. She was tired but her body did not yearn for sleep; it yearned for John. She tossed and turned on the clean, crisp sheets. She stretched but her reaching fingers reached . . . nothing; her questing fingers found . . . nothing. She almost jumped right out of her nightgown when the strident ringing of the telephone shattered the stillness of the night.

'Holly, it *was* you. Why didn't you leave a message?'

'Where were you?'

'It's Sunday. My parents. Remember.'

'I wish you were here.'

'Why didn't you come here, silly girl? Are you working tomorrow?'

'Of course. I'm not sure what to do yet.'

'About what? Look, I'll come over and sleep at your place and we'll talk about it.'

'I'm tired, John.' Suddenly she was, very tired.

He laughed. 'No one is ever that tired.'

He hung up. She looked at the electric clock beside her bed. It was only just after midnight. Thank goodness she had changed the sheets. Quickly she pulled them up and straightened the duvet.

Should she open wine?

Don't be stupid. That's seduction. No one is being seduced here. You are waiting for your fiancé. They were going to talk. Coffee, coffee was the answer. First she took the box containing the rubies from under her winter woollies and slipped the necklace on under her nightie.

Grow up, Holly.

But she left them on.

She would be reasonable, and while waiting for John to hurry across Glasgow, she would think. The paintings had to be of considerable value. She would have them valued, and then would sell them. An exhibition. That was what she had decided. She would have an exhibition as she had promised Tony when she had scattered her ashes from the point at Torry Bay. The paintings would sell to collectors, to galleries. Von Emler would help with that and could be paid from the proceeds. The jewellery could be sold, probably at auction. She could leave that to Tony's lawyer. The cottage? She would keep the cottage – at least for a year or two. If she could get John there again he would love it;

she knew he would, and then it could be their summer home.

At last she heard a car drive up to the front of the building and there was John. Oh, she loved the look of him; the way his hair flopped forward over his brow, his slight stoop, his funny snub nose. She went into his arms as soon as he opened the door and he dropped his overnight bag and hugged her to him. She walked backwards as he half carried, half pushed her towards the bedroom.

'John, wait.'

'Why?'

Why indeed. She wanted it too, didn't she, wanted him, not *it*.

It was not quite as she had imagined but it was good, such a build-up of tension and then that wonderful release. When it was over she realised that he hadn't even seen the rubies.

'John, how could you miss these?' she said later when his breathing too had slowed down.

'I never miss these.' He smiled as his hand encircled her breast again.

She pushed him off and sat up. 'These, John.'

He lay looking up at her, at the delicate red stones snuggling between her breasts. 'Wow, where did you . . . are they real?'

'What do you think?'

'I think you should always dress just like that.' He laughed.

'Perfect with jeans.'

Holly laughed too. Was that what Tony had meant?

'They are real.'

He got off the bed and walked across the floor and she watched him as he walked into the bathroom. Nice rear view. He came back wearing his towelling robe and brought hers. 'Are they valuable, sweetheart? They're not diamonds?'

'No, they're rubies but they're good stones; they were Tony's favourites.' She looked up at him. His eyes were on the stones. 'I want to keep them.' She spilled out the history of the boxes of jewels, the gifts to Tony from her one true love.

'Of course, but' – he hesitated – 'a gift from some man to your aunt. We could sell them and then you could choose something . . .'

She could read his mind. Fougère had been Tony's lover; ergo, there was something faintly distasteful about his expensive trinkets.

'Tony loved Blaise Fougère, not *some man*, all her life. I'm sure she thought of herself as his wife. She hoped I would enjoy some of her jewellery and these were her favourites.'

He reached out his hand. 'Keep it, if you like it. Makes my pearls look insipid though.'

'I promise never to wear them together,' said Holly as she closed the shower door behind her.

'Why didn't you call in sick and get the whole thing done while you were there?'

Holly had showered, and they were drinking coffee at the kitchen table.

'Now you will have to go back there and supervise the evaluation; and who says you can trust the agent? He wasn't asked to the funeral and anyway, everybody knows agents are crooked as hell.'

'Like lawyers,' interrupted Holly.

'Okay, but it's more sensible to be there. Get the paintings valued, two opinions probably, sell the jewellery at auction, and put the cottage on the market.'

'I won't sell.'

He slammed his mug down on the table with such force that coffee slopped over the edge. 'No one has a cottage in Argyll, for God's sake. The south of France, Holly, Tuscany, Spain.'

'I'm too tired to talk about it just now. It's getting late, John,' finished Holly as she stood up. She walked to the sink for a cloth and wiped up the spilled coffee. 'It's left a mark.'

John ignored the stain. 'I've had a thought. All the paintings have this opera singer in them?'

'Right.'

'Does he have a family?'

Family? Did Fougère have a family? 'I have no idea. Until you asked, I don't think I had really assimilated that he was real; he was just somebody in a painting.'

'Forty paintings.'

'If there is family they might have some feelings.'

'Strong feelings. Look, I'll see what I can find out, and you should talk to Tony's lawyer and find out what he knows.'

'If Tony was right and no one is left alive who cares then

it'll be easier to decide what to do with the paintings.'

'Great. Now that's settled I'd like a fresh look at those rubies.'

But for some reason, perhaps just that he had waited for her to clean up the spill, Holly was in no mood. 'I'm already showered, John, and we have work to go to in a few hours.'

They lay without touching until the alarm clock woke them at six.

Fences to mend. 'You have the bathroom first, John, while I make coffee.'

'I'm sorry about this morning, Holly. Did I sound selfish? I didn't mean to, and I do try to understand how much that little cottage means to you. But it's not right for us, Holly, and when we can afford a second home – God, we're keeping two apartments as it is – I want somewhere in the sun.'

Two apartments.

'We have two apartments, John, because you won't set a wedding date and because your parents don't approve of hanky-panky.'

'I can't hurt them.' Suddenly he grabbed her and held her close. 'It's different now, Holly. With your little nest egg perhaps we could think dates. Life was too unsure before, but I have some news for you too. I have a chance of being selected as a candidate at the next election. It takes money, Holly, and now we have it. It's the beginning for us, Holly. We'll talk about it tonight. Come over to my flat after school; we'll have dinner and make plans.'

She toasted some bagels and wondered idly if it was a smaller sin to lie to your parents than to confess that you were living with your fiancée. What size of a sin was it for a perfectly healthy person to 'call in sick' just to have time for business?

Damn it, I'm becoming so holier than thou.

Then there was no time to think until the school bell rang at three thirty, and even then she was too busy correcting jotters and repairing at least some of the damage incompetent supply teachers – or was this the headmaster's handiwork? – had done in her absence to think about levels of hypocrisy, inheritances or anything else. She stuffed her briefcase and caught the underground train to Hillhead. At a butcher's shop on Byers Road she bought a roasting chicken – John would surely have some wine – and then she found salad greens at a greengrocer's.

When John arrived just after seven the chicken was roasting, the table was ready, and Holly and her list were in a chair beside the window.

'Much better view from the house at Torry Bay,' she said with a smile as he bent to kiss her.

'I'll open some wine.'

A few minutes later he handed her a glass. 'Holly, I was thinking, and I have come to the conclusion that you should take a leave of absence and get this business settled. We could go up together this weekend, if you like. Perhaps we should bring the jewellery and the paintings here.'

Holly stood up. 'The chicken,' she said.

He followed her into the kitchen. 'They could be stolen or the cottage could be burned down.'

'It could be hit by a meteorite, John, but I thought I would leave everything there until I have decided what to do. I can't make up my mind. I love my job, warts and all, and don't particularly want to give it up.'

He put his arms round her and she leaned against him. 'No one wants you to resign: I said, for the moment, you should take a leave of absence.'

'It will take me weeks to clean up the mess my supply left. If ten per cent of what the children said is true—'

'For heaven's sake, Holly. They're not your children; you owe them nothing. If these jewels are real and if these paintings are valuable, then you just can't leave them in an empty house. They've been there for years, certainly, but Tony was there, and she's dead, Holly. Sweetheart, I don't want to be a bully but you must see that I'm right. Unless we can do everything this weekend. Could we get the paintings into two cars?'

She shook her head.

'We can bring the best ones, surely.'

'I don't know which they are. John, I haven't seen all of them. They're stacked five, six deep against the walls.'

'Probably rotted.'

'The house is sound.'

'I'll hire a van.'

'And where do you suggest we leave forty valuable paintings? They're safer in Achahoish than they would be in Glasgow.'

He pushed her away from him so roughly that she almost fell. 'Do you want my help, Holly, or am I going to be put away in a drawer with my pearls while you run around in some poncy soprano's rubies?'

Holly looked at him. Who was he?

She picked up her briefcase. 'The chicken has about thirty seconds left before total meltdown. The same might be said of our engagement.'

He grabbed her before she reached the door. 'Sweetheart, sweetheart, please. Forgive me. I didn't mean to push you.'

She forced herself out of his grasp. 'I need space, John. I have to have time to think, to evaluate.'

She knew that he was still standing in the doorway listening to her shoes clattering on the stone of the outside stair and she stopped and looked up. 'He was a tenor, one of the greatest the world has ever known. I looked him up on the Internet at school.'

For someone who had just told her fiancé of – what? – five years to get lost, she felt remarkably well. She could feel the rubies inside her well-cut and totally dull blue cotton shirt and she smiled. Perhaps she was different since she had begun to wear the 'poncy soprano's' rubies.

By the time she had reached her flat she had decided to apply for a leave of absence to begin as soon as the school district could find a suitable replacement. She had also decided to go to Torry Bay every weekend possible. Perhaps Mr von Emler would consider coming at a weekend since it was imperative that an accredited expert see the paintings without delay.

John did not ring her, she had not expected him to do so. He was sulking and these sulks always took a day or two. She was glad because it gave her time to assess. Too often she had dampened down her longing for Torry Bay and Tony because of John; now, although it was too late for Tony, she could respond to those faint tugs at her heartstrings.

The next day she forfeited her lunch break, discussed her situation at length with her head teacher and then applied for a leave of absence. When school was over, she bundled up some papers, stuffed them into her briefcase and hurried home in time to ring either the lawyer or the agent before the close of office hours.

By the time she had reached her flat she had decided that the number one priority was the paintings and so she took a deep breath, sat down at the kitchen table with a mug of lemon and ginger tea and rang the agent, Otto von Emler.

He had not known of Tony's death and was shocked. 'I knew Tony Noble almost all my life, Miss Noble. I think I may safely say that I was responsible for much of what was good in her life. That she left no instructions to tell me—' He broke off, obviously quite distressed.

'There was no one there, Mr von Emler, only old Mrs Fraser from the shop at Torry Bay – she found my aunt – and my aunt's lawyer. You may understand more clearly when you see what Tony has left in her cottage.'

His voice changed. He had sounded old and tired but now the tone was that of a young, vibrant man. 'A painting.' He almost breathed the words. 'Tony has left a new painting. So often she hinted and half promised and for years, nothing.'

'There is an attic full of paintings, Mr von Emler.'

She could hear him blowing his nose resoundingly and she smiled, thinking that she could almost see the huge linen square he would use.

'May I see them?'

'Your name was in my aunt's address book. Since you know her work better than anyone I hoped that you would consider flying up to Scotland to see them, perhaps to evaluate them.'

'I hate to fly and I have other painters. Had you waited one more week, Miss Noble, you would have had to wait until the spring. No one goes to Scotland after October, didn't you know that?'

She ignored that and had the feeling that he had expected her to ignore him or at least to pay little attention to anything he said that had nothing to do with art, that is Art with a capital A, the life force that motivated him.

'This weekend, Mr von Emler?'

'I'll fly to Glasgow, Miss Noble. Meet me there.'

She did. He said very little on the way to Torry Bay. 'I prefer cities,' he said as they drove into the magnificence of Scotland's west coast. There was really nothing to say to that. She had a sneaky feeling he was starring in a script he wrote for himself, for fun.

When they reached Achahoish he sat forward on the edge of his seat, as full of anticipation as Holly herself used to be, and as they headed down to Torry Bay all his affectations slid away like melting snow off a warm roof.

'Her bay,' he said and his voice was quiet as in church. He said nothing as she parked and opened the door to the cottage.

Hollyberry. Welcome home.

'If I could see the paintings, Miss Noble.'

He spent hours in the attic. Holly offered him tea, coffee, whatever, and he behaved as if he did not hear her.

'Damn it all, I am starving,' she said at nine in the evening and went storming up to the studio. He was sitting on the floor in his Armani suit – it was Armani if it didn't have a collar, wasn't it? – just looking at two paintings.

'So young,' he whispered as she walked in. 'So full of joy, of promise.'

Dents de Lion. Blaise, dressed only in shorts, was rolling in a field of glorious golden dandelions.

The Performing Bear. What did it mean? It was of Blaise but he was wearing a clown's costume and there was a chain around his neck. It was a disturbing picture and Holly shivered.

'Yes, I like that one,' she said, pointing to the dandelions.

'Like, Miss Noble? You do not *like* a painting. You are possessed or you walk away.'

'I am possessed,' said Holly quietly, and went back downstairs to scramble some eggs. This odd little man would obviously be there all night.

Holly ate her eggs on warm buttered toast while she sat by the window and watched the supreme artist paint the bay. First he tried the effect of dark brooding purples and then he made the sea dance with joy as he coloured it gold. The sky he streaked with red and pink and all with a dusting of gold left over from the sea.

She took Otto coffee and a sandwich before she herself went to bed and told him that the main bedroom was prepared for him; but in the morning he was back in the attic and there was only a small indentation on the white cover to show where he had rested for a while.

He came down while she was making coffee and sat looking out of the window while she worked.

'A major exhibition, with your permission, Miss Noble,' he said at last. 'I always hoped, but still, now they are here and they are her finest paintings. One or two I have seen before but she would not sell them.'

'And now you know why?'

'No, I don't even pretend to understand and I am too exhausted to think. Will you drive me to the airport?'

'Of course.'

'And you will trust me?'

'My aunt trusted you.'

'Yes, she did. I will take this legacy and together we will give Tony Noble the place she deserves. The first thing is to have the paintings shipped to my London gallery; there I can study them at leisure and value them. Only then will we decide what to do, but they have waited too long already. I will take all the time that is necessary but no more than I need.'

'How long is long, Mr von Emler?'

'Otto,' he said almost automatically. 'I don't just ring a man who has a lorry. These are works of art; I need to get the best shippers and I need to supervise. First I have a major show in London to deal with. I expect they will all sell and so when they are gone I will bring Tony's work down. If God is good they will be out of here before the winter.'

'Mr von . . . Otto, do you know anything about Mr Fougère?'

He almost buried his nose in his coffee. 'I'm so tired, Miss Noble.'

Holly smiled. She felt he was playing for time. 'Holly,' she said, and it was his turn to smile.

'Holly. Yes, I know about Mr Fougère but I have no permission to share such knowledge. I suggest you ring Tony's lawyer. If she told him nothing then I will reconsider what I know.'

He accepted some toast but ate it absent-mindedly. The sandwich was still on the floor and so, as far as she knew, he had eaten nothing for almost twenty-four hours. 'When I have mounted this exhibition, Holly, I can die. Do you understand that? I have watched her since I was sixteen years old and I knew, I knew she was painting. Tony had to paint – oh, not the pictures she did for the tourists, the swans at Torry Bay, flowers sometimes, all with merit, you understand. She was too fine, too good, ever to do less than her best, but the paintings with her blood in them we saw only once or twice and I knew. I knew,' he said again and his whole

60

small body was tense with passion. 'And at last I have seen them and I will not sleep a wink until they are properly mounted and hanging where the world can come to pay homage.'

He stopped talking and, his energy drained, looked his age.

He looked up at her and smiled wickedly. 'Thank you, Holly, for the most wonderful night of my life.'

4

---❖---

Godalming, 1938
DENTS DE LION

They swept round the corner on their hired bicycles.
Suddenly Tony uttered a cry and screeched to a halt.
'Look, Blaise, have you ever seen anything so beauti-
ful?'

His heart thudding painfully – she had yelled so
loudly that he had been sure that she was hurt – Blaise
looked. 'I see fields,' he said cautiously. He could see
nothing that merited such spectacular braking. 'And
many weeds on the verges.'

'*Crétin*,' she said. 'Weeds are flowers that someone
doesn't like.'

He nodded judiciously. '*Bien sûr*. My father would
not like these. Look at the heads; in a few weeks there
will be seed heads blowing all over the fields to bring a
thousand times as many next year. They should be cut
down.'

Her hand slipped into his. 'They're beautiful, Blaise.
Look again.'

And he looked, but this time he looked with Tony's eyes and he saw hundreds of brilliant golden heads flying atop strong green stalks. The meadow rose in a slight incline and some dandelions marched along the skyline, outlined against the clearest of blue skies. Blaise laughed. 'Yes, Tony, *ma mie*, they are very beautiful.'

They left their bicycles under the hedge by the side of the road and climbed into the meadow. Hand in hand they wandered up to the skyline and saw more of the field laid out before them. It too was ablaze with dandelions.

'*Les dents de lion*,' said Blaise. 'They are the teeth of the lion.'

'*Dents de lion*, dandelion. I never knew that,' said Tony. 'Aren't they beautiful?' She laughed like a little girl, lay down in the lush grass and rolled down to the bottom of the incline.

What could he do? He shouted with laughter and followed her example and when he bumped into her at the bottom of the slope it was only natural that he should begin to kiss her greedily, hungrily, and then his body blotted out the sky and the field and the dandelions and Tony moaned and pulled him closer until all she saw was his face with its beautiful green eyes gazing into hers. At last he collapsed on top of her and made as if to roll away but she held him with surprisingly strong arms and they lay together until they began to feel cold.

'That was quite something,' she said, as without embarrassment they searched for discarded clothing.

Blaise said nothing.

Tony looked at him. 'I wondered what it would be like and I wanted the first time to be wonderful and it was. It wasn't the first time for you though, Blaise, was it?'

'No,' he said sadly, 'and it should have been.' He sat down and clasped his knees with his hands. He did not look at her but beyond her as if he were seeing the past and the future. 'I am greedy, *ma mie*. I want to share everything with you. I should have waited and then we could have discovered it together.'

'Was it wonderful, the first time, for you, I mean? Was she very special?'

'At the time she was. She was my mother's maid and twice my age. She was very kind to a young boy and did not laugh.'

'Good. Come on. We had best find our bikes or we'll miss the train back to London. I hope your parents didn't fire her.'

'Fire? Oh, to dismiss. No. Perhaps they were glad it was someone . . . clean. I was always falling in love, Toinette, and with the most unsuitable people.'

'But you didn't *love* them?'

'No. Most of them terrified me. The friends of my parents were, how you say . . . racy, some of them.'

'What bliss,' said Tony as they clambered back over the fence. 'To know racy people, I mean. I have led such a *dull* life, Blaise.'

He looked down at her serious little face and his heart contracted. 'Oh, madame is so old and still so inexperienced.'

'My parents are such worthy people. And so dull.'

He looked at her questioningly as he methodically rebuttoned the back of her blouse. As usual she had done it up any old way. And as was usual with him each button fitted obediently into its allotted slot. 'Is worthiness dull?'

'No, of course not, but they manage to make it sound dull so that one always wants to do the exact opposite of what they suggest.'

She laughed up at him and as always when she laughed her plain little face changed, becoming animated and elf-like and he caught his breath.

'I know nineteen isn't old but if I am to become a great artist I must have lots of experiences.'

His heart, that a second before had been so exultantly beating, checked in its mad thumping. 'So, I am an experience.'

She stopped and looked up at him. 'No,' she said seriously. 'You are life.'

He caught her to him. 'And you are my eyes, Toinette. You will show me the beauty in simple things and you will make me stop and look and be aware of something outside my voice.'

'If you want me to be.'

'I will need you, Antonia Noble, all the days of my life, to keep my feet on the ground, to show me the difference between weeds and flowers.'

She kissed his throat. 'There is no difference, Blaise. You must look at everything with wonderment and love.'

'You will have to teach me.'

'I will be there, *ma mie*,' she said, stealing his endearment. 'Always.'

They put their bikes on the train and went back to London, holding hands and without talking, each of them aware that everything was changed between them. They had been friends for almost twelve months and they had kissed before: Blaise, after all, was French and used to saluting his acquaintance, but the kisses had held little passion.

Tony looked at him and smiled as she relived their moments in the field. So that's it, she thought. I'm not a virgin: I'm a woman, Blaise's woman.

For almost eight months they had been inseparable, meeting after classes, cycling south from Tony's boarding-house, crossing and recrossing the bridges of the Thames as Blaise looked for '*un appartement*', touring the museums and art galleries and spending evening after evening in the gods at Covent Garden. Blaise could afford good tickets but Tony could not and since she would not allow him to pay for her, he swallowed his pride and climbed the steps with her. He had not realised, he said, that he was in training to climb Mont Blanc. They sat in teashops drinking tea and eating scones and they talked and talked. They discussed art and music. They spoke about their families.

Blaise adored his parents, especially his beautiful, sophisticated mother, and he loved his baby sister, Nicole. He told Tony of their country house in the

Lot – 'There is a village there called Fougère' – and of his home in Paris.

'We live on the rue de Passy in the 16th *arrondissement* – that is how Paris is divided, into districts; we say *arrondissements*. We live in what is call an *hôtel particulier*, a tall thin house, three or four floors, and all for one family. There is a little courtyard in the front with glorious iron gates, so pretty. Paris is part of every artist's education, Tony. *En effet*, you must return to Paris with me in the vacation. I will take you to see the Bois de Boulogne – I went near there to l'École Marymont, very good, *très* – how you say – strict, but with good music, although that is not why I was sent there. It was the place to go. And on Thursdays my nurse or sometimes Maman, would take me to . . . *guignol* . . .' He looked puzzled. '*Guignol* is . . . *les marionnettes*, puppets, very famous, and after we would cross the river and go to Angelina, a café on the rue de Rivoli.' He sniffed the air. 'Almost from here, I can smell their hot chocolate. Oh, yes, ma Toinette, you must come to Paris.'

'I should like that,' she said seriously, and her heart was heavy in her breast because she could hear her father.

'French, a French boy. You will come home where we can look after you, my girl. Isn't it enough that we have to sit here and worry while you're at your art school meeting who knows what kind of Bohemian, smoking and drinking.'

Blaise had introduced her to wine and now she

67

decided that as soon as she could she would start to smoke. What bliss. Super-sophistication, and now sex.

They looked at one another as they approached Tony's residence. They did not want to part.

'I will take you to dinner, *chérie*, a proper meal, not a "Blaise, this is ridiculously expensive", meal. Go, I will return for you at eight o'clock. I hope there is hot water in your so austere residence.'

She smiled. 'Would a woman who makes such delicious bread expect me to bathe in cold water?'

She did not drift upstairs. She ran, jumping as many stairs as she could and drawing horrified looks from one or two of the older residents.

'Artists,' sniffed Monica English-lit. Bailey who lived among her books of obscure poets on the third floor.

Tony cared nothing. She locked herself firmly in the bathroom and threw off her clothes. She was preparing herself for her wedding night and everything had to be perfect.

At last, followed by a tidal wave of steam, she came out and hurried to her tiny bedroom. Nail scissors are not really ideally suited for cutting hair but she managed and Blaise tried not to laugh when he saw the uneven mop of red curls.

'I will even it off for you, *ma mie*, if you will not permit me to pay for a salon cut.'

They went in a taxi to the Ritz – 'but, of course the Ritz, Toinette' – and because Blaise was a Frenchman they spent a great deal of time discussing what they would eat but afterwards Tony could remember only a haze of smells and tastes and his green eyes smiling at her from across the table.

The summer evening was perfect and so they walked back to his hotel. Other lovers strolled through Green Park and they smiled at one another in understanding. At last they were there and with their arms around one another they went slowly upstairs and she was in his bedroom and knew that it was the right place for her to be. They kissed and undressed one another, not with feverish haste, but with slow deliberation, uncovering each delight in turn and worshipping at its shrine until they could bear no more. He lifted her in his arms and stood for a moment looking out at the moon as if he were offering a sacrifice and then he laid her gently on the bed and taught her all she wanted to know.

'I love you,' she gasped as dawn broke.

'*Je t'aime*,' he whispered. 'And I will love you all my life.'

They were very practical.

'It is not the time for marriage, *ma mie*,' Blaise said. 'We have too much studying to do.'

'We could be terribly modern and just not get married.'

He was shocked and sat straight up in the bed. 'But this is nonsense. Of course we will marry. It is the right, the only thing to do. I regard you as my wife now and one day we will marry before the mayor and before the priest, but for now I must sing and you must paint.'

'I can paint anywhere,' she said as she memorised the

curve of the muscles of his arm. 'I shall paint you while you sing.'

'If you would allow me to buy a decent ticket for the opera you would see that that is impossible. I am very ugly, me, when I sing. There is so much hard work, so much – how you say *déformation*? – distortion, strain on the muscles, the jaws, and neither do I stand still. How can you capture the pain of singing?'

'I shall try. I shall paint the joy and perhaps when I am very good, the pain. The pain doesn't hurt, Blaise?' she asked anxiously.

'No, I cannot explain. Only a singer would understand. It is like to run very hard, very fast; to sing well exhausts. That is the pain but also the joy.'

She sighed happily and lay back down, her arms behind her head.

He looked down at her and desire stirred again. 'You are with no shame,' he teased, 'flaunting your charms in this way.'

'I have no shame with you. Not a soul has seen my body, except the doctor, bits, since I was about seven and now . . .' But she could say no more because his mouth was on hers and she exulted as she responded to him.

'I don't think my mother ever did this,' she said when they were capable of speech.

'She must have done.' He looked down at her again. 'Tony, there must not be babies. I know what to do. Next time I will be . . . prepared. I am too greedy tonight and we must hope. It is not the end of the world if . . .' He hesitated to talk to her. She was young and inexperienced. He was the one who should have thought. He shrugged. He would handle it. Now he needed to sleep.

'Go to sleep, Toinette. We have classes tomorrow and you will ask your parents if you can visit my family in the *vacances*.'

But, held in his arms, she was already asleep.

Her mother was torn between worry that some nameless harm would come to her daughter in France and gratification that that same daughter should have found favour with a young man like Blaise. His parents owned two houses, think of it. She wondered if they had different sets of bed linen or did they carry their blankets from house to house?

'And cutlery,' she said out loud to her husband one evening as he sat correcting essays.

'Cutlery, Judith?'

'This young man's family. Do you think they have two sets of everything?'

'I will not have my daughter adopt a hedonistic lifestyle. She will not go to France under the protection of this young man. A singing student? Only one in a million is any good and their morals are extremely dicey to say the least. And he's French?' Charles Noble almost shuddered. Everyone knew they ate frogs. What kind of civilisation bred men who ate frogs? 'He'll get nowhere, Judith. Opera, if it has to be sung at all, should be sung by Italians, so much less embarrassing for everyone.'

He reflected that Antonia's situation could have been worse. She could just as easily have met an Italian. He would thank divine providence for that small mercy when he said his prayers before bed. 'Now, I will listen to no arguments. I believe I am a loving father and in other circumstances, had she made friends with a pleasant French girl of similar background, I would have found the money to finance a holiday. Travel, I have been told, is beneficial.'

'We could invite him here, Dad.' Tony's brother, Frederick, raised his head from his battle with logarithms. 'There must be decent French people and if Antonia likes this chap he must be fairly nice. Let us see him before you let Antonia travel abroad. Let him see that she comes from a respectable family and so, if her being an art student has given him any ideas, he'll see the error of his ways.'

The parents looked at their prodigy. Did the Bible not say, 'Out of the mouths of babes?'

Therefore Tony received a letter that told her that although they could not, at this juncture, countenance a visit to a foreign country in the company of a young man of whom they knew only what she had told them, they would be delighted to welcome Mr Fougère for a weekend visit.

'The summons.' Blaise laughed when she had told him. 'I am fill with terror.'

'You'll be bored to tears,' mourned Tony. 'We'll have fish on Friday evening. On Saturday we'll go to the tennis club to watch Freddie – that's my brother – and

72

my father play father-son doubles. The tea is good. We'll have dinner and play bridge. On Sunday we'll go to church and have lunch at the inn. Oh, God, you're a Catholic.'

'You need not say it as if it was the same as "You're a leper." Don't worry. I am also French and will compromise.'

'And Blaise, dearest, darling, sweetest Blaise, you know you can't come into my bedroom.'

He drew himself up to his full height and glowered down at her. 'Madame, you insult. I am a gentleman.' Then he dropped down beside her on the bed and his hands began their searching. 'And I will be the perfect guest, but for now I will be very not perfect.'

'Imperfect,' she tried to say, but it was muffled by his lips.

The visit was quite as bad as Tony had expected. She tried hard not to be caught looking at Blaise. Her eyes would give her away. But her father knew: she was quite sure. He was cold and studiously polite, but then he was always like that with strangers, wasn't he? Besides, not only was Blaise a stranger, he was a foreigner.

Her mother was worse. She gushed. Tony drew wicked little cartoons. Her mother sat with open mouth while a host of silly remarks came rushing out.

'A singer. How nice. You must sing for us. "One Fine Day." I do so adore that.'

'French, Antonia tells me. How clever of you to speak English.'

73

And then the horrifying nightmare of the hostess. 'I hope you can eat English food.'

Freddie behaved like a missionary out to convert the heathen even if Blaise was not a heathen but a baptised Catholic. Perhaps for the Freddies of this world that was even worse.

Blaise was naughty and called Freddie the Archbishop ever after.

Tony lay tossing in bed, thinking of Blaise in a room just two doors away and hoped and prayed that he would forget that he was a gentleman. He did not and being a practical Frenchman had gone to sleep as soon as his head had touched the pillow.

He had worked hard to avoid having to sing.

'I am not warmed up,' he had told Mrs Noble, who had hurriedly put another log on the fire.

'His voice, Judith, his voice,' Tony's father had said tetchily and Blaise had taken pity on her and asked her if once again she would show him the garden that reminded him of his father's. It did not. His father's rose garden was a masterpiece that covered over six acres but, as he reminded Tony as their train chuntered them back to London, 'I am a gentleman and gentlemen always try to put other people at their ease. Courtesy, *ma mie*, costs nothing.'

5

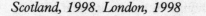

Scotland, 1998. London, 1998

A dozen red roses were delivered to Holly at school. The children in her class were not the only ones to hoot in derision – or envy.

'Mending fences, are we?' asked Fiona Gilmour, the school secretary who had signed for the flowers. She handed Holly the bouquet together with a large empty plastic ice-cream carton. 'Left the crystal at home, I'm afraid. This'll have to do.'

'We had a row,' confessed Holly. 'Thanks for this, Fiona.' She took the flowers to her classroom where they stood looking incongruous all afternoon but still filling her with delight each time she looked at them.

Once home and the flowers carefully arranged in her best vase, she rang John's office.

'I'm sorry too,' she said after she had listened to John's breast-beating. 'Look, John, Tony's agent came up to the cottage and had a preliminary look at the paintings. He thinks they're good. On Saturday I'm seeing Mr Gilbert again.'

'Great, I'll go through with you.'

She hesitated.

'I'm a lawyer too, Holly,' he said, and his voice was stern and wounded at the same time. '*Your* lawyer. Perhaps I should be there.'

'That would be lovely, John, except – it's just that he's taking me to his club on Princes Street for lunch. No office hours on a Saturday. He's doing me a big favour and I'm grateful and can hardly ask if I may bring a guest.'

'No, I see that, although bear in mind that lawyers don't do favours unless they expect to get something out of it. If these pictures are any good, Holly, you're quite a client.'

She said nothing. There was some truth in what he said but she wanted to believe Henry Gilbert was merely being kind.

'Is it the New Club?' he asked at last.

'Yes.'

'Very nice. I'll be here afterwards if you want to talk. I love you, Hol. I miss you.'

'Me too,' said Holly and, after she had hung up, wondered if she had told the truth.

Henry Gilbert, Tony's Edinburgh-based lawyer, had spoken to Holly at the funeral but she remembered nothing at all about him. Tall, thin and somewhat austere, she thought, with striped trousers and a dark jacket, a caricature of the Scottish lawyer.

She met him in the elegant foyer of the New Club, that sacred bastion of legal men which sits on Princes Street and stares balefully out at passers-by. He was nothing in the least like a caricature and resembled nothing so much as a very merry garden gnome. He was small and bouncy, had a completely bald head but a delightful soft white beard and his eyes twinkled, especially when he saw his guest gazing in awe like a child at the view of Edinburgh Castle.

'Would you like a quick tour, Miss Noble?' he asked, and taking her acquiescence for granted guided her along. 'There are some fine paintings and books and, of course, that priceless view.' The castle, in all its magnificence, seemed to fill the windows. 'Next time, you must bring your camera.'

Twinkling eyes or no, Henry Gilbert was also extremely astute.

'You have had time to look at your legacy, Miss Noble?'

'Yes, and there are questions.'

'You are now a wealthy woman, and I congratulate you. Your aunt loved you very much and we discussed her will several times. You have her jewellery?'

'Yes, but of course I couldn't keep it.' She wondered how to begin to explain.

'If you wish to sell the jewellery then I can help you with that, although I believe she did hope you would keep some of her favourite pieces. She thought you might suit the rubies and then the diamond earrings – she was sure you wore earrings.' He looked at her shrewdly. 'It's insured for almost a million.'

Her stomach had dropped on the floor. 'A million . . . whats?'

'Pounds naturally,' he said almost severely. 'Are you all right? Good heavens, you do look peculiar.' He gestured to a waiter. 'Let me get you a brandy.'

'No, I'm all right. It's just that . . . Mr Gilbert, almost all the jewellery is in my handbag and I have just walked here from the parking lot under the castle.'

Now he spoke lawyer-speak. 'Highly irregular and very foolhardy, Miss Noble. But it was also foolish of your aunt to leave it at the cottage. Never mind, I was aware of the jewels and their approximate value. I did not know, however, about the paintings and there Miss Noble made a mistake, if I may say so – most unsatisfactory – but I have had some people tell me, and this without their seeing them, of their probable worth. If they are genuine, as I'm sure they are, they are very valuable. Miss Noble was one of the most respected painters of her day. You probably know that in the years just after the war she became quite a cult figure in London society. Everyone who was anyone wanted her to paint him or her: a bit like Sargent or Raeburn.'

'I should have asked you about this when I spoke with you, Mr Gilbert, but did you know of my aunt's relationship with Blaise Fougère, the French tenor? The paintings in the attic are portraits of him.'

'I was your aunt's lawyer, Miss Noble, not her confidant. I know, however, that she painted Blaise Fougère for the Paris Opera House in 1952 and for the city opera in New York in 1949. That, by the way, was later gifted to Covent Garden. New York commissioned a second portrait in 1960 but she never delivered it. After 1960 she painted less and less and almost always landscapes or seascapes.'

'She loved Turner's paintings,' Holly contributed, a catch in her voice. 'She said that looking at *Ancient Rome: Agrippina Landing with the Ashes of Germanicus* and *Venice: Storm at Sunset* was worth an entire term of lectures on colour and light.'

He coughed and fiddled with his pens. He did not understand colour and light. The law, now, that was easy to understand. He coughed again. 'If,' he began sternly, 'as I said before, the paintings are what we think they are, and I see no reason why they should not be,' he added hurriedly as he correctly interpreted her quick look of anger, 'they will be much sought after. Perhaps the agent knows the provenance of each work. All I can say is that I am told that the Fougère Foundation is connected with the Hartman Corporation and I will research further if you wish.'

A waiter arrived with their order and Holly almost sniffed appreciatively – breakfast seemed such a long way away. She picked up her fork. 'The Hartman Corporation? Sounds like money.'

Henry Gilbert supervised the pouring of the wine before he spoke. 'The usual term, I believe, is filthy rich. Your worth, my dear Miss Noble, even after selling the paintings, is nothing compared to the money of the Hartmans of this world.'

Holly wriggled on the seat uneasily. She had no interest in the Hartman Corporation but if someone there was connected with Blaise Fougère they should be told about the paintings.

'The name means nothing to me, Mr Gilbert, but I would like to inform any relative of the existence of the paintings; the subject matter must be of interest. I could arrange for someone to view the paintings, perhaps even to donate one to the foundation or whatever it is.'

The lawyer looked somewhat startled. 'You are under no obligation, Miss Noble, and I'm not sure that this isn't highly irregular. I said I was not Miss Noble's confidant. That is true to an extent; she did, however, speak to me of her hopes for you. She was very proud when you decided to work for that charity in Africa but she worried that, like your father, you were cutting yourself off from other young people. He married, rather late in life, I believe, and she hoped that you would . . .' He stopped and smiled. 'Meet a nice young man, fall in love and marry.'

'I did,' said Holly wryly. 'Twice. Fall in love,' she added as he looked a little surprised. 'As for Africa – I loved every minute; I do not regret the years I spent there.'

'Good, now let us enjoy this delicious monkfish, and after lunch I will take the jewellery, by taxi, and lock it in the vault at my office.'

Holly strolled through Princes Street Gardens to the parking lot where she had left her car. Her heart as well as her bag was lighter and she was able to enjoy the gardens where, even in late September, colour cheered from flowerbeds. There were one or two hardy souls walking up the paths from the gardens to the very walls of the castle – somewhere up there surely there had to be a gate – and a few early autumn leaves floated in the puddles left by rain in the great dry fountain. She promised herself that next time she too would take one of those wandering, climbing paths and see where it led.

She drove home and rang Otto at his gallery.

He prevaricated. 'One assumed, Holly. I have already told you and I can say no more than that.'

Holly was deeply disappointed. She had been so sure that if anyone could tell her anything about Blaise Fougère and his place in Tony's life it would be her agent. 'You've seen the paintings. They tell the whole story of their love for one another, Otto. Do you know anything about Fougère, why they never married? If they loved one another as much as these paintings show that they did, why were they not together?'

'Fougère married, in the early forties, I think, or perhaps just after the war.'

'And there are no paintings during the war years.' Holly was excited. 'I saw 1937 and then the sixties or was there one in the fifties?'

'There were paintings, Holly. We sold landscapes for her, some portraits, and her swans.'

'Swans? I don't remember her being keen on swans but I suppose pretty seascapes with swans appeal to people who don't really know too much about art.'

She stopped talking, crossed her fingers, and went on with what she felt was important. 'I believe Mr Fougère had no children.'

'No.' Holly held the receiver and listened attentively but heard nothing but air. Why was he finding it difficult to speak? What did he have to tell her?

'No children?'

'Holly, there's a nephew.' He stopped talking, cleared his throat and began again. 'There is a nephew from the marriage of Fougère's sister, Nicole, to an American, Bradley Hartman, a member of a wealthy Pennsylvania family. Started in mines, earned enough to go into politics, and diversified. Nowadays there are more strands to the Hartman money than there are paintings in my gallery. The senator died about eight years ago but there is the son, Taylor Fougère Hartman. He'll be in his early forties I would say, and is certainly one of the richest men in America, having inherited everything from his father's family, his uncle, and his French grandparents.'

'I know; filthy rich, according to Mr Gilbert.'

'What you realise from this exhibition will be less than a tax write-off for Hartman.'

Holly sighed. 'So I'm told.' She had no interest in Taylor Hartman or his money, but since he appeared to be Blaise Fougère's only living relative he should be told about the paintings. 'I feel we should tell him of the existence of the paintings; the subject matter must be of interest to him. Wouldn't it be nice if he could tell me something about Tony and Blaise and perhaps there's a painting he would like to own. I could give him one.'

'Give Hartman a painting?' He was stunned. 'Holly, I have, as it happens, met him and can give you a number for his office in New York, but he can afford to buy. Don't be hasty. Don't worry about the Hartmans. They can take care of themselves.'

'My aunt loved Blaise Fougère. I'm sure she knew, what's his name, Taylor. Taylor, what a silly Christian name. Whatever his name is, Otto, Tony would want him to see the paintings.' She could feel an inner frisson of excitement. The paintings were becoming more than just a legacy. 'Otto, apart from their artistic value, they're a social document. Don't you see it? They tell a great deal about a famous man during a long life. He's so happy in some of them but he's so unhappy and almost disillusioned in others. It will be fascinating to research his life with Mr Hartman.'

Later she was to feel that this was the understatement of the entire twentieth century. It took weeks even to approach the inner sanctum where Taylor Hartman reigned supreme. His secretaries' secretaries had secretaries, and not one of these people would allow Holly anywhere near him.

Holly told John of her frustrations. He had taken her to dinner at Rogano, her favourite restaurant, and they were relaxing with their after-dinner coffee. Holly was torn: she felt that she was drifting, like one of the swans at Torry Bay, in no particular direction but at the whim of the tide; in this case, John's stronger personality. On the other hand, there was her considerable investment in the relationship over the past five years. She could not abandon that on what might turn out to be merely caprice.

They were, therefore, no longer at ease with one another and John was on his best behaviour. He was the perfect date, charming, courteous, attentive but not pushy and he very carefully said nothing at all about Holly's inheritance until she brought it up.

'If you found that there was a horde of unseen masterpieces featuring someone in your family, John, wouldn't you want to see them, possibly to have one as a special memento?'

John held his brandy glass in the palm of his hand and inhaled the aroma. 'I'm trying to think like a woman, Holly; I'm not being sexist, believe me. Part of my brain says that the very rich Mr Hartman has all the mementos he wants and so why does he want or need a painting, especially as a gift from you. He's not one of your waifs and strays, Hol.'

'That's not the point.' She leaned forward and he saw the excitement in her eyes. 'It's not a painting, John; it's a Tony Noble.'

'Wish I could excite you as much as this corporate executive does.'

She put her hands on his. 'Oh, John darling, it's not him; it's the paintings.'

'You're different, Hol.'

She sat back, astonished. 'I'm not. Try to understand. It's not the money. Never ever did I think Aunt Tony had any money. She lived so simply and I can't remember when she last sold a painting. I know they're real but I just can't take it in. But it's not the money; it's, oh, darling, don't sneer but I just feel something in the cottage, some atmosphere. It's as if I've been given a sacred duty.'

'And a million quid's worth of jewels.'

'I never think of them. One day I will, I suppose, and it'll dawn on me that they are real. I just can't come to terms with all this. Fougère has a foundation. Maybe there should be a Tony Noble Foundation for artistically talented children. There have to be really gifted children out there who are too poor for lessons.'

'How about the Holly Noble Foundation for indigent lawyers who want to get into politics so they can do something for everybody's children.'

She looked at him over the rim of her coffee cup, and then sipped slowly. 'John, the money is not relevant. Of course you have my full support, you have always had that, but I have to do this, see it through for Tony. Then I can think about money and investments and all that kind of lawyer-speak.'

'I thought I was speaking fiancé-speak.'

Was she being unfair? Serenely floating swans, if she remembered correctly, were paddling away like mad under the calm unruffled surface of the water. That's what she was, paddling furiously, trying to keep her head above water.

'Don't pressure me, John. I have so much on my mind: especially guilt. She was there for me, John, all through my childhood when my parents didn't really want to be bothered; she was my support through university and first boyfriends, and I just didn't bother to spend any time with her lately.'

He signalled for the waiter. 'And that's my fault, I suppose.'

'No, it's mine. I'm responsible for me and for my actions, and I'm not too happy with myself. I owe her.'

'Because she left you her Lothario's presents.'

At that her eyes widened in shock and he spoke quickly. 'I'm sorry, I'm sorry, Hol, but I'm having a hard time here too.'

His voice rose and Holly squirmed inside as she saw other diners looking, smiling, and wondering. She walked quickly before him out of the restaurant and waited while he paid the bill. 'I'm going home, John. I need time to think.'

'Don't think too much, Holly,' he said, turned on his heel, and left her in the middle of the pavement.

She looked after him for a moment and then walked to the road where she was lucky and found a taxi immediately. Don't think. No, she had to think – about so many things, but mainly about Tony and her life about which her niece had known nothing and about her love for Blaise Fougère. She made a mental list. First: somehow get in contact with Taylor Hartman.

Shrewd and more worldly-wise than Holly, John had decided that Hartman himself had decreed that he had no interest in Miss Holly Noble. He waited three days and then sent Holly more flowers and followed up with a visit.

'I hoped you'd let me drive up to Torry Bay with you this weekend.'

Holly stared at him. Torry Bay and John. She buried

her face in the flowers to give herself time to recover from the disloyal feeling that she did not want John at the cottage.

'I don't know, John; it's kind of you but . . .'

'We're both tense, sweetheart, and I think it's this Hartman fellow who's at the bottom of it. Once you've told him about the exhibition, you'll be relaxed.'

'He refuses to return my calls.'

'Tell one of the minions you plan to run a story in a tabloid about the affair.'

Holly was shocked. 'But that's unethical, and dishonest. I want him to see the paintings and have first choice, but if he expresses no interest then I intend to show them and sell them – apart from the ones I shall keep.'

He laughed. 'All the ones that have you in them, I suppose. I bet you were the sweetest little girl.'

Holly jerked away from his teasing fingers. 'I might keep a painting called *Uncle Fire* but not the others. There are some sad ones that I like. I'll have to think.'

What is wrong with me? This is my fiancé. We have been practically living together for five years and now I feel I can hardly bear to have him touch me. Get a grip, get a grip.

She turned into his arms and relaxed against him. 'You're right. I'm too tense. Let's drive up, just for the afternoon – she did not want to sleep with him in the cottage – and I'll show you some of the paintings.'

The following week an account of the discovery of the paintings was printed in the *Daily Mail*. Within hours of its publication Taylor Hartman was on the line from New York. To say that he was furious would be a gross understatement.

Holly, unfortunately, had absolutely no idea what he was talking about and was shocked when he told her. She asked herself, who could have sold such a story? Someone in Mr Gilbert's office, in Otto's? She did not want to face any other scenario.

'Mr Hartman,' she quavered, glad that the width of the Atlantic prevented him from seeing or even hearing her knocking knees, 'you must believe me – I did not give that paper this story and I have no idea who did. The only people who know about the paintings are of the highest—'

He interrupted. 'At least one isn't, Miss Noble. Demand a retraction and an apology immediately. These paintings, if there are paintings, are certainly not of Blaise Fougère. The idea is preposterous.'

Holly's knees were beginning to behave and her tongue had unstuck itself from the roof of her mouth. She would not be bullied. 'Kindly listen,' she began but he was already talking.

'Do you have any idea of the number of women who claimed to have had an affair with my uncle in his lifetime, Miss Noble?' The voice was full of repressed anger. 'And every one of them proved a liar. The opera world is full of sick groupies who create fantasies for themselves. Blaise Fougère was a gentleman. He was devoted to my aunt and would never have done anything to hurt her.'

'Antonia Noble was an eminent British painter,' said Holly. 'There are two famous paintings by her of Blaise Fougère—'

'Yes, yes, I know,' he said impatiently. 'Chocolate-box covers, both of them, sickly sentimental. *Lohengrin* in Paris and an absolutely nauseating *des Grieux* now in London. You should go see it – it stinks.'

'No doubt you are also a renowned art critic, Mr Hartman.' Holly was now quite calm; Tony had never been sentimental or sickly sweet. She loathed Taylor Hartman. 'The point is there are over forty canvasses of Mr Fougère in my house in Scotland. They are signed and dated and none of them is a costumed portrait. They are pictures of a great singer *en vacances*, as it were. The first one was painted in 1937 and the last in 1990.'

'An obsession,' he said after a pause. 'A diseased mind. Opera singers, especially the few really great tenors, attract them.'

'There is some fabulous jewellery too, Mr Hartman. My aunt's lawyer assures me that it's valuable. As to the paintings, I am in several of them and my aunt would never have put me in a fantasy. These are genuine and the world deserves to see them.'

There was silence for a while and Holly let the wires hum while he thought of his next strategy. 'You're going to tell me you knew him well, that he held you on his knee?' The voice was sarcastic, full of loathing and, surprisingly, of hurt.

'I remember nothing about him at all, Mr Hartman.'

'Where are they?'

Holly laughed. 'They're in a place called Torry Bay which is near Achahoish in Argyll.'

She thought she heard a gasp before he swore fluently but quietly in French. 'That's so God-awful it has to be true,' he said at last in English. 'Have you photographed them?'

That had never occurred to her. 'No.'

He swore again but in English and obviously in exasperation. 'Well, do it, Miss Noble, and then call me at this number and I'll meet you in London. I can be there in three hours . . .'

'I work for a living, Mr Hartman, and I can't just drop everything to suit you.'

'I'm dropping everything to suit you and your cartoons, Miss Noble. Call me.'

She rang John to tell him of her surprise phone call. 'Out of the blue, John; after all the trouble I have taken to contact him, the phone rings, I pick it up and it's a very angry Taylor Hartman. He says his British lawyer told him there was what he termed "an inflammatory article" in the *Daily Mail*. "Paintings prove love nest", or something like that. But how could there have been anything? Surely Mr Gilbert . . . Otto . . .'

'Agents, Holly. A bit of sensation and the price goes up.'

'I can't believe that of Otto. He was so . . . moved by the paintings.' She stopped talking, for the thought that wanted to come into her head was too awful to express or even to contemplate. She shook her head as if to chase it away. 'Hartman is prepared to fly in to London to see photographs of the paintings although he seems to think there's no credibility in my story. He says other women claimed to have had . . . known Blaise Fougère.'

'Perhaps they did.'

'Blaise Fougère loved my aunt.'

'Oh, come on, Holly. Your aunt never left a tiny cottage in Argyll. It's fantasy, Holly. Hartman knows it and you won't accept it. You cannot argue with the Hartmans of this world. If he tells the press you're a sensationalist, he'll make a fool of you and your aunt and of me, Holly, and my chances of getting into politics will go right down the tube. Holly, sweetheart, sell the damned cottage and the paintings and let's get married.'

Holly stared at the phone as if she could not understand what she had heard. Married. How often during their relationship had she longed to hear those words? How many times had he sweet-talked her into agreeing to postpone it?

'I'll go to London, John. While I'm there, I'll see Otto. Now, if you'll excuse me, I'm off to buy a Polaroid.'

Two weeks later she telephoned Taylor Hartman and this time was put straight through. She told him she had photographs of the paintings and they arranged to meet, for her sake, the following Saturday.

He had a suite in the Park Lane Hotel and Holly visited him there.

'I meant a professional photographer, Miss Noble,' he said after sitting for several minutes quietly looking through the photographs and handing them back. 'I'll have to view them. I can see they are of my uncle but the photography is so amateurish that it's impossible to judge the quality.'

Holly tried not to be insulted. She was considered a fair photographer but she had never photographed paintings before. She would not allow this man to annoy her. She had been stunned to see how much he resembled his uncle. The body was leaner but he was just as tall and the face harder perhaps but still very handsome. She would not permit herself to be attracted to him. He was so used to being courted. Life, and Miss Holly Noble, had a nice little surprise in store for him.

'As I told you the paintings are stored in an attic in my aunt's house in Argyll. I intend to sell them: unfortunately I cannot keep all of them.'

'There are letters in my uncle's hand, some real proof?'

'No. My aunt had obviously cleared out what she did not want to be found. She left me a letter that led to the paintings. If it makes you feel any better I do not intend to make an issue of the relationship that undoubtedly existed between Mr Fougère and Miss Noble.'

He looked at her shrewdly. 'The "Great opera singer's secret life" was just a ploy to get my attention.'

'I did not sanction the release of that story, Mr Hartman. I told you that I know nothing about it.' She took a deep breath and smothered the suspicion that kept popping up. 'To be honest with you, I believe it would never have been released had I had any reply to my letters or telephone calls.'

'Good grief, my dear girl. Do you think my staff have nothing better to do than reply to every nut who sends me a letter?'

She had thought that might be a part of a rich and powerful man's argument and had prepared an answer of which she was quite proud. 'Courtesy costs nothing. I take it you have some minion who could print out hundreds of little "Mr Hartman thanks you blah blah, but unfortunately blah blah" and I am not your dear girl. Now, if you would like to see the paintings, I am in Achahoish almost every weekend and can meet you at Torry Bay.'

He stood up abruptly and she had the distinct feeling that it was to prevent himself from strangling her. No, Mr Hartman was not used to being thwarted.

He walked to the window and stood looking down at the London traffic that tried desperately to fling itself past the huge hotel in the frustrated hope of beating just one red light. 'Hard to believe all that traffic is down there.'

Holly said nothing.

'Miss Noble. Concorde brought me here. I had intended to fly back this evening: I have a very important meeting in Washington tomorrow.'

'Have a pleasant flight,' Holly said and picked up her bag. She could feel him drawing himself together.

'Miss Noble.' Was he speaking through gritted teeth?

She dared not look. 'I will postpone my meeting and fly back to this God-forsaken place with you.'

Should she tell him that she was in London so seldom that she had hoped to go to the theatre, an art gallery? Better not.

'I had a return flight booked for tomorrow.' She indicated the telephone that stood on the antique desk by the window.

He smiled. 'Allow me to make the arrangements. I can't wait for scheduled flights. You had better check out of your hotel so we can fly up as soon as possible, view the paintings and make some decisions. Where may I contact you?'

She gave him the number of her hotel and, feeling as if she had been steam-rollered, hurried from his suite. How could Tony have lived with someone as high-powered and arrogant as any relative of Taylor Hartman would probably be?

'Blaise was so much nicer,' she said out loud in the lift and earned a doubtful look from the elderly dowager who was gliding down with her, 'and obviously she had him in small doses,' she finished to herself.

Later that afternoon Taylor's private secretary telephoned her. His car would pick her up in exactly thirty-five minutes. They would proceed to the airport where they would board a private plane that would fly them to Argyll. A car would be waiting to transport them to Torry Bay.

Thirty-five minutes? Why not a plain old thirty? Taylor Hartman was precise. He did not believe in wasting time. She vowed to be ready and she was. Her bill paid, she was waiting in the foyer when a large chauffeur-driven Bentley pulled up at the front door. Hartman was inside and she was pleased to see that he was not quite so successful corporate executive as he had been earlier. He was wearing a casual suit with a pale blue polo neck sweater and loafers. Holly felt overdressed in her smartly tailored grey suit.

His eyes gave no hint of what he thought of her clothes and she decided that she did not care. She had not dressed for Taylor Hartman but for comfort. Obviously he had done the same.

'Do you always travel by private plane, Mr Hartman?' she asked as they approached the airport.

'No,' he said shortly and then, as if ashamed of his abrupt answer, he elaborated. 'Concorde isn't private but it's the quickest way of getting from New York to London. My time is valuable and so a private plane allows me to work with my secretaries without interruption. Who knows, Miss Noble, perhaps if I keep the peasants' – or is it the minions' – noses to the grindstone while in the air, I may allow them some free time to see the sights when we set down. Are there sights in Argyll?'

'None that I think will interest you.'

'You know absolutely nothing about what interests me, Miss Noble.'

That was such a well-deserved put-down that she stayed down until they were in the air. She had always liked flying but to be in a privately chartered plane was exciting. She tried – and failed – not to show it.

'The ground looks just the same from the window of British Airways,' he said with a smile and she found herself for one moment prepared to like him.

She laughed and sat back. 'I know, but I just can't get over the fact that a plane gets into the air in the first place.'

They did not fly to Glasgow as Holly had assumed they would but to a small private airstrip near Oban. A car was waiting. For the Taylor Hartmans of this world a car would always be waiting.

'Ever been on a bus?' Holly asked unkindly but he did not think her remark worthy of comment.

Quite right too, she decided.

Hartman was looking at a map and discussing the route with the car's original driver.

'He's not coming with us?' Holly had been ushered into the passenger seat – she had assumed because she knew the way – and now Hartman was trying to find enough room for his long legs in the space behind the wheel.

He buckled his seat belt and glanced over at her. 'Your virtue is quite safe.'

Holly flushed and subsided. She almost wished that she had never decided he had some small right to see the pictures. They drove for an hour in a sun-warmed silence. Autumn in Argyll was on its best behaviour.

Hartman broke the silence with an exclamation. 'Do you mind?' he asked and before she could say anything he had stopped the car and was getting out. 'Ancient stones,' he said as he closed the door.

Intrigued, she followed him as far as the dyke. Her skirt was too short and tight to allow her to follow him into the field where a circle of great quiet sentinels stood waiting for someone to discover their secrets. Hartman, oblivious of the damp ground and the dried grass that pulled at his expensively tailored trousers, was walking around the stones, touching them, viewing them. He turned and saw her at the wall and smiled. He was very attractive. She would not smile back.

'A *sight*,' he said.

'Blaise was here,' she called across the field. 'Tony has . . . had several books about Pictish stones. They're at the cottage.'

She turned and went back to the car and several minutes later he followed her.

'Can we call a truce for the rest of the day,' he said. 'I'm starving and I want to eat at that little inn back there. Would you care to join me?'

It never occurred to her to say no. There were only a few tinned goods at the house.

They retraced their steps to the small hotel and Holly was surprised by the quality of the food and the cooking in such an out-of-the-way place. Hartman was not.

'I always look for places like this. Sometimes you get a real bummer of a meal, but most times it's great regional cooking. Now I feel much more ready to fight you over the paintings.'

'I didn't have to tell you about them,' Holly said, but without rancour. Something in their relationship had changed subtly. Was it the breaking of bread together?

They talked about the stones and the Picts, that ancient people who had lived in the area and carved their strange messages on the great stones, until they were almost in sight of the house. The road meandered up and around the glen and then it stopped for a moment at the top of the hill before plunging breathlessly down to the bay.

'Achahoish,' said Holly, her heart full of its beauty and its association, 'and there's Torry Bay.'

Hartman stopped the car, looked at her quickly and then away again. '*Merde*,' he said and then he was quiet.

Holly looked too and tried to see the view as Taylor Hartman had seen it, completely unknown, a surprise, but she could see nothing that could cause such a response. She had forgotten most of the French she had learned at school but she remembered enough to know that *merde* was certainly not a compliment.

She looked again and smiled with happiness as she saw the few houses snuggling into the valley and the purple and green of the hillsides. She saw the sea curling around as if holding the bay in its arms.

He said nothing as they drove to the wall of rhododendrons that made a huge arc around the cottage and its garden.

'Sometimes the sea meets each wing of the rhodies. It can be quite bleak but it's absolutely glorious in the spring, a wall of pink and lilac.'

Still he was silent. She left him with his own thoughts and went to open the front door.

'It's quite small,' she said when she found him at her

side. 'Look round if you like. I'll open the attic where the paintings are.' She looked at him measuringly. 'You might want to bring some of them downstairs to the living room. There isn't much room up there.'

She went upstairs and unlocked the attic door. The paintings still stood, their faces to the wall and then Hartman was there, bending his head to enter. He reminded her of something.

You cannot expect me to stand up in here, ma mie. *This is for little sprites, like you and my Hollyberry*.

She looked around but the ghost, if ghost it had been, was gone, and Hartman obviously had heard nothing. He went to the first painting and held it from the wall. He said nothing but just stood and then he looked at a second painting and Holly left him and went downstairs to sit in the window and look at the sea.

She heard him moving around, cursing as he bumped his head and then she heard him on the stairs.

'Holly,' he shouted. When had she become Holly?

'Turn right,' she called and soon he was in the room, his size and the large painting filling it up alarmingly.

'We can't leave them here,' he said. 'There could be a fire or a burglary.'

He propped up the painting against the table. It was of Blaise sitting in a field of dandelions. 'What's Godalming?'

'A little town in Surrey near London.'

'I like this,' he said. 'My uncle very rarely let himself be seen so at ease. The painting is quite crude, of course. The gold is perhaps a little harsh.'

'When did you last run half naked through a field of dandelions? It looks just fine to me.'

He laughed. 'I'm perfectly sure you didn't mean to imply what you have just implied. I'll be back.' And he was gone, leaping up the old oak staircase and returning more slowly with another of Tony's paintings.

By nine in the evening Holly was beginning to grow rather nervous. Hartman was as gripped as Otto had been and seemed unaware of the time and it was at least two hours back to Glasgow. She went upstairs and found him sitting cross-legged on the floor.

'It's getting late.'

'Got anything to eat in the freezer?'

He seemed astonished to discover that there was neither food nor freezer. Holly went to the kitchen to see what she could find.

'There's a farmhouse just round the bay a little. I'll see if they'll sell me some eggs.'

'Great,' he said. 'If you fix us something to eat, I'll spend some more time on the pictures, although it is really impossible to view them properly like this – we'll have to discuss where and when I can do – and then I'll make some calls and find a hotel. You don't mind staying over one night? Use my cellphone if there's someone who'll be worried.'

No, there was no one who would be worried but how was she to tell him there was no hotel for miles?

'There's no hotel for miles.'

He was unperturbed. 'I wonder if there's an old razor or a toothbrush in the bathroom. Won't matter. My secretary did tell me to be ready for anything: he'll be so pleased to be able to say, "I told you so." '

Holly shrugged, changed into some flat shoes and walked off to visit their neighbours. She was not afraid to spend the night in a remote cottage with a complete stranger. She was a mature woman, not a child. It just wasn't done though. She wondered what he would say if she told him that.

'Good heavens, how medieval. Now, I've checked the bedrooms and you may have the little one. If you object to being turfed out of the main bedroom feel free to share.'

'Very funny,' said Holly with an attempt at lightness.

'There are women who would jump at the chance. Come on, Holly, I'm too tall for that sweet little bed.'

'You know perfectly well I'm not talking about the rooms.'

He looked at her innocently. 'What did you manage to rustle up?'

'Rustle is about the right verb. We have some eggs, some venison sausages and some home-cured ham.'

'Sounds wonderful. Any time you're ready.'

'I can't cook,' said Holly angrily. That was not strictly true but he was used to fine dining in first-class hotels. She could not cook for him.

'Believe me, you have got to be better than me. Look, I'll fix the table and wash up after. How's that for equality?'

The sausages were just a little too well cooked but he did not complain about that or the instant coffee.

He pushed himself away from the kitchen table and leaned back in his chair. 'I could get used to the simple life.'

'Not in a force ten gale, you couldn't.'

'Maybe I'm at my best when pitted against the forces of nature.'

She did not rise to that bait so he began to talk about the pictures.

'Thank you for allowing me to see them. I'm not admitting that my uncle posed for any of them but they are extremely good paintings and if you are agreeable I would like one or two for my private collection.'

'They're real: the relationship was a reality and very important to each of them. Admit it.'

He looked away from her towards the window. The sky outside was lilac and pink. 'I knew him all my life. I would have known,' he said bleakly.

She said nothing. 'I would have known.' Had she not felt exactly the same herself? 'They're genuine. Choose your favourite. I have my own almost decided.'

He said nothing but was obviously deep in thought and she allowed him some space.

'I won't fight about that,' he said at last. 'It's what to do with the bulk. Would you consider storing them properly until I can do some research . . . and come to terms with what they're telling me?'

'That shouldn't be a problem.'

'I'll make some calls,' he said, getting up and moving over to where his mobile phone sat on the dresser.

'I have already made perfectly good arrangements, Taylor.'

He smiled and it was not so sweet a smile as he had awarded her earlier.

'Taylor,' he said. 'I wondered when you would use my name. To show us that we're equal.'

'Where the paintings are concerned, I am in absolute control.'

'I'm not going to steal them, for God's sake, but I want them properly stored and professionally researched and valued.'

Until that moment, no matter what John had said, Holly had never seriously considered their actual monetary value. To her they were a long letter from Tony. 'To me they are absolutely priceless, Mr Hartman, but you wouldn't understand that.' She walked past him to the door.

'There's some washing-up liquid under the sink. Goodnight.'

She would have felt wonderful if she had not heard him laughing as she walked, with ramrod straight spine, up the stairs to the smaller bedroom.

6

THE PERFORMING BEAR

'Love me, Toinette, love me.'

He was undoing her blouse and she gave herself up to the magic of his hands, his lips. 'I adore you, Blaise. I will always adore you.'

Later she sat wrapped in his bathrobe and listened to his humming while he prepared them a meal. 'I have never heard you sing, Blaise,' she said reflectively. They had been together for nearly two years but never had she heard him sing.

He stopped whisking his eggs. He was surprised. 'But I sing all the time, *ma mie*. I was singing now.'

'You were humming; and sometimes you warm up, but that's just like gargling or water going down the drain.'

Omelette pan in hand, he bowed low as if for a compliment. 'I sing on the bicycle.'

'To yourself, or sometimes you shout, "*En passant par la Lorraine avec mes sabots*," but that's not singing, singing.'

'It is my most favourite song and I, Blaise Marie Fougère,' he said, again bowing to her grandly, 'never shout. I am a tenor, from *tenir*, to hold, not some word for to shout.'

She examined her toenails critically and decided to paint each one a different colour. 'You told me that already; when may I hear you sing?'

'It is better that I make you sing,' he said, slipping his hands under the robe and running them over her warm responsive body.

'The omelette,' she said before it was too late.

He laughed and released her.

The omelette and the salad of fresh herbs were delicious. Blaise had moved into a small inexpensive flat on the other side of the river at the end of his first year of study. It meant that they could stay together without feeling guilty. He could make omelettes, he could concoct salads, and he made the most delicious coffee. Tony could cook nothing palatable. All her creativity was expended on her canvasses – or in loving Blaise.

All week she lived at the students' residence for which her father paid, but from Friday evening until Sunday evening she stayed with Blaise. She knew that she would have to tell her parents, but since she was well aware that they, and her brother, would disapprove, she kept putting it off.

'You haven't answered me,' she said as she watched him walk around the tiny kitchen area. She loved watching him. His body was as expressive as his hands and as expressive as she was sure his real voice would be.

'What I loved most about her,' he said looking at an empty chair instead of at Tony, 'was that in all our life together she never asked me to sing.'

Tony launched herself from the bed in a tangle of too long bathrobe and threw her arms around his waist. 'Beast, beast,' she wailed. 'You are talking as if it's all over and we were only friends.'

Calmly he put down the hot coffee pot before taking her in his arms. 'Tony, Tony.' He laughed. 'I was pretending that I was very old and very famous. All my public life I will meet people who will treat me like an automaton; you know, Drop in the penny and the performing bear performs. Every song I sing, I will sing for you, Toinette, but I cannot sing in this little apartment because I will wake the babies and the old people and would have to return to the so stuffy hotel where I cannot sing either.'

'But it's as if you are keeping something from me, a special part of you. I show you my paintings: that's laying bare my soul, Blaise. I need to see your soul.'

'Such melodrama. Are you sure you are not French, my Antoinette? No, no,' he said, holding her tightly as she tried to pull away from him. 'I am wicked to tease.' He held her against him for some moments while he thought. 'Come on, put on some clothes. We will go to find a place where I can sing for you. Then we will return and you will sing for me. That is a good bargain, no?'

She blushed furiously and hid her hot face against his chest. 'I should feel wicked, Blaise. My parents will say that I am wicked but I don't feel wicked. Being with you feels right.'

'It is right, for both of us, *ma mie*. We are the two halves of the coin, the sun and the moon. You, Tony, are the glorious burning energetic sun and I am your pale satellite who thanks you for your light.'

She looked at him in wonder. He was the sun and she the insipid moon but she would not argue. He was going to sing, really sing, and she was, at last, going to hear him.

She dressed warmly. It was cold and they were going to hide in the park after the gates had closed. He was crazy; she was insane. They would go to jail but she could deny him nothing. It was her fault after all. She wanted to hear him sing full voice and at this stage in his career an empty locked London park was the only place he could find where they would be, for a little, undisturbed.

They crossed the river and went to Hyde Park, which Blaise knew closed at midnight. There they would be safe from prying eyes. They strolled around in the twilight. Mothers and fathers and grandparents were collecting their charges and ushering them out before the park keeper locked the great iron gates. They heard voices: 'You come away from that swan right now, Alf, or I'll clip your ear.'

As innocently as possible they managed to slip behind the bandstand and there they sat, their arms around each other for warmth and comfort until they were quite sure that the park was empty. They did not speak but listened to the park fold in upon itself to rest until the morning. Trees sighed as evening breezes attempted to play and, from a distance, they heard the noise of traffic, a bus, a police car with its klaxon blazing, sounds that were part of the very fabric of the great city.

'What do you smell?' Tony whispered.

'You, the cleanness of you. Is there such a word?'

'Cleanliness.'

'Of course, and wood smoke. Already someone has found some leaves or something from the garden.'

'I smell chips.'

He laughed and then he stood up. He bowed to her. 'You wish?'

She nodded and he said, 'Welcome, Madame and all the little creepy crawlies, to the first official recital of Blaise Marie Fougère, tenor.'

He walked lightly up the steps to the bandstand and stood in the moonlight while he listened to the orchestra playing in his head. He began to sing.

Nothing had prepared Tony for this first experience. He sang in French, '*Je Crois Entendre Encore*', the delicate tenor aria from Bizet's *Les Pêcheurs de Perles*, the pearl fishers. Her French was not good enough to understand all the words but she did not need a translation. The words poured in a golden stream into the silver night. She did not know that he still had much to learn of technique, that the power and purity for which he was to become world-famous were still in their infancy. It did not matter.

One aria over, he began another, this time in Italian: '*Una Furtiva Lagrima*' from Donizetti's comic opera, *L'Elisir d'Amore*. As it rose to its climax in one great long breath she began to cry. She knew so very definitely that he was not and never would be hers. He would never belong entirely to her. He belonged to the world and she knew that there would be weeks, months, when she would sit and wait to receive whatever was left to give her. But something deep inside told her that he would need her to be there. For his sanity he would need to know, without question, that she would be waiting always, ready to give and give again.

He stopped singing in some consternation and jumped down. '*Ma mie*, that is a happy song. I have sing it badly. You cannot see that I smile in the moonlight. See me smile.' He was beside her on the grass, holding her, kissing her eyes, her hair.

'I know. I was crying because it was so beautiful,' she lied. 'I feel almost as though you are not real, Blaise, not a human being at all, and I have touched something almost mystical.'

He snorted with anger as only a Frenchman can. 'Shall I show you how human I am, my Tony? Who better than you knows that I am just a man with needs like other men?'

Plus a once-in-a-lifetime talent. She thought it but did not say it. For her he must be Blaise the friend, the lover, not Fougère the tenor.

'Sing one of those rousing ones,' she demanded. 'Remember that opera we heard at the Garden?'

'We have hear several. I will sing "*Di Quella Pira*" from *Trovatore* but my voice is too young and I will no doubt crack, but better here than at class when the maestro will sigh and wonder loudly if France does not have a school where Frenchmen can go to torture professors of their own race.'

He did not crack. He never got as far as that last ringing triumphant note, for suddenly there was strong torchlight shining on his face and a large policeman was holding the torch.

'What do you fink you're doing? How did you bof get in here?'

'Officer, how wonderful to see you,' said Tony, fluttering her eyelashes. 'I can't think how we got locked in,' she added as she looked down modestly and allowed him to come to his own conclusions. 'We were trying to get someone's attention.'

'Very unusual way if I may say so, miss. Your friend, foreign is he?'

'French.'

'Ah, well then,' he said, as if Blaise's nationality explained everything. 'Come along. You ought to be had up but I won't report you this time.' He looked sternly at their set faces. 'I'll remember you bof if I sees you in here again.'

'Thank you.' Tony watched him lock the gates behind them. 'Come along, Blaise,' she said and, still without a word, he followed her.

'Tell your friend he could make a nice little bit down the pub of a Friday night if he learned someink in English.'

To Tony's relief Blaise spoke but she was distressed by what he said; their first difference of opinion. 'Where did you learn to lie so well, Tony? I was prepared to pay a fine. That is all it would have been. My father is with the law in France.'

'You're shocked. It saves trouble, that's all.'

'I am prepared to pay when I do wrong. That is justice.'

'Money, money.' Their evening was being spoiled.

'I was not referring to money. In this case, perhaps a night in jail.'

Now she was shocked. 'My father would never hold his head up in public again if his daughter went to jail.'

'Toinette, I would not allow you to go to jail. The idea was mine. They would have telephone my father. A reprimand, no more.'

She said nothing but walked on, legs suddenly weary. Blaise stopped and held her close. 'I will take care of you, Tony, always.' Suddenly he laughed. 'And see, if my professors are in the right and I have no future, I can make a nice bit down the pub. We will not starve.'

She threw her arms around him, binding her eagle to her while he was still unaware of the true power of his wings. 'You will be the best, Blaise. Millions of people will pay anything to hear you sing.'

'Funny little Tony. I have so much to learn before I will be allowed on to a stage.' He held her away from him so that he could look down into her eyes. 'But, Toinette, when I am there, I will need you with me. You fill all my senses. Without your love I will sing with technique but without heart. Love me, Toinette, always.'

'With my last breath I will tell of my love for you, Blaise Fougère, for the man, my man.'

'My woman,' he said and she exalted in her power as she heard the passion in his voice.

She was painting the sun and the moon into a background of a portrait of Blaise when she heard that Germany had invaded Poland. She could not, with any accuracy, have found Poland on a globe but she knew where Germany was. Blaise had been muttering things about German aggression for over a year now but Tony had soothed and comforted him and made him think only of his studies or of her.

He had not heard the broadcast. There was a pile of open books and scores on the desk in front of him and he was concentrating. His powers of concentration fascinated her. He would sit there, making notes, humming lines, until severe stomach pains told him that he was hungry.

Tony was almost the same when she was painting: she just had to try once more to get it right, to show the young softness of his arm, the play of light on a leaf, the rustle of wind through grass.

She turned off the radio and that, of course, since she did not want it to do so, disturbed him.

'Is it time for dinner, Toinette?' he asked, but his eyes were still on the open score.

'What does your stomach tell you?'

'I am not listen to my stomach. I am listen to Beethoven.'

She looked at him and picked up her brush. She decided not to tell him. She would keep him here for ever. Never again would she switch on the radio. She would be happy here, with him, for ever and ever, Amen.

But he would not be happy. And that was all that mattered.

She went over and pulled his head back against her stomach. 'Germany has invaded Poland.'

He stayed, his head against her belly, for some time.

'Bastards,' he said in English and then a long stream of fluent and, thankfully, incomprehensible French.

'Did I not tell you, Tony, last year when Daladier and Bonnet came to London to talk about Czechoslovakia and in December when Ribbentrop dirtied the ground of Paris with his "There is no territorial question between France and Germany", did I not tell you that it was just a matter of time. There will be war, Toinette, another world war that will make the war to end all wars like a squabble among children.' He jumped up. 'Come, get a coat. I must talk with my papa.'

She liked to clean her brushes before abandoning them but she went with him, leaving the brushes and the paint to harden and spoil. If there was to be war, and there could not be, spoiled brushes would be such a small worry.

He held her hand and pulled her along through crowded September streets that somehow seemed tense and sad. The world was waiting.

He found a telephone box, put in his coins, and asked for his number. She watched him shovel coins into the box and then talk and laugh and talk and cry. Then he was quiet and hung up the telephone but he did not move and she dared not ask him why. The telephone rang and again he talked and listened and the only word she seemed to understand was Papa.

When he put the receiver back the second time he stood for a moment weeping and then he pulled her to him and cried into her hair and she was terrified and cried too. That made him stop. 'Tony, Tony,' he whispered, kissing her hair, her eyes, her nose. 'I have frighten you. Come, we will go somewhere nice to eat.'

'We can't. You have no tie and there is paint on my skirt.'

He held her from him and looked at her as he laughed without mirth. 'Dear God in heaven. Hitler is rampaging like a wolf all over Europe and we worry about ties and paint. Oh, my Toinette, if *le bon Dieu* permits, I will make sure that these are your biggest worries. Now I will be the well-brought-up young man and I will go back in the flat and wash my face and put on a tie and then I will take you in a nice restaurant to drink wine and to dance.'

But he did not. They went back to the flat and he closed the door and she turned into his arms and quickly, methodically, he took off first her clothes and then his own, and he took her to the bed and they made love until they cried out together in mingled ecstasy and pain. Never had he been so rough; never had he been so gentle; and Tony tried to match his passion, his grief, his love, his regret. Afterwards they slept and when they woke it was Sunday morning and it was dark.

'Now I am listening to my stomach, Tony. What is in the pantry?'

They rose, as they were, and found bread and cheese and tomatoes and red wine. Blaise brought her his shirt and he put on his shorts and they sat on the bed and ate and drank and talked.

'Did I hurt you?' He could not look at her.

She put her hand on his knee. 'No.'

He sighed. 'I am glad. It is fact, Toinette. Papa is sure that France is about to declare war on Germany. He wants me to stay here but I must go back to France and fight for my country.'

She threw herself into his arms and red wine stained the sheets. 'No, no. I will not let you go. You are too valuable. Civilisation needs the arts, Blaise. Your voice will heal wounds.'

He held her and rocked her as if she were a baby. 'But how could I live with my own wounds, *ma mie*? I must return to France. I must go home to enlist. Do you understand? I have not yet done the military service.' He gave a Gallic shrug. 'It has to happen and so – I will go now. Try to understand, *ma mie*, the more fast I go, the more fast I will come back. In two or three years I will be more mature, my body and my voice, I mean. This will not stop my career.'

'Unless you're killed. Don't go, Blaise,' she begged, all pride forgotten, clutching him. 'Your father is rich and important; he can keep you out of it. The war machine doesn't need you and I do, I do.'

He stopped her cries with his mouth and when she was moaning in his arms he loved her gently until dawn broke quietly over London. He held her in his arms as she slept and he lay playing his favourite opera over in his head, his beloved *Fidelio*. 'I will return, Toinette, and I will sing Florestan for you, and Alfredo and Rodolfo, and one day Parsifal and Otello and even Tristan. We will conquer the world together, *ma mie*, you with your painting, me with my singing, and the world will be a nicer place because we were in it.'

She woke and looked at him. 'Marry me today, tomorrow; and give me a baby because you won't come back, Blaise. It was too beautiful, too perfect not to be spoiled.'

He took off his signet ring with its deeply carved B.M.F. and put it into her hand. 'Tomorrow I will buy a gold chain for you to wear this round your neck. When the war is over, I will ask for it back and I will replace it with a wedding ring, and then there will be babies, *ma mie*, lots of fat little babies who will sing as they paint. Is that not a glorious picture to hold in your head?'

'I will hold it in my heart,' she said.

7

Torry Bay, 1998. Glasgow, 1998

Taylor had been perfectly amiable in Argyll. He had wakened her at the crack of dawn and driven her down roads where mist lingered to the airport. They were in Glasgow before eight o'clock. 'A decent cup of coffee,' was all he said as she stumbled out of the car.

'I go direct from here to Washington,' he said curtly. 'You have my New York number. Ask for Chandler, Chandler North; he will tell you where I am.' He looked round to where a uniformed driver was waiting. 'The car will take you home.'

She had not expected that last courtesy. Her neighbours would be interested to see her arrive in a chauffeur-driven car. Quite a change from her old Fiat or even John's more stylish Audi.

She was absolutely exhausted and sat down at her kitchen table to catch her breath, and without the overwhelming strength of Taylor's size and personality she had time to think.

Damn. Otto. She had intended to see him while she was in London, at least see his gallery.

A very groggy voice answered on the ninth ring just as Holly was looking in growing realisation at her watch.

'Miss Noble, it is not yet nine o'clock on a Sunday morning. I went to bed at three.'

'I'm so sorry, Otto. It's just that Taylor has been here.'

'Taylor. Wait.'

She waited.

'I can't think without my glasses. You said Taylor as in the Hartman Corporation?'

'The very same.'

'Tell me.'

'He rang me. Seemingly there was a rather lurid article in the gutter press.' She did not ask if he knew about it; she was perfectly sure he would not stoop to such actions. 'He asked me to photograph the paintings and meet him in London – you know these jet-setters, fly in, fly out? He was quite rude about the quality.'

'Of Tony Noble's paintings? The philistine.'

She laughed, and relaxed. 'No, about my photography. I flew down on the shuttle, had time to check in to my hotel and went to meet him. Next thing I am on a private jet flying back to Argyll. The important thing, however, is that he has seen the paintings and I think he wants one or two.'

'What did he say about their authenticity?'

'I take it you're asking if he believes in the relationship?' She waited but he said nothing.

'He asked if there were letters. There are none.'

'Are you sure, Holly? Have you – forgive me, my dear – have you searched?'

'Her lawyer gave me a letter at the funeral. It led me to the jewellery and the key to the attic. I saw no other papers apart from a few sketchbooks. Otto, are you free yet to pack and appraise the paintings?'

'I will make myself free. I want them out of Scotland before the winter. Are you able to join me?'

She thought of school where they had still not found a replacement and she thought of John. No, she was not free. 'Whenever you can come, Otto, will be fine.'

'I'll ring you in a few days.'

'I more or less promised Taylor that I would keep him informed: no point in alienating him, is there?'

But he merely said goodbye and hung up.

The unseen but all-powerful Chandler had been informed of their progress. London in March was impossible. Mr Hartman had to be in Japan. May perhaps. Would Miss Noble agree to a private showing with no publicity? The family were anxious to avoid any scandal. Scandal? That made Holly really angry. Tony had not been ashamed of her love for Blaise Fougère. Each of them, Tony and Blaise, had kept quiet about their relationship for their own reasons. If Blaise was anything at all like his arrogant nephew, he was the one who had wished to keep the affair such a well-kept secret. He was the one who had allowed all the publicity that said he was a devoted husband whose eyes never strayed. That pose was a lie as the paintings showed.

She was so angry about the word scandal that the word family failed to register.

'Chandler, I think I should talk to Mr Hartman.'

Taylor had telephoned sounding cold and remote and they had had a real argument.

'Look, Holly, not every artist has a relationship with her subject. No one has ever associated Blaise with her, even though she was commissioned to paint him . . . He was the nicest guy in the world; maybe they were friends.'

Holly interrupted. 'Don't be silly. Friends? They were lovers and you know it and your silly pride won't let you accept that.' She could almost see him. He would be standing up as he yelled at her, possibly pacing up and down on expensive carpeting. She would not join the hundreds of people who allowed Taylor Hartman to browbeat them.

'I will not have my uncle a subject for gossips. He spent his life protecting my aunt, and his privacy. His will asked me to protect his . . . reputation as he protected it; it's a sacred trust. He still has an enormous following.'

'Of people who loved to hear him sing. Do you think they're suddenly going to stop buying discs if they hear he had a . . .?' She had been about to say mistress but that was not Tony's role.

'Holly, you don't understand—' he began.

'I understand being patronised, Mr Hartman. I'll remind you again that I had no legal obligation to show you the paintings and I will show and sell them when I feel the time is right.'

She had hung up on him, assuring herself that handing Mr Hartman such a salutary lesson was good for the moulding of his character. Mulling over the conversation later she could only recall the words 'protecting my aunt'.

Several weeks later Chandler contacted her. Mr Hartman would prefer that the paintings be shown in New York. He would be most grateful.

Would he indeed? Holly's initial response was to say no and Otto had agreed. 'I smell deviousness, Holly. The same international buyers would come if I hung them in the kitchen at Torry Bay.'

That incongruous picture had made them both laugh.

'I would like Tony to have an international reputation . . . but as a painter, Otto, not as a mistress. I am right? The paintings are good?'

'Some of them are great, darling girl.'

She almost wept but, glad that Otto could not see her eyes, spoke briskly. 'Good. Now let us arrange a date for the opening. The Hartman Corporation will be informed like any other prospective customer.'

That conversation over, it was time to deal with John. 'John, how are you?'

He answered her question with one of his own. 'Where are you, Holly? Achahoish?'

'No, still here at the flat.' She stopped and then rushed on. 'I could make us some dinner and we could talk.' She hated herself for begging, but surely there should be no false pride where love was. She had promised to marry John; they could work this out. Compared with Taylor Hartman and his faults and failings, John was a paragon among men. She had probably misjudged him.

'I have some work to finish. Say eight.' He sounded so cold, so dismissive. Then he said, 'I've missed you, Holly.'

Her heart swelled with relief. They would work it out. 'I've missed you too,' she said, which was not really true because she had had time to think of nothing and nobody but Tony and her legacy. The telephone rang again almost immediately.

'How are you, Holly?'

Holly sat down, almost clutching at the table for support. What on earth did he want? 'I'm quite well, Taylor. What do you want?'

'Want? Why do you always have to yell at me? I call to say hi, how are you? And you jump down the line.'

'I can't be blamed if your reputation precedes you. Naturally when I heard your voice, so unexpectedly, no wonderful Chandler smoothing the way, I assumed you either had bad news for me or you wanted something. Why did you ring?'

He was quiet for so long that she began to think he had disconnected. 'God knows,' he said at last. 'I guess I got to feeling bad about my attitude, thought maybe I should have tried to explain my position better.'

'Perhaps you should,' she agreed sweetly.

'God damn it, Holly. I'm not used to grovelling.'

'Then get used to it. It suits you.'

And naturally he slammed down his receiver.

Holly sat for a minute not feeling particularly pleased with herself. He had behaved, for once, like a normal human being, and she had ruined it for him. Strangely that made her feel rather excited. She confessed to having enjoyed her contretemps with Taylor.

'Damn. I'm thinking about a man I do not like in the slightest when I should be involved in preparing a meal for the man I . . . love, the man I adore.'

She took great care with the preparation of the meal and the table. At the last moment she turned the lights up: it had looked too deliberately seductive. They were engaged to be married but their last meetings and conversations had been acrimonious. But they would come to an understanding: she was sure of it. John was not Taylor and she was not a meek female who could be dictated to by either of them. She and John would reach an agreement or the engagement would go no further and their evening would not end in the way their romantic dinners usually did.

He was over an hour late. She refused to think that he was teaching her a lesson. He was a lawyer and often worked late.

'Holly, I'm sorry,' he said, enfolding her in his arms. 'Those damn papers had to be read. Forgive me?'

'Of course.' Holly smiled as she took the wine he had brought and carried it to the sideboard. 'I have tuna steaks marinating so if you open the wine we can have a glass while it's cooking.'

'Tell me about your progress,' he said as he obeyed her. 'If you'd like to, that is.'

'Of course I want to tell you. I have resigned as from Friday. That was such a difficult decision to make. When this is all over I might need a job and good teaching jobs don't grow on trees.' If she had expected him to say something reassuring she was disappointed and went on. 'Otto is coming on Monday to start packing the paintings. Earlier this evening I spoke to Taylor who is making grumbly spoiled millionaire noises.'

He gulped his wine and refilled his glass. 'Why?'

Carefully Holly turned the fish. It stayed whole and she smiled triumphantly. 'Because a newspaper columnist is saying that there was a *relationship* between Tony and Blaise Fougère and Fougère's publicity people had created the myth that he was as pure as the driven snow, never looked at another woman, totally faithful. Their carefully constructed idyll is crumbling around his family's ears and they don't like it.'

'Can't you just deny a relationship? Say it was professional, artist–subject.'

'Let's eat this while it's perfect,' said Holly, putting two blue glass plates on the table. She had brought them from the cottage and there was a slight catch in her throat when she continued. 'I have ambivalent feelings about everything now. Tony seems to be telling me that she wants her paintings exhibited: she wants her story told. She kept her relationship with Fougère a secret but not because she was ashamed. I believe she pandered to his paranoia, his wish for privacy.'

'What's paranoid about wanting one's private life to be private?'

This from the man who had probably hinted at scandal to the newspapers. Courage, Holly. Challenge him. Did you do it, John? Ask him, damn it.

Holly looked at John cynically as she helped herself to some salad. She took a deep breath and tried. 'That's rich coming from you.' She hated herself for being unable to ask outright. What a weakling. This is no basis for happy marriage. 'You lawyers do talk with forked tongue. I sympathise with Fougère but Tony is an underrated artist whose work deserves to be shown.'

'And sold.'

'Exactly. They should be in art galleries, opera houses perhaps, private collections all over the world.'

Holly put down her knife and fork. Three months ago, three years ago the question now hovering on her lips would never have occurred to her. It had to be asked. 'John, if I share something with you in complete confidence can I rely on you to keep it that way?'

'Good God, Holly, I'm a lawyer. I deal with client confidentiality all the time.' He was angry and his silver fish fork, another treasure from the cottage, fell on his plate with a clatter.

'I'm not a client, John,' said Holly quietly.

'No, you're my fiancée, the woman who has promised to marry me. You trust me enough to sleep with me but not to confide in me.'

Holly could see the pretty picture she had painted of her future dissolving before her eyes. 'It *was* you who told the press the subject of the portraits.'

He stood up and threw his napkin after his fork.

'Sure, it was easy. Hartman would have ignored you; you'll never learn how to manipulate people.'

'Because I wouldn't want to learn. How could you do something that you should have known is completely against my principles?'

'Don't be so naïve. When you're ready to grow up, you know where to reach me.'

Did he expect her to run after him, to beg, to say she was sorry? Her knees were trembling and she felt sick but she would not do it and he reached the door, picked up his raincoat from the chair where he had thrown it, and left. Still she stood, smelling the tuna which was growing cold on the plates, and the garlic bread which they had not even touched.

Relief was the strongest emotion she felt.

She sighed and then laughed. Her fiancé had just walked out and she felt more relief than regret. A showdown had been coming for months now. Had that been a showdown or merely a skirmish before the big deciding battle? 'Damn you, John,' she swore softly. 'You know you were wrong and I'm damned if I'm going to let you ruin a very expensive piece of fish.' She poured a second glass of wine and took it with her as she popped her piece of tuna into the microwave oven. John's she scraped into the bin.

She would not let herself think that there was a parallel with her life there somewhere. She would eat, then she would open some of the boxes of letters – family archives brought from her parents' home and so far totally ignored – and tomorrow she would go back to Torry Bay to see what it told her of the love between her aunt and Blaise Fougère.

The letters revealed nothing. That is, they told her nothing of the love affair. Instead Holly read of her father's doubts when Tony sank her savings into buying the cottage from her landlord. She read interminable accounts of her own progress in painting, swimming, and later sailing but not painting. No child, it would appear, had ever constructed a finer sandcastle.

What a prodigy I was, Holly thought as she wiped away tears. She had taken that devoted love for granted all her life and had been too busy, too determined to be in love with John, even to visit her aunt. How could I have done that? How could I let one man take me over to that extent, to where I was an automaton doing his bidding?

Where's a good cliché when you need one? Bite the bullet. Dive in at the deep end. These would have to do.

She drove to Argyll, to Achahoish, and on to Torry Bay and the house, her house, the house she knew now that nothing would persuade her to sacrifice. I'll live here; possibly do supply teaching or volunteer work. When I sell some of the jewels I'll put in central heating and be quite comfortable. Add state-of-the-art television set and video to the 'must-have' list.

'I likes a nice clean murder story on the telly, I do.' She laughed as she drove.

How had Tony managed through all those bleak and lonely winters? She had never seemed to feel the cold, out walking every day up to that little headland she had painted so often. Holly felt an urge to go up there, to stand where Tony had stood so often, but it was dark and cold. She unloaded the car, promising herself that she would visit the headland first thing in the morning. She went upstairs to Tony's bedroom, the room that she had shared with Blaise Fougère.

'I suppose I should sleep here now,' Holly said out loud but she could not bring herself to put her things there. She opened the wardrobe and began to sort through Tony's clothes, clothes for two lives. Tony had not stayed, a recluse, in Torry Bay. She had visited Edinburgh, London and Glasgow for her own art shows and she must have visited other countries with Blaise. At least it appeared that she had been with him in Paris, Milan, Bayreuth and even New York and San Francisco because several of her major canvasses were set in these cities. Holly resolved to study Tony's passport.

She took out a huge pile of heavily beaded cocktail dresses and threw them on the bed. So much for her naïve idea that Tony had lived a quiet life. Some charity would surely be happy with such a windfall. The dresses had concealed a few carefully packed outfits that Holly assumed were either more valuable or just favourites. She opened the bags to reveal sweaters, slacks and shirts. She recognised the bulky dark blue Guernsey. Blaise Fougère was wearing it in the painting called *Grief*. That brown shirt he was wearing in *Uncle Fire*. Holly held the sweater against her face and a faint smell of soap and shaving cream came to her. Tony had not washed the sweater after he had worn it for the last time: she had wrapped it up carefully and put it in the deepest recess of her wardrobe.

'She loved you so much,' she told the ghost who had worn the sweater. 'Did you love her or did you merely use her?' But if there were spirits in the little cottage they did not answer her. She looked down at an evening gown. It was exquisitely beaded, the work of an artist, and its glitter reminded Holly of the valuable jewels hiding in Mr Gilbert's safe. If she looked at them again, what would they tell her? She would want them to say, 'We were to tell her how much she mattered,' but she was afraid they would speak only of a rich man's ability to assuage his guilt. Tony had never worn real jewellery or perhaps she had worn it only when she was with Blaise. A memory tried to push itself forward. There was a jewel that Tony wore always and with anything but what was it? Holly could not remember; it was not her favourite rubies. She would leave it for now. If the memory was important, it would return.

Back downstairs she sat for a while looking at the moon playing on the surface of the bay. Tony must have sat here day after day, night after night: Blaise Fougère too. They had loved here in this room. She could feel their presence; sense their love. And suddenly she knew that the love was for her too. They loved her: they approved of what she was doing.

'I want the world to know that Tony was a superb painter, Blaise. She kept these magnificent portraits hidden to protect you, to protect your wife, but you are dead now, all of you. You will not be hurt by the story the paintings tell. The millions who revere the memory of Blaise Fougère, the tenor, will not abandon you because you needed the love and support that Tony gave you all your life, for it was all your life, wasn't it? Whatever the truth of your private life, how could you have coped, how could you have been the joy that you were to millions without Tony? You knew that she was here, patiently waiting, sublimating her phenomenal talent to foster yours, taking whatever you could offer and giving you, gladly, everything she had in return. It's her turn now and you want her to have it, don't you?'

Hollyberry.

'I won't let either of you down, I promise.'

It was after eleven, only just after six in New York. Thank God for mobile phones. She would have a permanent line installed, together with the central heating. She dialled the country code, the area code, and the number.

'Hello, Taylor. It's Holly.' She spoke as if they had not had a recent fight. She was beyond that now. 'I'm at Torry Bay. His clothes are here, some of them. He loved her; he's told me that . . .'

'When?'

He did not sound surprised that someone should ring him all the way from an isolated community in Scotland. That was a twentieth-century miracle that the Taylors of the world took for granted. 'My uncle has been dead for years. When did he tell you?'

He would laugh her to scorn but she did not care. 'Just a few minutes ago. I'm not saying I've seen a ghost but I feel his presence here, hers too. They want me to fight you, Taylor. I will show the paintings to the world.'

He was scornful. He was so worldly-wise, so sophisticated. His uncle must have been just like that. Tony had no chance against the power of his personality but she, Holly, was made of sterner stuff.

'I guess you're at the cottage,' he said.

'Yes.'

'Don't get rid of anything till I get there.'

She panicked. 'I don't want you here: I was merely letting you know my plans.'

'I'm letting you know mine. I'll leave New York as soon as I can get clearance.'

He arrived less than forty-eight hours later when she was up at the headland looking out to sea. She had found a little hollow which protected her from the wind but which still allowed her to see the glorious view.

'Love me, Toinette, love me.'

'I do, *mon ange*, I do, but we are so near the cottage.'

He was undoing her shirt, one of his that he had left on his last visit. 'I can't wait,' he said.

Tony and Blaise were there with her. Holly sat down and looked at the painting spread out before her. It could have changed very little since her aunt had first seen this delightful place. It had to be the peace, the atmosphere that had drawn them both back again and again, that had caused Tony to make her home there in the first place. I could be a million miles from Glasgow and John, New York and Taylor. How much more valuable for Blaise. Here there was no stress, here there was Tony and acceptance and deep love. That's what I want. Acceptance and love.

She heard his voice and stood up. I'm talking of peace and acceptance and love and what do I get? Taylor Hartman – and there's still no food in the place.

'Here,' she shouted.

He had parked his rented car at the door and was standing, so corporate executive, watching her as, in her oldest skirt and jumper, she walked back reluctantly from the sea.

'Why did you come, Taylor?' she asked aggressively. 'There is nothing for you here.'

He laughed. 'Chandler ordered a hamper from Fortnum and Mason's. It was waiting at the airport.'

'I wasn't talking about food as you jolly well know.'

'As you jolly well know,' he mocked. 'Holly, Miss Noble, I would like to see what you tell me are my uncle's effects. Pretty please.'

Holly pushed past him and went to the door of the cottage that was now so unpeaceful. 'A few old sweaters. You can't possibly want to take them with you. They certainly would get in the way of that Madison Avenue you're wearing.'

He looked down at his pinstripe suit and smiled at her. For a second he reminded her of the *Sea Sprite*. 'Milan, actually. I could introduce you.'

She slammed the door in his face but he would not be

kept out. After a few minutes he knocked on the door. 'That was childish, Holly. Actually you look really adorable but I promise not to make any more un-called-for remarks. I also promise to share my hamper.'

She said nothing.

'Bet you were going to have beans on toast.'

She opened the door. 'You may come in and look at the things in the wardrobe, Taylor, but only because you have come such a long way, which, by the way, is an obscene waste of money . . .'

He grabbed her and turned her towards him and for a moment his furiously angry face looked into hers. Holly was just as annoyed. Then he laughed and let her go. 'I'll write a cheque to your favourite charity, Miss Noble, but, not that it is any of your business, I loved Blaise Fougère – I thought, more than anybody. And not that it's any of your business, I thought he loved me best too.' He took a deep breath. 'Damn it all, I can't deal with you when I'm tired. I would like to see his things,' he finished almost humbly.

'The bedroom.'

He walked past her and went upstairs and she sat in the big chair in the window and waited for him. He was quite some time and his face was very white under his tan when he eventually joined her.

'May I see the notes your aunt left, and the jewels, Holly?'

She retrieved her precious letters and handed them to him. 'The jewellery is in a vault.'

'Not important: I was interested only in the style.'

The letters he read over and over. 'She sounds nice, your aunt.'

Holly made to speak to him but he had jumped up and was already at the door.

'I'll get the food,' he said, 'and then I'll drive back to Glasgow.'

'Taylor.'

He stopped.

'You may use the bedroom tonight. You must be tired.'

His back was to her. 'I don't think I can, Holly, but thank you; there's just too much to take in.'

When he came back with the hamper it was obvious that he did not want to talk about Blaise or Tony or the paintings. But she had to ask before he left.

'The clothes, Taylor?'

'Give them to charity. See you sometime, Holly.'

She watched him drive away and as she walked back to the house she asked herself whether that was a threat or a promise. She stood for a moment at the door and then opened it slowly and whispers on a sigh reached her.

Darling girl.

Hollyberry.

8

---✦✦---

London, 1939

Britain declared war on Germany on 3 September
1939. Australia, New Zealand, and France joined her.

For two days Tony had waited, hoping against hope
that somehow everything would be all right. There
could not be war. Blaise could not abandon his career
to become a soldier. It was unthinkable. If he left her she
would die. She knew it. He was more important to her
than the air she breathed, the food she ate. Even her
painting came second to her need for him.

'Paint, Toinette,' he ordered her. 'When I am away I
will take courage knowing that you are here making
beautiful things. Paint my babies, our babies, five, I

think, five fat little babies, two boys for you and three little girls for me to spoil.'

To please him she made sketches of plump little cherubs with paintbrushes in their hands and streaks of paint on their dimpled little behinds.

'This one is going to be world-famous,' Blaise told her seriously as he pointed to a singing cherub. 'She has the voice of an angel. What a Tosca she will be, and when she is between roles she will paint masterpieces. Come, give her a little baby easel.'

But Tony cried and he held and comforted her until she was again in control.

'It mustn't happen,' she said – but it did.

The Slade was moving from London to Ruskin College, Oxford. 'I won't go. Who cares about painting in a world gone mad?'

Blaise soothed her. 'Is this the same Toinette who tells me the arts civilise humanity? It is not far from Oxford to London, Tony. You must go and we will see one another when we can. Good practice, *ma mie*, for an operatic career.'

He himself did not leave immediately. His parents were as distraught as Tony and tearful telephone calls and tear-stained letters from his mother forced him to remain, much against his wishes, at the Conservatory.

The year 1940 came and in late March Monsieur Reynaud became Premier of France, but if la belle France had hoped that this would stop the inevitable it did not. On 14 June, when Tony and Blaise were beginning to talk about a summer break, not, alas, their aborted trip to Paris, German troops entered the French capital. Blaise was filled with despair and Tony tried hard to forget her own terror and to think only of what it must be like to know that your parents and your little sister are living in a city that has been invaded.

'They will go to the country, Blaise, you'll see.'

'My father's business is in Paris. Many of his clients are Jews. He will not leave.'

'Knowing that you are doing so well' – for Blaise had recently taken part in a college recital – 'will help them.'

He turned away from her and she wanted to throw her arms around him and help him but his body language was saying, 'Leave me alone in my despair.'

She did not know how to reach him. She stayed in London where sometimes Blaise sat for hours staring at something she could not see, filling the flat with over-loud music, and at other times he made love to her, almost desperately, as if he could not get enough of her, and then he would weep and she would hold him and soothe him until he fell into an exhausted sleep.

Then one day she returned to his flat and he was gone. There was a letter that she could not read because her eyes filled with tears that made the words blur on the page. She did not need to read it; she knew what it said. He had returned to France. It was not what she had expected. It was worse. He had gone to join the Free French and would contact her if and when he could. In the meantime his father had paid the rent on the flat for two years and so, if Tony would enjoy it, she could use it whenever she chose.

'I will imagine you in the flat, painting, trying to cook, *pauvre* Toinette, and sleeping. That will make me very happy. You are so beautiful when you sleep.'

For the next year Tony lived two lives. During the week she was Tony Noble, art student. She attended classes and lectures in one of the most beautiful cities in the world and she did not see its beauty. How could there be beauty where Blaise was not? Never did she so much as sketch one of the fabled 'dreaming spires'. She returned to London as often as she could, at first by train, then bus and sometimes even perched on the top of a lorry load of vegetables. She began to hate the flat; it was too empty, too quiet. Even if she played his records of Beethoven symphonies, there was still an awful silence.

Today there will be a letter; I just know it.

Next weekend there will be a letter, I can feel it.

If there was a letter, and occasionally there was – a few fragile tissues signed, '*Je t'aime, ma mie*' – she would stay for a night and she would clean the flat. The very dust mocked her loneliness. It would dance in a ray of sunlight before languorously settling back down on to the furniture.

'You are helpless,' it told her, 'helpless and hopeless.'

No, she was not hopeless. She had this fragile message.

No, no, the paper is fragile; the message is strong. He will come back and, in the meantime, I will learn to paint.

There was one teacher who terrified her. Tony was small and he was not much taller but, with a paintbrush in his hand, he was a giant – and he knew it. He would look at her work, scream vitriol at her, and then take the brush from her hand and show her. It took weeks for her to accept that this meant that he thought she was worth bothering about, but she never recovered from her fear of sudden noises.

'Too much bluidy atmosphere,' he would say in his thick Scottish accent. 'Not enough bluidy clarity.'

Oh, please, could he not teach without swearing?

'What the hell are you painting? A man or the Decline and Fall of Bluidy Civilisation? Study the Florentines, for Christ's sake, and be *precise*. Your painting starts long before you touch the fucking canvas. Mix the paint *on* the palette. That's where the painting starts.'

Her upbringing had not prepared her for anything like this and, without Blaise's arms to support her, she considered fleeing back to staidness, quietness, dullness. At least there one's nerves suffered in a more conventional way.

'What are you painting with, Miss Noble? What are you trying to convey? A photographic likeness? Go and buy a bluidy box camera and stop wasting my valuable time. Oh, ho, the mouse has spirit. She doesn't like that. Good. Good. Paint with your guts, Miss Noble. Look at the way the light falls on your subject and paint what you *see*. That vision must seduce you as a lover seduces, so that you will do anything, accept anything, to get it right.'

She could bear no more. She would leave the Slade and paint pretty pictures of Oxford colleges to sell to tourists when the war was over. At night she painted the babies she and Blaise would have: she painted them on clouds floating in a blue sky. She opened all the little mouths and let the golden notes fly. She could not paint Blaise. She did not know where he was or what he was doing. His infrequent letters told her of nothing except his unchanging love. How she missed him. The pain was like a toothache. Only the sufferer was really aware of its intensity. Once, when her pain seemed unbearable, she missed classes and hitched to London where despite the emptiness she felt close to him. They had lived and loved in this apartment, and they had laughed and cried too.

She was at the apartment on the August night when the boarding-house where she had first lived received a direct hit. Mrs Lumsden and Monica English-lit. Bailey and all the others were killed. They were the first people to die whom Tony had actually known and she tried to mourn. She remembered Mrs Lumsden and her bread, the sandwiches she had made for Blaise, but her heart was too aware of its own suffering to make room for that of anyone else. She hated her inability to feel but accepted it.

She heard that de Gaulle was fighting from London for a free France. Was Blaise with him? Was he near her? The French Government under Marshall Pétain was set up at Vichy and then that same government broke off diplomatic relations with Britain. Nothing mattered except Blaise.

Tony took her paintings and the several prestigious awards conferred on her at graduation by her college, locked them in the attic at her parents' home in Surrey and then, against her mother's wishes – 'You're foolish, Antonia; you have already had one miraculous escape. I just know you won't be lucky a second time. Stay here, stay here where it's safe' – she returned to London where she did war work and painted . . . nothing.

How can I create anything when I am dead inside myself?

The rent was paid until the end of June but Tony could not consider taking over the lease; her feeble earnings could not begin to cover the cost of the flat. She would leave London; perhaps, in the circumstances, it would be better to go somewhere, anywhere, far away to wait until the war was over and Blaise returned. She wrote to him but again he did not answer and at the beginning of May when pink and white blossom waved defiantly from trees all over London, she packed up his few belongings and her own and, without contacting her parents, she went to Waterloo station to find a train, any train, going as far from London as possible.

That night there was one leaving that would eventually reach Glasgow, a city that was as familiar as Timbuktu but it did not matter where she was. Several times on that interminable journey she wondered if she was not a little mad. Would a completely sane human being push herself on to a train that was crawling – when it moved at all – back and forth across the English countryside? The carriages were overfull of passengers and Tony sat on her suitcase all the way to a station she thought might possibly be Birmingham – there were no signs – and blessed the foresight that had made her wear her second-best pair of lisle stockings. Kit-bags bumping against her defenceless legs tore, not only the stockings, but the skin on her shin bones too. At wherever it was she moved into a carriage vacated by some soldiers, but the smell of unwashed humanity and cigarettes made her look back on her sojourn in the corridor with something approaching nostalgia. Across from her were squeezed a rather large woman with a basket that, from the blessedly healthy earthy smell, surely carried potatoes, two women in uniform and three small, often fretful, children with unwashed faces and runny noses. Tony tried to avoid looking at the noses but mentally chastised herself when she saw the labels pinned to their coats.

'Where are you going?' she asked the older girl.

'We're not to talk to strangers,' said the girl. 'Our gran's meeting us at Crewe. She's a grand baker our gran,' she added, as if her virtuous silence had tried her sorely.

Tony smiled. She wished she had a gran meeting her in Crewe. No, she wanted only Blaise. If these little children could brave the unknown as far as Crewe she could go farther to find a refuge until Blaise returned. She closed her eyes and when she opened them again the children and the large lady were gone and the train was sitting quietly in a siding.

'Don't ask,' said the young woman beside her. 'It's too dark to see a bloody thing.'

Tony needed a cup of tea, the use of a lavatory, and a hot bath, but not necessarily in that order. She got none of them for several hours but at last, cold, stiff and incredibly weary, she stumbled from the train that had finally reached Glasgow. She later sketched but never painted the NAAFI canteen where she was able to strike the first two off her wish list. Holding the mug around its bowl for warmth, she looked at a dilapidated poster and found an idyllic background for a perfect painting. She could not pronounce its name; neither could the ticket clerk but between them they found the most direct route to Achahoish.

Blaise was on a mission to London that May night. For twenty long minutes they were in a crowded railway station within touching distance of one another – and they did not know.

Blaise had successfully delivered the waterproof packet that he had carried from France and his orders were to return immediately.

His work done, his mind was free to think of Tony. She was here, possibly asleep in his apartment. He imagined the exquisite joy of seeing her for just one moment or of hearing her voice, but his orders were clear: Return immediately. He was almost ashamed when he heard the air-raid warning. He could not now attempt the return journey; no one would expect it. He could walk through the streets to find her. She was his life, his sanity. In all the time that they had been apart he had received only three letters from her, letters that showed they were a small part of a great rainforest of letters, in which she spilled out her love, her longing, and he had answered them but had no way of knowing if his letters ever reached her. It did not matter. His Toinette knew that she had his heart. She knew that he would come back.

He was filled with longing, to see her, to touch her, to hear her voice. They could have, possibly, a few hours together but they would be grateful, for that was more than most lovers were allowed. But London was changed. Great areas of this side of the city had completely disappeared in the horrifying raids of the previous September: streets that he had known so well were no longer there.

He had lost his way and he turned looking desperately for a marker. The river and St Paul's should be behind him. 'If I keep them there, I will know where I am.'

Finding a specific street in an air-raid is not easy. Blaise stood stock still and watched as the front wall of an entire building dissolved in front of him. One moment there was a huge looming shadow, then a ball of flame that showed an old man making a hot drink, a baby in a crib, silent furniture, and then they were all sucked into a hell on earth and he thought he would be drawn in there too. The noise was indescribable. The dull droning of aircraft was so permanent a part of his experience that he noticed it only when it stopped, but no one could ever get used to the sound of a bomb disintegrating life. The fire services, the air-raid wardens, the ambulances were already there, and he joined in automatically.

There was no fear, no time for fear. One saw, one acted. Then, at last, someone said, 'There's no more you can do here, lad,' and the reaction set in, and once again his mind was full of Tony.

He had to get to her. She was in this madness somewhere and he had to find her.

Dear God. It was true. How he would laugh with Toinette. The British and their tea.

'Here, lad, get this inside you.'

A warden, his face dirty, his clothes torn and smoke-grimed, pushed a tin mug into Blaise's shaking hands. He could have been twenty: he might have been sixty. There was no way to tell who was under that layer of dying London. 'Bloody Bomber's Moon tonight, lad. Bastards are peppering all round the Elephant and Castle with incendiaries. Freeman, Hardy and Willis is ablaze, and Spurgeon's Tabernacle, Dean's Rag Book Factory – fires are spreading.'

Blaise did not answer. He nodded his thanks. For almost three years he had spoken very little English and he did not want to risk having to waste time explaining.

I am more alert than I thought, he decided, if I can think about that. Must be training.

He finished the tea that tasted surprisingly good and waited until, in the utter chaos around him, he could slip away without being observed. He had all the papers that would satisfy the authorities but he had so little time. He had to get to Tony. Suddenly he was terrified. What was he doing, drinking tea and wasting time? Their London was being obliterated around him and Toinette was in the midst of it.

He knew the Elephant and Castle; it was their pub. Freeman, Hardy and Willis was just round the corner from the flat. Toinette had laughed. 'Boots and shoes? They should be solicitors with a name like that.'

He began walking again, and this time his mind did not remember London before the war. It did not relive precious hours with Tony. He needed to think only of how to get to her. It was quite easy to see where he was going. There were fires burning out of control and he allowed himself a moment of despair as he used their flames to show him his way. Would there be any city left in the morning? Of course there would be. Nothing could destroy London. Almost every civilisation had already tried and failed. Hitler would fail too.

His heart knew a second of joy as he turned, he thought, into his own street. His mind refused to accept what he saw. Where the street had been there was a huge smoking crater, and there were ants scurrying around everywhere. But their running was methodical and ordered and when they spoke, they spoke calmly, and, in order to be heard, quite loudly but they did not shout.

As he reached them the ants metamorphosed into ARP wardens and fire-fighters. Blaise stopped one, an old man with a face grey from exhaustion.

'Where is the street?' he asked desperately. 'Where is the street?'

'In that 'ole, Frenchie.' The warden looked at him and there was compassion on the dirty face. He took off his helmet and Blaise saw the curly auburn hair of a young man. 'No survivors, lad, if you was looking for someone.'

'My wife.'

Blaise looked into the crater and was amazed at how calmly he was behaving. Toinette was somewhere in that crater. She was dead and, therefore, since she was his heart, he was dead too. That was why he was so calm. He was dead.

'Sorry, Frenchie, you can talk . . .'

But Blaise had turned and was walking away and this time his mind was full of Tony. Tony as he had first seen her, when, pretending to be absorbed in *Lohengrin* he had watched her walk across the grass and begin to sketch him, Tony in the dandelions when he had first loved her, Tony sitting cross-legged on the bed in his apartment, Tony, Tony, Tony.

'I too am dead, my Toinette, but what is left will love you for ever.'

9

London, 1999

'A gallery in Bayreuth has asked for an option on all the swans, Holly.'

'Why? They must have some connection with Blaise but a very nebulous one and, besides, there are many swan pictures out there.'

Otto was not really listening. '*Lohengrin*. We'll call them the *Lohengrin* series.'

'But he seldom sang Lohengrin. It's hardly a role associated with him like Cavaradossi or des Grieux.'

'Pity she didn't keep letters or a diary.' There was a hint in his voice, hoping, always hoping.

'No diary, and the letters she kept were from family or from galleries, even one or two from you. And your father.'

'My father. How splendid. May I see them?'

'Of course. I'll give them to you.'

They were relaxing after an excellent lunch in Otto's magnificent London flat. Holly was lost in the depths of a peach-covered armchair looking up at a ribbon of orchids that were exactly the same colour. She had been disappointed to discover that such exquisite things had no scent. In her opinion all flowers should smell of flowers. Otto's manservant had poured coffee in his usual silent way and had then disappeared. Holly looked after him.

'Where on earth did you find Phil? He's a marvel.'

Otto put his finger to his lips in that gesture she hated.

'MI5 listening to you, Otto?'

'Stranger things,' he said enigmatically. 'But Phil is – was a Tibetan priest. He escaped to India with the Dalai Lama in 1959 and has been in England since the early seventies. God knows how old he is. He looks just the same to me as when I first interviewed him. He does everything, you know. I don't even have to think, and that means I can concentrate on making my artists rich and famous.' His gesture embraced the glories of the drawing room and the view beyond. 'Wouldn't you like a little place like this, Holly?'

Holly, who had pulled herself out of her chair and gone to the window, thought the room was the most subtly beautiful one that she had ever seen in her life. It managed somehow to look both like a picture in a magazine and a home, even though she knew that no piece of cake had ever been abandoned under any of these delicate silk cushions. She glanced out at the amazing city and then thought of the cottage at Torry Bay. 'You play too hard at being facetious, Otto. I'm happy with Tony's cottage.'

Otto joined her at the window and brushed an

imaginary speck of dust from the softly toning curtains. 'I wish I had visited her there, too stupid, but she was so private about it.' He turned and smiled at her. 'I hear that even the elegant Taylor enjoyed his little stay. What did you do to make one of the richest men in the world happy in a teeny-weeny pied à terre?' he added wickedly.

Holly decided to ignore the innuendo and returned to her chair. 'Why, Otto, I gave him sausages for supper and made him wash up.'

He had just lifted his tiny porcelain cup to his lips and he choked on a mouthful of coffee. 'How very bourgeois of you, Holly.' He looked at her measuringly as she sat sipping her coffee innocently. 'No matter. The paintings aren't from the Fougère series – she painted hundreds of swans – but they were in the attic. Some years before she died she hinted that she was preparing an exhibition. Possibly she didn't mean these to go with the major works but she lost heart. We can still cash in.'

Holly stood up. 'I hate it when you talk like that.'

'How we are naïve. Holly, I am a businessman. I hope I am also an artist. For Tony I want worldwide acclaim; for you I want as much money as possible and no, I will not give my cut to your little foundation, whatever it is. The paintings are good – Tony painted them. They are not in the same league as the portraits of Blaise but they are fine examples of her style, her incredible facility with light, colour. Do you want to consider selling them as a series?'

'I have never really examined them carefully. It

seems that the question is, are they all part of the *Lohengrin* series or are some of them merely paintings of Scottish scenery complete with swans?'

'Mr Hartman to see if you are at home, sir.'

They had not heard Phil open the door. Holly felt her heart race as she looked at Otto. She had not seen Taylor since he had left her in Argyll. Her raging pulse told her that she was looking forward to seeing him again.

'Show Mr Hartman in.' And as Phil did so, 'Well, this is an unexpected pleasure. Taylor my dear, how nice of you to drop by. Another cup, Phil, please. Taylor, you know Miss Noble?'

Holly could tell that Taylor was as surprised to see her as she was to see him but he recovered more quickly. 'Hello, Holly.'

'Taylor.'

He turned back to Otto who waved him to a sofa. 'You are just too frightening when you tower over one, Taylor, and I will not be intimidated in my own sitting room.'

Taylor smiled and sat down, crossing one elegant leg over the other, completely at ease. 'I apologise for my height, Otto. Holly, I'm glad you are here. There must be some way of contacting you at the cottage. You gave Chandler your Glasgow number but not your cellphone.'

Holly found herself teasing him again. 'They'll take a message at the shop.' It had worked for Blaise. But Taylor was not Blaise and Holly was not Tony. Blaise had loved Tony and she had loved him. Holly did not love Taylor, she did not even like him, and he disliked her too.

There, she had admitted it and it did not hurt at all.

Taylor looked at her for a moment and she found herself blushing. Was he thinking the same thing? 'Cellphones, Holly, the Internet, e-mail, etcetera. That journalist, no, sorry, legal-eagle boyfriend of yours surely doesn't like you to be so incommunicado. I would be worried sick. If I loved someone,' he added hastily. He was embarrassed, not a condition with which he was familiar and he did not like it.

Holly was enjoying his predicament so it was left to Otto to help his unexpected guest. 'I was just telling Holly that a gallery has asked for an option on the *Lohengrin* series.'

'One question. Does Holly make more money if they are sold separately at auction or as a job lot?'

He sounded like John. Money, money, money.

'There are other considerations, Mr Hartman.'

He almost groaned. 'Mr Hartman again. Holly, only people with no money make holier than thou statements like that. Surely you spent enough time sweating in Africa to know that the more money a true philanthropist has, the more he can do for humanity. You want maximum cover?'

Holly was confused. One part of her wanted to know how he had found out about her work in Africa; another part ached to argue, 'I am not a philanthropist,' but that was what she wanted to be, basically, wasn't it? She finally said only, 'Of course.'

He was looking at her, an expression she could not read on his handsome face. 'Then make sure you get it off to a great start. This is a one-off Holly.'

Holly stood up. She was furious. He knew she was annoyed. 'I must be off, Otto. You and Mr Hartman have great deals to do, I'm sure.'

Taylor ignored Otto. '*Miss* Noble? Happy now? Yes, I will have coffee, Otto, black. Miss Noble, I stopped by Otto's apartment to see if he knew a way of contacting you. We need to talk about having the paintings valued and shipped.'

Otto coughed. 'Dear boy, all is in order.' He reeled off the names of three world-renowned authorities. 'Every one a masterwork, according to them. We decided to bring the paintings straight here before having them evaluated. They were unpacked a week ago and the last valuation was carried out today. They are hanging in my storerooms.'

'I expected to have been told,' said Taylor stiffly.

'Why?' asked Holly. 'Their value has nothing to do with you.'

'I have no interest in their monetary value, Miss Noble, but I thought you might just consider letting me see them as they were unpacked. In fact, I do believe we did discuss the matter. In case you have forgotten, they are purported to be portraits of my uncle.'

'They are, but what's that got to do with anything?' Holly almost shouted.

'You must be the first to see them, dear boy,' Otto said swiftly. 'In fact, we could go to the storerooms right now. Remember though, Taylor, a storeroom is just that, merely four walls, and the lighting is not right. They have not been *hung*.'

'I know what you mean and I would still like to see them. Do I have your permission, Miss Noble?'

Holly decided to be gracious. 'Of course, and you may even choose the one you would like me to give you.'

She smiled sweetly as she saw his jaw clamp shut and turned, still smiling, to Otto. 'I'll come too. We'll have to decide whether to hang them chronologically, the unfolding of the love story, as it were. Have you finished your coffee, Taylor?'

She smiled again as she heard the delicate cup clatter against its saucer and decided to behave; she had goaded him enough.

Since Taylor's car was outside they took that and drove to the great warehouses where Otto stored works that were awaiting showing or shipment. Holly said nothing as they drove.

'It's quicker to walk in big cities,' she observed at last and Taylor, relaxed again, laughed at her.

'If you think this is bad, visit New York or Tokyo, but I think London is worse than New York for traffic hold-ups. Your streets are so narrow.'

Holly thought about her almost-decision to live in Torry Bay. 'There is only one street in my town,' she said, 'and there are only traffic jams when American tourists try to rush through.'

She saw that she was making Otto nervous. Taylor,

after all, was a favoured customer. She could not imagine what imp of mischief was forcing her to goad him.

What is he to Hecuba or Hecuba to him?

Swiftly she stopped the little record player in her head. The end of the line was 'that she should weep for him', and she certainly had no intention of shedding tears over Blaise Fougère's arrogant nephew. She felt his eyes on her and looked at him and flushed, she knew not why.

'You do know what the Hartman Corporation is, don't you, Holly?'

'Of course.' What a strange question.

He said nothing.

The heating in the warehouses was controlled so that the paintings were kept at the optimum temperature. Holly felt her excitement grow as she prepared to see the paintings again. When Otto's hand-picked staff had unpacked them she had been feverish with delight. Almost every one was too big to show to advantage in the cottage at Torry Bay but here, in these huge rooms with the stark white walls, the explosion of colour and light was tangible.

'Look at them,' she breathed. 'They're beautiful.'

'Magnificent,' Otto agreed.

Taylor said nothing. He began to walk slowly down the room, familiarising himself with the work. He had not seen all of them before; that had been impossible in the cramped conditions at the cottage. He had looked at a few, one at a time, and in unfavourable light. Holly forgot that she did not like him and went with him, exclaiming, pointing out things that she had not noticed before and that he too might not have seen.

'Look, Taylor, at the rainbow . . . do you see, how clever.'

'Why is there a chain around his neck? The title is so strange too.'

'Oh, the swan, look at the swan; she's writing messages.'

The paintings were in no particular order. They had been packed just as the removal men had found them in the attic and they were unpacked and hung in just the same way, following one another on to the bare walls: 1978 following 1990, 1947 side by side with 1982, Torry Bay nestling against Bayreuth, Vienna giving elbow room to New York, a very young Blaise in a bandstand beside a more mature Blaise in a field of clover.

'It's mind-blowing,' said Taylor at last.

Holly turned to him, face radiant, eyes sparkling. He agreed with her. 'They're breathtaking, aren't they?'

'They're obscene,' he said. 'A sick mind. I knew him better than anyone except my mother and she . . .' He stopped without finishing and turned to Otto. 'We would have known. If you don't want to take a cab, come now.'

'We'll find a taxi, dear boy.'

Taylor said nothing. He walked out and Holly stood listening to the sound of his, no doubt expensive, handmade shoes on the concrete floors. Then she turned and looked at Otto who was smiling happily to himself.

'What's wrong with him?'

'Who knows, darling girl? Maybe his chauffeur was on overtime.'

Holly was incredulous and furious. 'He called them obscene.' She almost chocked with anger. 'What a swine he is, Otto. How can they be obscene?'

'Holly, let Uncle Otto tell you something about the male species. They become extremely miffed if their little balloons get burst. Taylor Fougère Hartman assumed he was the only person his uncle cared about, and *voilà*, an entire series of paintings that shows a hidden life, people and places of whom Taylor knew nothing.'

'How childish,' said Holly, and then remembered guiltily that she too had been surprised and not a little hurt to find that she had not been the only love of her aunt's life. Naturally she said nothing of this to Otto.

'We might as well look at them all and enjoy them while they're our secret, Holly.'

Holly looked, really for the first time, at paintings of Blaise Fougère his fans would hardly recognise but would love. Blaise pensive. Blaise laughing. Blaise with the weight of the world on his broad shoulders. Blaise in his beloved Paris, in New York, in Vienna, in London, and countless paintings of him in Torry Bay. The *Lohengrin* pictures . . . some, Holly saw at once, now that she really looked, were merely paintings of swans, but others were pictures of the swan prince sailing across the sea, carrying, it was to be hoped, the maiden's longed-for lover on his broad back.

'Look, Otto.' And she showed Otto what she had been excited to show Taylor. 'If you have very good eyesight and peer very closely you can see that this is not a smudge but a golden crown. He was on his way back to her in the end, I know it.'

'We'll put them all in together then, shall we, darling girl?'

'Otto, you have no soul.'

'Such a nuisance in business.'

A few days later Holly and Otto met to select the photographs that might be used to illustrate the catalogue for the exhibition.

Holly was seated at Otto's desk going through several heaps of professionally produced photographs.

'There is such a big gap over the war years and beyond.'

'We know he was a soldier.'

'Yes, but the war was over in 1945. Even if we allow several months for combatants to return, there are no paintings, in this collection, of Blaise until 1953. You would think if he loved her, really loved her, he would have gone to her as soon as Paris was liberated.'

'We must assume that they lost touch during the war. He was working undercover for de Gaulle and for some reason she went to Scotland. If she loved him, surely she would have left a forwarding address.'

Holly picked up a photograph. 'I love *Dents de Lion*. I may keep it, especially since Taylor has his eye on it.'

'For shame, Holly,' said Otto but he was not serious.

He too felt that the rich Mr Hartman needed some salutary lessons. He was much too fond of getting his own way.

'Why, Otto?' Holly went on as she turned over the photographs. 'Why was it so long before they found one another? Look at his face. He adores her. Why didn't he go looking for her?'

'He may have thought she was dead. Didn't I read somewhere in that trashy paper that his apartment block in London was razed to the ground before his very eyes?'

'He didn't check that she really was dead? He didn't rake through the rubble with his exquisitely manicured fingernails to see if she was there?' John would come looking for her, wouldn't he? He would turn up on her doorstep as often as Hartman seemed able to do, wouldn't he?

Otto examined his own beautiful fingernails. 'I hardly think he had time for a manicure fighting to free France.'

'That's not the point, and you know it. It's the appalling waste that gets to me. Waste of her life, her child-bearing years. She loved children. What about that and then her potential to succeed as an artist? She deliberately kept her greatest work hidden. He went swanning around the globe leading this double life and she stayed in a tiny cottage in Argyll when she could have been world-famous. Why did she do that?'

'Love.'

'Very one-sided.'

'He was married.'

'Why? Why did he marry someone else when he was in love with Tony?'

'Maybe he met Eleanor during the war, had a relationship with her, got married, and then when the marriage went wrong he decided to resurrect his first real love. The date of the first personal postwar painting is 1953. Yes, it would take a few years for the gilt to wear off.'

Holly scooped the pictures up and thrust them back into the envelope. 'Except, if he thought she was dead as you were saying two minutes ago, how did he find her?'

'Where are you going?'

'Covent Garden. It was something Taylor said. I'll tell you about it later, unless you want to come.'

'I would adore to be seen going into the Opera House with a beautiful young woman but I have a gallery to run and besides, it's not a matinée. Who would be there to see me?'

She looked at him sadly. 'You are an old fraud, Otto. Come on. I want to look at the *des Grieux* and you are the only person I know who can tell me how good or bad it is.'

He gave in as she had known he would and less than half an hour later they were standing in an upper corridor well away from the lovely staircase of the Royal Opera House.

'I have to admit he is drop-dead gorgeous, Otto, but I don't really like it; there's something wrong with the expression. Reminds me a bit of his supercilious nephew.'

Otto did not take the hook so she examined the painting a little longer. 'Was he really that pretty or did she just gild the lily a little?'

Otto looked critically at the painting. 'I was quite young at the time this was painted and I had seen him only in some French thing they were doing at the Garden, but I would say she painted what she saw. His physical appearance was out of the ordinary; indeed, interest in his looks rather than, as he saw it, in his voice was one of the things that drove him to hide himself. Nowadays opera stars will do anything to be noticed. Fougère was not only intensely private – and I'm quoting my late father here – but he felt that his voice was the only thing about him that should even remotely concern his audiences. A little naïve, I think.'

Holly looked again at the beautiful young man in the wine-coloured jacket and neckcloths of snowy pink satin. The ribbon tying back his dark hair was the colour of his eyes. 'I must say a hero who looks like that does more for my blood pressure than a little fat Italian.'

'Then you are not really a lover of the art form. Your little Italian should make you believe he looks like Fougère.'

Holly laughed. 'We had better go, Otto. Can't stand here admiring pecs all day.'

'Yes, I can,' said Otto, but he was smiling. 'Now tell me what being allowed into the hallowed inner sanctum to see this painting has to do with Tony.'

'The date, Otto: 1949. According to the archivist

Eleanor's family commissioned and donated the painting. Did my aunt paint him knowing he was married and if she did, why did she paint him? She must have known,' she went on, answering her own question. 'It's hardly the kind of thing you can keep a secret.'

'Unlike an affair,' broke in Otto.

Holly ignored the remark. 'But why did he marry Eleanor and not Tony?'

They stopped for a moment on the glorious staircase. 'It's beautiful.'

'It is nice enough,' said Otto dismissively, 'but nothing compared with the Staatsoper, or at least what was the Staatsoper.'

Since Holly had never been to Vienna she could not argue, but mumbled something and went on down the stairs, childishly imagining herself in a beautiful gown with miles of softly swirling skirts.

'We will never know the full story of Blaise and Tony,' she said sadly.

'Had she wanted us to know more, she would have left diaries.'

'Ah, but she did, Otto, and they are all in the exhibition.'

10

---◆◆◆---

Torry Bay, 1942. Surrey, 1942

She looked from the window on to a field: her gaze ran across it until it reached the sea. The sea was grey. Grey water bounded in the first instance by grey rocks and then further out by grey clouds. Grey, grey, grey, like her spirit. As she watched, however, slowly, slowly the grey clouds began to dissipate and she saw pink and pale blue.

Her breath caught in her throat as she saw him, his head held high as he sailed towards her across the bay.

She got up from her cramped position on the floor and ran quickly down the stairs and, still in her pyjamas, she let herself out of the side door and ran down to the beach.

He was still there looking towards the house, almost as if he were watching for her.

'Hail, my Lord Lohengrin,' she said as she reached the shingle.

The swan dipped his head in the now silver-grey water, pulled it out again and turned from her, and a shower of water diamonds flew around him as he sailed.

She barely breathed, willing him not to leave, and at last he stopped and settled in the water a few feet from the shore.

'I'll feed you,' she whispered to him. 'In the bad weather you'll be able to trust me, I promise.'

She was cold, her pyjamas were damp, and she was painfully aware of her bare feet.

'Please don't go,' she pleaded, but when she reached her bedroom window and looked out the swan was gone.

'He'll come back,' she whispered. 'He must.'

She washed in cold water and dressed quickly and her heart was light because she knew she had done the right thing. This was her place, her nest. Here she would wait.

She realised that she would starve to death if she did not earn some money. The first thing to do was to find a job. She had one marketable skill, her painting. Ergo, she must paint and she must sell. She would paint the swan and she would sell him. For the first time in years she felt motivated. She wanted to paint.

No, that was now an indulgence. She would have to paint in her free time.

She walked up to the village. If she was going to live here for ever then she must get to know her neighbours.

The village was no more than a street that wandered haphazardly around the bay. There were a few houses, a village shop combined with post office, and a slightly grander house that said, 'Doctor's Surgery'.

She went in.

There was no one in the waiting room. She wondered idly if it was because of the grudging welcome of the splintery wooden chairs (two) and the obsolete magazine (yes, one), and the absence of any art on the walls, not even a reproduction. Were prints not handed out to general practitioners with their medical degrees? She had little experience of doctors' surgeries; after all, her father had been a teacher and a teacher's salary did not exactly lend itself to frequent visits to one's local GP. In her mind, however, there was a vision of the painting *The Angelus*, and surely only a doctor would hang that in his waiting room. She knew no priests.

'Hello. What can I do for you?'

The resident doctor presumably. His appearance did not immediately fill Tony with enthusiasm but then, she reflected happily, she was unlikely ever to need his professional skills.

'Nothing,' she said, holding out her hand. 'I'm Tony Noble and I've just rented the cottage at Torry Bay.'

He looked disappointed for a moment. 'Good lord. You don't look like a lunatic. The entire village is talking about the eccentric millionaire who has moved into Torry Bay. I had hoped you were a patient. I'm Simon McRae, the new doctor.'

'Very new,' she said, looking at him closely.

He had to be about her own age, early twenties. He was smallish, thin, and badly in need of a decent haircut. Blaise would have thrown up his elegant hands in despair. Simon's jacket, like his hair, had seen better days.

Suddenly he reminded her of Blaise. Blaise who was tall, handsome, well dressed, sophisticated and articulate in several languages.

'It's your eyes,' she said with a smile. 'They're kind.'

He blushed a flaming red that did nothing for his appearance. 'Sorry?'

'Don't mind me, Doctor McRae. I assure you, if I ever need a doctor, I shall yell, loudly.'

'Please, Miss . . . Noble, was it? Won't you come in? I was about to have a cup of tea and some toast. I should sign you up as a patient if you are going to be staying long.'

'The rest of my life, I should think,' said Tony, and her voice was sad but burdened by acceptance. 'I was living in London, wanted out. I saw a poster and the word Achahoish, which I did not pronounce properly. I got on a train, and here I am.'

'I'm sure we are all very glad. London must have been hell.'

He saw her animated face grow bleak.

'Hell,' she echoed.

'But it couldn't be worse than . . . that . . . place you're renting.'

Tony smiled. 'It's not the Ritz. I got a lift on a lorry – I'm quite good at lorries – and the driver took me to a farm where they let me sleep on the sofa, very scratchy. Horsehair. But they, the farmer and his wife, own the cottage and they've let me have it and I'll do odd jobs on the farm till the war's over or till their son comes home from Burma, if he ever does, God help him.'

He took her into the tiny living room. 'Everything comes with the surgery,' he explained as Holly looked round. 'It's my uncle's. Would you believe they took him and he's forty-three.' He said that as if it were a great and advanced doddery old age. 'They wouldn't take me because, well, my eyesight's not too swift and Uncle Henry gave me this practice to keep for him while he sorts out the enemy. Very good at sorting things, Uncle Henry.'

'I should loathe your Uncle Henry,' said Tony as she demolished a raspberry jam tart. 'Why did you want to go?'

She asked as if it were vitally important that she should know.

'A man does,' he said after some thought. 'You want to be counted; to be able to say, I did my bit.'

'What makes you think your bit has to be done "over there"? I . . . know someone, a Frenchman. He needed to be counted, but perhaps, like you, his skills are more needed somewhere else, or when it's all over and all the wounds still have to be healed.'

His face brightened. 'He's a doctor?'

'A singer. The greatest tenor the world may never hear.'

He was quiet for a while and they sat drinking the weak tea.

'A different kind of medicine man,' he said at last and Tony knew she had found her first friend.

'I need a job.'

He seemed perplexed. 'This isn't exactly a hotbed of

industry, not out here. You might get something on the land.' He looked at her and gew more perplexed. 'You don't look as if you could sling a sack of feed around.'

'No brawn,' she agreed. 'I'm a painter.'

'Everyone does their own here,' he said gloomily. 'Oh, you mean a real painter. I say, how marvellous. I can't draw a straight line.'

She laughed. 'Then you're well on your way. No, I was looking for something menial. I don't mind doing my bit where I can, volunteering, although I'm afraid I have no skills, apart from those I learned at the Slade. I want to paint my swan but I need to eat. I thought I might clean house or wait tables.'

Suddenly Tony realised the enormous foolhardiness of what she had done. Her parents were, as usual, right. She should have gone back, clutching her prizes and her diplomas, and tried to earn a living from home.

She was home. With certainty she knew that. Something had spoken to her as she had seen the remote peninsula on the poster, it had cried out to her when she had found the cottage, and it had soothed her quietly this morning when she had seen the swan.

Lohengrin had come to her across the water. If she stayed here, Blaise would come. If he were still alive, he would find her.

She smiled and Simon McRae's heart contracted in the most unmedical way. When she smiled she became a changeling. She became beautiful.

'I inherited Jessie from Uncle Henry,' he said, 'or I'd hire you like a shot. Mrs Douglas – she who baked those raspberry tarts – used to have a girl before the war to help sell sweets and ice creams to holidaymakers but there haven't been many tourists lately.' He stood up and opened a door. 'Come on,' he said. 'I've an idea.'

She followed him into a narrow stone passageway and through a door that opened on to a formal and very gloomy sitting room. It was a brown room, brown walls, brown carpets, brown curtains with ghastly unhemmed blackout ones hanging between. The windows were in need of a good wash with vinegar and so were more grey than brown. That did not cheer up the room.

'You don't paint pictures like these, I hope?' he asked.

'Good heavens, no.' The walls were covered with dark brooding paintings of mountains, gullies, dying Highlanders or dying deer, and still-life studies of dead rabbits, ducks and pheasants.

'I never sit in here: all that blood and all those eyes. I don't suppose you'd,' he began and got no further.

Tony was walking around looking at the heavy pictures in their heavy frames. 'You poor thing. Uncle Henry wouldn't be too pleased if you threw some of them away?'

'No. I mean, yes he would not be happy.'

Tony went on shuddering at some of the pictures and smiling with joy at others. 'One or two of these are worth an absolute fortune, but if they make you gloomy, banish them to the spare bedroom. Will he allow you to paint the walls?'

'Shouldn't think so. It's been like this since my grandfather's time.'

'And his,' laughed Tony. 'Never mind, I shall lend you one or two of mine until I can paint you something bright. My cottage is much too small for some of my canvasses.'

He almost whooped with joy. 'I was trying to ask you to paint something for me – wasn't quite sure what to say.'

Tony smiled at him. 'Silly you. Now I must go and speak to . . . Mrs Douglas, was it?'

He walked with her to the door and when she had gone he returned to the sitting room and saw that it was even darker and gloomier since her light had left it.

Chrissie Douglas had a teashop near the harbour. She laughed with wonderful warm Glasgow humour when Tony asked her if she needed help.

'I need a bloody miracle, hen. Here I am, the best baker in the whole of Scotland and the last paying customer in here was in 1940. What brought you up here? You're no' in trouble, are you? Glasgow would be better for that.'

Tony noted the euphemism for 'you're not pregnant, are you?' and smiled ruefully. She would have welcomed such trouble. Blaise, where are you? The swan was a good omen. Think of the swan.

'No. I'm a painter, an artist. I graduated from the Slade.' Obviously the name meant nothing to Mrs Douglas. 'It's an art school in London – rather famous.'

'I thought you weren't from round here.'

'I am now. I've rented the cottage on the point.'

'My God. Highway robbery. This war's brought out

the worst in people. That place is falling down and should be pulled down. You've been done, lassie.'

'The view is incredible.'

Chrissie Douglas looked at her pityingly. Her home had an insecure roof but nice views: an artist, right enough. 'The view won't keep you warm in the winter. We'll have to think of something.'

'I'm going to paint. Maybe you'll be good enough to let me show some of my work in the tea room?'

'Aye, the two of us can admire it, and the canon when he comes in for a cup of tea, and Doctor McRae.'

'That's three more than are admiring it just now,' said Tony lightly. Everything would be all right. She would paint, the war would end, the tourists would come back and one day she would hear from Blaise.

'I'll send for you if a ship comes in, hen. The war can't last much longer.'

But it could. It went on but at last the tide was turning. In September 1944 Tony read that the Allies had captured Paris in August. Was Blaise there? Was he even alive? Yes, of course he was. She would feel it if he were dead. She wanted to stay at Torry Bay for Christmas and thought about using the uncertainty of travel as a good excuse, but a feeling of duty not of love caused her to repeat the dreadful experience of that spring. The train, when she did get a place, was colder and even more crowded than the one that had brought her north two years before. It did not help when her parents and Frederick threw up their hands in horror at her appearance.

'When did you last eat, Antonia?' her mother wept over her.

'Mummy, trains are impossible. I had a sandwich and was grateful to get it. I eat well at Torry Bay and I'm working and selling.'

She did not say that her single sale was to a travelling salesman from Liverpool and had earned her ten whole shillings.

She did eat well, even if her meals were repetitive and simple, and she was warm enough. There was plenty of driftwood for the fire and seaweed used cleverly helped her keep the kitchen fire going all night. She slept in the kitchen all winter. To lie full-length in a clean, warm bed was a joy she would not express to her disapproving parents.

'Your hands, Antonia? What are you doing with your hands?'

'Painting, Mummy, and collecting wood, stripping walls and furniture, all sorts of things: gardening even.'

'Do tell us more about this doctor?'

She could smell the hope from her mother.

'He's a good friend, Mummy, like Chrissie Douglas and the canon.' Whoops, she should not have mentioned the canon.

Freddie said nothing but her father swelled with disapproval. 'A Catholic?'

'Roman.' Worse and worse.

Her father sat down heavily. 'You're not going to his church?'

Should she tell him that she had not gone to any church for years? Had she been in Achahoish this Christmas, she would have gone to the canon's church. Longing, for Torry Bay and Chrissie, Simon and the canon, swept over her and almost swamped her.

'No,' was all she said but Freddie looked at her disapprovingly.

'Whatever happened to your Frenchman?' he asked, as if he had suddenly remembered another of her transgressions.

'He went back to France to fight,' she managed to say steadily. 'I haven't heard from him for years.'

'Just as well, dear,' soothed her mother. 'No future in singing, I shouldn't think. A doctor now . . . oh, he's not Scotch, is he?'

'Of course Simon is a Scot.'

Her mother offered her more potatoes. 'Well, it could be worse, dear.'

Stifled, Tony stood up. 'Yes, he could be a French singer. I'm tired; I'll go to bed.'

She was aware of their hurt, anxious faces but she had to get out of that room. How had she ever thought she could go back, even for such a time as Christmas? In her bedroom, unchanged since its redecoration when she was fourteen, Tony sat cross-legged on the bed and experienced again the childish fantasy that she was a changeling. In spite of her sadness she giggled to herself. 'I'm not a changeling. I'm a cuckoo. Poor Mummy, poor Daddy, and poorer, poorer me.'

She should have stayed at Torry Bay. She should have spent Christmas with Chrissie and gone to midnight mass at the canon's tiny chapel. Chrissie gave Canon Gemmell home-baked scones and tea every time she could get him into the tea room – 'somebody's got tae feed the poor man' – but nothing would have got her into his church. Her honesty was refreshing.

Everything about Torry Bay was refreshing. Simon, Chrissie and the canon were her friends and one or other of them had found a way to the cottage at least once a week to see how she was, to comment on the state of the cottage, to admire or wonder at her paintings, to lend a hand when she was working. She, of course, did the same for them.

She had painted views of the village and the bay for Simon and had loaned him *Sea Sprite*. Chrissie had paid her ten shillings to wait tables and wash up after the Women's Rural Christmas lunches and the Rural had invited her to come to their meetings.

How to say No without hurting feelings?

'Do you know I'm doing most of the repairs to the cottage myself. I need every minute.' Not very good but it would have to do.

Two local tradesmen had come down to do major work on the cottage – 'keeps us busy' – and she painted what she called 'chocolate-box covers' for their wives, and that led to a few commissions which would keep her from starvation until the war was over.

Canon Gemmell had studied at the Scots College in Rome. He was a cultured man and Tony found herself wondering why the Church had sent a multilingual academic to minister to a few crofters and fishermen.

'That's a snobbish viewpoint, my dear Tony. There are intellectuals among the crofters, men and women too, very knowledgeable about the arts. There isn't much to do here in the winters besides reading and listening to the wireless.'

She would not go down without a fight. 'You don't need Italian and German to speak to the villagers.'

'I did before the war. There were two Italian families and a German family living here. Two have been deported and one is in a camp. There will be fences aplenty to mend when the war is over.'

'Will it ever be over?'

He had smiled at her. 'Yes,' he had said simply.

He never pried, never asked her, as Chrissie had done, why she had chosen to live in Achahoish. She was there. That was enough and he let it be known that he was there, if needed. He did realise that she was a trained artist and they spoke together about London and its galleries, for he had travelled and seen great paintings in most of the European capitals and so her education went on.

'This is not a good place for someone without an income, Tony. You will have to exhibit. Let me take *Sea Sprite* to Glasgow.'

'He's not for sale.'

'To show him.'

'No.' She smiled to soften her rejection of his kindness. 'You can take *Lohengrin* when he's finished.'

'Lohengrin? Wagner's Lohengrin?'

'Mine. He's a swan in the bay.'

Cannon Gemmell decided not to ask why she called the swan Lohengrin. 'There are several swans in the bay, Tony. Which one are you painting?'

'There are between twenty-seven and forty-one swans at any time in the bay, Canon, but Lohengrin was there on my first morning here. Seeing him . . . cheered me. I look for him first thing in the morning and last thing at night. Silly to be dependent on a swan, but, when I see him, I just feel that everything is going to be all right.'

'I look for God first thing in the morning, Tony, and last thing at night, and every moment in between.'

She squeezed paint on to her palette as if what she was doing at that moment was the most important thing in the world. Then she screwed the top back on the tube and placed it neatly beside its brothers. 'I hope you always find Him, Canon.'

'Is that Lohengrin?' He gestured to her easel.

'No, you'll recognise him when you see him. This is merely a chocolate-box picture for my parents' Christmas present.' She could not admit that she had been glad not to have been able to visit her parents for years. 'They have sent me the train fare.'

'When the tourists come back you can make a nice living painting these chocolate-box pictures. You don't sound too enthusiastic about Christmas.'

'I'm very enthusiastic about Christmas. I went to a French church in London once with . . . a friend. It was lovely. The priest progressed in with all the children of the congregation before the mass and the smallest one was carrying the baby, *le divin enfant*. It was rather sweet. First things first. God, then presents.'

'Very practical race, the French.'

'Yes.'

She would say no more and he would not press her. 'Have a lovely holiday with your family, Tony.'

But she did not have a lovely holiday. Sometimes she felt older than her parents, older than time. Sometimes she wondered how she had lived with them for seventeen years without going crazy. Often she panicked. I have nothing in common with my parents, with my brother. I do not understand them and they do not understand me – but they will not try. Surely parents should try.

Freddie was the perfect son for them, uncomplicated, perfectly programmed to conform. It seemed to Tony, as yet another train groaned its way back to Argyll, that the relationship with her parents, with her brother, worked better when she stayed away from them. Perhaps if *Lohengrin* sold, if she received some kind of recognition . . . But would they still be suggesting, as they had suggested several times during the holidays, 'Isn't it time you got a proper job, Antonia, married a nice young man?'

'I am married,' she had told them baldly. 'I was living with Blaise and even to look at anyone else would be unfaithful.'

Her mother had cried. Her father had gone white with anger. 'Living in sin? Our daughter: and your brother about to be ordained. [The enormity of that]. You are selfish and self-centred, Antonia. You always were. You have ruined your chances of a good marriage, and for what? To give yourself to a bloody frog who had his way and then discarded you . . .'

'He's dead, Daddy,' her mother had sobbed. 'He has to be dead.'

Dead? Discarded? No. She would know if he was dead and he would never discard her. One day he would sail back across the waters that divided them on the back of a swan.

She had to believe that.

11

London, 1999

Guests started arriving unfashionably early; so many rumours had been circulating about this major showing of previously unseen works by Tony Noble.

'Well, they're certainly in for a surprise,' said Otto von Emler, the owner of the gallery, to the artist's niece.

Holly looked around the huge gallery, at the white walls on which Tony's lifelong love story was hung, and sighed. 'I hope this is the right thing to do, Otto.'

Otto took her arm and turned her to the glass-topped table on which several bottles of the finest wines were waiting. 'Just think of all the lovely money for good causes. Now come and have a drink; champagne, *naturellement.*'

Holly took a long last look at the walls and went with him. He was right. Of course he was right. This was what Tony had wanted. Wasn't it?

Marcelline Sandhurst was the first art critic to arrive. She stood in the glass doorway as still as if she herself were one of the exhibits and took one long measuring look at the walls. Her well-cut red suit reflected itself several times in the doors and the mirrors and resembled – had she only known it – nothing so much as a jagged bloody scar across the white walls.

'Holy shit,' said the urbane Marcy and reached for her mobile phone.

Gleefully Otto clinked his glass with Holly's. 'Didn't I tell you, my angel? It's started. That was not a comment on the skill of the artist.'

Holly put down her untasted wine. 'She can't be calling in her critique?'

'She's ringing Amy Rosenthal: they are such good chums.'

Holly grimaced. Amy Rosenthal was a notorious and therefore highly popular and expensive gossip columnist.

'I had invited Miss Rosenthal,' confided Otto, 'but she claimed a prior engagement.'

'Good.'

Otto looked at her pityingly. 'How we are naïve. She will be here almost before Marcy has disconnected.'

'I don't think I can bear it.'

Otto looked down at her and smiled because he liked small, frail-looking women; they made him feel protective and superior. 'We went into all that. The questions will start and the speculation will go on and on and the paintings will sell and sell.'

'I'd prefer that they sold because Tony is a wonderful artist.'

'But of course that's why they'll sell, but when the

punters see the subject, the object of a life's work, they'll understand why so few paintings were exhibited in the artist's lifetime and that adds an extra frisson of excitement. It also explains the prices I'm asking for the works of a painter most of the world has forgotten.'

She did not want to ask but she did. 'Has Taylor accepted the invitation?'

Otto tried to fill her wine glass but was not perturbed when she rejected him. 'The Taylor Hartmans of this world don't accept or reject invitations. They come if the mood takes them.' He sipped appreciatively from his glass as he eyed her speculatively. 'Why? Were you hoping to see him? I must say that if I were an unattached woman I'd be hoping to see him too but he's not for you, darling girl.' Otto posed for a moment and eyed himself critically in a mirror. He adjusted his handkerchief just so. 'What do these pirates have that makes them so irresistible? He would eat you for supper and spit out your little bones; you're too naïve, Holly, too trusting, and while we're on the subject, you don't make nearly enough of the canvas you were given.' He looked at her to see what effect his words were having and saw the clear eyes merely watching, waiting for him to finish. He shrugged. 'Hartman has the pick of the world's rich and famous, Holly, women who give as good as they get. Spoiled, you know, from the moment he was born. His uncle absolutely adored him, the son he never had.'

Otto, once so reticent, was now like a river in flood. 'Spare me.' Holly winced and gulped some of her wine. Thinking about Taylor, which she did far more often than she wanted, or talking about him, was a certain way to ruin a pleasant evening. He was the most . . . No, she would not allow him to insinuate himself into her thoughts. She looked at the door and at the throng of people who had all arrived at the same time. 'I think I'll stay in your office for a while, Otto. You go and do and say all the right things.'

'Coward,' he said, but he was smiling as he went off to greet each of his guests effusively.

'Not a coward, Otto,' Holly said to his retreating back. 'Just not my scene.' She looked in the mirror quickly and had to agree with Otto. High time she had a decent cut. She would get round to it one of these days. She looked out into the salon. Through the thick glass she could hear only a low, happy party rumbling but she could clearly see the expressions on the faces of the people who were walking around. They were impressed, surprised. Was it surprise at the subject or surprise at the talent, or amazement that the artist had painted these pictures over so many years and yet none had been seen or even rumoured of before?

The telephone on the desk beside her rang loudly and she looked for guidance to Otto. Where was his secretary? Otto himself had heard the ringing and was waving to her, gesticulating. She nodded and picked up the receiver

She recognised the voice, having heard it – usually raised in anger – several times before. It was strong, forceful and powerful, like its owner, Taylor Hartman.

'Get me Otto,' he ordered.

'I'm afraid Mr von Emler is in the middle of a private showing,' Holly began.

'He can be in the middle of anything he wants,' said the voice. 'Tell him to come to the telephone, now.'

There it was again, that damned annoying fluttering low in her stomach. Nausea, that was what it was, plain old nausea. She breathed deeply, felt better and was able – almost – to shout down the telephone line. 'You are the rudest person I have ever had the great misfortune to meet, Mr Hartman. I will see if Mr von Emler can answer the master's summons,' and she pressed the hold button so hard that she broke her carefully nurtured fingernail and cursed fluently.

She went out into the hordes of people who were drinking, eating the amazing canapés, and talking, talking, talking about the magnificent portraits. Holly managed to catch Otto's eye.

'Taylor Hartman is on the telephone. He wants to speak to you now.'

Otto excused himself from a very wealthy socialite – my, the pull of an even wealthier one – and hurried to his office. He spoke for some minutes, listened for even longer and then hung up the receiver. Then, like a man about to make a very important announcement, he went to the wine table and tapped a crystal glass with a tiny pickle fork.

He wiped his perfectly dry brow with a silk handkerchief and then was ready to speak. 'Ladies and gentlemen, an anonymous buyer has just called in with a bid of' – he paused, ever the showman, until he was sure that every eye was on him – 'five million dollars, American, for the entire collection.'

There was uproar and more mobile phones than Holly had ever seen at one time were pulled out of handbags and vest pockets.

'Anonymous, hell. Five gets you ten it's . . .'

'But this is outrageous . . .'

'Hugo, I just have to have the dandelion one. I have to have it. Outbid. Do something . . .'

Holly could hear parts of frantic conversations and in the middle of all the bedlam Otto walking around, calming, cajoling. She went to him.

'Otto, they are not all in the sale.'

He was almost dancing with excitement. 'I know, Holly. Isn't this fun?'

Holly was frantic. This was totally unexpected. 'But why does he want them? He can't want all of them.'

'He did say something about putting the lot in the nearest incinerator.'

Holly gasped. 'You haven't sold them to him.'

'Dear dear Miss Noble, I can't sell without your authorisation. Calm yourself. You are about to make an absolute fortune.'

He left her and went round soothing his guests, chatting, promising who knows what until everyone had left, but for the staff and Holly. The waiters, fascinated by the strangest end to an art show in London's chequered history, tidied up and they too left.

Holly and Otto found themselves alone in the great

studio with its soaring walls and then the door opened and there was Taylor Hartman, a throwback, thought Holly, from a more undisciplined age. Like Marcelline Sandhurst he stood framed in the doorway for a moment, a painting come to life, but unlike Marcy he did not pose for effect. He was looking for his prey. He saw it where it faltered, shaking, and strode forward, looking at Holly as if he would like to break every bone in her body. Vainly she tried not to show him that she was trembling and she would not examine the source of her fear.

'Hello, Taylor,' she managed quite calmly, if a little squeakily. 'How nice of you to come. You're wasting your time though; you can't have them. I reject your bid.'

She turned and walked into Otto's office and almost fell into his chair.

Taylor did not slam doors; that was not his style. He followed her in as quietly as a big man, who was also very angry, could.

'Why I came to talk to either of you I do not know. I should have had the opening cancelled. I asked you for a discreet private showing – carefully vetted, selected art lovers. You would make the same amount of money but no . . .' He gestured into the gallery with its amazing arrangements of expensive flowers. 'Instead you want this, this flagrant display. The thought of gossip columnists gawping at my family turns my stomach. I told you what I felt about this sordid little love affair, Holly, and I will not allow the Fougère name to be gossiped over by every empty-headed woman in the country. God knows they gave my uncle a hard enough time when he was alive. Now we're on a damage-limitation exercise. Take the damn cheque. You're giving most of it to charity anyway so you should be pleased. These paintings will not be shown and my family will not be flavour of the month in the world's gossip columns. I could take out an interdict or injunction or whatever it's called here.'

The nausea was gone. She was herself again; ready to deal with Taylor. 'To do what? Make the paintings even more interesting. Besides, Taylor.' Here Holly, surer of her ground, stood up. A bad move. He seemed even bigger and more threatening when she was standing trembling in front of him. 'Oh, do sit down. You're cutting out all the light.'

He sat down smiling, aware of her discomfort. He must always be aware of his effect on people. 'You were saying?' he asked politely.

'No court would issue an injunction. I own the paintings outright and have the artist's authority to do exactly as I please with them.' She was right, wasn't she? Tony's letter said so, didn't it?

He stood up again and headed for the door but there he turned. 'Otto, explain the facts of life to our little ingénue, and you, Holly, I hope you read the contract this crook has written. Make sure he gets only that to which he is entitled.'

He walked out and the vast gallery that had seemed so full now felt empty.

'Unkind,' breathed Otto, 'but he is upset.' He smiled and turned to Holly. 'Let me take you to dinner and we'll discuss this little contretemps.'

His luxury car paid for, no doubt, by Otto's hefty but legal commission was at the door when they stepped out. 'Now, not a word about dear Taylor until we have ordered. All I will say at this juncture is that it never pays to spoil children.'

'Isn't London pretty?' Holly asked, more for something to say than anything else. Her mind was full of Taylor. Taylor, who had tried to thwart her plans at every move; Taylor, who was so sure of his attraction. Not to this girl, Hartman.

'Pretty? Holly Noble. Can you really be Tony's blood relative? She had such exquisite taste. London is shabby; she is majestic. But she is certainly not pretty. Girls on calendars are pretty.'

They had arrived at the restaurant and so there was no need for Holly to say anything.

It was not a pretty restaurant; it was gilded and glorious and the food was excellent. For all her size Holly had a formidable appetite and Otto, who ate barely enough to feed the proverbial sparrow, laughed as she tucked in.

'Now,' he said when at last she sat back to enjoy her coffee, 'let us examine the offer from Taylor.'

'He can't have them to destroy them, Otto. That would be sacrilege.'

'He is hot-blooded and hot-tempered and does not like to be crossed, but he is also aware of the intrinsic value of these paintings. The artist could have been world-famous had she exhibited more in her lifetime. He will not burn them.'

'What will he do? Five million dollars – what's that in real money?'

'Three million pounds – give or take.'

'That will nurture a lot of talent.'

Otto had no interest in her plans for the money. She could finance a hedonistic life or, as was more likely, she could donate it all to charity.

'The paintings should be seen, not because of what they tell us of Mr Perfect Husband' – he saw Holly wince and reached over to pat her hand – 'but because they are great art. She was a genius, Holly. Her paintings have stood too long wrapped in old sheets. I want people to see them, to admire their colour, the incredible light and shade. Taylor will keep them locked away somewhere and that is cruel. They should be enjoyed.'

'I don't mind his having one or two if he intends to hang them, look at them, but he may not have all of them.' She leaned forward intimately across the table. 'Otto, what if he takes out an injunction?'

Otto frowned and twirled the brandy around in his glass. 'He'll try. I have no doubt that his lawyers are already searching to find just cause. Ruthless streak in the Hartmans. Beware of wolves in sheep's clothing, even if it's Armani or Dolce and Gabbana. Pity we had so little warning. You had spoken to him.' It was not a question.

'I haven't seen him since he was with us in the

storerooms. Naturally I was in touch with Chandler North. Taylor and his "discreet, private showing". How dare he handpick buyers for Tony's work? I shall just have to try to make him see that he's being unreasonable. It was not "a sordid little affair". He can't have been looking at the paintings properly. Nineteen thirty-seven, Otto, 1937 was the date of the first painting, and Blaise was still visiting her just before he died. They must have loved one another very much.'

He knew the answer but still he kept hoping. 'She left no letters, no diaries? They, together with the paintings, would be priceless.'

She shook her head; no one should ever see the sketchbooks with their sometimes acerbic comments. 'As far as I know, just the note with the jewellery.' She crossed her fingers, a talisman against suffering the deserved effects of lying. 'We're not a good family for keeping letters; my parents kept very few, not even mine. Anyway,' she dismissed his question, 'the paintings tell the whole story.'

'But paintings don't talk,' Otto argued bitterly.

Holly laughed. 'What a very strange remark for a world authority on painting to make.'

His smile was rueful. 'You deliberately misunderstand me. They do speak to us but if they could talk, really talk, what a story they would tell. Holly, dear, have you searched the house thoroughly?'

Holly looked at him. 'Otto, has it occurred to you that I have a home and commitments and a . . . relationship.'

'An unsatisfactory relationship, my dear. Why isn't John here with you? If he loved you . . .'

'You have no right, Otto. How dare you judge John? He had a court case. He's not like Taylor . . .'

'He's too like Taylor, selfish, self-centred, used to getting his own way. I bet he's not happy with your plans.'

'Of course,' she began and he laughed. How dare he. They had met only a few months ago and now he was the number one authority on Holly Noble and her life.

She did not want to admit that he was right. She was still wearing John's ring, unable somehow to take it off and return it. That was so final, so frightening. She hated to think that she was hanging on to an unsatisfactory relationship because she was afraid of the void its absence would cause. John was not pleased. He was displeased with the amount of time she had spent away from Glasgow over the past few months and he was not ecstatically happy that she planned a scholarship in Tony's name, but he was not like Hartman. Not in the slightest.

John, dear John. Naturally he missed her; he needed her. Perfectly natural too that, after all their years of hard work, he should feel that her unexpected inheritance should help them achieve their ambitions.

'There's enough, John,' she had cajoled him, 'enough for everything, your plans, Tony's memorial. You'll see.'

'My private life is my own concern, Otto,' she said now. 'I offered you these paintings because you were Tony's agent. Don't make me change my mind.'

'You can't. We have a contract.'

Why did a man always have to have the last word?

As soon as Otto had dropped her off at her hotel, remaining, with old-world courtesy, in the foyer until he was sure that she was safe in her room, Holly rang John. Again her fingers were crossed, but this time it was so that John would react as she hoped he would and not as she was sure he would.

'Five million dollars. I can't believe it. My God, Holly, even in sterling that's incredible. You sold them.'

'No.'

Silence. And then, 'Clever little Holly. He'll go higher. Maybe even ten.'

'I won't sell them to him.'

At that he had shouted so loudly that he had almost no need of a connection. 'Why not, for God's sake?'

She had wanted to cry. How could she love someone so much who was so different from everything she believed in? Desperation? Was that really what kept her in this relationship? Apathy, acceptance, fear? 'He's threatening to burn them.'

'What do we care? Keep your favourite ones. Be quite a talking point in the future – and it will up their value so what does it matter what he does with them?'

Her heart sank like a stone dropping into a pool. It was over. Stupid, stupid Holly. What a wonderful judge of men you are, to be sure. John would never understand. Tony, her beloved Tony, spoke to her from every painting. In every canvas she laid bare her heart, her soul. She had entrusted her life, her love for Blaise Fougère to Holly. Why? Surely because she knew that, basically, Holly was like her. Holly would understand what the paintings meant. Holly would cherish her legacy.

'Goodbye, John,' was all she said. She wanted to add, 'For ever,' but felt that smacked of melodrama. But she had to act. She had to stop running around like Scarlett O'Hara saying that she would take care of it tomorrow. She had thought and deliberated till her brain felt fried and she was no further forward. She faced the fact that she had given her heart – and everything else – to John too quickly and that she had sublimated herself to his driving ambition. How could any woman resist who was told that she was wonderful, beautiful, desirable? For a time she had felt all of these things. Had it all been a mistake, a costly mistake that would only cost more the longer she let things drift?

Everything was a mess: her private life and now her hopes for Tony dashed almost before they had had a chance to blossom. She would not cry and she would not cave in. A little setback, Tony, but we'll do it. We'll show these paintings and we'll make Taylor acknowledge you. Just you wait.

12

Torry Bay, 1945. London, 1946. Surrey, 1947

The war was over and the letter never came. 'Either he is dead or he no longer wants me. If he has forgotten his promises I will not beg and plead. I have my pride.'

Tony was not the first woman to find pride a very uncomfortable bedfellow. She finished throwing bread to the swans, took a deep breath and just enjoyed looking around her, marvelling at the way the purple-grey of the hills met the blue-green-grey of the water. 'I will try to paint that but first I will discover if he is alive and not in any kind of need.' She knew that if she found Blaise in a hospital, in a mental home, wounded mentally or physically, she would care for him. He was her husband, her life. It was as simple as that.

She went to the canon.

'This has got to be the most inhospitable garden in Argyll, Canon,' she said as she saw him kneeling down on his arthriticky old knees, scrabbling at the stony earth that grudgingly gave him a few cabbages every winter.

'Oh, one of these days I'll grow a rose, my dear. Help me up and tell me what I can do for you.'

When they were seated side by side on the garden bench outside the door and the old man had conscientiously brushed the earth from his trouser legs, she told him that she had decided to paint seriously. His ascetic face lit up with joy.

'My dear child, you have always painted seriously. I think you mean you are prepared to exhibit.'

She nodded.

'Then you must go to London. Can you afford a hotel?'

'My parents live in Surrey.'

He had forgotten, having become so used to Tony alone, that she had spoken once of her family. 'Good. There is an Austrian refugee making quite a name for himself. Gallery owner, agent, von Emler, Klaus, I think. I saw his gallery a year or so ago when I was visiting in London. What can you show him?'

'Some of the swans are perhaps good enough, and some landscapes.'

He looked at her with his gentle understanding eyes. 'Your best work is *Sea Sprite*.'

Tony looked back at him and her broken heart looked out of her eyes and he saw it. 'I'm sorry, my dear, you know best.'

'There are others,' she said, thinking of *Les Dents de Lion* and *Bébés qui Chantent* in particular, 'but there is a good reason why I'm not ready to exhibit them. Perhaps I never will.'

'You're the artist, Tony.'

'You have a very fine face, Canon. I hoped I might do you and then Chrissie, the aristocrat and the peasant, but don't tell her I said that.'

She painted two portraits of the canon during the winter of 1945. In one he was sitting in a high-backed carved chair, wearing his robes, and looking, as Chrissie said, 'as holy as all get out'. In the other he was wearing his oldest clothes and appeared to have been caught for a split second in the middle of digging his garden. Chrissie she painted in her apron and her pink fluffy slippers, and these two paintings became the yardstick by which all her commissions – and there were many of those – were judged.

'No,' stressed the great and the good, 'a camera can catch me like that. I want the real me like that old chap in his garden.'

But before that Tony had to paint the portraits and show them to this new dealer who was as anxious to find business as she was to give it to him. It took her almost a year. When she was ready she telephoned her parents from the Chapel House. They did not ask about Blaise but then they never had.

'Will Freddie be at home?'

'We thought you had quite forgotten you had a brother. He will be ordained next summer. We hope you'll be at home for that.'

'Of course, Mother. Nothing would make me miss it. I can't come down from Scotland every weekend, you know.'

'There's no need for you to be living up there anyway.'

Oh, there is need, but she could not say that; could not say that, without Blaise, Scotland, Argyll, her lovely Torry Bay was the only place where she could breathe.

'I'll tell you everything when I get there,' she said desperately and put down the telephone. She found a ten-shilling note in her purse and left it on the table. It had been a long conversation, she had no idea how long, but the canon would say nothing unless it was far too much to pay.

She travelled to London to see Klaus von Emler with three portraits, two small landscapes and one of her swans. It was one of her *Lohengrin* pictures. They were marginally better than the paintings of mere swans. Canon Gemmel's friend, Father Donald MacDonald, met her at the station and helped her carry the paintings to von Emler's small gallery and there Tony met two people who were to affect her life almost more than any other except Blaise himself.

Klaus von Emler did not live up to his aristocratic name but looked more like Tony's idea of an old grandfather. His sixteen-year-old son, Otto, would one day look exactly like everyone's idea of what an art dealer should look like. He was small and slim and very blond with rather lovely blue eyes, the very type of youth for whom German dictators had been searching. Surely no need for such a beautiful boy to be taken from the Fatherland, but the von Emlers never said why they had chosen to leave Austria and Tony never asked them. Never in the fifty years that she knew the family did either one of them ever go to Germany or Austria. Not even a singer like Blaise Fougère could tempt Otto, an avid opera lover, into the exquisite Vienna Staatsoper and he made few remarks about the backgrounds of any pictures Tony painted in either of the two countries.

At this first meeting he smiled at her shyly and said nothing as his father examined the paintings.

'You have talent, Miss Noble,' said Klaus at last.

'Oh, Papa, she's a genius,' said young Otto before he could stop himself and the father laughed.

'Such a poor businessman,' he teased his son, 'but already he knows more about paintings than I do. We will be honoured to arrange a show for you, Miss Noble. It will take some time.'

Tony gave him her address at Torry Bay and the canon's telephone number and then she took the train to Surrey. It was as well that her heart was singing at the knowledge that she was to have a London show, that a mere boy had called her a genius, that she had friends like the canon and Father MacDonald, for the visit home was not a success. She was thin, her mother called her scrawny; her hair had not benefited from a hairdresser's care in several years – Tony hacked it off with scissors when it fell into her eyes – and her clothes were not only too loose but out of style.

'And don't say, "There was a war on." We have standards, war or no war. Now, before you see any of our friends I will see if anything can be done with your hair.'

Poor Mummy, thought Tony. She deserved an obliging, conforming daughter and she got me.

'And while we are talking, Antonia,' said her father – Were they talking? Had they ever? – 'I would like to know how you have been living for the past few years. I have given you every opportunity to ask me for a little money.'

Good heavens. Did he think she was on the street, on the game? She had a wicked desire to burst into tears and ask for parental forgiveness but she controlled herself. 'I sell paintings, Daddy. You spent a great deal of money to send me to the finest art school in the world. Now, at last I am going to have an exhibition in London. You will come?'

'That man? The singer.'

The pain struck her again just behind the breastbone. 'A casualty of the war.'

Her father had the grace to look slightly discomfited. 'Antonia, we only want what's best for you,' he pleaded.

'No, Daddy, you have always wanted what you decided was best for me. Now, tell me about Freddie.'

Thank God for Freddie. They could go on all day, all night. They asked nothing about the exhibition and since she knew nothing, she said nothing. She told them she had to go back to Scotland and went back for a day to London. She went to Covent Garden. During the war it had been used as a dance hall. Would it ever reopen as an opera house? She went round to the door on Fountain Street, the door that led to the countless stairs that she and the complaining Blaise had climbed night after night in anticipation, in excitement, hand in sweaty hand, friends, lovers, music critics, not Blaise but 'Mam'selle, the great connoisseur'.

'The tenor's good, Blaise, but he's not nearly so good as you.'

She went to the Slade, its latest students soon to return from exile in Oxford. Some of her classmates had died in the war but some must be painting somewhere. She would find out. She went to Blaise's flat. She could not find it. The area near the Elephant and Castle that they had loved so much was no longer there or totally unfamiliar.

Had I not left London, I would have been killed. That awful fate seemed remote. She could not get worked up about the girl who had waited in that flat for her lover. She seemed to have nothing at all in common with the Tony Noble who looked at rubble where her heart had been.

Mrs Lumsden? A cold hand seemed to squeeze her heart. Mrs Lumsden was dead, and the secret of her wonderful bread with her. When it happened I was too lost in my own misery to react properly. I will mourn now, dear Mrs Lumsden.

She wished she could push the train home to Torry Bay. It seemed to groan and moan at every incline. She did not see the fields and shattered towns of England; she saw Mrs Lumsden's twisted body in the ruins of her house and she saw Blaise Fougère's body in the ruins of their flat. He was dead. He had come back to find her, had gone to the flat and been killed. One sad story among a hundred, a thousand, a million. One more chance. When she came back for the exhibition she would try again to find him.

She was on a train heading back to London for Freddy's ordination, which would follow the opening of her first exhibition, when her mother had a telephone call.

'Mrs Noble, I do not know if you remember me. My name is Blaise Fougère.'

Judith Noble listened, saying nothing, thinking, thinking. *She has come through. She has a chance to do well, to be famous, and here comes that Frenchman who turned her against us, ruined her life. And Freddie's ordination on Saturday.*

'Mrs Noble, you are hearing me? I'm sorry if it has been a shock but I lost touch during the war and I saw our *appartement* and they said everyone was dead, but I keep hope. I am going to be in London soon and I think, I will try one more time.'

Judith steeled herself. She did not want to do it, and heaven knows what Freddie, dear Freddie, would say if he knew, but it was for the best, being cruel to be kind, better for everyone. 'You were wrong to hope, Mr Fougère. You saw the street?'

His heart plummeted; he had hoped. 'Yes.' He could never speak of what he had felt, experienced, as he had seen the hole where his life had been.

'They told you then?' *Oh, he had to help her. She did not want to tell a real lie. Her son was going to be ordained on Saturday. Didn't he realise that? She did not want to tell an outright lie.*

'No survivors, they said, but I kept hoping, praying . . .'

'Let her go, Mr Fougère. I'm so sorry to hurt you.' She was not lying. She did not want to hurt him and she had never actually said that Tony was . . . she could not even think the word. 'Goodbye, Mr Fougère.'

Blaise heard the click as she disconnected and then he heard the humming on the line, but he stayed holding the receiver for some time before he could put it down.

His sister found him with the receiver still in his hand. 'What's wrong, Blaise?'

'Nothing, *chérie*, I had hoped to meet an old friend when we go to London, but she is . . . not there.'

Nicole laughed. She was too young to remember her brother's phone calls telling his family all about the miracle of true love. 'Then you can spend more time with that lovely American girl who makes cow's eyes at you. Don't you like her, Blaise? She's crazy about you.'

'Don't speak like that. It's not ladylike.'

'Pooh. It's true, and she would be a good wife for an opera singer. She likes travelling or she wouldn't be in Paris. I bet she follows us, or you, rather, to London.'

But he could not think of Eleanor Ridgeway and her flattering adoration. Toinette was dead. Her mother had confirmed it. He had seen the craters made by the bombs. He had heard them say, 'No survivors,' and he had wanted to believe that it was a mistake. There would be, for him, a miracle and Toinette would appear out of the dust and rubble. He saw that Nicole was concerned for him. He must make her laugh; he must turn her into the happy teenager that the war had forbidden her to be.

'Who said you were to come to London with the French National Opera? Who said this new tenor who is going to set the operatic world on its head wants his giggly little sister with him while he devastates London?'

'You did,' she said.

He capitulated, as she knew he would. 'Take care of your mother and your sister,' Papa had said during the war, 'just in case.'

When Blaise Fougère made his debut at Covent Garden his parents, his young sister and a very wealthy American family were in the audience.

13

London, 1999. Glasgow, 1999

Without the noise and bustle of the opening night, the gallery was almost like a cathedral. There was a breathless hush that was almost solemn. Sunlight streamed in the huge windows and for a few minutes Holly watched the dance of the dust sprites. A clerk sat at a computer in a corner but no one moved and no one spoke. Holly turned and saw Otto seated at his desk in his glass-enclosed office. She was surprised to see how the rays revealed his age, as artificial light did not. She smiled gently. Even in the face of disaster Otto was a happy man. Whatever happened, he seemed set to make a great deal of money.

As do you, Holly, she told herself. Even though John is livid about the Tony Noble Foundation, there will be more than enough to finance his political career and anything else we want – once we sell the paintings. She shook her head impatiently. Damn, damn. Had she not decided to say goodbye to John?

Never settle for second best, darling girl.

Voices in my head, even here in London. I'm tired.

She was tired of thinking about John. She dismissed him from her mind and began to wander around in the sunbeam lanes looking at the paintings, each one titled, each one dated. The doors were closed. No one could come to look, to buy. Today they belonged only to Holly and she gloried in them, discovering something new in each one. Every so often she stopped and allowed a painting to invade her heart and mind completely.

Tony created this, Tony, and I never knew, never suspected her brilliance.

She might keep this one, the first she had uncovered. *Sea Sprite*, 1937.

The sprite's wicked green eyes smiled at her from the whale's back. Holly put out her hand and very gently followed the line of the boy's back from his neck down, down to his waist, the curve of the buttock.

'Naughty girl. You shouldn't touch a painting. The oils on your skin are so destructive.'

She had been so involved, or perhaps the carpets were so thick, that she had not heard Otto's approach.

'I know, but he looks so real.'

'Nice butt.'

'She chickened out. The top of the wave hides his . . . butt, as you call it.'

'Nineteen thirty-seven. As far as we can tell they had only just met: she probably hadn't seen it yet and so let that wonderful wave cover it, just a little tantalising glimpse there.'

'What do you think of the painting really, Otto?'

'It shows promise and that makes it so exciting. You can see that the artist is young, inexperienced, the colours are quite crude: they don't sing.'

'She loved him, her sprite?'

'Probably, but she didn't know it. She was what, seventeen, eighteen, a schoolmaster's protected, cherished daughter up from the country. He, the very indulged only son of an upper-class French family, sophisticated, far better educated than your aunt. What happened to those innocent young lovers in the field of dandelions, Holly? Why didn't they marry?'

'I don't know, Otto.'

'What did Taylor say?'

'Very little and most of it offensive.'

Holly moved away from the painting of the desperately young and untroubled sea sprite. Would she keep it? No, she would have the *Dandelions* just to spite Taylor. That was the one he had said he wanted most, wasn't it? Someone else too? One of the rich and famous who had been invited to the exhibition had wanted the dandelion picture. Two people would have to be disappointed. Oh, to be able to keep them all and to learn their secrets. Or was that voyeurism? This was the story of a love affair: a marriage in everything except name, for they had remained lovers, or so it seemed, for over fifty years. Had they married, Holly and Taylor would have grown up together. Horrid thought.

The bell on the locked front doors rang as if it resented the force with which it was being pushed.

'Good heavens,' said Otto and hurried, without losing his dignity, across the miles of carpeting to answer the summons. 'Dear dear, Mr Hartman, the poor bell may never ring again.'

'So sue me. Good, Miss Noble is here. You wait in the gallery, Otto. My solicitors are on their way with an injunction. Right now I want to speak to Miss Noble.'

Holly's heart, which had been behaving very oddly, now took complete fright and seemed to flip over.

Nonsense, nonsense, it can't do that. Be calm.

'Good morning, Mr Hartman,' she managed, and turned to escape into the office but he followed her in and closed the door firmly on Otto who could only look at them shouting at one another but who could hear nothing.

'You are a bully, Taylor, and I will not be bullied. Your lawyers have no grounds for an injunction. The paintings are mine.'

'Sit down, Holly; you're not going to like what I have to say.'

She stayed standing.

'Then I will. Holly, in my uncle's will he specifically charges me with guarding his privacy. I have been granted a temporary sympathetic injunction; it's what they call an equitable remedy. You can't show the paintings while I'm collecting the information that proves they hurt . . . Blaise's family.'

Holly looked at him but could no longer see his eyes. He's avoiding me; he has something to hide. 'Nonsense.

These pictures can't hurt his reputation and they will certainly enhance my aunt's.'

Taylor stood up and went towards the door. 'You are ridiculous. Aren't you ashamed to have the world know your aunt was no better than a . . .?' He saw her face go white; he had gone too far and he knew it. 'I'm sorry. I have no right to judge, but I am one of my uncle's executors and I must carry out his wishes. Besides, I have to worry about my mother and my aunt.' He stopped suddenly as if he were unsure but then he started again. 'I never thought I would be glad that my mother was ill. She had a fall earlier in the year and I'm able to keep a great deal from her but I can't monitor her telephone calls. Now this damn circus has gone worldwide and though I managed to make sure no stupid woman showed her that fool tabloid, I can't think of one acceptable reason for keeping the *New York Times* away from her.'

She looked at him. 'Empty-headed women, stupid woman. You don't like women much, do you, Taylor?'

'Spare me the psychoanalysis. It was a stupid woman who ran these delightful pieces that got into your so-called better press this morning.' He threw some news-papers on Otto's immaculate desk. They opened as they fell. She read the headline and tried not to wince: THE ARTIST, THE SINGER AND THE SOCIALITE.

Taylor was still talking. 'My mother is elderly and she adored her brother. I won't have her memories sullied; and there's my aunt. Life treated her so badly and he went to great lengths to protect her. She deserves to be left alone.'

This was too much. 'She was treated badly? By your uncle, I suppose. He married her when he was already in love with someone else. Why, Taylor? Rich, was she? Did he need her money to finance his career?'

Holly gasped at her cattiness. What a terrible thing to say. She was angry with herself but she was also furious with John and Taylor and even Blaise Fougère. 'She clung on to someone who was in love with another woman. Vindictiveness must run in the family.'

He looked down at her and he sighed and it was as if all his anger left him. He seemed to sag as he sat down on the edge of Otto's desk.

'How well he kept her secret. Tony told you nothing of her?'

She shook her head. Nothing she had heard prepared her for what Taylor now said.

'Eleanor Ridgeway Fougère was insane, Holly.' He stopped as if he could not bear to continue and then he looked straight at her: 'She died in a secure asylum a few weeks before Blaise died. She had been hospitalised for nearly fifty years. My uncle adored her and never once contemplated divorcing her. That's real love, Holly. He gave all the time and received nothing in return but still he stayed faithful. I cannot . . . I will not believe these paintings were painted from life. I'm sorry. Tony Noble met Blaise Fougère in New York – once, only once. The *des Grieux* and the *Lohengrin* have different dates but they were painted at the same time.' He looked into the gallery and threw out his hands in an all-encompassing gesture. 'This, this is fantasy, a fabrication. My uncle

loved his wife and protected her. I have to do the same –
for both of them. These paintings will not be exhibited.'

She could say nothing, do nothing. By the time her
brain began to function again he was out of the office
and on his way to the street where, no doubt, another
car waited.

'Well, my dear, that was one very angry man.'

She could not look at Otto. Her stomach was churn-
ing with the horror, the tragedy of it. 'Did you know,
Otto? Did you know about his aunt?'

He did not look at her directly. 'The world's best-
kept secret. She was . . . reclusive. There were rumours, you know, alcohol, drugs. For the first few
years they were seen everywhere, all the smart parties,
the right resorts. He couldn't get enough publicity. The
golden voice married to America's golden girl and then
it all went wrong. She lost a baby. They were going to
try again. Then she disappeared off the face of the earth
and he hid from his public, didn't give interviews, didn't
do stage door lines. All that served to do was make him
more popular than ever. The mystery combined with
that glorious voice and the body. You know, my sweet,
a Rodolfo who looks a bit like Byron and sings like an
angel instead of a small fat Italian with horrible breath.
The more he ran, the more they pursued. Even when he
stopped singing, still they hunted him. Can you imagine
what it must have been like? He left the theatre and
there were hundreds of screaming women, and photographers, waiting to catch him, Mr Perfect being imperfect, being human. He entered a hotel and they

stood outside timing him. I think he resorted to disguise for a while and he had a group of devoted retainers who acted as decoys. He was unable to eat in a restaurant, swim in a hotel pool, shop.'

'Tell me you didn't know about his wife.' Holly stood up. She was going to be violently ill all over Otto's minimalist desk in a moment but she had to know before she ran.

'I've told you all I know – and what I know I read in the newspaper. You tell me about his wife.'

But Holly had run for the bathroom; no, Otto insisted on calling it a powder room though the only powder used in there went down the toilet bowl. When she came out she refused any help or sympathy and went straight back to her hotel where she lay fully dressed on the bed for hours, thinking, thinking. If it was true, and it probably was, then it was tragic. But what about Tony?

No one is alive now who cares one way or the other.

But you're wrong, Tony darling. Taylor is alive and he cares very much.

Holly lay quietly while her stomach schooled itself, and worked out that Tony had allowed her career to take second place to Blaise's career – because she had loved him. She had had some recognition during her lifetime but she had deliberately withheld the work that might have made her both famous and notorious, yet in her last note to her niece was she not hinting that she would like the paintings exhibited. Holly had been told that she could do what she wanted with them. They were hers to sell or to keep and selling meant showing. There were gaps in Tony's painting career: she would have to look carefully at the dates on the paintings and the places in which they had been set and then go through family papers to see if they told her anything. Tony had not liked her younger brother very much, but she had loved him, and they had been in touch until his death.

But I can't have Otto's gallery closed for weeks while I fight the Hartman empire in court. No way can I afford that and he knows it, the bastard. I'm sorry about poor Eleanor but she's dead and nothing can hurt her.

She pulled the duvet cover over herself and fell asleep and woke later in the evening with a headache. Her mouth felt as if it had a coating of fur and she was ravenously hungry.

Serves me right for not cleaning my teeth.

An hour later, feeling much better, she left the hotel and walked until she found an open newspaper stand and then a coffee shop. Good coffee made the stories of the abortive selling of the paintings almost bearable. The ghastly publicity had started. There were two articles on Blaise Fougère and one headed MYSTERIOUS BRITISH ARTIST. LOVERS OR SUBJECT AND PAINTER. she was unable to find THE ARTIST, THE SINGER AND THE SOCIALITE.

The journalist had not seen the paintings, for which blessing Holly said a small prayer of thanks. She read the articles about the tenor twice while she ate with relish a hot panino, redolent of pesto and cheese, and was slightly ashamed that she was still able to take such enjoyment in her food.

I hadn't eaten all day, she excused herself as she read.

The journalist was unaware of the true sad fate of Eleanor Ridgeway Fougère, whom she believed had died a recluse in a New York mansion. There was a slight hint that all was not well with Mrs Fougère and a carefully worded theory was put forward, but money and her husband's dedication had proved successful against the morbid curiosity of the masses. Although rumours abounded, some of them cruel, Eleanor's secret had died with her. Perhaps the truth would have been kinder.

I'm so sorry, Eleanor, but Taylor is fighting for you. I have to fight for Tony.

She rang Otto and found that he was still in his glass sanctum.

'It's been bedlam here all day, Holly. Take a taxi over and I'll drive you back to your hotel later.'

She did as he asked.

'Bedlam? How could there be bedlam in an empty room?'

'Every paper in the country seems to have been on the telephone today. Any reporter I have ever informed of a launch wants a scoop. I have been offered money, Holly,' he added with distaste in his face and voice. He shook his head as if he could not quite believe he had been so insulted. 'Everyone anywhere with any pretensions to being a connoisseur wants a preview. This temporary sympathetic whatever it's called is exactly that – temporary. The judge will throw him out of court. Tony's paintings will go all over the world.'

'I'm going back to Scotland, Otto.'

He went as deadly white as his walls.

'You must buy a purple suit, Otto. You're lost in this place.'

Oh, Holly, deliberate cruelty twice in one day.

He looked pained but not insulted. 'I blend, Holly dear, which is what the astute gallery owner should do. My artists shout, my paintings—'

'Sing,' Holly interrupted.

'Exactly.' He smiled in surprised approval. 'I am here merely to encourage my clients to buy. Now, don't tell me you are running away from Taylor. My lawyers are fighting back. In a week or two, with all this lovely free publicity, I will be able to sell anything. Not that I would, *naturellement*. One has taste, one has standards. But everyone will want me to represent him or her. Out there another Tony, painting away in a little garret, half starved . . .'

'Come off it, Otto. Tony was never in a garret and she was never half starved.'

'Of course not. She had a rich lover.'

Holly was perfectly sure that Blaise Fougère had never 'kept' Tony Noble. That was not Tony's style. If they were lovers, they were equals. She would go back to Scotland to look through the rest of the boxes she had not cared enough about to open when her parents had died in that stupid, senseless accident on a narrow Himalayan road. Maybe, a little voice whispered, she would rake through her feelings about John. Maybe. First things first. She would put Tony first. Tony had always . . . No. She had thought that she, Holly, had always been first with Tony but all the time there had been this secret, more important, more powerful love.

She took a deep breath. It was do-or-die time. Holly and Tony: each had had enough. 'I'm going to Torry Bay, Otto, to live.'

He saw that she was serious. He got up from his chair and almost ran round the desk to her. 'Holly, my dear, you can't leave. It's just beginning to get exciting and I can't make decisions without you.'

'You don't need to make decisions. I'm taking the paintings off the market until I've done some research. Pack them up and send them back to Achahoish, if you like.'

He grabbed her arm. 'I would adore to be free to send them anywhere. I'm afraid, too, that you can't just take them off the market. They are literally wards of court. No one, including you, their rightful owner, can do anything with them without the permission of the court and for the moment Taylor has the court in his pocket.'

'I'm perfectly sure he'd sue and win if he heard you say that, Otto. I'll be as fast as I can. In the meantime I can't sell them but Taylor can't buy them either and that makes me feel absolutely wonderful.'

She returned to her hotel in luxury, courtesy of Otto who had been kind to her and determined to take no offence at her rudeness. She slept as soundly as the most untroubled of babies, checked out early, and caught the first train back to Glasgow. It was clean, well staffed and ran on time. Bliss.

On the way north she mused that she had been a drifter all her life. The present was not as she wanted it to be, but then it was not too awful either. She was not, however, getting any younger, and was still drifting, looking for the perfect man who would help her build the perfect home, the perfect family, breed the perfect babies.

Damn it; I'm thirty-seven years old.

Over thirty years of drifting, Holly, over thirty years too long.

Torry Bay, she realised, had never been her second home. It had been, quite simply, her home, the one place in the world where she was accepted as she was, the one place in the world where she had always felt completely welcome – and safe. She would stop blaming her parents for their inadequacies, their inability to show her that they had loved her, that she did not come in second place to the mission station they were running at any particular time. She would accept that she had in fact inherited a few good qualities from her parents, qualities that had shaped her life. Why would she have spent her first few years after university teaching in children's homes in Africa if they had not taught her to care about those who were less well off? If they had also taught her to worry incessantly about what constituted a real family, a real home, well, that was something she would have to learn to deal with. She would ring John and tell him about her concerns and worries, facts on the table.

Damn it all, another cliché.

But, and here she was adamant, she would not allow herself to be sweet-talked into accepting things the way they were. Weakly, she allowed herself to remember and tally all John's good points. It was a formidable list.

I'm crazy. Why am I even thinking of giving all this up?

She reviewed in her mind some of the paintings that she had seen for the first time in the storerooms: Fougère in a field of clover, under a rainbow, desolate in a rowing boat, and a Fougère, who could never have been a romantic fantasy, helping a little girl to make a walkway of shells while Tony dozed against a rock.

Toinette, ma mie. *Hollyberry, Hollyberry.*

The voice in her head was as real as if he were sitting beside her.

Refuge from the Storm.

What strength there was in that painting. The storm raged around the couple on the headland, that little headland from where she had thrown Tony's ashes.

Did you want me to do that, Tony?

Darling girl.

For the rest of the journey she looked out of the window and tried to see nothing but the landscape before her.

She heard her telephone as she let herself into her flat and then she heard her answering machine. It was John. No time to think. 'Hello, John, I've just got in.'

'I read about it in the papers. I should have been there for you; I'm sorry.'

'I didn't ask you, John.'

'Can't we talk, Holly? I don't want to throw five lovely years away because of some silly arguments.'

'John . . .' she began.

'No sex. Just talk. Please, Holly. Look, I'm sure there's nothing to eat in your flat. Let me take you to dinner, a pizza, or spaghetti somewhere. We need to talk.'

They agreed to meet in a little Italian restaurant they liked near the Theatre Royal. Holly was determined not to allow memories of lovely evenings there to interfere with her decision to become more assertive in her relationship.

'Tell me more about the exhibition,' he said after they had ordered.

'I told you it was a madhouse; so many people turned up. Every reporter in London was there. I heard people talking about the paintings, choosing the ones they would just have to have. There were some of those ghastly society reporter types and I hid from them in Otto's office. Everything was going along swimmingly and then Taylor phoned and ruined everything.'

A waiter put a plate of garlic bread on the table and Holly remembered that she had eaten little on the train. She could hardly bear to wait until he had gone through the ritual of opening the wine.

'Doesn't that smell take you straight to heaven, John?'

John was not too interested in food. 'Have you thought any more about his offer? Perhaps you should reconsider.'

'He knew I wouldn't agree. I don't want his money.'

'What exactly do you want?' John asked aggressively.

'Recognition of Tony's genius. If her greatest paintings are hidden away or destroyed, her greatness is merely hearsay.'

'I can't believe it.'

'Believe what?'

'That there are actually people in the world who can throw millions of pounds away.'

Holly smiled at him. 'I take it you mean that to buy them and burn them is throwing away money. To give him his due' – no, she could not share his family secret – 'to give him his due, I don't think he would destroy them. Or am I the person you see as nonchalantly throwing away money?'

'It could be our future. That's what you're throwing in the river.'

Was it the wine, the satisfying flavours of perfectly cooked food? Holly knew for a certainty that she had no future with John. She put down her glass.

'I'm selling my flat, John, and moving to the cottage. I'm not running away; I'm not Tony. I need civilisation and I'll come back – some time – but right now I need Torry Bay.'

'You're out of your mind. What's happened to you, Holly?'

'Nothing, except that looking at Tony's incredible paintings has opened my eyes.'

She stood up and handed him her engagement ring. 'I'll send the pearls back tomorrow.'

'Pearls are tears.' Fougère was right.

14

Torry Bay, 1949. New York, 1949
DES GRIEUX

'I'm sorry, Klaus. Who did you say? It's such a bad line.'

Tony was in the canon's hall trying to understand a telephone call from her agent, Klaus von Emler. Klaus's accent and the poor connection were making every second or third word disappear.

'It's a wonderful opportunity, Tony. They will send you to New York which is where he is for the winter; well, November and December.'

'Who is in New York, Klaus? I'm not sure that I heard you properly.' Tony's hand was shaking as she held the receiver and she sat down on the hard wooden chair.

'Fougère, Tony. He is a singer, a very great one and the opera house wants you to paint him as des Grieux. That's a character in an opera.'

Tony did not reply. Des Grieux, the tenor role in Puccini's *Manon Lescaut*. She had seen the opera with Blaise before the war. He would be superb.

'Blaise Fougère?' she managed at last.

'Yes.'

'He wants to commission me?'

'Some rich family is donating it to the opera house. Have you heard of Fougère? I took Otto to hear him in *Rigoletto* a few years ago . . . just about the time of your first exhibition, Tony. Yes, when the Garden opened again after the war. Such a voice. Tony, can you hear?'

'Yes, I hear.' He was alive; he was singing and he had forgotten her. Her parents were right. He had used her when he needed her and then dropped her. She could not take in what Klaus was saying. He had been in London, singing at Covent Garden, when she had had her exhibition. How could he have been in the same city and her not know?

'I'm too busy, Klaus,' she said and hung up because she could no longer speak. All the banked-down pain was pushing its way to the surface. She had to get away. She could not scream with pain and disillusionment in the canon's front hall. She closed the front door as quietly as possible and hurried down the lane and on to the path that led to the bay. When she was out of sight she began to run and run until she was sobbing for breath and there was a stitch in her side. The swans were in the bay. They disregarded her. They had no need of her when the water was full of food. Swans, they were just swans. Tony sat down in an abandoned heap on the stony beach and watched them.

They're swans, she told herself. Swans, not disguised princes and no knight in shining armour is going to come sailing across the sea on the back of one of them. What a fool I have been. Did I make any effort to keep in touch with him? I wrote a few letters that he never answered. I had no address for his parents but when the war ended I could have gone to Paris and looked at telephone directories and I could have written to every Fougère who was a lawyer. That's what he said, 'My father is with the law.' I could have put an advertisement in the paper. I could have fought but I sat up here like a romantic fool and waited for a bloody swan. I can't believe what an idiot I've been. He's alive and he's successful and Toinette, his precious Toinette was no more than a sexual convenience while he was at the Conservatory.

His ring. Oh, God, I thought this was my wedding ring. How could I have been so naïve? She lifted the gold chain over her head, stood up, and threw the ring as far as she could into the sea. She was humiliated to see it plop into the water just a few feet from the shore. Without taking off her shoes she began to wade in. She was going to pick it up and throw it far, far . . . No, she wanted it back. It was her wedding ring. She had to find it. She found herself panicking as the waves refused to give up her treasure.

Please, God, let me find it and I'll never swear again.

The swans hissed at her angrily and paddled off to calmer water as she walked up and down methodically looking. Her skirt was soaked and her shoes.

'Oh, shit, oh, shit. I don't mean to swear but I haven't found it and shit isn't a swear word. Oh, help me, please help.'

At last she saw the chain lying on a stone almost at her feet. She picked it up and held it close to her breast and then she kissed it, dried it lovingly on the tail of her shirt, and slipped it on again over her head.

I didn't fight hard enough. Did I believe, deep down, that I wasn't good enough, special enough for him? Is that why I left London without leaving a thousand messages? Klaus says he is great, acclaimed. But I knew that ten years ago. His first letter said: 'Trust me.' But I did trust you, Blaise. I waited . . . dear God Almighty, I waited for a bloody swan, and he told me, many times, he told me that he was just a man.

The canon was waiting for her at the cottage and her heart contracted as she saw how he had aged. He stood up when he saw her coming and said nothing at all about her wet clothes.

'Hello, my dear. Klaus rang back.'

'Come in and have a cup of tea, Canon. Give me a second to change my clothes.'

He followed her into the cottage and when she came downstairs she found he had already put the water on to boil.

'I owe you an explanation,' she began, but he interrupted her.

'You owe me nothing, my dear, except a reviving cup of tea. Klaus worried that you did not understand the importance of this commission.'

'I understand. I was . . . afraid.'

'Forgivable, understandable even, but remember, Tony, that you are the one who is being sought out now. You have a reputation: no need to be afraid of the rich and famous or of your own talent. That's a very insidious fear. Many geniuses have it.'

'I'm not a genius,' she began and again remembered Blaise's voice. 'You must have the ego. If you do not believe you are good, how can you expect the world to know?' 'I'm good, Canon, and maybe I will go to New York and paint Mr Fougère.'

'You must, and if he should invite you to the opera, my dear, go. I believe he is being touted as the voice of the century, the new Caruso, the new this, that and the next thing. Poor man, instead of being allowed to be the first Fougère as you, Tony, are the first Noble.'

She laughed. 'I too learn from the magnificent dead, Canon. "Listen to the magnificent dead." A friend said that to me, many years ago.'

'I like that, the magnificent dead. And so will you come back with me and ring Klaus?'

She nodded, poured him a second cup of tea, and, mindful of Chrissie's worries that he did not eat enough, found a biscuit hiding at the bottom of the bread tin and put it on a plate.

'What fine friends I have,' he said and she noticed that he was seemingly unaware that the biscuit was stale.

It appeared, according to Klaus, that a wealthy sponsor in New York wanted to donate a portrait of the French tenor, Blaise Fougère, to the city opera house. New York had tried to snap him up just after his debut in Paris but had missed the boat and had to wait until he had debuted at Covent Garden. The opera company and the wealthy family, which was one of its major sponsors, often underwriting the entire cost of a new production, wanted Fougère to make New York his base. The portrait was only one of the little inducements being thrown his way.

'The Ridgeways saw your portrait of Lord Butterstone and were extremely impressed. If you recall they bought a small landscape.' Tony did not recall. She paid little or no attention to where her paintings went. She created them for someone else to love and then created more to fill the empty space.

'Klaus. Does Fougère know the name of the artist?' She could hardly bear to know the answer.

'I really don't know, my dear, but I believe it's to be a surprise gift for him.'

It will be a surprise all right, thought Tony.

She decided to go. She tried not to let her heart hope that he still loved her, that there had been some horrid misunderstanding, that he had ached for her as she had for him. She refused to allow herself to imagine his dear face lighting up with joy, his arms reaching out for her. She would be dignified, the artist everyone wanted. She would show nothing of her inner turmoil, but if there was any way to fight for what she wanted she would fight.

I wear his ring. I will wear it in New York and if he ignores it then I will know the fight is lost and I will throw it at his feet and get on with my life.

She was sick all the way across the Atlantic. She had

never flown before and was not afraid. In fact she was barely aware that she was in an aircraft thousands of feet above the earth. She was sick with the fear of final rejection.

If he had wanted you, he would have found you years ago.

They'll tell him the painter is this new Tony Noble and he'll refuse to sit. Tenor angst, they'll call it, and send me away with a nice placatory cheque.

Blaise was sicker than she was. He was not told until he returned to New York from San Francisco. He stood, stunned, in the middle of the drawing room of the Ridgeways' magnificent mansion. He could not believe it. It was a joke in bad taste, a nightmare – insanity.

Sarah Ridgeway had expected her protégé to show some gratitude. The painter was fairly expensive, even though she was quite new, and there had been the extra expense of the transatlantic flight and, naturally, a decent hotel. 'We hoped you'd be pleased, dearest. We saw her paintings in London when you debuted and thought, I just bet that painter could do a decent job of Blaise.'

He looked desperately at his brand-new secretary who did not understand his reaction either. 'Noble, you say, Tony Noble. It can't be a woman.'

Henderson Ridgeway laughed heartily. 'My goodness, my boy. Don't tell me you don't like women artists. She's the up-and-coming portrait painter. When we said at the club we'd hired her, everybody,

225

but everybody asked if there would be time for them to sit too, but she's all ours this trip. All yours, that is, and the management wants des Grieux, your debut role.'

'You're just darling in the costume, Blaise dear,' said Sarah Ridgeway, 'and I just bet it will cheer up our little Eleanor to see you again in all that lovely velvet and satin.'

Eleanor. My God, Eleanor. 'Yes, I must go to see her at once.'

'No, don't be hurt, honey, but she really doesn't want to see you yet. Doctor Kermaly is taking care of her. A little rest and she'll be fine. You and Stefan here have so much work to do. We thought we might ask Miss Noble to dinner. We could all meet her then.'

'No. Not tonight, Sarah. There is too much mail for me, and I want to see Eleanor.'

'Of course you do, my dear. Henderson and I will take Miss Noble to dinner and we'll set up an initial sitting. Will you trust us to do that?'

She was at the door before he remembered that they had spent hundreds of dollars to donate a portrait of him to the opera company. 'Thank you both. You are too good to me.'

'Nothing's too good for our favourite tenor,' Sarah said and blew him a kiss.

As soon as the door had closed behind them he turned to Stefan. 'Find out where Miss Noble is staying and get me a car.'

'She's at the Carlisle, Monsieur.'

'You are definitely going to be indispensable, Stefan.'

He hurried out and found the car drawn up at the kerb. 'Downtown, please, the Carlisle.'

He was as nervous as the night he had made his debut; no, more nervous. Then, what was the worst that could happen? He might forget the words; he could crack on a note. But this, this. He was still having difficulty believing that it was true, that all this time she had been alive and he had not known. He had mourned her, and had then decided to go on and make some kind of a life without her, and now she was back from the dead.

'Miss Noble's room, please,' he asked the reception-ist and waited for the few seconds that it took her to connect him with the room.

'Hello.' Her voice was just the same, well modulated but slightly nervous.

He tried to speak but no sound came. He tried again and this time the voice obeyed him. 'Tony? Toinette? Is it you?'

He heard her gasp and then there was silence and he could imagine her standing there, holding the tele-phone.

'Blaise? Where are you?'

'In the foyer. May I come up?'

Again there was silence and then quietly, slowly, she gave him the number of her room.

The lift seemed to crawl. It stopped at each floor and one or two people looked at him but he did not see that they wanted him to smile his acknowledgement that he knew that he was recognised. He hardly saw them at all and could think only of Toinette. His pulse was racing, his heart was pounding. At last, at last he was on the seventh floor. He stood outside her door for a moment. Somehow he had thought the door would be open and she would be standing waiting. He knocked.

The door opened and Tony stood there. For a soundless lifetime they stood looking at one another and then with a groan, almost of pain, he opened his arms and she ran into them.

'She told me you were dead,' he said, and kicked the door closed behind him.

15

Glasgow, 1999. Torry Bay, 1999

On the next afternoon, Holly went to see a local estate
agent and arranged to put her flat on the market. It had
not, in the end, been such a difficult decision. Torry
Bay called to her and, without her job that she had
loved, and John, whom she had thought she loved,
Glasgow meant little. There were friends, of course,
good friends, and leaving them behind would be hard,
but Torry Bay was only a few hours away and friends
would visit and she would return to the city often, to do
all the things that she had always loved to do and that
she could not do in a tiny remote cottage; when this
crazy business was behind her, she might even buy a
new flat.

On the way back to her flat she posted the pearls and
stopped in at several small shops to buy some odds and
ends to tide her over at Torry Bay: a firm green
avocado, some crisp fresh lettuce, tomatoes on the vine
that brought the smell of Tuscany into a rather grey
Glasgow street.

A very small blue car was parked outside her building and Taylor was leaning against it as he watched some boys play football on the quiet street. Her stomach churned with what? Fear, excitement, some animal instinct she refused to call simple lust. He looked . . . good, standing there. Where had he been? How impossible had it been for him to get to her apartment? John lived a few stops away on the underground and he had never just turned up and yet Taylor who lived, she thought, in New York seemed to pop up frequently. She wished she could believe it was her charm.

'What do you want now?' she asked crossly.

'Nice to see you too,' he said as he straightened up.

She flushed. 'Why are you here, Taylor? You've changed your mind and you're sorry you made such a fuss about nothing.'

'Protecting the people you love is not nothing, Holly. If you were about to make some coffee I could use some. It's quite a hairy drive from the airport.'

'And you haven't a penny left after renting that car?'

'Amusing. May I join you for coffee?'

'I have tea at this time of day.'

'For God's sake, Holly. Anything but vitriol would be fine.'

She looked at his tired face and she heard her shrewish voice. What changes there were in her in such a short time; she was no longer overawed or intimidated by Taylor Hartman. 'I'm sorry. Of course you can have coffee, but what do you want?'

He followed her into her flat. 'This is nice but the

walls aren't big enough.' He did not say 'for Tony's canvasses'.

'I'm moving,' she said casually as she filled the percolator.

'Getting married and moving to where? Across town?'

How did he know so much about her life? 'That's none of your business, but as it happens I'm going back to the cottage. I'm going to sit on that headland and think.'

'I hope Tony left you a fur coat.'

She laughed and he laughed too. If she didn't dislike him so much she could quite like him. 'Politically incorrect.' She took two mugs from a cupboard above the sink. 'I can make you a sandwich. Avocado, lettuce, tomato, and I have some nice cheese somewhere.'

'All of them, please. That's my ultimate sandwich.'

He sat at the table in the kitchen while she sliced bread and avocado but said nothing until the sandwiches were ready. 'My mother wants to see the paintings.'

Surprised, she looked down into his eyes as she put the blue plates from Torry Bay on the simple blue checked cotton tablecloth. She had not noticed his eyes before. They were dark, but not brown or black; they were green. 'Damn,' she said and blushed. It was such an insufferable cliché. She had looked into his eyes and felt she was drowning. She pulled her head above the water. 'Why?'

'She said she owed it to her brother.'

No one is alive now who cares one way or the other.

'And even though she's so old, she'll make the effort.' Holly did not quite believe in this fragile invisible mother.

He looked down at his hands as if unable to meet her eyes. 'I told her I had closed the exhibition, that I had tried but been too late to stop it altogether.'

Holly sighed. 'Why so vindictive, Taylor?'

'I am not vindictive.' He smiled at her again and she was aware of his practised charm. 'All my girlfriends will tell you that. Seriously, my mother wants to see the paintings, to meet you.'

She looked at his hands as he reached for his plate; the long suntanned fingers, the expensive watch. She pulled her eyes away.

'Did she know – about her brother and Tony?'

He put the sandwich down untasted. 'There was no Blaise and Tony.'

'Don't waste it.' She watched him eat.

'Great bread.' He finished a second bite. 'Will you meet her?'

Nicole Fougère Hartman. She would know for sure, if anyone did. 'Where is she?'

'Right now she's in Paris. She has an apartment there.'

'She's not too frail to make the journey?'

Was there a faint blush of embarrassment under the expensive tan? 'Perhaps I misled you and I'm sorry; I thought it was . . . necessary. She fell . . . skiing.'

Holly laughed. 'What a fraud, Taylor. I had a vision

of a little old lady on a Zimmer frame or even in a wheelchair.'

He had the grace to look rueful. 'I don't like to lie, Holly, and I didn't – exactly. She has been ill.'

'I suppose justification comes easily to businessmen.' She stood up abruptly and moved away. 'There are things I have to do at Torry Bay. Have her talk to Otto.'

He left the table and stood, towering over her. He made no effort to distance himself from her and she could see a pulse beating in his throat. No tie. How casual. She almost jumped back.

'Why did you come – really?'

'Thanks for the sandwich,' he said and he was gone. She heard his feet pounding on the steps, the car door, and then the noisy attempts at starting the engine, silence, then success, and finally the low sound as the car moved away.

She stood in the kitchen and lifted the mug he had been using. The unfinished coffee masked any scent of him; or, no, there was something faint. She slammed the mug down so hard that the coffee slopped over the side on to the tablecloth.

'Damn, damn, damn, and he's eaten my supplies.'

Holly was filled with urgency to get away. She could not think in Glasgow. There were too many intrusions. She almost ran around in her haste to pack the few things she would need. From the kitchen window a yellow primula reminded her that spring was on the way. She could not leave it to die. She watered it and put the flower, pot and all, into a plastic bag.

A few hours later, even after stopping to restock her provisions, she put the plant between some stones on the windowsill at Torry Bay.

Holly 1970 . . . Holly 1972.

April in Argyll. It sounded like the title of a movie or a book: *April in Argyll*. The morning after her arrival Holly walked down to the cove and sat watching the swans. Somewhere near here the hens must have their nests and soon the bay would be full of brown cygnets. She would stay for the cygnets and she would stay for the light, which was like no other light anywhere, so soft, so gentle. She would stay for the air which was cool and clear and for the warm wind which sometimes blew across the bay carrying the smell of the sea, or the scent of wood smoke from a cottage fire somewhere near. She would stay for the peace which came 'dropping slow'. Tony had loved the peace. Holly had read the letters and read the notes on the sketches and 'I love it here' was what Tony said most.

'Morning, Lohengrin,' she called to the stateliest of the swans and he dipped his head.

Impossible that he was the same swan and there was certainly no golden crown upon his head. If Tony waited for a swan, what am I waiting for? Knights on white stallions are notoriously scarce in this day and age. A memory of Taylor's hands holding the sandwich disturbed her for a second but she banished it. How peaceful it was without the worry of John and their relationship.

'Can I love someone if I am relieved to be away from

him?' she asked the swans who, in their serenity, ignored her and so she answered herself. 'No, I do not love him, not as Tony loved Blaise.'

Tony had never been at real peace without Blaise. The paintings told Holly that. The letters were less communicative. Those in answer to Tony's were full of domesticity and church matters. Those from Holly's father complained about Tony's 'selfish' wish to divorce herself from her family, 'to spend the little money your paintings are earning in buying this ridiculous run-down cottage miles from anywhere'. This from a man who was a missionary. Sometimes they dealt with the child Holly.

You know how difficult it is for us to have Holly here. We want her to have a British upbringing. It was quite thoughtless of you, my dearest sister, to arrange a show at her school holiday time. Now we will be forced to ask the headmistress to find someone to look after the child. She cannot come here. Naturally we would love to have her with us; she is our dearest child, but, on second thoughts, perhaps you could arrange to take her to London with you. Gilda and I do not want the sophistications of the city for ourselves and are only too aware of the traps that lie in wait for young girls – we need not remind you of those – but we are aware too of the cultural opportunities in our capital city and visits to museums and art galleries, perhaps even the ballet at Sadlers Wells, would be educational . . .

Just one of many letters from parents who found their 'flock' easier to deal with than their only child. Holly had felt even worse about the letter when she had checked the dates with the schedule of Tony's exhibitions and found that none had taken place at the times suggested in the letter. Tony had not wanted her; it was as simple as that. She tried to banish the hurt as easily as she had banished Taylor. Blaise had been there and his needs came first; there could be no other explanation. She refused to countenance the thought that the need was mutual.

She did love me and my parents did love me in their fashion. No one loved me with the passion that Tony obviously had for Blaise Fougère. What would it be like to be so in love, so loved that no one and nothing mattered but the beloved? If John had loved me the way Tony loved Blaise . . . if I had loved him . . .

'I want to love recklessly, totally, oh, I want to,' she told Lohengrin, but he had heard it all before, drew up his proud head, and sailed away.

She did not know where the hours went. The days were getting longer and the evenings stretched beautifully out to the bay. She woke early and tidied the cottage, cleaning out the fireplace, a task she remembered sharing with joy when she had stayed with Tony. Then she laid a new fire – the evenings were chilly yet – and went out. She walked and walked and spent a great deal of time looking for the tiny yellow primroses that hid among the roots of trees, or sitting watching the play of light on the water.

She watched the swans, aware that Tony had watched them, communed with them. Darling Tony, how could you wait for him so faithfully? You knew the story of Lohengrin was a myth; but still you believed Blaise would come back.

Sometimes she thought she heard a loving, laughing voice.

When it's right, you'll know it, darling girl, and you'll wait till the end of time if need be.

Holly was too practical for such nonsense. She knew she was not hearing voices and if she were then she would seek help, probably from a psychiatrist. Still, it was a joy to curl up in Blaise's chair before the fire in the evenings and look through Tony's sketchbooks, laughing sometimes, smiling often and too often reduced to tears.

A sketch of Blaise in a rowboat and the words, 'such pain'. Two figures, unrecognisable, on the point. The man tall and broad, the woman sheltered in his arms, tiny. The words, 'peace, shelter'. She remembered that painting from the aborted exhibition. The child Holly with a doll. *Joy.* Whose was the joy, Tony, yours or mine? I hope both.

But it could not last for ever. Letters came from John, from Taylor and even from Otto. How dare they disturb her peace, remind her of the world outside.

Forgive me, Holly. I love you and need you and will try to understand about the cottage. Please come home. It will soon be time for the nominations.

Would she feel differently if, instead of writing a letter, John had driven out to Torry Bay, carrying her engagement ring and the little string of pearls?

Darling Taylor has been here twice, in person, so terrifying. One might almost think he was becoming a resident. I am very skilfully – and tastefully – keeping the story in the public's fickle beady little eye. You'll thank me but you can't thank me from the wilderness.

Fight fair, Holly. Come back and argue with me or I'll come to Torry Bay. I owe you lunch.

She ignored them all and studied and restudied the family letters. None of Tony's relatives or friends ever alluded to her relationship with Blaise Fougère. There were cryptic remarks about 'problems encountered by young girls in big cities', worries about the progress of the war from her grandparents, but no mention at all of Blaise Fougère. Did they know he existed? If they did, what did they think? Where was Blaise during the war? He was a Frenchman studying in England. Did he stay, but if he did why did he not marry Tony? He loved her. His eyes in the early portraits told the world of his love. Why did they never marry?

16

New York, 1949. Torry Bay, 1949. Surrey, 1949
DISILLUSION

Tony had not wanted, sought, to have an affair with a
married man. He had not said, when she let him into her
room, that he was married. They had been capable of
no rational thought. Years of frustration and heart-
breaking sorrow had disappeared for a while under the
surging tide of desire. When he had told her about
Eleanor she had been furious, not that he had married
but that he should have come to her and loved her.

'Get out, get out,' she had screamed at him. 'You
have made me a whore.'

Her anger frightened him and he imprisoned her
hands. 'No, oh no, *ma mie*, never, never. Listen, Toinette,' he had beseeched desperately. 'Listen to me,
please. You never wrote; the building was destroyed.
She told me you were dead. Obliterated. I looked up
that word. To blot out; erase; leave no traces. All that
was left of you was in my heart, in my blood, under my
skin. I mourned my wife, my wife.'

He let go and stood as if waiting for another blow. And she dealt it.

'So you jumped into bed with someone else?'

She knew the look of pain that crossed his sensitive face was because of her crude language.

He went on, feverishly, the words spilling out, trying to make her understand. 'I met Eleanor in Paris after the war. I believed that you were dead and so I stayed in Paris and resumed my studies. I was the right voice at the right time; doors opened quickly. The Ridgeways were making a tour and they heard me sing. I was invited to New York. Eleanor fell in love, maybe with my voice, and I was lonely, Toinette. I thought you were dead. I had tried to find you. Did you try to find me?'

What could she say? I waited for a knight in shining armour to sail across the sea on the back of a swan. She prevaricated. 'I wrote to every address you gave me; you never answered.'

The telephone rang. It was the front desk.

'Mr Ridgeway is coming to take you to dinner.'

Tony looked in horror at the receiver. Mr Ridgeway. Dinner. 'Thank you,' she said dully and hung up.

'Mr Ridgeway is coming. What can I say? I've got to get out of here.' Wildly she began to throw things back into her suitcase.

'Toinette, please. Stop, Toinette. Look at me.'

'Why? Why should I look at you? What will I see when I look at you?'

'Me, Blaise, the same Blaise.'

She slapped at his words and began to cry and tentatively he put his arms round her and held her but still she stiffened against him.

'Tony, I'm sorry. There are no words but please, stay, paint the picture.'

'I'd rather die.'

He winced. 'Tony, it's a job, nothing more. Can you think of it as a job? An opportunity? Stay for a few weeks. Paint the picture, a tenor in a fancy costume, no more. Then you can leave my life and I will leave yours, I promise, if that's what you want.'

'How dare you. Of course I want.' She looked at him and her eyes were full of contempt. 'You make me feel dirty. I never felt dirty before.'

He went white under his tan.

'Get out.'

He stumbled backwards to the door, his hand held out before him as if to protect himself from her hatred. In the corridor he waited until he was composed and then was forced to hide again as the lift disgorged his wife's father. He waited and heard Tony say politely, 'Do forgive me. I'm not quite ready.'

He skulked like a criminal until he heard them leave and he stood and watched the floor indicator until he saw that the lift had stopped on the ground floor. Like a very old man, he walked down the stairs, and took a cab to his home. The next day he began his sittings with Tony. It was her least successful portrait and the Ridgeways were disappointed and embarrassed at being let down, as they saw it, by society's favourite young painter.

'It's not you, Blaise. The eyes are . . . calculating.'

'It's a painting of des Grieux,' he tried to defend her.

'Then you should have told her the story of the opera; des Grieux is a young man blinded by his love for an unsuitable woman. He could have used a dose of calculation. Hyped up, these British painters.'

He said no more. He did not say that Tony loved and understood the sad story of the Chevalier des Grieux. Neither did he say that Tony had refused to speak to him at all during the sittings and had not explained why she had decided to complete the assignment.

Later she told him that his father-in-law had told her a little of Eleanor's story and that she had feared to add to the young woman's grief by refusing to paint her husband. She had left the studio where she was painting as soon as she had completed the work. She was unhappy with the painting because to her it resembled neither Blaise nor des Grieux. She had not liked the expression in the eyes of the portrait because it was not the expression she had seen as she worked. Those eyes were sad, but the sadness was borne bravely. She wanted to paint what she saw but her fingers refused to do what she told them to do.

He wrote to her and Klaus forwarded the letters but she did not read them and burned each one as it arrived. It was the boy, Otto, who gave Blaise the address of the cottage, a sin for which he refused to ask his father's forgiveness.

'They love one another, Papa. I want her to be happy.'

'He is married to someone else.'

'You are old-fashioned. Nowadays it is correct to admit to a mistake.'

'Clients expect integrity.'

'She is not my client, Papa. I prefer that she is happy.'

'Stupid boy.'

Blaise knew better than to write to Tony again. He waited until he had a few days between performances at Covent Garden. Stefan booked the trains. He said nothing, but Blaise could tell that his secretary thought he was out of his mind.

'I'll sleep on the train, Stefan. You know I can sleep anywhere, like a cat.'

It was his last chance. He had to explain, make her understand. He could not bear that she should hate him. He refused to admit that he wanted her to love him. He loved her but then he had always known that he loved her.

'Her mother told me she was dead.'

As the train lumbered through the hills and valleys he wondered what could have made her mother let him believe such a terrible untruth but he could come to no rational conclusion. He decided not to think about it any more. He would think about what he would say to Tony. Eleanor was stable. Perhaps, if she got really well . . . no, he would not think about anything at all. He would take refuge in music, in Beethoven, in Mozart. The music filled his head and thrust out everything else, except that last image of Toinette.

'You make me feel dirty.'

It was raining when he arrived in Argyll and he took a taxi from the station to the village. All he deduced from his map studies was that it was likely that Toinette lived near the sea. He did not ask to be taken to the cottage at Torry Bay. It was a small community; he would not cause Tony embarrassment. The rain had stopped obligingly and he saw, for the first time, the incredible beauty of Scotland after rain. The light was so soft and beautiful that he felt his heart, heavy for such a long time, lighten. Above him a rainbow arched across the sky and he saw that at the rainbow's end was a cottage, small and square and bulky, with a blue door and blue windowsills where fat pots of petunias lifted drenched heads to the emerging sun.

The blue door opened and a woman came out. She walked away from him towards the sea and he saw the swans.

Dare he? Dare he?

' "*Mein lieber Schwan.*" ' He began to sing the delicate melody that Lohengrin sings off stage to the bewitched swan.

She stopped and stood looking at the sea and then slowly, as if she could not believe what she was hearing, she turned. Would she run to the cottage and close the door firmly against him? She stood and looked up at him, and the rainbow seemed to frame her. He stopped walking and only his voice went towards her and then she smiled.

'You had better come in,' she said. 'You've come such a long way.'

He did not try to touch her. They sat at the kitchen table for hours drinking coffee that she had made and they talked, and the next day he was gone.

She smiled. She had not promised him but she had promised herself. She would see him again.

No one in New York had had any idea that she was painting two pictures, the one the Ridgeways wanted and were paying for but which was not Blaise and the other painting, her secret painting which she started really because she was disillusioned with the work she was trying to do while the subject in his maroon velvet frock coat and pale pink satin shirt was sitting there in front of her. Tony would have liked to work longer on the painting of des Grieux. Ideally she would have preferred to finish it at Torry Bay; she felt that the real Blaise would emerge from the canvas if she could get him away from this stifling hothouse atmosphere, but the Ridgeways were used to getting what they wanted and Tony was too distressed to argue. Instead she suffered the agony of being in the same room with Blaise for hours at a time, unable to touch him, or even talk to him naturally.

Not that she wanted to talk to him, of course, or touch him. He belonged now irrevocably to someone else, to a woman with whom he had stood before God and man and promised to love, honour and obey. She could not settle to her work. The woman subjugated the artist and when he was there casually poised on the exquisite period chair, her skin, her blood relived those first feverish moments after he had entered her room. She tried to nourish her anger.

'He treated me like a whore. That's how he sees me.'

She refused to confess that she had clung to him as avidly as he had to her. It was better to see him only as a mythical creature, unreal. During the hours when he sat for her she painted the stiff figure of des Grieux and she could not get him right. She hated the painting and would have destroyed it but the Ridgeways wanted des Grieux and were determined to get him. At night she painted Lohengrin and the earnest young face that emerged from the canvas was otherwordly, pure, visionary. The recreating of the legend exhausted the artist who, like a wounded hare, limped back to her home to recuperate. She did not even tell Blaise when the commissioned painting was finished, but when she was ready, when she could do no more, she checked out of the hotel and took a yellow cab to the airport, the second painting, unfinished, rolled up in her flight bag.

There was work waiting for her but she could not paint. She was drained and she had learned not to struggle when she was empty but just to wait until her stores of energy adjusted themselves. She spent the time on the shore watching the water and the swans and she tried to think only of the play of light on water, or the incredible way in which each feather grew just in the right place, exactly the right size so that it lay without disturbing its neighbours, but as her body rested and recharged its batteries, her mind went over and over her talk with Blaise and she remembered the words she had forgotten: 'She told me you were dead.'

Because *she* had told Blaise that Tony was dead, Blaise had married Eleanor. It was as simple as that. Her life was ruined – as was Blaise's – because *she* had said that Tony was dead. Who was *she*?

It was time that *The Singing Babies* and *Les Dents de Lion* were brought home and there was money at last to transport them. She wrote a brief note to her mother.

Her father met her at the station in Godalming. He was not usually perspicacious and she was surprised when he asked, 'What's happened? You look different somehow.'

'It's the New York experience,' she tried to joke. 'It's an amazing place, Daddy.'

'I was never too happy about you going all the way there just to paint a picture.' Same old Daddy.

She did not tell him she had been asked to return by several prominent people. She was, she had been told, 'hot' and since she felt ice cold, she found this mildly amusing.

Her mother was over-jovial. 'Here comes the world traveller.' She smiled but the smile, or so it seemed to Tony, was uneasy, unnatural. 'There was a piece on young artists in *The Times*, Antonia. You're mentioned and so I saved it for you.'

They ate dinner and Tony sat quietly while her mother chatted vivaciously about Freddie and all the doings in the village and everything except Blaise Fougère.

'He's married,' she broke into the non-stop chatter about the tennis club summer dance.

'Who?' began her father and then stopped and looked from his wife to his daughter. 'I'll go and look at my cauliflowers.'

Obviously he had not been party to it. Tony waited for him to escape and then she turned, very calmly, to her mother. 'Why, Mother, why would you tell him such a thing?'

Judith began to whimper. 'It was for the best, dear,' she whispered.

So it had been her own mother who had betrayed her. Tony realised painfully that she had hoped all along that her suppositions had been wrong. She stood up carefully, like a frail old woman. 'I love Blaise Fougère with every atom of my being. I have loved him for ten years and so I think it's fair to say that I will always love him. I will never ever forgive you.'

She walked out of the room leaving her mother sitting at the table and when she heard her break into a paroxysm of weeping she did not turn to comfort her but carried on upstairs to pack her paintings. When that was done to her satisfaction she went to her old room and lay down fully dressed on the bed. Tomorrow she would get a taxi to take her to the first train for London and then she would go back to Torry Bay. She would never set foot in this house again.

Her father knocked on the door around ten in the evening. He stood, ill at ease, at the foot of the bed. 'He'd heard you were killed, Antonia. Mummy thought you were doing so well with your paintings, better not to start things up again.'

She said nothing.

'She did what she thought was best for you. That's all we have ever tried to do.'

Tony sat up in the bed and looked at him and he flushed. 'You have done what you have wanted to be the best for me. You have never considered what I thought was best for me.'

He was angry now. Right was on his side. 'We let you go to that arty, crafty school.'

'Yes, you did, and I will always be grateful for that. Pity you are so embarrassed by the swan the school created, Daddy. You never really believed in me. I can just hear the conversations. "We'll let her go, Judith, get it out of her system. Then she'll come back, settle down with a nice chap from the village." Wasn't that right?'

Her words were so accurate that he coloured furiously.

Tony lay down again. 'Goodnight,' she said dismissively.

She was gone before they woke in the morning and she never saw either of her parents again. She painted a strange picture that she called *Disillusion* and since no one knew anything about it, later critics decided it was disillusionment with her lover that had inspired the painting. She was in Vienna with Blaise when her father died of pneumonia. Two days later her mother, worn out from weeks of devoted nursing, died peacefully in her sleep. The broken-hearted Freddie knew no way to reach her, and the funeral was over before his sister returned to Torry Bay. As usual she took refuge on the headland. They were dead and she had never forgiven them. She tried to forgive now but the words meant nothing. Instead she grieved for them, for Freddie and for the 'might have been'. She knew that Blaise would never be her husband, the singing babies would never be born, but Lohengrin had returned to find her waiting. So he would always find her.

17

Torry Bay, 1999. London, 1999

'You will never guess who rang me this morning: Nicole Fougère Hartman. She has invited you for lunch.'

'Why? What can she want from me?'

'No doubt she will tell you at lunch.'

Holly said nothing and in the silence she could hear rain lashing against the window and the wind howling because it was caught in the old chimney. She would have to find someone to look at that. When the wind blew she either had a raging fire that threatened to set the house alight or great gusts of smoke filling the little rooms.

'You have fallen off the planet?'

She heard Otto's mild voice in her ear and brought her mind back from her domestic problems.

'Sorry, Otto, there is a gale blowing here. Has Mrs Hartman deigned to tell you where I am to have lunch; perhaps the pub her son found up here?'

'Naughty, naughty. No, she rang from Paris to ask for your telephone number; she has an enchanting

251

apartment on the Ile Saint Louis. Blaise used to take her to a puppet show when she was a little girl and they'd walk across a bridge near the island to have pastries and hot chocolate at a special café. She said, "I told him I would live there when I grew up, and he promised to buy me an *appartement* – and he did." Generous man, Blaise Fougère.' Otto sighed, no doubt remembering the beauty of Madame's apartment. 'I thought I'd get in first and warn you, although Taylor did alert you?'

As it happened, Nicole Fougère Hartman waited until evening to ring and although she was expecting the call, Holly jumped nervously.

'Were you expecting my call, Miss Noble, or may I call you Holly?' She took Holly's assent for granted and went on. 'I plan to return to the States soon but will stay in London for a few days first. I would like to see these paintings and to meet you.'

What to say, what to do? How to react? With charm, with honesty? 'Mrs Hartman, did you know my aunt?' she asked abruptly.

Mrs Hartman sounded surprised when she answered. 'No, my dear, but I knew of her. We can talk if you will be so kind as to meet me in London. So clichéd, but I stay at the Ritz; Blaise always stayed there when he was in London.'

Holly had been thinking all afternoon of what to say to Blaise Fougère's sister. She had even written a list of questions but she found herself being very gently but expertly side-tracked. She tried again. 'Can you at least tell me what you know of the relationship between your brother and my aunt because it was real, wasn't it, and Taylor knows?'

'So many questions. So much more pleasant to speak face to face in a lovely room.'

Holly admitted defeat and agreed to travel to London. Then she telephoned the Royal Overseas League in London because her father had always stayed there in his later years, and because it was within walking distance of Mrs Hartman's hotel. She was assured that a room would be waiting for her and so, with some reluctance, she packed for a few days away from Torry Bay.

The rain had followed her from Argyll and she looked out of the breakfast room at the club and watched raindrops bounce off the leaves of the trees and slide down the iron railings that led to the delightful little garden. The silent maid brought her breakfast – fresh fruit salad, warm croissants and tea – and she turned her attention to her fellow guests.

I wonder if anything has changed since Daddy stayed here? That fireplace is the same; the columns holding up the roof are the same. Some of the old dears look as if they could have been here thirty years ago too.

She looked at one couple. They were dressed alike in corduroy slacks, checked shirts (flannel) and shapeless Aran jumpers. So burned were they by countless eastern suns that it was now almost impossible to tell one from the other: only the huge diamond on the fourth finger of the left hand of one hinted at her gender. Holly wondered if she herself was an incongruity. Or was she beginning to look like a typical single British female who was approaching middle age? There were healthy and heavy single females with loud voices that seemed louder in the hallowed and hushed Buttery. Apart from the voices they could have been from any time, but sitting neatly by each chair was a large rucksack and Holly wondered at their use. Perhaps these ladies should have received one of the Reverend Frederick Noble's letters on 'the dangers facing unaccompanied females in large cities'.

She finished her breakfast, went up to her tiny but comfortable room to tidy up, and then left the house, accompanied in fact by the large ladies with the large rucksacks.

'Lunch,' they yelled at her, pointing to their rucksacks. 'London's such a rip-off these days.'

Holly smiled but said nothing and they had obviously expected nothing, for they swung the bags on to their broad shoulders and set off, no doubt, to *do* London.

Holly walked up to Piccadilly, past the Ritz and into Green Park. As always it was busy but today everyone was either bent down against the rain or fighting for control of an umbrella. Holly, who hated umbrellas in cities and saw no need to use them in the country, walked down one path and then realised that she would look like a drowned rat at her meeting and so she turned and hurried out of the park and round to the side door of the Ritz in Arlington Street.

If anyone accosted her she was prepared to use the

magic name, Hartman, but nobody paid her the slightest attention and she found a beautifully decorated Ladies' room off the main hallway and went in there to tidy up and to repair the damage caused by wind and rain. She looked at the result in the mirror, shrugged in despair, and walked up to the hallway across from the Palm Court restaurant where she found a comfortable chair where she could sit to wait until it was time for her meeting.

Blaise had stayed here. Had Tony? Had this beautifully appointed hotel been one of her special places? Had they sat in the Palm Court, sipped tea and danced to the music of the Palm Court Orchestra? No, too public. She thought she heard a faint sigh and looked around but there was no one there, no ghosts smiled from behind exquisite arrangements of pink orchids.

Poor Tony. She had lived alone and she had died alone. While Blaise Fougère relaxed in pampered seclusion at the Ritz and hotels like it in other parts of the world Tony had lived in a cottage at Torry Bay and . . . died alone.

Tears pricked at Holly's eyelids and she tried to decide whether she was crying for Tony or for herself. I don't want to die alone and unloved but I don't want to marry the wrong man either.

Did you love her, Blaise Fougère?

Love never dies, Hollyberry. I had to go ahead but I waited for her.

Did you love her?

Ma mie.

Holly looked around. A woman in a glorious green silk dress was looking at her questioningly and Holly rose and half smiled but the woman turned and hurried away.

Now I'm talking to myself in public places. Holly got up and went in the opposite direction that took her to some display cases of jewellery. She looked at these for a few minutes, wondering if she looked as if she could possibly afford them, decided she did not and returned to the hall.

I have more diamonds than I know what to do with anyway.

'Miss Noble?'

A frock-coated porter was beside her. Was she about to be arrested?

'Yes.'

'Mrs Hartman wonders if you would join her?'

Holly had not expected to feel quite so nervous when she was ushered into the sitting room of Taylor's mother's suite. Her first coherent thought was that the Fougère genes were very strong; Taylor's mother resembled both her brother and her son, although the once black hair was silver, and unlike her brother and her son she was small-boned and fragile but not frail. She looked like a woman very much in charge of her life.

She kissed Holly first on the left cheek, and then on the right. She had lived in America for nearly fifty years and she was still French.

'Toinette's niece. I am happy to meet you at last, little Hollyberry. Come, do sit down and we will have some coffee.'

Holly did as she was bid. 'Thank you, Mrs Hartman. I hope you will now reassure Mr Hartman that these paintings were done from life.'

'Coffee?'

Holly took the cup, noting that it was very delicate and probably Crown Derby. She set it down on the table and said very deliberately, 'Mrs Hartman, I want to be civilised but I have travelled a long way to meet you. You knew Blaise's name for me and I think that fact alone proves the authenticity of the paintings and the relationship. I would like to know when Taylor will lift the injunction or whatever it is that one does with bans.'

'I would like to see the paintings, Holly.'

'The world could have seen them if your son had not been so . . . so . . . childish.'

Nicole Hartman laughed. It was a lovely sound. 'What did you call him, Blaise, I mean, so sweet, like a child . . . Uncle Fire?'

'He told you that.'

'*Bien sûr.*'

Holly felt sad. 'I don't remember him at all.'

Nicole waited for a moment to give Holly time to compose herself. 'The coffee, it is all right?' She waited while Holly picked the cup and saucer up again. 'He told me everything. He had to have someone to talk to; *ça va sans dire.* Everyone needs someone, Holly, but a great artist, whose emotions are stretched and torn every day, needs a *confidante, un confesseur,* no, more than ordinary people.'

Holly again looked directly at her hostess. Her accent was almost American; after all, she had lived there for a very long time, but when she spoke her hands gestured with her, and she was most undeniably French. 'Then will you tell me why Taylor doesn't know, or pretends that he doesn't know?'

'But he did not know.' She shrugged expressively. '*Ça ne le regarde pas*; it was not his affair.'

'But why not now?'

'How angry you sound.'

'Of course I'm angry. His not knowing has caused me – and others – a great deal of discomfort. It's unforgivable that Otto's gallery should be closed.'

Nicole shrugged. 'Otto will recover,' she said complacently. 'When the ban is lifted he will make a fortune. I did not tell my son, Holly, because I did not know of your inheritance. I had had a little accident and Taylor thought to protect me from worry.' She looked at Holly from over the top of her fragile little cup and smiled. 'He is a thoughtful man, *n'est-ce pas*? He worshipped Blaise and has worked hard to protect his reputation and to keep his sad secret.'

'I'm sorry about your sister-in-law, Mrs Hartman, but Taylor is rich and powerful and will fight for her. Tony has only me. She sacrificed herself for your brother and he abandoned her in an isolated cottage – and I did too. She died alone, Mrs Hartman, and I can't forgive your precious Blaise or myself for that.' Holly sat back, embarrassed, in the comfortable chair, feeling that she had made a fool of herself but might as well finish. 'The paintings show that he loved Tony. Why then did he marry Eleanor?'

Nicole Hartman had not taken offence and Holly was sure that if they had been closer her hostess might well have patted her hand and said there, there, or its French equivalent.

'Mrs Hartman, your son does not believe my aunt and your brother were lifelong lovers. The paintings refute that. You know the whole story, don't you, and you must tell him.'

Holly had not meant to be so blunt. She had gone over and over opening sentences honing them to perfection and this was not it.

Nicole Hartman smiled. 'Taylor does not *want* to believe it and that is an entirely different thing. In his heart he knows. *Sûrement*, my dear, you have lived long enough to know that life is not simple. He was at the beginning of his training when he met Tony, his Toinette, 1937 I think, and he was . . . oh, how can I explain. For Blaise Tony was *un coup de foudre*, a lightning bolt. As we French say he was quite *bouleversé*, turned upside down. Of course the war taught us to think less of ourselves but in those days, for a Fougère to live with a nobody, a penniless art student, was unthinkable. But a choice between Blaise with his Antoinette or no Blaise was no choice – my parents capitulated. He remained in love with Toinette until the day he died.'

'But you never met her.'

'No. She never visited us but he went to see your . . . grandparents, it would be and met . . . Frederick?'

'My father.'

'*Très digne*, yes, worthy. He was destined for the Church, no, but for us the wrong Church. He is a bishop now, *sans doute*.'

'He has been dead for a long time, Madame. But, please, Blaise . . . Why?'

'Why did they not marry?' Nicole shrugged. 'He thought she was dead. He went to London in the war and found the hole where his apartment had been. Oh, *quelle douleur*, what grief. He was a madman, scrabbling in the dirt for his Antoinette. I was a child; it was a black time, the war, and he did not tell me all but later . . .' She sat still, thinking, remembering, and at last Holly became impatient.

'Please, Mrs Hartman, if you know, please tell me why he married someone else. The paintings . . .'

'Ah, yes, I would like very much to see all the paintings, without Otto, or Taylor. He is so disturbing, Taylor, so energetic and exhausting, but I have sent him to San Francisco on business. You will take me to see the paintings?'

Holly was having a hard time picturing Taylor as someone who could be sent anywhere by anyone. 'Of course, if I can but – Madame?' Holly was shaken but she had to know more. 'My aunt moved to Scotland during the war. Why did Blaise not try to find her? Surely . . .'

'But she told him she was dead, *chérie*. Who would doubt the word of a mother?'

No, it could not be. Holly gasped. 'My grandmother told him . . .?'

'Her parents did not like a French singer, a Catholic, any more than my parents liked Tony.'

'But to lie.'

'Who knows? Let the dead sleep, Holly. My brother loved Toinette all his life. He married poor Eleanor, mainly I think because he was too tired to say no.' Nicole Hartman sighed. 'He married her because he needed a stable relationship; most men do. He did not want one-night stands. He wanted a home and children. Toinette was dead. He was distraught, unable to train, to function even. Eleanor adored him; her family were influential at a time when we wanted out of Europe. The war changed him as it changed so many. Before he used to say, "To be great you must believe in yourself," but then all those years without music, without training, without practice . . . If, *peut-être*, without his Toinette he could have believed in his own greatness, maybe he would have taken another route, but he married Eleanor and he loved her till the end. He was faithful to her you know, until he met Tony again.'

'But not as he loved Tony?'

'No, love like that is once in a lifetime – if you are very lucky. You have heard him sing, Holly?'

'No. My aunt did take me to performances but never to his and she never, as far as I can remember, ever mentioned him.'

'You did not think it strange that someone who had painted Fougère, who loved opera, never mentioned the greatest tenor of them all?'

Holly shook her head. 'Are all children self-absorbed,

Mrs Hartman? I loved Tony, I loved being with her but I never once wondered what her life was like when I was not with her. I assumed she waited for me . . . and all the time, she waited for him.'

They were both silent, lost in their own sad thoughts. At last Nicole shrugged and continued. 'After the war, the Ridgeways, Eleanor's parents, commissioned Britain's exciting new portrait painter to paint their so famous son-in-law for the Opera House in New York. They could not tell Wagner from Scott Joplin but they were patrons of the arts. Eleanor was different. She loved music and she adored Blaise. I never really believed that she thought of him as a real man; it must have been very annoying for him, always to be spoken of in a hushed whisper.'

'But why didn't he divorce her and marry Tony?'

'Because she is . . . because . . . *comment* . . . how do you say?' Even after all these years in the United States, Nicole Hartman thought in French. 'She was insane,' she finished simply.

'I know and that's terrible but, forgive me, Mrs Hartman, it doesn't really answer my question.'

'He felt guilty.'

'Why – because she lost a baby?'

Nicole nodded sadly. 'Babies. Blaise felt that the pregnancies were his fault and so he vowed to protect Eleanor and to keep the press away from her, for her sake not his own. Poor chivalrous Blaise, the knight in shining armour. His princess understood nothing. In the last years of his life she did not even know who he was and yet he continued having her clothes made just as she liked them when she was young and beautiful; he continued to visit her at least once a month. No matter where he was in the world he flew back, exhausting himself, and Tony stayed in her little cottage painting those magnificent pictures waiting for him to throw her the crumbs. That is what *ma mie* means, you know. My little crumb. She was the breath in his body, Holly, his heartbeat, that is what he meant by *ma mie*.'

Holly tried to remember Uncle Fire, the big man who had walked with her into the sea and she saw his face as he had looked back at Tony. 'I know,' she said quietly.

'I hope she knew he was on his way to her when he was killed. I don't know, but I believe he had finally made up his mind to make a life with Tony. He changed all his plans and flew to Britain when he was not due to sing there for six months. What else could he be doing but going to Tony?'

'Would you have been angry, Mrs Hartman, as Taylor supposes, if your brother had divorced Eleanor?'

'Taylor thinks that?' Mrs Hartman signalled for the maid to take away the coffee. 'We should have had drinks, Holly. Shall we go downstairs for lunch and we can continue to talk.'

They went down into the opulent dining room with its splendid draperies and exquisite floral arrangements.

So this is what it's like to be rich, thought Holly as they were served immediately.

Mrs Hartman smiled at Holly's expression but mistook the reason. 'Lovely, isn't it. I feel quite dowdy.'

Holly, looking at her hostess, realised for the first time that Nicole was dressed very simply and that the austerity suited her. Her whole style spoke of lack of embellishment; one tailored grey suit, elegant shoes. Her jewellery too was understated, a gold wedding ring and plain gold studs in her ears.

'You will forgive me if I say I am surprised that Taylor has revealed so much of himself to you, Holly. I had no idea he thought that I would oppose a divorce. Frankly I would have welcomed it. It was Blaise who would not consider divorce. Not that he did not love Tony but . . . men can be so stupid sometimes. His honour would not let him divorce Eleanor. Had she been mentally stable he would have divorced her *immédiatement*, like a shot. *Pauvre* Taylor.'

'You are the second person to refer to your son like that, Mrs Hartman, and, if you will forgive me, it's the last adjective I would use to describe him.'

Nicole laughed. 'But he too is wasting his life, Holly. I should not tell you but maybe it will help. In college he loved a girl who loved his greenbacks, more than she loved his green eyes. He is looking for a woman like Eleanor to love chastely and devotedly when he should be looking for another Tony who will love him as fiercely as he loves her. It was . . . difficult to make him believe in my brother's love for your aunt. Discretion can be such a nuisance.'

Holly assured herself that she had no interest in

Taylor Hartman or his aborted love life. 'Discretion? Another word, if you'll forgive me, that I wouldn't use in connection with your son.'

Mrs Hartman laughed. 'Not Taylor, *chérie*, Blaise. He was almost paranoid about privacy, you know, for himself, for Eleanor, for me – our parents died soon after the war, you know, and I lived with him – and yes, he wanted privacy for his beloved Toinette. He did not want his problems gossiped over and, besides, he was sure that the miscarriages were the cause of Eleanor's condition although, frankly, I'm sure she was unstable before they were married.'

Holly thought of her own longing for a child. 'Did he want a child badly?'

'I never thought so, but I was a girl when he married. He would have enjoyed being a father; he adored Taylor and from his expression in some of those catalogue photographs, he was fond of you too, but it was not a compelling force with him as it was for Eleanor. I am not particularly maternal myself and it is hard for a woman like me who has her prize chick really to enter into the feelings of the woman who cannot have children. You are an only child?'

This was a turn to the conversation that Holly could well have done without but she answered truthfully. 'Yes, my parents were missionaries; they married rather late and I've always felt that my arrival was something of a surprise and not a particularly pleasant one.'

'And you have no children?'

'No,' answered Holly shortly. This was something

she would not discuss with a woman she had only just met.

Mrs Hartman recognised her stress. 'What an astonishing amount of feeling can go into such a little syllable, Holly.'

When they had finished their meal Nicole rose. 'Come, we will have coffee in my sitting room. I want you to tell me more about yourself. You live in the city, but you have decided to go to that little cottage, miles from civilisation. I should like to see this place that so many people find so attractive.'

'I'm not Tony. I won't live there permanently; in the meantime I intend to modernise.'

'And the paintings?'

'Will go to museums and galleries all over the world. If you would like to choose one . . .'

Nicole Fougère Hartman could not hide her expression of surprise. 'My dear, you do not plan to *give* me a painting.'

'If you would like to have one . . .'

Nicole shook her head sadly but she was smiling. 'Taylor was right in one regard. He said, "She is giving me a painting out of goodness, not because she wants anything from me." You have no head for business, *chérie*. Even from the photographs I can see that there are several pictures I would give anything to own and I have a great deal of *anything*. Will you show them to me now, today?'

'I'm not sure that I can. They are wards of court, whatever that means.'

266

'You cannot sell them until the court decides their fate but they are still in the gallery, no?'

'Yes.'

'Then we will call dear Otto and tell him to open the door. He knows how to be quiet, Otto, not like my Taylor who must always charge in head first. Otto is like me, subtle. You watch how we get our own way.'

'Doesn't Taylor usually get his own way?'

'Of course and especially with women. His tactics are . . . different. Be warned.'

Holly fumed over that last remark all the way to the gallery. Otto, in a favourite subtle suit, appeared at the kerb before the driver could get out of the car and opened the door to one of his best customers. They greeted one another in French and then remembered Holly.

'I thought you were German, Otto.'

'Unkind. You know perfectly well I am Austrian, but, unlike the British, we real Europeans speak more than one language.'

'Children,' admonished Mrs Hartman. 'You would not believe that Otto is exactly my contemporary, Holly.'

Holly said nothing. Taylor had described his mother as elderly, and Otto had known Tony when he was a boy. It must then be so. She decided to take charge; after all, the paintings did belong to her and later she would ask Otto why he had never told her that he knew Nicole Hartman well.

'Mrs Hartman would like to view the paintings of her

brother, Otto. I would be grateful if you would show them to her.'

'Of course, dear ladies.'

He opened the door and ushered his visitors into the cathedral-like rooms where Tony's passionate paintings still graced the walls. They bombarded the senses with their colours, their phenomenal use of light, their messages. He loves her; he loves her not; he loves her.

Nicole Fougère Hartman walked slowly along through the galleries looking at a part of her beloved brother's life. She said little but would stop often and gaze at the images, occasionally sighing or even laughing, smiling often. *Sea Sprite, Les Dents de Lion, Uncle Fire, Rainbows* . . . She stopped beside a picture of a graceful swan, his head held high gliding into a safe harbour; she looked closer. 'Ah, *la pauvre petite*,' she murmured. '*Je comprends; c'est Lohengrin.*'

'*C'est plutôt triste.* So sad,' she whispered before others, and then she came to a large canvas. It was called *Rainbows* and was, of course, of Blaise, who stood on the point at Torry Bay. Behind him the sky was aflame with several rainbows.

'I should like to have this painting, if I may, Holly.' Nicole's eyes were wet with tears. 'I feel like a voyeur, you know, to see so much intimacy.'

'That is the genius of the artist, Madame,' said Otto quietly. 'You can see now why these paintings must not languish in an attic or be destroyed.'

'Taylor is not a philistine, Otto. Once he has learned to accept what the paintings tell him, he will be reasonable. After all, the love of a man for a woman is very different from the love of a man for a child. Taylor has lost nothing.'

'I confess I had a similar feeling, Mrs Hartman, when I first saw the paintings. I thought Tony loved only me.'

'I have not lived as long as Tony but longer than you, and I have loved and still love many people, Holly. I pray that you and Taylor can say the same. All love changes us, betters us, *n'est-ce pas?*'

'Changes us, yes. I feel that when you love someone you are never the same person again.' Holly thought sadly of her shattered dreams. 'You cannot return to being the person you were before, even if the love dies. By having loved, one is irrevocably altered.'

'Goodness, such philosophy; but altered for the better, yes?' Nicole, still drinking in the beauty of the painting, asked.

'I do hope so.'

'Then you are the gainer. Love is a strange thing. Here I stand falling in love with a painting and so I am not the woman I was when I walked in because this painting, and of course, the artist, have reached out and touched me.'

Holly looked at her, at the expensive couturier suit, the hand-made shoes, at the tears on her cheeks.

'That is exactly how I feel about the paintings. They called to me.'

'And Blaise, does he call to you?' Mrs Hartman asked seriously. 'He is very beautiful, no, and such a talent.'

'I am enjoying getting to know him,' said Holly diplomatically.

'My son is very like him,' said Mrs Hartman enigmatically while she pulled on her gloves.

Holly refused to say anything.

18

Torry Bay, 1957
GRIEF

Tony was sick with excitement and then she was sick
with fear. But most of all she was sick because she was
pregnant. How had it happened? They had been
careful, hadn't they? She had been in London for
the whole of June and almost every night Blaise had
managed to steal away to be with her. It had been
wonderful, just like being married. He went out to
work and then he came home; they ate supper and
went to bed. Or sometimes they went to bed and then
ate supper, or perhaps they just went to bed. She had
tried to be relaxed, to pretend that they were old
married people, to pretend that no reporters were
waiting in the shadows to discover their secret and
make from it a tawdry headline. Twice she had been
to receptions at which he was also a guest but they
had parted quickly, fearing that someone would see
the looks that passed between them that said, 'I love
you, I need you, I want you.' They had made a game

of it. Famous tenor meets almost famous artist.

'We must have Miss Noble paint you again, Maestro.'

'That would be a pleasure. As you say, I am familiar with Miss Noble's work.'

'I should be honoured.' This last from Tony, thinking of the great storehouse of paintings that already existed.

Later, in her bed, he would talk of work and pleasure, and he would make her sing, and then they would lie pleasantly exhausted listening to London waking up.

'It's not waking up, *mon cher*. London never sleeps.'

'Thank God it dozes a little, like Paris. But Parisians wake to the smell of bread and flowers, and Londoners wake to petrol fumes and smog. I wish we could go to Torry Bay and smell the sea.'

'When we are old, we will wake every morning in Torry Bay, Blaise. I know it.'

With the sound of the sea in their ears and the smell of the sea in their nostrils they would sleep at last until it was time for Blaise to dress and go to his hotel to pretend that he had been there all night.

Blaise's secretary, Stefan Lazlo, was their ally. Did he approve, disapprove? Tony did not know and Stefan said nothing, never showed his feelings. All that was sure was his unquestioning loyalty to his employer.

There had been no time to go to Scotland. Blaise had gone from Covent Garden to Bayreuth to sing Wagner for the first time and Tony had resisted the temptation to go to hear him.

'All eyes will be on you and better that you concentrate on Wagner and not on me.'

She had gone to Torry Bay to wait for him and now she was not alone in her waiting. On one of those magical nights a baby had been conceived. Would it be the soprano who would set the musical world on its ears with her Tosca?

Suddenly Tony felt cold. She was pregnant but she could not have this baby. For a few minutes she had indulged in daydreams. Blaise would be thrilled. He would see that the only thing to do was to divorce his wife and marry the mother of his child.

'I can never divorce her, Toinette. Her inability to give me a living child destroyed her mind. I will never leave her.'

No use to rail and cry that Eleanor had left him, that she would not know, would not care. He could continue to pay for her care; he could visit her as often as he did now. Tony lay in bed and waited for her stomach to behave. She would write to him. No, she would go to Glasgow and telephone him from there. If she rang him from Torry Bay, the whole of Argyll would know within hours that the artist who lived at the point of the bay was no better than she should be, and that the partner in her disgrace was that whiter than white perfect husband, Blaise Fougère. The carefully constructed lie of a perfect marriage that he had built up would crumble around him, and more importantly from his point of view, his wife's sad secret would become fodder for the gossips.

But his baby, my baby, is more important. Eleanor will never know, never understand.

Her family will suffer.

They are suffering already.

Do they deserve to suffer this blow too?

She argued with herself over and over.

If they really love Blaise, they will be happy for him.

Frighteningly she found that she was beginning to hate Eleanor and even once wailed, 'Why won't she die?'

Blaise wrote from Bayreuth. Wagner's *Tannhäuser* was an unbelievable challenge. He was finding it so difficult. There was prejudice because he was not German but he would work and work with the *répétiteur* on the language and his interpretation of the role.

I can't give him another major problem when he has so many already, but I can't wait until the end of the run.

She went to see Simon.

He did not judge. 'You are at least two months pregnant, Tony. What has the father to say?' For a second she saw deep disappointment.

'I haven't told him. It's . . . difficult.'

'Suppose you'll be getting married.'

'No.'

'I advise you to tell him.'

Tony did not try to explain. She looked at him. 'I have decided on termination.'

The words tried to float out of the window but they were too heavy and ugly. They hung for a moment and then fell into the silence.

'No.'

He took her hands, hands that were cold with fear. 'Tony, that's a human being inside you, another . . .' He searched for a personality. 'A Van Gogh.'

'You could have chosen a more sympathetic example, Simon.' Tony attempted to laugh. 'Van Gogh was as nutty as a fruitcake.'

'Another wee Tony. That would be nice. A miracle is happening inside you and you can't throw it back in the face of the Almighty as if it were something washed up by the tide on Torry Bay. "So sorry, God, it's not quite convenient." It's a real, live human being, Tony. I heard a story once about this woman. She'd had several children, all of them handicapped in some way and then she found herself pregnant yet again. "Get rid of it. You can't afford it." She refused. "It's God's gift," she told them. Do you know the name of the baby who was born, Tony? What was his name?'

She covered her ears with her hands. 'Shut up, shut up! You have no right to talk to me like this. Tell me the medical options, *Doctor*, nothing else.'

'There are no options in this office, Tony. I promised to respect life, not to destroy it.'

She got up and walked out. She did not speak to Simon for months.

'If it were done when 'tis done, then 'twere well it were done quickly.' Shakespeare's Scottish play. How apt. Blaise had twice sung Macduff in the Verdi opera. Termination, abortion. Abortion, termination. To abort. To terminate. Dear God, forgive me. Baby, forgive me. She must not think of a baby, not a real baby. If she imagined a real live baby with his father's looks and his beautiful voice floating around inside her, she would go mad. *Bébés qui Chantent.* Singing babies. Which one are you? This naughty one on the cloud who is spoiling his sister's painting? This serene little one who is putting paint on the clouds instead of her canvas?

Tony packed a suitcase, locked up the cottage, and left. Two months later she came back. She went to Chrissie's for milk and bread.

'Tony, I've missed you; you never said you were having a holiday. But you never took painting stuff with you? A real holiday, was it?'

Of course, everyone in the community knew everything about everyone. The village knew her movements, wondered in whispers about the man who was seen from time to time on the point, about where she was going when she was on her way to meet Blaise, asked about the success of her exhibitions . . . 'Saw a bit in the *Glasgow Herald*. We'll have to start treating you with more respect.'

Chrissie had always known when to pry and when not.

'You look a bit peaky, Tony, tired like. That's the trouble with holidays. I always need a holiday to get over my holiday.'

She tried to smile, to answer. 'That's it. Too much sun and late-night restaurants. A few days at Torry Bay will put me right.'

'I'm here, Tony, like always.'

'My friend,' said Tony.

She heard the murmurs from other customers as she left with her purchases. 'She's seen no sun the last few weeks. Strange people, artists.'

She reached the haven of her cottage and in the following weeks tried to decide whether or not she should tell Blaise, triumphant Blaise who had confounded the critics and forced the Germans to accept him in a Wagner role. She examined her body and hated it because it gave no sign. It was still slender but unmarked and somewhere, surely, it should say, 'A baby was aborted from this womb.' But it said nothing. She could see no change at all and therefore was it not true that Blaise would see no difference? She wanted to ask Simon if there would be changes inside, change that Blaise might notice, but she could not bring herself to walk into the village to talk to him.

I must tell him. He has a right to know.

Don't be stupid. He did not want the baby. Remember how careful he was.

Do I want him to grieve with me, to share my suffering?

Possibly, probably and you have no right to such indulgence.

Bayreuth. Next stop Vienna, her favourite city. Then it was Tokyo and after that Australia and home to New York for Christmas.

'Come, Toinette. I miss you so. You love Vienna. Come to see the city.'

'I have an exhibition in Glasgow. I'm too busy.'

'Come to Tokyo. We can have a few days in Kyoto. How I would love to show you Kyoto.'

'Next year.'

'From Tokyo I will go to Sydney and then to New York. Come to New York, *ma mie*. I cannot live without you.'

How could she tell him that she was too afraid? At night she lay longing for him or dreaming of him, dreams that were satisfying while they lasted but which left her bereft and desolate. During the day she painted like a madwoman: countless studies of his hands, his eyes. She painted her swans and she painted babies, babies that she scraped away with her palette-knife before falling weeping onto her bed.

Please, God, forgive me. I made a terrible mistake.

Mistakes can be rectified. Her mother had told her so. All that was required was that one promised never to make the same mistake again, and to say sorry.

'Sorry. Sorry. Sorry. I will never do it again.'

Her mother was wrong. Perhaps it worked if you had said something nasty to your very best friend.

'I'm sorry I said you were fat and I'll never ever say it again.'

Too late. Too late.

He arrived on 16 December and she was so happy to see him that she fell into his arms without thinking.

'*Ma mie, ma mie*, you are so thin. You have lose too much weight. You are working too hard, Toinette. We will go to New York and get fat together.'

She could say nothing, just lie in his arms feeling his warmth, drowning in the smell of him.

He took her silence for acquiescence, picked her up and carried her upstairs.

She forgot everything but her love, her need. She responded to his desire, his passion, clinging to him with her arms, her legs. Together they climaxed and fell asleep exhausted.

Later his fingers traced her breasts, her stomach. 'How you are thin, Toinette. Why, *ma mie*? You have been silly about food and pass all your time painting. Now we will spend Christmas in New York and instead of painting me you will be loving me and we will have the perfect holiday.'

'I had an abortion.'

The words came out of their own volition. She had not thought. She had made no definite decision but now the words were there and the air grew cold around them. His hands that had been holding her dropped to his sides and he lay still. She lay beside him wishing the words back but they refused to come.

Her body, hot and sweating from love, grew cold, but she was afraid to reach for the covers and she remained quiet, growing colder and colder.

Perhaps he remembered that he was a great tenor, that thousands of people were eagerly looking forward to hearing him sing. He could not afford to catch cold. He got up from the bed like an old man and walked to the window. There he stood looking out at the storm that was broiling itself up in the bay.

It echoed his anger and, he realised, his overpowering grief.

'You killed our baby. How could you do it?'

Never in her wildest imaginings had she dreamed that he would say anything quite so cruel. She stared at his broad back and the anger that she did not know that she had been suppressing for so long boiled up and spewed itself out. She jumped from the bed, ran to him, and began flaying his back with her fists, knowing as she beat him that he hardly felt her blows. She was a mouse, a mouse beside a lion, and the lion could kill.

'Our baby?' she asked. 'It was my baby. You were just there for the conception. Any man alive with working equipment could have done the same thing. You come here when it suits you: you screw me out of my mind for two or three days and then you leave. I don't hear from you, sometimes for weeks, and you have the audacity to say, "our baby".'

'Sometimes your lack of real breeding shows, Antonia.'

He began to pull on his discarded clothes and she watched him angrily. When he was dressed he ran downstairs and went out into the storm.

Where was he going? What was he going to do? Blaise. Blaise.

She searched for her clothes and pulled them on with fingers that seemed helpless and then she followed him downstairs and out into the wind. It caught her and tried to push her back into the house. 'Blaise,' she screamed. 'Blaise, forgive me. Come back, please come back,' but if he heard he paid no heed and she turned back to the cottage.

She was soaked to the skin and she almost crawled up the staircase to their room. She pulled off her clothes and crept into the bed where she lay cold against the colder sheets and remembered the love and joy of just a moment ago. She wept and, weeping, fell asleep and so she did not hear him return. She did not hear him stoke up the fire in the kitchen. Neither did she hear the old springs groan as he lay down on the settee in front of the fire; nor did she hear him cry for his dead child.

When the outside storm was over he got up and pulled on his jeans and the hand-knit sweater she had bought from the fisherman's widow and he went out and down to the sea. Their rowboat was there, high above the water line and he pulled it down the shingle to the water. Then he began to row, out, out, out as if he might be able to row out to his opera house where all the tragedies were scripted and where they were over when the curtains came down and the tumultuous applause ceased. He rowed until he was exhausted and then he shipped the oars and sat there in the rocking boat until Tony found him.

His face was white and she knew he had not slept. She did not call him but stood, the wind whipping her skirt, and watched him. She would never forget his face, never, even if she never saw him again and she was so horribly sure that she never would. He hated her. She saw his eyes as he had looked at her when he had cried out for the dead baby and she knew that nothing she could say or do would console him and that he would never, ever be able to understand her desperate action. The boat with its silent, broken passenger drifted on the lightly bobbing waves and then he looked up to the sky so blue and clear now after the storm and he sighed. He picked up the oars and began to row back to the shore and she stood waiting for the blow to fall on her unprotected head. He pulled the boat up and, as always, left everything shipshape. Only then did he turn to her although he must have known that she was there. 'It is over, Antonia. I am going away and I will not be back.'

She would not beg. She would not throw herself down and clutch at his legs to be dragged screaming up the shingle to the cottage. If she had believed for one second that such tactics would have been successful she would have resorted to them. She was not proud: he was her life and when he left she might as well slit her wrists and let her blood drain into the sand, for she could not conceive how her heart could continue to beat if her life left her.

He turned and went back to the cottage and when he had gone inside she ran up the little hill behind the house to the shelter where they had lain so often, talking, making love, dreaming. Curled in a foetal position she waited until she heard his car start up and then she flung herself up on to the rock and watched him drive out of her life.

Tony did not weep. Some grief is too deep for tears. She lay back down in the hollow and stayed there sleeping and waking for the rest of the day.

The early darkness drove her stiffly indoors.

It was as if he had never been. His clothes were gone, his books, his music. His shepherd's crook that they had laughed about was broken and tossed nonchalantly on to the fire. She stirred the embers and watched it burn. When she had aborted the baby she had thought that she could experience no greater pain but the pain that ravaged her now tore at her belly and her entrails just as the abortion had done. She thought, she prayed that she might die from such pain but she did not die.

It was weeks before she painted. She had thought to paint her own grief but the painting that came was that of a man bowed by grief sitting in a rowing boat, staring helplessly out at what was and what might have been.

When the lawyer's letter came with the cheque in it that would keep her comfortably for the rest of her life, she almost destroyed the painting. Such appalling anger struck at her.

'How could he?' she moaned, and she raised the palette-knife to gut the painting, to destroy his grief, but she could not and instead she did her best to tear the cheque into as many pieces as possible.

Before she sent the pieces back to his lawyer she put the painting with its face to the wall in the attic and never looked at it again.

19

---◆---

Holly decided to undress, wrap herself in one of the club's comfortable bathrobes and order room service. A steak sandwich, a glass of red wine and coffee; she would put her feet up, watch something inane on television, and then have a long soak in the bath. An evening of absolute bliss beckoned.

The room telephone disturbed her before the first bite. Who, apart from Nicole and Otto knew that she was in London?

'How did you know I was here?'

'It's lovely to talk to you too. My mother actually. I called to see how travelling had affected her and she told me all about your lovely lunch and your visit to the paintings.'

'And?'

He sighed. 'Hey, Holly, you know sometimes I wonder why I try. I am mid Atlantic—'

She interrupted him. 'You can't make calls from mid Atlantic.'

284

'It's easy when you own the plane.' He was quiet and Holly waited for a moment, furious with herself for being so antagonistic. 'Maybe this call wasn't such a great idea.'

'I'm sorry, Taylor, but you can't expect me to be thrilled to hear from you; unless,' she added with a note of excitement, 'you're calling to say you're lifting the ban.'

'No. I'm on my way to Paris.'

He stopped talking but she was full of a sense of disappointment and, strangely, of betrayal.

'And?' she prompted.

'I thought you might like to meet me.'

'Where? Paris?'

'Of course, Paris.'

Holly looked at her lovely sandwich that was growing cold and at the cooling coffee. The sandwich might still be edible; the coffee would be undrinkable. Damn Taylor.

'Taylor, let me tell you about the working classes,' she began but he interrupted.

'Spare me. Paris is a few hours, at most, from London. Get a single. I'll fly you back when I go pick up my mother.'

'Do you want us to meet so that we can discuss what your mother has told me?'

'Never occurred to me. I actually thought you might like to see the *Lohengrin*; painted in the same year as the *des Grieux* but definitely a girl's painting.'

She hung up and immediately snatched the receiver up but the connection was terminated.

Double damn. You are your own worst enemy, Holly Noble, but he is arrogant believing that I would just jump to see him.

She heard the telephone again while she was in the tub and, telling herself that she was convinced it was Otto with important information, she got out, wrapped her towel around her and went to answer it.

'Hanging up is so rude, Holly.'

Holly stood there, telephone receiver in one wet hand, and laughed. 'Taylor, what's the hidden agenda here? You live – that's if you are ever anywhere for any length of time – in New York, but almost every time I look out of my window, there you are. Explain.'

There was silence for while. 'Damned if I know,' he said at last. 'Maybe I just like you, Holly Noble. You're so . . . you're real, Holly.'

Real? Not beautiful, fascinating, intellectually challenging. Damn him.

'And you are impossible and I am going to hang up on you again. It gave me tremendous pleasure to cut you off,' she lied. 'Actually, I think the experience will be good for you; you will thank me one day for pointing out, a little brutally perhaps, that you and your singing uncle are mere men.'

'Was,' he interrupted. 'He was a mere man. That was what was so incredibly exciting about being in the same room with him. He just had to walk into a room for everyone to fall silent. In a restaurant other diners would stand when he walked in and clap until he sat down. He hated it but I couldn't breathe for excitement.' He stopped as if once more aware that he was giving too much of himself away. 'I was calling, politely, to ask you if you would like to see the *Lohengrin*.'

Oh, the temptation. To fly to Paris to see the only painting of Blaise Fougère as Lohengrin, painted by Tony at the beginning of his amazing career.

'You won't even have to see me, Holly. I have work to do.'

'In that case,' she began and he laughed. It was a pleasant sound.

'Call me when you've made your reservation. Chandler will pick you up and I'll arrange for you to be allowed in to see the painting.'

He did not wait for thanks and she was left with the receiver in her hand and the sound of emptiness. She became aware that she was cold and still damp in places but inside – she was so warm.

She booked a return flight. The indispensable and unfailingly efficient Chandler met her and drove her to the opera house. He gave her a handwritten note from Taylor.

Have dinner with me this evening. We can compare notes on the undoubted quality of the painting.

Naturally she wanted to refuse but just as naturally, since the note was deliberately written in a way that was sure to annoy her, she accepted.

France was proud of Blaise Fougère. The painting had been moved in 1989 from its original home in the

287

magnificent Opéra de Paris Garnier to the new Opéra Bastille and was hanging where every opera-goer was bound to see it. Holly stood for a long time drinking it in. Taylor was so maddeningly, infuriatingly right, of course. It was a girl's picture. She would die before she admitted it to him. Lohengrin stood, the knight in white shining armour, his sword in his mailed hands. Behind him there was a vast sea. Was it the sea as seen from the windows of the cottage at Torry Bay? Just behind the figure of the Prince of the Holy Grail was a swan, already turning to swim back to his land of enchantment.

Lohengrin paid no attention to the swan. He was looking forward, straight into the eyes of the viewer, and originally, perhaps, the painter. How young he looked and how vulnerable. He had suffered, oh, how he had suffered, but he would fight for right. The determination in his eyes was as strong as the accepted sadness.

No, thought Holly, I am reading things here that I want to read. She tried again. He looks sad, sad and decisive at the same time . . . Vulnerable.

It was a chocolate-box cover. The handsome prince was just too good to be true. He was beautiful, both strong and tender and that face, those eyes.

'Bastard,' said Holly out loud and received a well-deserved condemnatory look from the only other person in the corridor, a minor official of the opera house. Holly blushed. The expletive was not a common part of her vocabulary. She looked again at the painting and a similar face swam in and out of the one immortalised on the canvas. Had she sworn at Blaise or at Taylor?

Silly woman, she scolded herself. Taylor doesn't really look like Blaise and he doesn't behave like Blaise.

She made her way back to the little hotel near the Sorbonne where she had arranged to stay and got ready for her dinner with Taylor. Since she had brought no evening clothes with her she hoped he was not planning to take her to a restaurant where she would feel ill at ease; if he, like his mother, dined at the Ritz or the much applauded La Closerie des Lilas, she was in trouble.

Chandler drove her to a small inn on the way to Versailles.

'You know me, Holly, always looking for places where the food is great. I hope it meets with your approval and selfishly I hope Marin will be content not to expand.'

'It's more elegant inside than I had expected,' said Holly, looking at the snowy tablecloths and crystal glasses.

Taylor smiled and called the waiter, and Holly sat half hearing his faultless French and wondering what she could tell him about the portrait of his uncle. Should she admit that it disturbed her almost as much as the *des Grieux* had done?

'She painted them at approximately the same time, in the same year anyway, and the *Lohengrin* is painted with so much . . .'

'Adoration?' Taylor suggested almost with a simper.

'Understanding,' said Holly crossly. 'Your mother said something very interesting about love.'

He laughed. 'Maman is French; she believes, therefore, that she is an expert.'

'You don't want to hear, do you, but it was sensible and perceptive too, something I hadn't thought about.'

He smiled tolerantly as if he were indulging a child. 'Share it with me.'

She had had no lunch and the warm, smooth wine had slipped easily down into an empty stomach. She smiled back at Taylor. Really he was very good to look at. 'She says love changes us. If you love something, even a cat, I suppose—'

'God forbid,' Taylor interrupted.

'Then you are changed and can never go back to being the same person. That's quite an important thought.' She stopped, flustered.

'If you say so. And what other deep thoughts did Maman share with you?'

She gathered her dignity together and looked around the busy dining room. 'No one stood up when you came in, Taylor.'

'I am a mere man, Holly,' he said indulgently, refusing to fight. 'All I have is money.'

'And good looks,' said Holly judiciously as she allowed the wine waiter to refill her glass.

Taylor laughed. '*Merci mille fois*. I was going to say many people have money. Okay.' He laughed as if he were embarrassed. 'Some have looks too but that . . . charisma, that power, that voice.'

'Can you sing?'

'Like a frog.'

'That good?'

He leaned back in his chair, elegant, soigné, sophisticated . . . amused. 'You have had too much wine, Mam'selle.'

Holly regretfully swallowed her last morsel of perfectly cooked asparagus and followed it with a sip of wine. She giggled. 'I know, but the paintings, Taylor. The *des Grieux* is almost as sad as the *Grief*.'

'No,' he said almost angrily. '*Grief* is a great painting; *des Grieux* is not. The artist was confused. When she painted *Grief* she knew what she was painting. Her personal grief is in it too.'

So he did know something about painting. 'I would like some coffee, please.'

He leaned towards her. 'Come back to my house, Holly. It's very pretty, with trees and little courtyards with beautiful gates; Maman says it's now too pearls and poodles but Blaise left it to me and I'd like you to see it.' He knew that his closeness was disturbing her and sat back. 'It's probable that Tony was there.'

She looked at him steadily and knew that she wanted nothing so much as to return to his town house with him. She decided that was the effect of the wine. 'Not tonight, Taylor. I think I'm a bit squiffy.'

He leaned forward again. 'You are absolutely adorable when you're squiffy. We're having fun together. Isn't that pleasant?'

'Please take me back to my hotel.'

He did not argue.

She was now very, very sober.

Next morning, having paid her bill, she left and took an expensive taxi to the airport. It was as if she feared that he would stop her.

From the airport she telephoned Chandler to say that she was going home and took a plane to London. She forgot to ring Otto to tell him what she had seen in Paris; she was full of an overpowering urge to get as far away from Taylor as was humanly possible. She wanted the cottage at Torry Bay and when she opened the door, and sympathy and understanding seemed to greet her, she knew that she had made the right decision.

She was home.

In the ensuing weeks it was as if Scotland were trying Holly's mettle. She had forgotten that a day of showers was, alas, often followed by a day of showers. Tony would have pulled on an old raincoat and braved the day but Holly was not made of so fine a steel. She stayed closeted in the cottage, reading, thinking and looking out at the bay. Then the postman cycled down the hill and brought her a letter from Taylor. Would she have opened it and read it had she known it was from him? The address, she noted idly, was computer-generated, neatly word-processed on a nice little label.

Goodness, will I get a Christmas card now that my details are secure in the bowels of Taylor's secretary's secretary's computer?

Another surprise was that the letter was handwritten.

Why should you be surprised, Holly Noble?

Because I thought he had minions to do all his writing for him.

Childish.

I know.

It had been a day for lighting a fire and curling up with a book. Holly held the heavy embossed paper in her hand, and peered moodily out on a rain-soaked landscape. Even the rhododendrons looked sorry for themselves as cold raindrops ran down their curled leaves, making countless little waterfalls onto their shallow roots. The sheep in the field huddled together miserably and a dense cloud of grey rain hid the sea.

I shall light a fire and then I shall burn this.

When baby flames were beginning to curl tentatively round the dry sticks Holly held the paper out, but at the last moment kept it back.

Had she had a telephone installed he would have talked to her. Had she had the courtesy to give him the number of her cellphone he would have called her. Instead he had written.

No doubt on your private plane as you flew from a sailing date with one beautiful socialite to dinner with another, scowled Holly, and decided that that thought was yet more childish than the one before.

She did not need to read the letter again. Already she had it by heart.

Why do we always fight, Holly? Maybe you should try to get along with me for Tony's sake. Running away was so childish. What in God's name did you think I intended to do to you?

Holly blushed when she read that. She had thought . . . oh, what had she thought? She held the single page out to the flames again and then stuffed it behind the cushion on her chair. A particularly inane way of behaving, Holly Noble. She would look at the pictures of the paintings again and compare them with her memory of the Paris *Lohengrin*. Holly loved it, 'girl's picture' or not. The subject looked like every girl's idea of the knight in shining armour who will come to rescue her either on the back of a white stallion, or, as in this absurd story, on the back of a bewitched swan. She decided not to think about Paris. Remembering Paris made her remember Taylor and those few moments in the restaurant when she had been so sure they were becoming . . . friends. Stupid Holly, to think that a man who has had the world given to him as a birthright might like Holly Noble. She picked up another of the photographs and stared at it, at the absurdity of it, the tall elegant man, the skinny little girl. She willed it to surrender its secrets. She tried and tried, racked her memory bank, but her memories of Blaise Fougère existed only in the paintings. She did not really remember him.

The fire was now blazing brightly and she put yet another log on the flames while she went upstairs to take a hot bath in the huge, deep, old cast-iron tub. There was a lovely memory there; why had she not noticed that the great iron feet on which the tub stood above the floor had had their toenails painted quite recently?

Did he laugh too, Tony? Did you allow him to suggest colour schemes for the feet? Was he like me with a penchant for purple?

The toenails today were a flamboyant green.

No, green is more like you.

If I sell the cottage will I stipulate that the successful buyer must paint the bath's toenails?

Holly laughed at her absurdity. Anyone who bought the cottage would no doubt rip the entire bathroom apart to put in modern plumbing.

Quite right too, but since I have absolutely no intention of selling the cottage I shall investigate the local plumber myself.

It was late so she pulled on a long-sleeved nightgown that she had found among Tony's clothes. It was as if she were held in Tony's loving arms and she poured herself a glass of wine and sat down near the fire. She pulled the letter out from behind the cushion and read it again.

'Why do we always fight?'

Because we don't like one another, that's why, Boy Genius.

Holly had been raised to be scrupulously polite to everyone and anyone.

'Courtesy costs nothing.' That voice came again and again from the past and so Holly had tended to be, if anything, overly polite to those few people she actively disliked.

'Courtesy can be a powerful weapon, darling girl.' That was Tony and the other voice was Tony's brother, Frederick, Holly's father.

Even the bay was now quiet. She sat in the window in Tony's scruffy old chair and looked out. No wonder Tony had been happy to stay here and to paint.

If I wanted to tell anyone how unbelievably beautiful this is, Holly thought, I would fail. I don't have a gift for choosing the only word that is right. What could I say? The water is calm and tiny ripples on the top are caressed by moonbeams so that it looks like, looks like a . . . a silk scarf nonchalantly tossed down. The sky is grey-blue or is it blue-grey and there's pink there, and there, just there where the clouds almost touch the water, I can see the merest sliver of pure molten gold.

Tony had not needed words. She had taken her palette and her brushes and transferred the picture to her canvas; no need for inadequate words.

I wish I could read everything in the portraits, but I think that perhaps I have read as much as you wanted me to know.

The cottage was so cosy and the firelight jumped and played on the walls and Holly sat in Tony's old nightgown and dozed. The embers stirred, then settled with a sigh in the grate and Holly woke.

It is *so* cold in here. Ask the plumber about heating too.

She stood up and stretched and Taylor's letter fell into the fireplace. She reached down for it and then threw it onto the embers; for a few seconds it sat there turning red and then it burned quite satisfactorily.

Spring-cleaning, that's the answer. Spring-cleaning and improvements.

She began next morning to clean the cottage from top to bottom. The ghosts who sometimes accompanied her up the stairs and into the attic were friendly and she did not fear them. She would be pleased to have their company. She was halfway up the stairs when she remembered. A ring. That was what Tony had always worn, not the lovely jewels reposing in stately isolation in Henry Gilbert's safe. Holly sat on the stairs and tried to conjure up pictures of Tony. Jeans, a man's shirt – Blaise's obviously, for comfort – and round her neck a gold chain with a heavy ring suspended from it. But oh, how many years was it since she had seen that ring?

Her memory was playing tricks with her because she seemed to have seen the ring recently but Tony had not worn it in the past twenty years. Blaise must be wearing it in one of the portraits. She would look at them again carefully when she returned to London.

She rang Otto to put him out of his misery.

He was ecstatic and just for a moment she felt pleased that her call should have given him such pleasure. 'Hello, my dear. How is it in bonny Scotland?'

'Refreshing,' she said dryly. She felt she knew Otto quite well. He was up to something. 'I thought I'd let you know my plans, Otto.'

'No need, no need. You just take your time to get your head together.'

She wanted to ask if he had been drinking, but Otto

rarely drank and never to excess. He should have been uptight about his inability to sell and here he sounded positively ebullient. 'There's nothing wrong with my head. I wish I could say the same about yours.'

'How we are nasty. What's the weather like up there?'

'It's a typical spring day. Sunny, refreshing, daffodils all over the place and primroses. Tony encouraged the little pink ones.' He had to have been drinking. 'Otto, why aren't you begging me to help you sell the portraits?'

'All in good time. Must go, darling girl. I'm having lunch with Amy Rosenthal. I shall tell her . . . all about your decision to stay in Scotland. I can just see the headlines.'

She had no time to say, 'Don't do that,' before he had hung up.

'Damn Otto.'

She went back to her cleaning. What should she do about Blaise's clothes? She had not taken them to Glasgow and now they hung there reproaching her. The doctor or the priest or the minister would know who, among the community, might like a warm sweater. Taylor didn't need them, wouldn't want them. He had been offered. The beaded cocktail dresses were rather dated. A theatre perhaps. There were exclusive and expensive labels on most of them. She had heard that bright young things scoured the markets for dated designer wear but she shrank from the thought of making even more money from Tony. She sorted them out while she held decisions at bay.

Hunger drove her downstairs. She made tea and a cheese sandwich and sat in the seat at the window looking at the view.

How unusual. There was a car coming down the hill towards the bay. Who could it be at this time of night? Poachers would hardly be so bold. She went swiftly to the door and locked it, feeling slightly silly. Then she turned off the lamp and went to the window. The car had come into the driveway. Something had to be wrong. It must be the police.

But it was not. The car stopped. The lights went out. The door opened. Taylor. It was Taylor.

A million feelings, thoughts, sensations, chased one another around in her head and for some inexplicable reason in the pit of her stomach. She had been so close to him in Paris – the wine had gone to her head. That was all; it was wine. She stood like a rabbit caught in a headlight unable to move.

'Holly, open up. Damn it all, I saw the light.'

Exultant. She tried unsuccessfully to stifle her excitement.

Yes, indeed, Taylor Hartman. Who else would travel thousands of miles and then swear at the person he had come to see?

Holly hurried to the door and tried to open it but for a second she forgot that she had locked it and struggled with it.

'God damn it, Holly, I have just flown three thousand miles. I need the bathroom and a cup of coffee.'

'Stop shouting. There, I forgot I locked it.'

Taylor was a New Yorker. Everything was locked in New York. 'How can you forget?' he muttered angrily as he pushed past her.

She closed the door, saying, 'Won't you come in,' politely to the now empty space at the door.

'Can I get you a cup of coffee?' she asked when he was downstairs again.

'Very funny but I had forgotten how remote this place is.'

'You could have stopped on the way, and telephoned as well as whatever else you needed to do.'

'I don't have your number, remember; you're harder to reach than I am. Please may I have some coffee?'

How meek he sounded. Better beware, she told herself firmly. When he was sweet and gentle he was at his most dangerous.

She ignored his request. 'Why are you here?'

'I needed to talk to you.'

She laughed. 'To find out why I didn't take up your offer of a lift? I do hope you didn't come from wherever you were just to do that.'

'I suppose there's no wine.'

She looked at him for a moment and saw lines of strain and fatigue on his face. Where had he been? Had he come from Tokyo, from Rio, to speak to her? There was wine. 'I'll make some coffee.'

She went into the kitchen and on the marble shelf in the pantry were two beautiful venison sausages and she decided to cook them for him. She put on the kettle and prepared coffee. No doubt he would complain about instant. He said nothing, for he had fallen asleep and she stood holding the tray looking down at him for a moment. How vulnerable he looked when he was asleep. She put the tray down with a thump. John had also been able to look vulnerable and put-upon when it suited him.

'I cooked some of those venison sausages you like; they're not burned this time,' she added diffidently.

He sat up, rubbing his eyes like a little boy and it was then that she saw the ring. Tony's ring, Blaise's ring. Taylor was wearing it.

'You're wearing his ring.'

He looked casually at his hand. 'He gave it to me for luck when I went to college. I always wear it.'

Holly flushed with embarrassment. She remembered his hands as she had seen them when he was in her flat and then again in Paris; she did not remember the ring.

He took the plate she was holding out. 'I'm sorry. I should have brought food.'

Immediately she bridled. 'It's not your friend Jacques Marin but it's good.'

'Holly, please, time out? I only meant it's rude to come uninvited and not contribute something.'

Holly sat down in her favourite window seat. She had pulled the curtains closed to look at wear and tear and now wondered if she should open them again. Usually she never closed them – the view was so spectacular. Closed, they made the room look intimate, but she knew that if she opened them he would be bound to say something provoking.

She sat drinking her coffee while Taylor demolished the sausages and the toast she had made to accompany them. At last he sat back with a sigh and wiped his mouth with a clean handkerchief; she had forgotten napkins.

'I remember that as having a spectacular view,' he said.

She opened the curtains. He was quiet for a moment.

'Better than I remembered,' he said after a while.

Had Blaise said something like that each time he returned to Torry Bay? Had Tony sat in the window seat watching him eat or admiring the ever-changing painting outside?

Holly got up abruptly. She was not Tony and he was certainly not Blaise. 'It's very late, Taylor. Perhaps you could tell me why you are here.'

'And then you'll turf me out?'

'Oh, stop being ridiculous; there is nowhere for you to go. You can have the big room. I've never been able to sleep there.'

'Thank you.'

Was that all he was going to say? He had flown thousands of miles – what had he said, three thousand miles, so from New York. He had been to London after Paris and then New York, then Tokyo, back to New York and here he was again. Did he ever sleep in his own bed? She wanted to rail about obscene amounts of money but she could not, for he had come to see her. Why? She would not ask. The idea of a private jet setting down on the bay made her giggle and he looked at her strangely.

'Where did you put down?' She was pleased with that, put down, sounded very knowledgeable and sophisticated.

'London. I couldn't get clearance anyplace else. Then a shuttle and a hired car. I'm tired, Holly, and I'm not at my best when I'm tired so please don't fight me. That's all you ever want to do, fight, fight, fight.'

That was so blatantly untrue that she bridled. 'Me? Me fight? Taylor Hartman—'

'See,' he challenged. 'I open my mouth and you're shouting at me.'

She stared angrily back at him and then capitulated. 'You're right. I'm sorry. Would you like to go to bed, Taylor?'

Hearing what she had just said she coloured violently but he merely smiled.

'No dishes for me to wash first?'

'They'll wait till morning.'

He stood up and went to the door. 'Is there water for a shower?'

'There's plenty of scalding water but no shower.'

'No big deal. Goodnight – and thanks, Holly.'

She did not move from her chair. 'Goodnight.'

A few minutes later she heard the sound of water cascading into the deep bathtub, and then Taylor's voice. 'Hey, that's neat. I just noticed the toenails.'

Holly was *so* aware of every move he made. When he was safely in the tiny bathroom she hurried up to her room and sat on the edge of her bed. She heard him yelping as he tentatively lowered himself into the bath.

303

Too late she realised that a perfect hostess would have warned him that the antiquated plumbing sometimes sent hot water through both sets of taps. She tried hard not to listen and harder not to picture him. Eventually she heard him open the window – much against its will – to let steam out and she heard him enter the room next door.

What was he doing? He was taking so long to get from the door to the bed. Was he on his knees praying? There was a bizarre thought. Was he standing looking out of the window seeing the bay as his uncle had seen it more times than Taylor could be made to admit?

At last she heard the creaking of the old springs and then nothing until the early summer sun played on her eyelids and forced her awake. 'Well, Achahoish, are you not determined to let our visitor see you at your best,' she said as the soft purply blue that was the Argyll landscape spread itself out for her admiration.

Taylor was already in the tiny kitchen and he handed her a mug of coffee when she went downstairs. She took it and sipped appreciatively. 'Thanks. Taylor, why are you here?'

'I don't know,' he said simply, but he turned away from her as he was speaking. Was that to hide his eyes? Surely the Hartmans of this world learn to lie with beautifully frank, open eyes. He went on, 'I always seem to do something wrong around you.'

'Like closing the exhibition.'

'It's temporary; Otto's lawyers are in there slugging too. I wish I could make you . . . never mind. If you have no plans for the day I thought you could show me Edinburgh. The art gallery there, at someplace called the Mound, has some of Tony's paintings.'

She was startled and ashamed that she had not known.

She looked at him. What was going on behind that surely deceptively friendly façade?

'I was cleaning, actually, throwing out old clothes.'

'That's better than a pleasant day showing off your city?'

'Edinburgh is no more my city than Los Angeles or New York, Taylor, but I do like it and, certainly' – she capitulated – 'looking at my aunt's wonderful paintings beats spring-cleaning. To be honest it never occurred to me that there would be paintings of hers hanging there.'

He waited without complaining while she changed and then he drove as fast as the law allowed towards Edinburgh.

'Is there someplace that we could get breakfast?'

She directed him to the Royal Overseas League on Princes Street. 'You're not a member of the Commonwealth but you may come as my guest.'

'A private club. Boy. We colonials love all that stuff.'

'Don't be facetious. You will love the breakfast.'

He did and when he had eaten he put his elbows on the table, folded his hands, and asked, 'Holly, tell me, why are you so hard on everybody, starting with yourself?'

'Now it's Doctor Hartman.'

He smiled and refilled her coffee cup.

'Am I hard on everyone? I don't mean to be – if I am. My parents were missionaries, but you knew that?'

He nodded but said nothing and poured himself more coffee.

'I suppose what we learn in childhood stays with us. I tried really hard to move away from my parents but the older I get the more I find myself adopting their principles. It's too easy for us in the Western world and we take too much for granted.' She stopped, aware that she was blushing. 'Drink up, Taylor. We're wasting time,' she said.

He smiled but he said nothing and as if conjured up by magic the waiter arrived with the bill. 'I should eat here more often,' he said as they walked down the flights of stairs to the street floor and out on to Princes Street.

'I had a girlfriend in college,' he said as they stood looking at the majesty of the city, 'who came to Edinburgh for the arts festival. She told me she walked around poking all those buildings; she was convinced Disney put them up the night before, just for her.'

'They're real all right. Taylor, how did you know there are paintings by Tony here?'

'Chandler,' he answered simply. 'Now what and where is the Mound?'

She went into tourist-guide mode. 'We can walk there through the gardens. Edinburgh, old Edinburgh where you parked, was divided from what became new Edinburgh by a lake, a loch, the Scots say. To get from one side to the other without going all the way round tradesmen piled rubble from the foundations of the New Town, basically, to make a walkway and that was called the Mound and that's it straight ahead.'

They stood at the end of one area of Princes Street Gardens and looked at the elegant and busy road that now joins the Old and the New Towns. On one side stood the two splendid galleries, the Scottish Academy in front and the National Gallery of Scotland behind. The eyes travel in the wake of constant traffic up the Mound to a row of buildings breathtaking in their beauty.

'I feel like prodding one or two of those myself,' said Taylor, but he had already punched the button on the traffic control.

As they entered the National Gallery Holly found that she was almost holding her breath. She had visited Edinburgh several times with Tony but she had never seen any of Tony's paintings there.

How utterly boring, darling girl. You see my paintings all the time.

Perhaps, after all, she had known that there were paintings there.

The huge landscape dominated a wall of one of the galleries. It was the view from the point and captured a winter squall. The waves had been whipped up by fierce winds and such was the skill of the artist that the viewer stepped back from the painting as if afraid of the power of the elements.

'You ever see the bay like that?'

'No. I was never there in the winter. See, there are pockets of snow near the point. Look, you just know that sky is about to offload all that heavy cloud.'

'Powerful work.'

They stood looking at the painting for some time. The gallery was empty but for a guide – or perhaps he was a custodian – who sat in a chair by the door studiously looking everywhere but at them.

'You interested in Tony Noble?' His voice startled both of them.

'Yes,' said Taylor. 'We were told there is another painting.'

'Aye. We have two. Priceless, I think, especially now the poor woman's dead. There was a docent round the other day with some students but maybe you're painters yourselves and don't need to be told.'

'We're not painters,' Holly answered for both of them. 'Just admirers.'

'A great artist, was what he said. Was well known just after the war, maybe till the late seventies but she produced less and less and rarely exhibited. The professor said he's read some paintings were discovered in America. But you're an American, sir, you'll know.'

'No,' said Taylor, his eyes very carefully studying *Storm at Achahoish*. 'They were found right here in Scotland. Where is the other painting?'

'Through there. It's an old man, nicest face you ever saw in your life.'

They went through the archway into a smaller,

rectangular gallery. They knew the painting immediately. It was of a tall stooped figure with an almost ethereal quality to the lined aesthetic face. He was standing, fork in hand, beside a small cairn of stones that he had removed from the obviously infertile soil. The painting was called *Vision*.

'Why that title?'

Holly looked at the painting and remembered the subject, not well, and not as the artist had portrayed him. 'He scratched a few old cabbages out of that inhospitable plot and yet he always hoped for roses.'

'That's the canon, then?'

Holly nodded. 'He was quite old when I met him,' she informed Taylor. 'He had retired and lived in a monastery near Oban.'

'Catholic, I guess.'

'Oh, yes. Roman Catholic.'

'And Tony?'

'Church of England. What about Blaise?'

'Catholic.'

Remembering her conversation with his mother she said, 'I suppose he didn't believe in divorce.'

She could sense his tension. He seemed to draw inwards inside himself and it was almost as if he were no longer standing there by her side.

'Look, she can paint. Okay. We knew that before.'

'You wanted to come,' she pointed out mildly. 'I had spring-cleaning planned.'

'Let's go back and look at the landscape.'

They returned to the first gallery and then Taylor

went to the gallery shop and bought prints of both paintings.

'Prints?' asked Holly in disbelief. 'The Hartman Corporation buying prints.'

'I don't intend to hang them, Holly, unless perhaps I could string you up between them.' But he was smiling.

They had spent just over an hour in the gallery. 'Let's go poke a building unless you're anxious to get back to your housework.'

No, she was not anxious.

'Can you walk in those shoes?' he asked as he started up the Mound. 'Tell me what's under here.'

Since he seemed to take for granted that her shoes were up to the allotted task, she explained as they climbed the Mound. 'I believe they have found bones, human remains.'

'Would you look at that?' He had stopped and turned back to look down on the elegance of the gardens, Princes Street, and the magnificent Georgian New Town. An attractive soft blue light seemed to hang over the city.

'That light used to be grey,' said Holly, 'from all the smoke from coal fires.'

That reminded him of winter storms. 'I hope you kept Blaise's blue Guernsey if you really intend to winter at Torry Bay; you'll need it.'

'I'm having central heating installed.'

'And a telephone?'

'Taylor, are you planning to ring me?'

'Every Christmas, to make sure you haven't been blown into the sea.'

They walked on into the Royal Mile. 'I know, I know, it's a mile between the palace and the castle so it's royal. Which way, up to the castle or down to the palace?'

Three hours later they had walked up to the castle, taken a guided tour, gone into the Camera Obscura where a fascinated Taylor had fed the machine copiously so that he could look again and again at the historical and architectural wonder that was this capital city, and had walked down the Mile again to the palace, stopping to see several historic buildings on the way.

'Heck, we're too late,' complained Taylor.

'Thanks be to God,' whispered Holly, who felt that at any moment she might buckle at the knees.

He heard. 'I warned you.' He looked around. 'Know what I'd like? Lasagne.'

'Isn't time important?'

'Not today. Let's find an Italian restaurant and then I'll drive you home.'

She tensed as she made quick calculations and he laughed. 'This isn't a seduction, Holly. We'll eat, I'll drive you home and then I'll find a hotel. Maybe I'll come back here. There are quite a few buildings still to poke.'

'It would be midnight at the earliest before you got back here.'

'What a touching invitation,' he said, 'but no. The parking lot cashier reminded me of a good hotel. I'll call while we're eating.'

Holly hardly knew whether to be annoyed or relieved. Yet Achahoish was a long way – even for a driver like

Taylor – and she did not want him in the cottage. Not tonight, not after a lovely day when they had been so relaxed and at ease, the spectre of the exhibition and Taylor's court orders so far away. Neither did she want to stay at a hotel with him. Besides, she had no luggage. His first-class hotel would balk at no luggage.

Damn him. She had to get back to Argyll. Could she rent a car? Of course: that was the answer. 'I'll get a car. Please. That'll be easiest.'

'Your thoughts are written all over your face, Holly. I will drive you home. One, I'm starving and so must you be. Two, I like driving. Three, what would my mother say if I abandoned my date?'

'This isn't a date.'

'Explain that to my mother.'

Better to say nothing.

He hailed a cab and asked the driver to recommend a good Italian restaurant. 'You do like Italian food?'

Holly nodded and sat quietly while they crept back up the Royal Mile.

'Ever been to the Festival Theatre?' Taylor asked. 'The restaurant is right there and I just wondered if Blaise had sung at the theatre. He did sing in Edinburgh.'

'Probably the Usher Hall,' murmured Holly.

'The Usher Hall. A pokable building?'

'Absolutely.'

The restaurant the cab driver had recommended was used to customers rushing in for a meal before the theatre and so it was less than fifteen minutes before

Holly found herself sitting with a large glass of wine while Taylor made his phone call.

He was smiling as he eased himself back into the restricted space behind the table. 'Great. I have a booking at the Balmoral. Isn't that a good Scottish name.'

'It's obscenely expensive.'

He looked at her for a moment as if he were about to retort and then he smiled. 'Funny Holly.'

The waiter arrived with their antipasti and they were too hungry to talk much. The antipasti was followed by spaghetti carbonara for Holly and lasagne for Taylor. With his pasta he drank water and Holly nursed her large glass of wine through the meal.

By the time the waiter brought coffee she was relaxed again and it was not so late as she had thought it would be when they left Edinburgh for Argyll.

They talked little. Holly's mind was too full of conflicting thoughts and opinions and she was content to look out of the window and watch Scotland flash past. At last they were well out of civilisation and heading into the artist's palette that was the west coast.

'No wonder they loved it so much,' she said at one point, but Taylor said nothing and Holly decided not to provoke him. He was once again the Taylor who, no matter what his mother, Holly, or his own brain said, refused to believe in the love between Blaise Fougère and Antonia Noble.

There was still light when they reached Torry Bay but he could not drive back to Edinburgh.

'Taylor . . .' Holly began.

'You know what they say about opera, Holly? It's not over till the fat lady sings. Goodnight.'

She stood at the door and watched until the tail-lights disappeared into the blue-black night.

20

———◆———

Torry Bay, 1957. London, 1957
FLOWERS IN THE STREAM

Tony hardly left the cottage for weeks after Blaise had
left. She knew he would not write and so she did not
climb the hill to the road and to the post box. There was
nothing else that she cared to receive. She stayed in the
cottage; she ate very little and she slept less. She did not
paint and she did not listen to music. She existed. She
was numb. She had cried and railed against life so much
when she had had the pregnancy terminated that she
felt there were no tears, no grief left. When she woke up
from her disturbed rest she was sorry to find that she
was still breathing, and she was surprised by the instinct
that forced her to eat a little bread, a dry cracker, a stale
piece of cheese. Blaise's wine was still there and she
wondered what would happen if she opened it, drank it
all, and then walked out into the sea.

I would probably fall asleep before I'd walked out and
then I'd wake up and be sick for days.

She left the wine inviolate and that decision began the

healing, if healing there was. One day when she woke up she was hungry and when she looked in the mirror she was ashamed of her uncombed hair and haggard face. She bathed and dressed in clean clothes and walked to the village for groceries.

It had no right to be such a beautiful day, but the sky was soft with that particular light that tells you that there has been rain. The hills smelled clean and the roads smelled fresh and the scent of the sea rose up on the warm air. Tony quickened her steps.

Chrissie looked at her and her old face crumpled.

'Ach, lassie, did I not tell you life's a bitch. I'll no' ask you a thing but I'm here.'

Tony returned the hug. 'I know,' she said, 'and that makes this almost bearable.'

She bought sausages and fish and bread and coffee and an apple that was so perfect that she wanted to take it home and paint it, but instead she ate it with chunks of the bread on the way home. Never had food tasted so good.

It had no right to taste so wonderful, but that thought only pierced her heart with a small arrow, and so she hurried home, pricked the sausages all over and when they were squealing happily in an iron frying pan on the stove, walked up to see if anyone had written to her.

There were several letters, some from friends made at the time of her first show and a heavier one from Frederick who fought daily with the conviction that she was a lost soul but still his sister.

Only the smell of burning sausages alerted her to the

near disaster in her kitchen and she ran through in time to throw the frying pan into the sink and to pull down the curtains at the window in an attempt to douse the fire.

Blast, blast, blast. I've burned my hands.

She remembered that she was a painter and now she had burned her hands.

There must be something I can do. But there was nothing in the medicine chest that remotely suggested that it might be useful in dealing with burns. She would have to go back to the village to see Simon.

He did not mention their fight. 'You look awful,' he told her kindly as he bandaged her hands.

'Well, it was either my hands or my home,' she said and he laughed.

'Your hands are just burned, Tony. It's the rest of what ails you that troubles me.'

'I've been busy,' she lied. 'When I'm painting I forget to eat.'

'A new invisible paint? This postwar era is truly remarkable. Tony, old friend, even at Major Cunningham's elegant drinks party last Christmas there was paint ingrained on your hands. It's over, is it?'

She said nothing but dropped her gaze from his face to his hands. She should paint his hands.

'Would he have divorced his wife?'

She shook her head violently. 'No. Yes. I don't know. Maybe. All of the above. But I couldn't win him that way, Simon. He would have grown to hate me, perhaps more than he hates me now, and he would have loathed the scandal, and so would I.' She stood up. 'Thanks for this,' she said and walked out.

When she reached home she threw the blackened sausages out for the seabirds and filled her burned pan with cold water.

I'm going to paint Simon's hands.

But memories of other hands came into her mind and the tears started again.

I'm in shock. I'm in shock. I will go to sleep now in my own bed. For she had been dozing in the big chair by the fire since he had gone.

She climbed the stairs and saw the unmade bed, its sheets still stained from their last loving. She saw the dust accumulating on the dressing-table.

Tomorrow, I'll tackle this tomorrow. And she crept into the little room at the top of the stairs and cried herself to sleep on the horsehair mattress.

Morning came. There were no curtains on the little windows to shut out the light and so strong was the northern summer light that curtains would have been useless anyway. Tony got out of bed and went the few steps to the window. Outside stretched a painting that was more beautiful than anything she could ever achieve. The rising sun on the sea, the sea as it caressed the shore, the mist that hovered almost lovingly over everything . . . they spoke of life. For the first time, it was all horrifyingly obvious.

I should have had my child and this should have been his room. He should have wakened here every morning and rushed to this window where every minute of every day there would have been a new painting waiting for him.

She knew he would have been a boy. She could see him down there on the shore, dancing in and out of the waves, her baby sprite, his limbs strong and brown like his . . . She could not say it and pain, worse than the pains of the abortion itself, gripped her again until she crouched down below the window and prayed to die. She did not die and eventually she got up from her foetal position on the floor, went downstairs and made coffee. She took it out to the rock near the door where she sat and let the morning sun begin to heal her.

I'll paint my grief, she decided.

One day she climbed up the hill behind the house and stood looking out to sea. Somewhere away over there, that's where he was. Was he happy? Of course he was happy. All he really needed was to sing. He could forget everything then, all the pain, all the heartbreaks, the regrets, and he forgot everyone: Eleanor, his wife; Nicole, his sister and Toinette. How long had it taken him to tear Toinette from his heart for the second time? Was it easier because she had murdered his baby?

My baby. My baby too. My son. My little son.

There were little blue flowers growing on the headland, pale blue petals, so lovely, so delicate. Forget-me-nots.

'Forget me not,' she cried desperately and threw the flower from her into the stream. It danced along. If it goes to the sea, it will reach him and he will remember and come back. The first flower stuck on a rock and would not

319

move. The current pulled the second under. The third swirled under the overhanging bank. No, no. They must be free to go to him, to reach the sea, then to sail bravely on, to join the waters of the great oceans. Otherwise he would never come back and this time she would die. Surely she could not bear to live without him, not again. But she would not die. It would be worse. She would exist in a pain-filled limbo where there was no light, no music, no art and no love. Feverishly she pulled more flowers, and then she knelt down by the water and patiently tore each perfect little flower from the parent stem.

'Forget me not.'

One by one the tiny blue flowers tumbled bravely into the turbulent water. Oh, to have the courage to throw the husk that was Tony Noble in after them, to end this purgatory. She pulled herself to her feet and stumbled back to the cottage. To exist at all she had to end it. They were upstairs, her unborn babies, her precious little cherubs. She looked at them: she heard their silvery little voices. And another voice.

'See this one. She has the voice like an angel. What a Tosca she will make.'

She would never sing Tosca because she would never be born, never conceived. Tony felt cold, so cold as she picked up her palette-knife, colder still as she hacked her unborn babies from their fluffy clouds. Then she took the lighter from her pocket of her trousers and set fire to the pieces.

'Stupid. Idiot. *Crétin.*' She started forward in dismay. 'The others will go.'

'Let them all burn. They are only dreams.'

'No, no. My babies.'

She reached for the burning pieces of the singing babies but was too late. She had murdered her babies twice. Simon found her and put out the fire before the other paintings, the house, and the painter herself went up in flames.

'No man is worth this, Tony.'

She tried to explain that she had not meant to burn the house down, that she was perfectly rational, that she had changed her mind and tried to rescue the painting. Her paintings were her children conceived in delight, born in mingled ecstasy and agony.

Such talk embarrassed him. 'Between sausages and paintings, you're determined to ruin these hands.'

She waited patiently for her hands to heal and then she painted Simon's hands and gave him the picture for Christmas. At dinner on Christmas Day he asked her to marry him.

'I've loved you for a long time, Tony, and I want to take care of you.'

She had expected the question but not quite so soon. There had been a death in the family; should they not wait a year? 'I still love him, Simon.'

'I know, but this can't be mended, Tony. He wants it broken. I love you and, in a way, you love me. We could be happy.'

'You deserve better, Simon. I can't marry you. I've always thought of myself as married to . . . the baby's father.'

It was not his way to probe. 'Hasn't he brutally divorced you?'

She tried to smile. 'By jumping over the broom handle? I divorce you, I divorce you, I divorce you. We've been friends a long time, Simon. Don't spoil it.'

'Think about it. It wouldn't be as it was with him but it would be peaceful, Tony, and perhaps we could have a child.'

She stood up. 'I can't. I must go, Simon. I have work waiting.'

He did not argue but walked her down to the cottage and waited until she was inside. Then he waited again until he saw the light go on upstairs.

She began to work on *Flowers in the Stream*. It took her three years to finish it almost to her satisfaction and still it was not right, but then they never were. Nothing was ever perfect, not now, not without Blaise.

Frederick wrote to her. He had met a nurse in the mission station in Africa. They were going to be married. She must come to the wedding.

Freddie the sexless, married. You bet I'll come, Frederick, just to see what humourless individual would take you on.

Her letter of acceptance was couched in more acceptable language. The wedding was to be in London in June. As the date grew nearer Tony found herself becoming quite excited. When had she last been in London? Three years, four? How ridiculous. She must visit the old galleries. One or two of them still kept in touch and Klaus and his new partner, his son, Otto, had asked her to remember them. Perhaps she'd take *Flowers in the Stream* or *Lohengrin*.

Frederick had sold their parents' house and since his fiancée, Gilda, lived in Bayswater, he was going into digs in the city for a few weeks before the wedding.

Gilda from Bayswater. How appalling. What would our parents have thought? Still, better than a French tenor, and I bet she's a virgin.

Tony was so ashamed of her narrow-mindedness and intolerance that she spent twice as much as was seemly on a wedding present and also gave them one of the *Lohengrin* series, a gesture she regretted when Gilda called it pretty.

She had been invited to stay with Gilda's parents but preferred to stay in a hotel in Kensington, especially since Gilda thought a hotel for family an unnecessary extravagance.

Dear God, prayed the unreligious Tony, please don't let her look like her name. It even sounds awful, Gilda, nothing musical about Gilda. Why did Verdi, the consummate musician, call a heroine Gilda? Nothing musical. Who cares? I shall love her because her name does not sing.

In the lovely bedroom of her hotel she unpacked quickly, had a bath – such decadence, a hot bath in the afternoon – and then, wrapped in a huge, soft, warm towel, smoked a cigarette. How wonderfully wicked and debauched. Freddie would adore to scold.

Cigarette finished, she dressed and went out. She had no plans but found herself heading for the Underground. She bought a ticket and in less than thirty minutes she was walking along towards Covent Garden. She would stroll through the market, have a cup of coffee. She found herself before the Royal Opera House.

When had she last been inside that exquisite building? Blaise had been singing Alfredo in *La Traviata*. As usual she had been circumspect. She had watched from the balcony and later, after he had signed the countless autographs and posed for the photographs, he had joined her in her hotel room. That surely, was when the baby had been conceived. Tony brushed away a tear. She had listened to no opera for three years but suddenly her head was full of it. His voice was there, full, rich, as if he were standing beside her. She shook her head. Was she really hearing him? Was he singing somewhere inside the building and the sound was soaring out to her? She listened. The only sound came from the market where traders were calling, and friends were greeting one another, and buskers were frantically trying to prove that they were worth watching.

Tony turned and almost stumbled away. She forced her internal machine to stop playing *Traviata* and it left only to be replaced by . . . this she could not bear. He was singing from *Les Pêcheurs*, the aria he had sung that first time in the park, her special song, '*Je Crois Entendre Encore*'. A critic had called it a 'nice enough little tune' and she had been furious. Could he not feel the heart being ripped from his body as the glorious voice seemed to jump with consummate ease from one level to another?

'He is complimenting me, *ma mie*, and Bizet, because he does not know how difficult it is for me to jump cleanly; no sand on my heels, see.'

He had gone but she would never be rid of him, never. She had to get away from here, from the opera house with all its associations. Freddie. She would think of Freddie and Gilda. There was a future for them, if not for her.

She did not look round at the building where she had experienced such incredible pleasure.

Oh, Blaise, forget me not.

She did not see the poster that told the world that Blaise Fougère would sing three performances of Nadir in Bizet's opera, *Les Pêcheurs de Perles*.

Blaise left the opera house by the unpretentious little door on Flower Street. He turned towards the market and caught a glimpse of a woman with head bent, hurrying away. For a second she reminded him so powerfully of Toinette that he gasped and held out his hand as if to call her back. Then he stopped and allowed his hand to drop to his side.

I have learned to live without her, without love. I am married to music, to the opera.

They were there, as always, hungry, rapacious. Why did they have to touch him? Was it not enough to stop him, to speak to him?

'Could I have your autograph and please a photograph? Maisie, you take one and then I'll take one.'

He signed. He smiled. Did they realise he was a

human being? They seemed to talk at him, not to him. They did not wait for him to reply. Others were different.

'Mr Fougère, your work gives me such pleasure.'

'Blaise, you're fabulous.'

'A photograph? Could you put your hand on my waist? They'll never believe it in the shop. You're just like a real person. Did you know that?'

He smiled, and signed, and signed, and muttered thank you, and then when he had managed to escape . . . no, to get away to his next engagement, he sighed, and Stefan looked in the rear-view mirror.

'We have time for a quick trip to Scotland?'

His employer said nothing and it was Stefan's turn to sigh.

Tony went to Frederick's wedding and said all the right things, and then when the happy couple were off on their honeymoon she found herself strangely reluctant to go back to Torry Bay.

She resisted the temptation to wallow in misery by revisiting old haunts; that one outing to the Garden had brought back all the grief and pain, and in the quiet hours of the night, a little of the joy. She could not bear it.

She telephoned Otto.

'Tony, my dear, we thought you were dead. Lunch? Dinner? Breakfast? You name it.'

She laughed. He had not changed. 'A chat would be fine.'

'We have a new gallery. I did tell you but you've never visited, never sent us anything.'

'Otto, I will come and I will talk about paintings.'

The new gallery on Bond Street was almost as elegant as Otto himself but much more masculine. As usual he matched the walls of his main salon, an indefinable creamy white.

'What do you wear in the winter, Otto?'

'Winter's easy, Tony. Woolly jumpers and fake fur. You look ghastly.' Solicitously he helped her to a seat but as usual he made sure that she did not clash with his cushions. 'You have been ill and I have harboured such negative thoughts. I have looked, Tony, yes, I am compelled to confess, and I have looked, but you're not selling with anyone.'

'I haven't been painting.' She did not deny that she had been ill. 'My brother was married on Saturday and I came down for the wedding.'

'And the opera?' She had forgotten that he had known her a long time.

He kissed his hands towards the windows. 'Fougère is guesting with the Royal Opera. You painted him just after the war, didn't you? I could get you another commission there, my dear.'

She could hardly breathe for the pain in her heart. To hear him spoken of so casually . . . to pretend that the name meant nothing . . . Torry Bay. Suddenly, happily, she ached for its clean air, its cold wind from the sea.

'I thought landscapes, seascapes.'

He looked vaguely around. 'Did you bring some work?'

She thought of the swan picture that she had given Gilda. 'Not really. I hadn't intended to come but I couldn't help myself and now I'm here and . . .' She looked at the paintings on the walls with disdain. 'You're stealing from the illiterate, Otto.'

He looked with her. 'Can you still paint better than any of them, Tony?'

She said nothing. Of course she could, with her eyes shut and her dominant hand tied behind her, she could paint better than any of them.

'There's always a plaintive cry for *real art*. Go home and paint me some pictures, Tony. Welcome home.'

Home to the world of paint and canvas and brushes and heartbreak or possibly immortality.

She was excited. She thought the excitement had gone but it was still there. She sat on the train and her mind saw blues and green and yellows and reds that sang clearly and defiantly.

I haven't lost everything if this has not deserted me. She took a pencil and whiled away the miles by sketching on the backs of the envelopes she found in her handbag. She drew Gilda in her wedding gown and made her almost pretty to please Frederick. She drew the little church where her brother had been married and she drew Frederick, so solemn, even more solemn – if that were possible – than on the day of his ordination. He had felt his responsibility heavy then; now he had taken on even more responsibility.

She hoped he would get more out of marriage than extra worries.

Heavens, two people and a church and I had decided to give up portraits in favour of landscape. I'll let the gift dictate.

Her pencil began to move again and a man wearing only a loincloth appeared. His hair was dark and flopped down over the eyes. She rubbed out the hair and then, unable to stop herself, drew it in again. She could not see his eyes. They would be green, green like the still, deep reaches of the water in the bay.

She tore the envelope across, once, twice, and tried a third time.

'That really was quite good,' said the woman across from her sternly and Tony laughed.

'Yes,' she agreed. 'It was quite good.'

21

———◆———

Torry Bay, 1999. London, 1999

This was where she was going to live; ergo, she must make it more comfortable. She was not Tony who dealt cheerfully with an open fire and almost primitive plumbing. Even now in summer it could be quite chilly and what was that wonderful word the woman in the village shop used? Dreich, that was it. Torry Bay could be dreich, damp and misty, in July. What would it be like in November?

She put on a jacket, locked the door, and walked up to the village. There was a plumber; he was out on a call but would be sure to drop in on his way home.

Holly returned to the cottage, got out the Yellow Pages and soon a very cheery voice was telling her of the advantages to be had from the use of a British Telecom land line.

'Just a telephone is fine, thank you.'

'We put in the line, Missus, and points where you want them; you have to buy your own phones at a shop.'

'But you'll come as quickly as you can?'

'Oh, aye, I've put you down; a few weeks, no more.'

'A few weeks?' repeated Holly to herself as a loud knocking at the front door startled her.

'Hello, Missus. We're Reid the plumbers.'

'Good heavens, that was fast.'

'We were on the way back for our tea.'

'Come in. I'm so glad you could come so quickly. You'll want to look round, take some measurements perhaps. Can I make some coffee; I mean tea?

They were inside. 'I sorted the water heater for Miss Noble,' said the older man by way of answer. 'She was aye talking about putting in the heating.'

'I don't know why she didn't,' began Holly.

'Quiet sort of a lady; we'll be under your feet a bit.'

'That's fine,' said Holly. If they had worked for Tony she knew they would be all right.

They had followed her into the tiny kitchen. 'It'll have to be the electricity and that's expensive.'

'It shouldn't cost a fortune to put central heating in a place this size.'

'No, no, the running costs. The electric is expensive, but we can do storage heaters and that'll save a bit. Is the rooms upstairs big?'

'One is, one isn't, and the bathroom.'

'Well, that's two big ones and three wee ones and you'll want to keep the fire. Nice and welcoming, a driftwood fire. Should take us –' they looked at one another in wordless communication – 'two days maybe.'

Two days and she would be warm; she could undress and have a bath.

'What about a shower in the bathroom?'

'Well, if the floorboards are up, you might as well get everything done.'

Only one member of 'We're Reid the plumbers' had spoken so far but the other smiled shyly at Holly every time she caught his eye over his coffee mug.

'When can you start?'

'We'll measure up and draw you a wee picture while we're here and then . . .'

'A week on Tuesday,' volunteered the quiet one.

Holly was unbelievably disappointed. Nearly two weeks. She had hoped that their appearance meant they were ready to begin.

'We'll need to order in,' explained the first one, 'and there's jobs waiting but,' he finished as he got to his feet. 'Say a week Tuesday and if we can we'll make it this day week.'

With that Holly had to be content. They measured all the rooms, consulted her about the size and positioning of radiators, and were gone with a promise that they would drop in a catalogue for the latest in showers.

The cottage settled quietly around Holly and it was as if they had never been. Scribbled notes on the kitchen table reassured her that she had not imagined them, for somehow the cottage seemed even quieter after their presence. They had filled the rooms up somehow.

She went off to buy her telephones and settled on a dark green one for the living room and a red extension for the upstairs hall. More sensible to put it in the larger bedroom but she could not yet bring herself to sleep there. Less than a week later she was surprised to have a visit from the telephone company.

'Well, if you aren't the luckiest woman to be where you are. Another hundred metres down the coast and the cost of installing a land line would be ridiculous.'

Holly smiled. Yes, she was the luckiest woman to be where she was. 'I haven't actually had time to think where this one should go,' she explained when they were in the living room. 'I'm having central heating installed.'

'No problem. You don't even need wires these days but if you're putting this wee green one in here, then across the room from where the radiator's going. You'll be wanting access to the Internet? Where's your computer?'

When he left Holly laughed at how she had disgraced herself. No computer; no interest in the Internet? What kind of woman was living at Torry Bay?

The next few days were fine and dry and she spent them walking along the coast collecting driftwood. She could hardly believe how contented she was. She was not cut off, for now she had her beautiful new telephones but no one rang; there was a radio but no television and so in the evenings Holly either listened to the radio or read. Most of the time, however, she thought. One day there was a note from *the* Mr Reid to say that 'the bits are coming in next week.' She would be delighted to see them, bits and all. Hallelujah. Soon

Torry Bay would be a cottage to be reckoned with. She wondered what its inhabitants felt about the renovations.

Darling girl. Hollyberry.

She told herself that she was not talking to ghosts but merely clearing her mind of what had been happening as she prepared for the upheaval that all the renovations would cause. Why am I dusting? Have you any idea the amount of dust there is going to be in here over the next few weeks?

She decided to go for a long walk to clear her lungs. She did not expect her lovely new phones to ring because she had given no one the number, but she switched her mobile to answering service. When she returned she burned herself some sausages but assured herself that that was how she liked them.

I wonder where Taylor is dining? He would be dining, not just having dinner. What if I had gone with him to the Paris house? Would I have felt Blaise's presence? Were you ever there, Tony?

Hollyberry.

I don't know what to do. I don't know what I want to do. Yes, I do. I want to make love to Taylor Hartman.

Damn it, I'm depraved or desperate or both. I'm certainly out of my mind. He is the most pig-headed, egotistical, solipsistic, conceited . . .

Hollyberry.

Oh, shut up.

Was there censure in the sigh, *Darling girl?*

Wonders of technology – she had messages, and

Sod's law prevailed. After weeks of silence someone had chosen to ring when she was out. She carried the mobile upstairs, ran a bath, and while she waited for it to cool, accessed her messages.

John.

'Holly, you've punished me enough, don't you think? We need to talk . . .'

She sat down abruptly on the edge of the tub. Who was John? The fellow who lived in Glasgow and who could not bring himself to drive for two hours to petition her. Taylor Hartman flew thousands . . . Enough, enough. I don't love John any more. I do not love John. I gave him back his ring – and his pearls. What more does he need? Do you ring people to tell them you don't love them or do you go and tell them face to face? I'll have to think about that one.

Otto.

'Holly, are you popping in again? Have you seen the German papers?'

Sure, Otto, they sell them on every street corner in Achahoish, she thought flippantly and then, Oh, God, why would he think I might want to read a German-language paper?

As far as Holly was aware she knew one German word and it translated as God bless you. This did not sound like a blessing. Shaky fingers managed to punch his number on her lovely red telephone.

'Otto, what German paper?'

He could not forget the instilled characteristics of civilised behaviour. 'Good evening, Holly, how are you?'

'Fine.' Enough courtesy. 'What German papers?'

'I assume all of them. There was, naturally, coverage at the time of the aborted exhibition but someone has been doing some investigations. Now new publicity – and this morning, so many offers.'

'It's been weeks. How can they cover an exhibition that wasn't?'

'Oh, you know newspaper people,' he said vaguely. 'Somehow they get a seed and the seed germinates and today, would you believe, I had a respected journalist from *Le Monde* telephoning for an interview. *Le Monde*,' he said again as if he could not quite believe it. 'Do you know I had quite underestimated the French interest? Unpardonable of me, given that he was French.'

'What are they saying?'

'They can't say anything when they know nothing; they are running some old stories and awakening interest, that's all. Not just in Blaise, of course, but whatever they can find on Taylor and the Hartman Corporation, and old press pieces on Tony are being reprinted with photographs of some of her lovely pictures. Lovely, lovely free publicity.'

She didn't want to ask but she had to know. 'Is there speculation about Eleanor?'

He was quiet, hesitant. 'She is mentioned, Holly, but the Hartman machine is powerful.'

'Otto, if you have leaked any of this I will never deal with you again.'

'Holly, I am going to make you rich.'

She hung up and went to sit, almost shaking, on the edge of her bed.

Damn, the bath. The water was tepid and she turned on the hot tap again and watched it flow until the temperature was just perfect. She poured in an over-generous amount of bath oil and lowered herself in.

I trusted Otto.

Darling girl.

Taylor will be furious and rightly. Oh, damn, I wish I had never met him. Tony, you were wrong; how could you have thought he wouldn't care. Did you forget Blaise's sister was still alive? Had grief impaired your judgement? She had never seen the slightest difference in Tony's attitude or behaviour. She had never suspected that for nearly ten lonely years her aunt had remained in her isolated cottage grieving for her lover.

No, Tony, you imagined he was with you.

Hollyberry.

I am imagining things too. I am imagining that Taylor could care for me. In Paris, in Edinburgh, he seemed . . . I don't know, approachable, nicer. I wish he were here now.

She looked down at her breasts, at her stomach.

Not bad, Holly Noble.

Slowly she raised one leg high in the air and examined it critically. She lowered it and raised the other one. Love or lust? I lust all right. I wish he were here. I don't give a hoohah if there's a difference between love and lust. I want him here. I have no pride, no shame.

Bébés chantants, Hollyberry.

Les bébés qui chantent, ma mie.

I want a baby, Tony, but not for you.

Oh, damn, this is so sad.

She raised the stopper and heard the water begin to drain away.

I will not turn into a melancholy old recluse.

She wrapped a huge towel around herself and went back into the bedroom. She pulled a cotton nightshirt over her head and climbed into bed. Then she remembered, climbed out again, padded across to the red telephone in the hall and dialled John's number.

'You have reached John Robertson.' Damn all answering services.

'John. I'm sorry. There is no nice way of saying it. I meant what I said. It's over. I am not coming back. I've accepted an offer on the flat.'

Now what? It's been great but . . .

'I'm sorry but please don't contact me again. Good luck with the election. I'm sure you'll win.'

It was hours before she slept.

The Reids arrived just before eight the next morning. Plumbers tearing out bathrooms and kitchens are easier to tolerate when one is not tired. 'You said,' began Holly as she stood holding her dressing-gown around her.

'I know, Missus, but we know how much you wanted to get the work done and the bits came in.'

The bits were standing for the entire world to see in the back of a truck that was parked right outside the door.

'We'll unload the bits and get started on the pipes.'

'Fine, but I'll need to make coffee first.'

'That'd be nice.'

I meant for me, said Holly to herself as she went back upstairs to wash, to pull a brush through her hair, and to dress in something warm. A summer squall was brewing and she had a feeling she would be spending quite a bit of time outside. Give them their due, once they had had their coffee – tea for me, Missus – they had worked really hard. It was just that there was so much to do and the house was so small. The only way to avoid the constant hammering was to walk for miles along the shore and the only thing to do while walking was to think about wasted lives and wasted opportunities and to resolve for the millionth time that 'It's not going to happen again, old son, it's not going to happen again.'

They stayed during their lunch hour that lasted approximately twenty minutes. They explained. 'We work for ourselves, Missus.'

Missus made a sandwich and went for a walk and saw several of Tony's paintings spread out on all sides. Here were some of the little flowers that featured in one of the sad paintings, there the clover flowers that bloomed in another.

The plumbers were leaving as she got back to the cottage. 'That wee phone thing has fair been ringing.'

I just bet it has. John must have been stunned.

It was Taylor. Taylor? Of course. She had forgotten she had given him her number.

'I called last night but you had it switched off.'

'Yes.'

'I wanted to know if a certain agent – one Otto von Emler – has been in touch.'

'Damn, damn, damn.' She hung up; she would not allow that arrogant man to ruin what had been a perfectly pleasant day. After all, as she looked around the devastation that was her cottage, she figured the plumbers had ruined enough.

No, Holly, this is the breaking eggs bit and there will be an omelette. The telephone rang again while she was in the kitchen.

If it's Taylor and I don't answer he is perfectly capable of coming here.

'Yes?'

'I was out of your hair, Holly, but you had to let the papers have these stories. Mother and I are returning to London next week. She says there is something she wants to tell you.'

'Then you had better have my new number. Long calls on mobiles are so ridiculously expensive, Taylor.'

She heard him suck in his breath. 'Thank you,' he said when he had noted her brand-new number. 'She'll be in touch. I will stay well away but I am toying with the idea of breaking Otto's neck.'

'Don't be silly.'

'One last chance. I give you personally five million dollars and you allow me to keep the paintings in a vault for twenty years. The Hartman Corporation will show them.'

'To whom? A few of your sycophantic rich friends. You can't buy your way out of this one, Taylor.'

This time Taylor was the one who disconnected. She had to get away from the cottage from the echo of his angry voice.

She picked up a sweater from the back of the chair where Blaise used to sit looking at the sea and sat down.

The gentle beauty of the hills, the terrifying awesome beauty of the sea calmed her and focused her mind. First things first. Tony's paintings would be exhibited and not after they had lain in some storage vault for another twenty years. She would go to London to see Mrs Hartman again and she would ask Otto to show her the articles in the foreign press.

Dear God, I have travelled more in the last few months than I have done all my adult life. Sensible really, to be away from the cottage while all the work was going on.

She did not disclose her plans but went in to Otto's galleries on the chance that he would be there. He was.

'Dear Holly.' He came forward and embraced her in the delightful smell of some expensive shaving cream. 'How lovely to see you. I take it this means Taylor is in town.'

'I would like to see the papers, Otto.'

Otto altered the position of an orchid on his desk a fraction of an inch. 'I have them here. Shall I read them to you? British education, so lacking.'

'I can manage the French. You read me the German.'

'It is no fun teasing someone who refuses to react, Holly.' He saw that she was in no mood for idle chatter. 'Very well. Here we are.'

He handed Holly some cuttings from various European papers and she trusted him to translate the German ones correctly. The French she stumbled through but refused to ask his help. All in all, they were more of the pap that had been printed in Britain and America at the time of the exhibition.

'Taylor is going to . . . "break your neck", I think were the words he used.'

'So violent, and it is nothing to do with me. I am sitting here, working hard for all my clients. I have given no interviews that I have not discussed with you, Holly, and remember that I have been in New York. I cannot starve to death while I wait for busy judges to lift the injunction.'

Holly looked at him with equal measures of annoyance and affection. 'You're an old fraud, Otto, but I have warned you that Taylor is angry and now I'm off. Nicole has something important she wants to share. You wouldn't know anything about that, would you? And, Otto, there is just one small detail.'

He looked up expectantly.

'Why didn't you tell me Nicole was a client?'

He did not even look abashed. Otto too had his ideas about loyalty. 'But my clients' names are not mine to bandy about, Holly, not without permission.'

She had arranged to meet Nicole for lunch at the Overseas Club because she was quite sure that Taylor could not follow her in there and because she wanted to return Nicole's hospitality.

They ordered lunch and sat quietly among the other

diners and it was as if Nicole had no idea how to bring up what she wanted to discuss. Holly was content for the moment to allow her to find her own way but eventually she asked, 'Madame, there is a break in the dates of the paintings. The 1950s are not well represented. Have you any idea why there are so few works from that time?'

'You told me that you have no children, Holly,' was the strange answer. 'I managed, with enormous effort, to produce one. I think I would kill for him,' said Nicole simply.

Holly looked at the tiny woman and thought of her son, Taylor, whose physical magnetism made him seem even larger than he was and she smiled.

'You underestimate mother love, Holly.'

'No, perhaps I'm jealous, Madame, firstly that I do not have a child and secondly that I can hardly believe my mother felt as you do. I wish it was otherwise.'

'Tony probably felt for you as I do for my son, especially since . . .'

Holly went cold. 'Yes, Madame.'

'Holly, do the words, *les bébés qui chantent* or *bébés chantants* mean anything to you?'

'I can translate them, Madame.'

'It was a painting; I never saw it but Blaise said it was a masterpiece, like one of those Italian masters, the naked cherubs on the clouds. Tony started to paint it before the war but either she destroyed it or she painted over it.'

'Why?' The question was barely a whisper.

'She had an abortion.'

Although she had already known the answer to her question, the confirmation made Holly feel desperately ill. She was cold and clammy and fought to control her heaving stomach. 'Why?' she managed to hiss.

'*Je ne sais pas* – I don't know. All I know is that Blaise came home and could not sing; he cancelled performances – something he did very rarely – but his voice, it was gone. He did not see her again for years. She had killed his Tosca, he said, his singing baby.'

Holly could bear no more. 'Excuse me.'

She managed to walk in a dignified manner through the tables of happy people and then rushed to the Ladies' room. Luckily it was empty. Nicole joined her there ten minutes later.

'I'm sorry, Holly. I was almost sure that you did not know and deliberated about telling you.'

Holly raised her tear-stained face. '*His* baby, *his* Tosca. My God, what arrogance, what conceit. What about Tony's baby, Tony's pain?' She shook her head wildly as if to drive away the horrifying images that crowded her brain. 'I can't handle how cruel your family is.'

Tentatively Nicole put her arms around the sobbing woman. '*Chérie*, we each look after our own. Blaise and Tony parted, their hearts broken, but we know their love survived. Of course I felt for Tony but at the time I had to succour my brother. Quite frankly I believed, and still do, that to nurture his voice for the world was my duty.'

344

'Everything Tony did was for your precious brother and his precious voice.'

'You cannot believe that she thought to abort would help his voice?'

Holly deflated like a little birthday balloon and she sagged against the slighter woman. 'I don't know. The answers are in the paintings.'

'Could you bear to go again?'

'Where is Taylor?'

Nicole looked surprised by the question. 'At this moment? I have no idea.'

'It's just that I would prefer him not to know that I am here; we parted . . . I don't know; we didn't fight but . . . and then we tend to hang up on one another.'

'You thought he might want to sleep with you? You are afraid of him. He told me.'

Good God, was there anything he did not tell his mother?

'He was hurt, Holly. I think I raised a gentleman.'

Holly could say nothing. Her feelings for Taylor were so confused. Had he said one single word . . .

'I am not afraid of him,' she said lamely but did not add, I am afraid of myself.

Nicole smiled. 'Let us have another private view. You are well?'

Holly, who felt that she would never be well again, acquiesced. This time they looked at the dates of the paintings. It appeared that one had been produced almost every year from the time the pair had met in 1937 till Fougère's death when the last painting had been dated. There were two large gaps: the last years of the war when Tony had sold what she called chocolate-box covers to tourists and when she had started her series of swan paintings, and the years between 1957 and 1962 which Holly now so painfully understood. Invisible and inescapable magnets drew them to the large painting that Nicole had picked out before. On first seeing it, Holly had thought it was a painting of an unsuccessful fisherman in an empty rowing boat. There were no fish, no oars. Holly felt her stomach revolt again as she read the title. *Grief, 1957.* Blaise's sister and Tony's niece viewed the painting of the bowed figure in the rowboat with deeper understanding.

Nicole was obviously thinking along the same lines. 'So much waste: so much tragedy. That one should go to a museum, Holly. I cannot bear to look at it. I feel his grief in my . . .' She did not finish her sentence but pushed her little clenched fists into her belly.

'What about this one, Madame: 1957–1960? Tony worked on it for three years. Is that why it is so different, a new style, and it's not Blaise.'

It was a landscape and had been painted up on the hill behind the cottage. There was the house or a suggestion of the house and a figure – again more of an approximation of a woman than a clearly delineated person – kneeling by the stream with outstretched arms, and on the surface of the water, twisting and turning in the currents, flowers, tiny blue flowers.

'It is, I believe, a companion to *Grief*, Holly, and

should go together. Look, it is Tony's grief. The flowers are forget-me-nots. Those years were hell for him. He ached for Tony and she . . . look at her pain. Men and their stupid pride: their honour. I tried, please, Holly, believe that I tried.'

'I can't take any more, Madame.'

'Of course. Let us see Otto for a moment.'

He was waiting in his pastel palace. 'Mrs Hartman is asking if you know anything about reopening your gallery, Otto.'

Otto smiled and threw out his arms evasively. 'I am content – *pour le moment* – to stay closed, dear ladies. Nothing prevents me from selling my other clients' work, and the interest in the Noble collection is escalating day by day. You will forgive me, Madame, if I say that to close me was not the most astute move the Hartman Corporation has ever made.'

'It is unlike Taylor to think with his heart, Otto. I hadn't realised how much he honoured my brother's memory. Let me remind you, however, that I am still part of the corporation and we did not close you; Taylor did.'

'Water under the bridge, *chère* Madame, water under the bridge,' said Otto expansively.

Nicole stood up and immediately Otto jumped to his feet.

'My car is outside, Holly. Shall I drop you somewhere?'

Holly looked out at the people hurrying or sauntering past. 'No, I think I'll walk, Madame. I'm in no hurry.'

Again that so French salute on both cheeks.

Holly smiled but would not be drawn and soon, having seen Mrs Hartman into her car, she began walking back to her hotel. Her mind was fully engaged with the story of her beloved Tony and the abortion and the knowledge that Blaise Fougère had told his sister of his grief.

Taylor had the audacity to talk to his mother about me. What a family for sharing their woes.

She blushed again as she replayed the scenario of Taylor saying quite baldly, 'She thought I wanted to sleep with her.' The thought of them discussing her, perhaps laughing at her, made her squirm.

Did Tony talk about sex with her mother? I doubt it and I certainly never used the word sex in the same room as my mother. Is Taylor right to be so open with his mother and was I too restrained?

Thinking and thinking as she walked along, Holly could not ever remember discussing anything except schoolwork with either of her parents. The facts of menstruation she had learned messily through experience and she supposed sex was the same. It was not something she had considered until she went to university and then it seemed to be the only thing she ever thought about. She was old enough now and experienced enough to laugh at herself, but she still felt a pang of pity for the young Holly.

What had Taylor said?

'Silly woman thought I wanted to sleep with her. Me?'

Or was it more . . . 'I'm sure she was terrified I was going to rape her. Me?'

However he had said it, the thought made Holly hot and cold at the same time.

Once again the immediate necessity was for flight. She checked out and rushed to Euston station as if something dreadful were pursuing her. Ten hours, two trains and a taxi ride later and she had reached her sanctuary.

At the front door she found Taylor asleep in the back seat of a rather small car.

22

New York, 1963. London, 1963. Torry Bay, 1963
REFUGE FROM THE STORM

'Blaise, why do you put yourself through this?'

He did not answer. He sat on the chair beside Eleanor's bed and he watched her sleep. Asleep she looked almost normal. Watching her sleep her husband could almost forget that she had just tried to kill herself, that it wasn't the first time, and that it was all his fault. He had wanted a baby, a son, a child who would live after him, one who might have his genius or an even greater one. He hadn't thought about that when they were young, when the war had just ended and he had begun to learn to walk down a street without ducking or dodging. All he had thought about then was loving her, forgetting in her the dreams he had had, making new dreams with her. He would be a great tenor; that was Toinette's dream too, so don't think about it, think about it as Eleanor's dream. They would have babies, singing babies, but these babies would not paint. So this dream of the babies was his and Eleanor's and he would forget the cherub with his voice and her mother's talent. He had loved Eleanor because they had told him Tony was dead, and then Tony – so alive, so desirable, so part of his skin, part of his blood, part of his breath – she had murdered his baby and so was dead again to him, and all that was left was the great tenor and this shell who occasionally roused herself enough to try to end it all.

'How amazingly fragile is a human being,' Blaise said and his sister, Nicole, so French, so practical, had looked down at the exquisitely night-gowned form of her sister-in-law and had said, '*Au contraire, mon brave*, as tough as old boots. If she didn't hold on so hard you would be free to marry Toinette.'

He had pushed away her loving hand, had turned his face away.

'Divorce her, Blaise,' Nicole hissed at the broad back that was all she could see. 'She doesn't know. She doesn't care.'

'It's my fault. She feels she failed me by not giving me a child. I will never desert her.'

Eventually he heard the tap-tap of his sister's expensive high-heeled shoes as she gave up and left the private ward. He smoothed the lace ruffles on the nightdress. He had them copied in Paris from her trousseau. She had liked that colour, that style, those falls of exquisite lace. She had been so pretty in her gowns, not desirable, although she had never realised that. Desire was Toinette in his shirt. Toinette in . . . Desire *was* Toinette.

To dress Eleanor in the gowns that had made her feel pretty was a small thing to do.

The nurse was there. 'She'll sleep a while, Mr Fougère. We could call you if there's a change.'

He did not look up. 'I'll stay.'

Tomorrow he had to go to London. He was going to sing *Otello* there for the first time. The thought made him feel sick but the nausea was generated by fear and excitement. He had to go – if Eleanor was well. He would be away for weeks; he would stay with her while he could.

On the plane he studied the score. He did not need to study it. He had been studying it for years but the plane was going to London and if he thought about *Otello* his mind would not be free to think about . . . anything else.

London. He had sung in every major opera house in the world. The Met owned part of his heart, the Paris Opera House another part, but Covent Garden owned his soul, although he was careful never to let Paris or New York know that. Deep down he felt that every great singer thought of Covent Garden as the pinnacle, number one. Vienna, Milan, houses where his knees still trembled as he walked on to their stages, the Metropolitan, Bayreuth, Paris, seductresses all, but Covent Garden . . . Less money, a dressing room that would have been a disgrace if its condition was not so funny, but it was Covent Garden, the only house whose floor he kissed each time he entered it for the first time. Not that anyone saw him. The staff at the Garden were used to singers and their rituals and waited while they visited all their hallowed places and so no one saw him walk on to the stage reverently as if he were in the presence of God, and who is to say he was not, and kiss the stage.

They would have shrugged their shoulders. 'So that's what Fougère does, is it? Who cares?'

He liked walking around London, more difficult now that television was making singers part of popular culture, but he could still walk in the park, the parks that he did not avoid because even his great will was not strong enough to banish the memories. He went to Bond Street and looked in the windows of the exclusive shops and galleries. He began to tremble and leaned against the plate glass for support. The window held one painting: *Flowers in the Stream*.

He recognised the headland, the little shelter where he had been so often with Tony, the stream. He recognised the style, even without looking at the scrawl of a signature. He could see her, a cigarette that she never drew on hanging from her lip, her hair a mess and covered in paint as stress made her constantly touch it. He recognised the tiny figure on the headland and only he in the world knew that he had dealt the blows from which the frail figure cowered as she tossed her little blue flowers into the stream. He could not enter the gallery. He hailed a taxi and went back to his hotel from where he sent Stefan to buy the painting.

'How high should I go?'

And he had looked at his secretary so coldly that Stefan, who was used to unflappable courtesy, had babbled something placatory and hurried out.

He had been almost afraid to return.

'It's not for sale. It's a come-on. Really quite unfair. You may commission from it and there are some nice landscapes.'

'You bought them.'

'No, sir. I thought—'

'I don't pay you to think. Buy them. Use cash. Try again for the *Flowers*. Think of a number, Stefan, and double it. I rely on you.'

Stefan, who had been with him since that first journey from the Old World to the New, was ready to weep when he returned. He had managed to buy one small view of Torry Bay. The others had been sold almost as soon as they had been hung in the gallery. The flowers painting was the artist's personal property and would be taken away at the end of the week. He had, of course, said nothing of the buyer who was interested in the artist's work.'

'When may I have the painting?'

'Saturday, Monsieur. The show ends then.'

He would send Stefan for the painting. No, he would go himself. No, Toinette would be there; he might just see her and the pain in his gut told him he could not cope with that. He no longer loved her, *ça va sans dire*, but there was no point in exposing old wounds.

What did it matter if the wounds were healed?

Of course they were healed but the skin on top of the scab was still painfully thin. He had a rehearsal on Saturday. As usual he was completely prepared and once he was on the stage he thought only of his work. It did not go well. It was the first time he had worn the armour breastplate and it constricted his chest; he could not breathe, never mind sing.

'There is room there for his chest expansion,' fumed the costume designer to the director. 'Chaliapin could get into it.'

'I know it and you know it but he doesn't know it.'

She took it away to adjust it.

He tried again. He felt strangled.

'I can't sing in this breastplate.' He tried to remain calm. He hated fuss of any kind and especially when he was causing it. 'Maybe it's the neckline. Can we lower the neckline?'

'I can lower it all the way to your damned diaphragm and you'll still complain that it can't expand.'

'You wear it yourself and sing Otello,' he shouted at her and stalked off the stage.

Blaise Fougère was not known for his tenor angst. Usually he was calm, he was always prepared and he thanked the staff of the opera house for their work.

'For a tenor he's not difficult,' was what the house staff said and now he had walked off and Hilary Stewart, one of the best designers in the business, was in tears.

The director looked at his Desdemona who was world-famous for her tantrums. She smiled at him sweetly.

'Tenors,' she said demurely. 'Well, I can't make love to the pot plants, darling. Shall we have lunch?'

'Lunch for the principals,' shouted the director and went off in search of his Otello.

He was in a rehearsal room with a *répétiteur*. The 'Exultate', Otello's proud boast as he jumps ashore from his ship, was ringing out again and again and again perfectly.

'You see,' he said, turning to the director. 'I am not difficult. That must be perfect and it is so difficult to get right with no build-up.'

'You were perfect. Could hear it booming out all along the corridor. Let's go across to the pub for a beer and a sandwich and then we'll try it again.'

'It's the armour.'

'Absolutely.'

Blaise took the young pianist's hand and kissed it. 'Thank you, Marian. I was so worried.'

'It's the armour,' she said.

'It's his head,' mouthed the director as he ushered his star out of the studio.

'Blaise, we'll relax, have a beer, come back and try again. Shoots the hell out of the afternoon schedule but heck.'

Blaise sat back in a darkened alcove in the pub and realised that he had managed to avoid having a free afternoon. Had he been free he might just have gone to Otto's gallery to pick up Toinette's painting. No, ridiculous, the armour constricted his chest expansion. They had no idea how difficult it was to sing the 'Exultate' cold. Let them try it. He had proved it was the armour. The original Moor of Venice didn't have to hit a note like that when he jumped off a ship. He sat up smiling and refused the offer of a beer. He needed nothing to relax him and if he did it would not be warm British beer.

Toinette. He could smell her. He looked around wildly but there was no one remotely like her in the pub. It was in his head. He was always relaxed with Toinette. One word soothed his tension, one touch . . .

'Do they have avocados? I had the best sandwich in San Francisco last season, avocado, bean sprouts, tomato.' He kissed his fingers.

'You'll have to go back to California, *mon ami*,' said the director, and they both laughed. 'I hate English bread though, don't you?'

Mrs Lumsden and her home-baked bread. Mrs Lumsden dead in the war. 'Some is fine,' he said quietly. 'This is bearable. When I've finished I'll buy some flowers for Hilary. She had my measurements wrong, yes, but it will be perfect now. *Pauvre petite*, I am sure she is, at this very moment, working hard.'

Yannis smiled. No way would he tell the tenor that Hilary was spending her lunch break eating yoghurt while she stuck pins in a full-length picture of Blaise Fougère. No prizes for where most of them were going.

The soprano walked off the stage in the afternoon.

'Your tenor is deliberately upstaging me, and in the love duet, which is so crucial for me, so important, he's making sure the audience can't see my face.'

She refused to come back unless Blaise apologised.

Blaise was intransigent. '*Non*. Call any soprano in the world, they'll say I never upstage. Besides, I'm not hiding her pretty little face. How can I when I'm beside her? Get her cover in. That will bring her out here so *rapidement*.'

The strategy served merely to have the soprano's manager call in her lawyers.

'Please, Blaise. I'm on my knees,' begged Yannis.

'Then get off them. This is ridiculous. I shall sing "*Gia Nella Notte*" with little Miss Sofrani, and I shall sing full voice. I may even kiss her, gently yet lingeringly, as we walk off stage to Otello's "Paradise". Yes, I will. I will then walk past Madama's dressing room telling the world how exquisite is the Sofrani and how thrilled I am that she is to have this chance. Then I am going to the gym.'

Hilary showed how grateful she was for his apology by slipping into the weeping soprano's dressing room and managing to suggest that 'your bloody tenor has the hots for Sofrani, Madama. Don't let him get away with chasing you off.'

Capitulation, not one hundred per cent gracious but capitulation.

'Admit that you did upstage me just a teeny-weeny bit, Blaise darling. I'm sure you didn't mean it and Yannis will just mark where you stand' – she stood quietly while the exasperated director made incomprehensible chalk marks on the floor – 'and now everything will be wonderful.'

It was, of course, because her voice was exquisite, she was beautiful, and she could act. A director is usually thrilled if the voice is there, but all three in a Desdemona is a gift from the gods.

Then the rehearsal was over and it was still only four fifteen and he had forgotten to tell Stefan to pick up the picture. He wanted to go to the gym. He needed exercise.

He walked to the gallery. The doors were still unlocked but the gallery appeared empty. The flowers painting was gone and a new group of canvasses were up on the pale walls.

'May I help you, sir?' He had not heard the gallery owner approach across the miles of deep carpeting.

'I bought a painting,' he began.

Otto von Emler clapped his hands together reverently. 'Monsieur Fougère, what an incredible honour.' The very young, very effeminate man spoke perfect French. 'So you are the real Mr Lazlo. I wondered . . . I was about to close the gallery but he paid cash, you see, and I thought he might have been caught in traffic.'

'Stefan Lazlo is my secretary. May I have the painting?'

'Of course and . . . yes, I hoped so.' He broke off as he looked over Blaise's shoulder. 'Tony, my dear, one of your admirers.'

Tony was standing in the doorway. When Blaise turned, she went quite white and grabbed the door handle again as if for support. She turned as if to leave but stopped.

Blaise took a step forward and then he too stopped. 'Toinette,' he said.

Otto looked from one to the other and many things became quite clear to him. 'I'll just wrap your picture,

Mr Fougère,' he said, but he knew that his customer neither knew nor cared what he was saying.

Tony had turned again, in control. 'Hello, Blaise. What a coincidence.'

'*Flowers in the Stream*,' he said. 'I saw it. Oh, God, forgive me, Toinette, forgive me.'

'Please,' she whispered, 'please don't do this to me. Take your picture and go.'

She turned again but he reached the door before she was able to get out. 'Toinette, I've never stopped thinking of you for a moment,' he heard himself babbling. 'I saw the picture, Tony. It's you. I know what it means.'

'It means you hurt me seven years ago; almost as much, I suppose, as I hurt you. But the girl in the painting no longer exists. You don't have to feel sorry for her. She's fine.'

'But I'm not, Toinette. I feel sorry for me.'

'That's good,' she said coldly. 'The catch in the voice . . . use that in *Otello*.'

She pulled away from him and ran out and he was too stunned to follow her.

Otto, who had watched everything through the glass walls of his office, came out, essaying a smile. 'I've wrapped the painting, Monsieur. A little gem. I wish she would sell *Flowers in the Stream* or other work like it, but it's just the landscapes she does for sale, and her swans.'

His distinguished customer said nothing. He was still staring at the door.

'I have one of the swans in my private office, Monsieur.'

Blaise put up his hand. Otto had seen it raised like that so often on the stage, a graceful gesture. 'Don't intrude,' it said.

He intruded. 'I don't want to sell it to you, Monsieur le Ténor, but I do think you should look at it. Please.'

Blaise looked at him and Otto saw the desolation in his eyes. 'You really ought to see it, sir.'

Blaise went with him.

The painting was small. Blaise recognised the bay and the headland. The composition was that of a picture postcard or even a holiday snap. Scottish scenery, view one. In the bay, but heading for the shore, was a swan, a magnificent and very beautiful bird. There was a tiny blur of gold just above its proud head, almost a smudged finger mark. Did the artist mean it? His heart, which had seemed to stop beating when Tony had left, began to race. He leaned forward and laughed. How did she do it? Close up, the little blur became a crown. He looked at Otto and smiled.

'Once she called it Lohengrin,' Otto said. 'When I asked her she said, "It's just a swan." But I don't think it's just a swan. *Au revoir*, Monsieur Fougère. Enjoy your painting.'

Blaise picked up his picture and tucked it under his left arm. Then he held out his hand and Otto shook hands with him.

'It's an honour, Monsieur,' he said and Blaise knew

that he was not referring to the successful sale of a small painting.

In the street he looked for Tony but he knew that he would not find her. He knew where she would be. Not tonight, and he could not get there anyway, but one day soon . . . He almost skipped to the edge of the pavement to hail a taxi. When he got back to his hotel he took the little painting and propped it up on his dressing-table. He touched the headland delicately.

'Don't touch, don't touch. There's oil on your fingers.'

'I know, *ma mie*, I know.'

Forgive me, Toinette.

Otello was a triumph. It had to be recorded. It had to be televised for future showing. His work was always his number one priority but he had to get away. He had to. At last he looked at his schedule, so carefully crossed and recrossed by the meticulous Stefan, and there were two whole days.

'I'm going to Scotland.'

'Very good, sir.'

'If I said I'm going to Mars, would you say, "Very good, sir," Stefan?' he teased the unflappable secretary.

'Probably, but I might just ask *how*. I'll reserve a car.'

On the plane he fretted. He must not read anything into her painting of the swan as the legendary Lohengrin. It was an artist's joke, no more. It did not mean that she hoped one day to see her love arrive on the wings of a princely swan to save her from all evil. She hated him. But then she had known he was to sing

Otello. If she hated him, would she still be aware of his schedule? She liked music. No doubt she had asked the Garden for a schedule of their forthcoming productions just as countless other opera lovers did. He would arrive in Torry Bay and she would not be there.

He arrived in Torry Bay and she was not there.

Until the moment he saw the cottage he had believed deep down that she would be waiting for him, ready to listen, to allow him to beg, and then to give him another chance. It was raining slightly and the cottage looked forlorn, unloved. The door was closed, the windows looked empty, bereft, abandoned, and just as he was sure he now looked. How foolish to come all this way in the middle of a difficult production. He had saved his pride though. No one but Stefan knew that he had made a fool of himself. He got back into the hired car and started the engine but he sat for a time looking at the cottage where he had been unbelievably happy and where he had suffered the worst pain. Or was that unfair to Eleanor? They had suffered pain together, the aborted babies, her insanity.

'Oh, Toinette, I need you so.'

The rain had stopped and the sun was already trying to dry the grasses. He turned off the engine and got out of the car. One last look from the headland. Perhaps the swan prince would sail across the bay to take Lohengrin back to the knights of the Holy Grail.

Dear God, it was beautiful. Until this moment he had not understood that Torry Bay as well as Toinette had become a part of him. At least he had the little picture.

He would carry it everywhere with him, another eccentricity like the pillow he took to every hotel knowing that he could not sleep if it was not there. He looked at the hollow.

'Love me, Toinette.'

'We are so close to the cottage.'

'I can't wait.'

He had to get away from here. In another second he would be sobbing like a child. He held up his hand, as he had done countless times on stages all over the world.

Goodbye, was what that graceful gesture said. The fans knew he would not return, no matter how they called and clapped, once he had held his hand up like that.

She was standing beside his car, an overnight bag at her feet. She looked up and saw him. He began to walk towards her, slowly, fearful of rejection. When he was closer he saw the expression in her eyes and he began to run.

He did not deserve her. He did not deserve her love, her compassion, her giving. She gave and gave and gave and never seemed to resent the unfairness of the giving. He knew it, he understood it, but he could not find the words in any of his languages.

'Toinette. Toinette.' He could not go on. All he could do was hold her, kiss her cheeks, her hair, her lips, anything he could reach.

'It's all right,' she said. 'I understand. *Je comprends, ma mie. Ma mie.*'

Ma mie. She had never ever called him that, or once

maybe, before the war. He held her, looked deep into her eyes and on the pebbled path he fell to his knees, his hands sliding down her painfully thin body until he was clasping her around the knees. He pushed his head against her belly, against the womb from which she had in physical and mental agony expelled his child, their baby, their singing cherub, and he wept. As always, she lifted him up, and comforted him.

'It's all right. I understand. *Je comprends. Je t'aime*, Blaise. I have never stopped loving you.'

'A baby,' he began. 'It was so . . .' He could not go on and stayed, his head against her stomach, feeling her softness, her warmth, smelling her special smell, that mixture of soap and paint and turpentine and fresh air that was his essential Toinette.

'I was wrong, Toinette, so wrong, and I have paid.'

She tried to pull him up. 'It's over and you're here. I was wrong too and I have paid. We have each of us paid, *ma mie*, but now . . . if you love me, we can go on.'

'I am nothing without you, Toinette. I am technique without warmth, an automaton. They say, des Grieux, Cavaradossi, Rodolfo, and I perform, but I am a man without a heart, Toinette. I left it here.'

'But you had mine, my dear. You always had mine.'

He stood up awkwardly, and she stood in the shadow of his body enjoying that once well-known feeling of belonging.

'There is no wine.'

'I brought nothing.'

She lost herself in his beautiful eyes. 'You brought yourself.'

'Which is nothing without Toinette.'

They turned, arm in arm, and walked slowly towards the cottage.

'Don't tell me how long,' she pleaded as they went upstairs.

'If you say it will be for ever.'

She said nothing but held his hand more tightly as they reached their old room and turned towards each other, their flesh burning as it had burned with un-fulfilled longing when they were younger.

He was gentler than he had ever been and more passionate, but this time, this time it was he who, at the moment of fulfilment, moaned, 'I am dying.'

Tony began to paint *Refuge from the Storm* while his plane was still in the air.

She painted their beloved headland: she painted the sky as it too often was in their little bay, glowering and lowering. She painted the seas, grey and whipped up by the winds that did not play but sought to cause havoc, and she painted Lohengrin and his extended family as they returned for shelter to the bay.

But on the headland she painted . . . yes, two figures, a man and a woman. The man held the woman in his arms, her head against his chest, his broad shoulders protecting her frail figure from the winds that raced in from the sea. He was her refuge. She lost herself in him and she never appreciated that hers was the strength that allowed him to cope with his life, which gave him the stamina to work, to study, and to be what he was. She had looked up *mie* in a French dictionary. *Crumb*. An endearment, she supposed. Her first French teacher had told her the French said '*mon petit choux*', my little cabbage, to those they loved. She assumed my little crumb meant much the same thing and only towards the ends of their lives did she understand exactly what she meant to him.

23

---◆---

Torry Bay, 1999

He was the last person in the world she wanted to see.
She had cried long despairing tears on the journey from
London, embarrassed when people near her either
moved away assuming she was drunk or offered to
help her.

'You want a cup of tea, Miss?'

The English and their tea.

No, I want Tony alive, married to Blaise and a
mother of all those *bébés chantants*. Had she shouted
that, they would really have thought her plastered or
crazy, crazy like poor Eleanor.

Now when she needed two aspirin and a hot bath,
there was Taylor, come to say what?

'Would you like to have dinner with me, Holly?'

Someone around here is crazy.

She stared at him stupidly. 'Dinner?'

'Yes, you know, soup and meat and two veggies and
dessert if you've been good.'

Anger came to her assistance. 'How did you get here,

you lunatic? Are you stalking me?' Taylor Hartman who did not like her at all seemed to pop up like a Jack-in-the-box.

He laughed. 'Don't be melodramatic. My mother told me you had lunch and that you went to see the paintings again. She told me you were at your club. They told me you had checked out. I broke every law in London getting to the station and still missed the blasted train. I thought all trains in this darn country were supposed to be late.'

Despite the headache that was threatening to lift the top of her skull right off she managed a smile. She looked at him and tried to focus. 'How did you get here?'

'This new thing, invented by an American; it's called the airplane.'

She was seeing three of him. None of them looked good. 'You're insane,' she said and immediately regretted her choice of words. 'I'm sorry; it's just that it's been a really shitty day.'

'A drink would help.'

'I really don't think I can face you tonight, Taylor.' She turned and walked away from him towards the cottage.

Once inside the tears began to flow again. God in heaven, get a grip, Holly.

She reached the cool, dark haven of her single room and lay down fully clothed on the bed. She was just drifting off to sleep when someone knocked on the door.

He couldn't. He wouldn't. Surely he doesn't think he's so irresistible.

'Go away,' she said furiously.

'Room service.'

She opened the door. Taylor stood there with a tray. On it there was a cup of something that steamed and a small foil-wrapped packet. Silently she stood aside to let him enter the room and put the tray down. He said nothing but left as quietly as he had come.

I don't want to like Taylor.

Hours later her new telephone rang. She was conscious of a warm glow of expectation low in the pit of her stomach as she hurried across the floor.

'We have to talk, Holly.'

'Where are you?'

'In that little inn where we had lunch: they took pity on a benighted foreigner. I explained that you had thrown me out and that I was too big to sleep in this dinky little car.'

'Thank you for telling my neighbours that, Taylor. All I want to know from you is when you are going to have the court order lifted?'

'I can't.'

'Today – yesterday – I found out that your precious uncle was a first-class bastard who put my aunt through hell. You knew about the abortion, didn't you?'

She heard him gasp. 'Abortion? It's not true. I can't believe it. He was—'

'So full of his career and his image that he let my aunt abort their baby and then he dumped her. Goodbye,

Taylor.' She slammed the receiver down, stood silently for a moment and then returned to her room and lay down.

When did it become easier? When did those women with their obvious flawless serenity achieve it? Did they just wake up one morning and spend the rest of their lives never putting a foot wrong, always saying the right thing, and walking elegantly in and out of each social occasion? Other people seemed to manage. Why couldn't Holly Noble get it right? Damn it all: there were books for everything these days but nowhere had she seen the title that promised the reader inner knowledge. Inner peace was promised in abundance: do yoga, burn candles, even soak in a hot bath. There lay inner peace, but when your whole life was turned upside down on its head all you got in a hot bath was clean, and maybe dry skin.

This last thought made Holly laugh and she got up, walked downstairs and opened the door to let the peace of Achahoish permeate the cottage. She went out and walked out to the point and looked at the bay that still lay wrapped in night. She turned and looked back at the cottage and saw the moon reach up behind the stone walls, setting fire to the roof, the chimney stacks, the rhododendron bushes. How unruly they were becoming. Tony had always kept them well cut back. They took what they wanted, rhododendrons, unless the gardener was very firm with them.

Suddenly exhaustion so intense it was almost tangible wrapped her in its folds and she struggled back to the cottage, climbed the stairs and fell face down on her little-girl bed. She woke six hours later furious, as she always was when she fell asleep without washing, and wished that she had found time to clean her teeth.

The front door stood wide open and two sheep were in the living room. One black face stared at her unconcernedly from where she lay demolishing the rug before the fire and the other presented a fine rear view as she stood with front hoofs up on the table. She had eaten a sizeable piece of the red and white checked gingham cloth and would no doubt have eaten the rest of it had her hostess not disturbed her. She dropped down, whirled round and skittered out the door, scattering black droppings widely in her wake.

'Oh, damn you, sheep,' yelled Holly and the other ewe jumped up and galloped after her sister.

'Not a job I relish on an empty stomach,' complained Holly as she seized the broom and swept the sheep's gift out of the door.

By the time she had made some coffee she was laughing. 'I wonder what Taylor would have done?'

She could picture him, tall, broad, oh so masculine.

'Damn it all; I don't care what he would have done.'

She took the coffee to the table, scooped up the remains of the tablecloth and threw it in the wastebasket. Then she realised that the sheep had come in not only because the door was open but because the Reids had not been there.

She rang the Reids' office.

'No point in coming, Missus. That was the wrong

bath that came. We should have the new one some time next week.'

Providence. Suddenly Holly felt like leaping in the air like the startled sheep. Her decision to remodel completely had been wrong.

'Just as well, Mr Reid. I've decided to keep the old iron one. I like its toenails. Will you please just do everything else around it.'

'It's your bathroom, Missus.'

It surely is, agreed Missus.

She made some coffee, closed the door and walked with her coffee to the point. On her way back, refreshed and reinvigorated, she saw the little red van belonging to the local postman turn off the road and crawl down to Torry Bay.

There were letters from London, Glasgow and Edinburgh. Mr Gilbert had sold several pieces for her and told her she needed to speak to a financial consultant about the best way to handle the money. Very nice. She would tell the financial wizard that quite a bit of her money would be needed to pay the Reids. The people who were buying her flat wanted it complete with furniture. Holly experienced a slight pang. So many hopes and dreams had gone into the purchasing and furnishing of her home. She squared her shoulders. Torry Bay was now her home and when the alterations were finished she would have fun painting her newly centrally heated cottage sunshine yellow. She had painted nothing in her entire life – not since her aborted attempts as a child with Tony: 'We'll find your talent, darling girl' – but surely she could slap paint on a bare wall. It would be a lovely summer project for the new Holly Noble.

Otto wanted to know her feelings about holding the paintings in storage. He was in his office.

'I lunched with Mrs Hartman before she flew back to New York; she says her son is still adamant about refusing to allow us to sell. Wants to compromise, I believe.'

'Yes, I should have told you. He wants to hide the paintings for twenty years. Then they could be exhibited, but I've decided I'm not prepared to wait. I want to see Tony's name in lights.'

'Even if it means completely alienating Taylor?'

'Why on earth should you think that his opinion matters to me at all?'

He laughed. 'Dear Holly,' he said and hung up.

Later Holly took her favourite long walk along the coast and her thoughts kept pace. John still refused to take his rejection seriously. He had decided magnanimously that she needed 'time to come to your senses'. Men.

She turned and looked back at the cottage. In the early evening dusk the light from the lamp she had left on in the living room shone with a friendly welcome. Her heart filled with emotion.

I'm happy.

Life was not perfect but it was damned good. Was it the cottage that had seen deep love, appalling tragedy and grief? The echoes of the tragedies were long since gone. All that remained in the old stone walls was the memory of all-encompassing love. Did its ghosts welcome her return as the little light did? She hurried back, relishing the idea of going home, home. What a beautiful word. Soon we'll be centrally heated and modern. There is nothing now that I lack.

Darling girl.

I can manage. Mr Right would be nice but I can manage.

Don't think, Holly, just relax.

She would paint the cottage and when she was bored she would walk on the beach and collect shells; she would light a fire and sit before its flickering warmth, reading. She could almost smell security.

A car was parked outside the cottage.

Please don't let it be the plumbers.

It was much worse. It was Taylor.

'Go away.'

He stood waiting for her to open the cottage. For a few minutes she stood looking at him. 'I'm not leaving, Holly, not till you explain. I called my mother. "Holly's right," she says. My uncle wanted children. Open the door or do we stand and yell at one another right here?'

She walked away from him and opened the door of the cottage. 'I have no intention of yelling at you, Taylor. I'm tired . . .'

'I'll wait.'

It was no use. She gave in. She walked before him into the cottage.

Hollyberry. Darling girl.

375

She smiled. 'Open the shutters while I make some coffee,' she said. 'You will need it.'

He did as he was bid and then sat looking out of the window at the sea. Idly he played with the stones. Holly 1964, Holly 1972. 'Cute,' he said and he smiled but his eyes were sad.

She put two mugs of coffee on the table. 'There's nothing to eat,' she said ungraciously and this time he smiled with his eyes too.

'I know your erratic housekeeping. I brought your supper, the one you wouldn't have with me last night. I even brought the wine.'

'I'm not having supper with you.'

'Whyever not?' he asked. 'Even the condemned man gets a last meal.' He picked up a mug of coffee and went back to the window. She could not see his eyes. 'Holly, my mother says you are right but I know my uncle would never have encouraged abortion. I know it.'

He turned. His posture reminded her . . . Blaise, of course; he looked like Blaise, the tall, muscled body, the casually worn expensive clothes. Only the eyes were different. She dropped her head and then raised it again and looked at him. 'Whether he spelled it out or wrote the cheque for the doctor's bill or did nothing doesn't matter. He let it happen.'

He sank down onto the window seat. 'He didn't know, Holly. If he knew, why *Grief?* Why Tony's masterpiece?'

That thought had not occurred to her. 'All right. He did not tell Tony to abort but it looks like she was so crazy about him, so anxious that he should not ruin his first Wagner, that she dared not tell him. The great tenor must not be disturbed. She loved him so much that . . .' She was crying again, nothing feminine and sweet, but great choking sobs that tore at her throat, red-hot tears that scalded her eyes as they flooded down to fill her mouth with salt. 'I hate him,' she sobbed. 'I hate him.'

Hollyberry. Hollyberry.

He was holding her and she stood held in the circle of his arms and felt his heart beat as she tried to slap him, slap him. 'There, there,' he said like a father holding a child, and she stopped fighting and lay quietly against him until her sobbing dropped to an occasional hiccup. 'I hate him,' she said on a sigh.

Darling girl.

She had stopped crying but still he held her. 'It doesn't matter what you feel, it's what Tony felt.'

'I know but sometimes I feel . . . oh, I feel sometimes as if I'm Tony, . . . as if I'm experiencing her pain.' She looked up at him and the eyes that looked down were Blaise's eyes. They did not mock or taunt but were calm and clear and gentle. 'I don't mean – really think I'm Tony – damn it, it's so hard to explain. It was 1957, Taylor. God only knows who did it, how appalling it must have been, how dangerous, and it was against the law too.' The frustration, horror and anger that had been building up remorselessly sought relief in explosion. 'As a good Catholic I suppose he didn't believe in divorce. Why did he let it happen, Taylor? Why did Tony believe it was what he would want?'

She could sense his tension. He seemed to draw inwards inside himself and it was almost as if he were no longer standing there with her. Had his uncle used this phenomenal self-control in his work? 'We can only learn so much by looking at the paintings. I thought I knew Blaise: you thought you knew Tony. We did and we didn't. Let it go. We're not going to find out all the truths. You're reading things into the paintings that aren't there, things you want to see to support your belief in this great love affair.'

'Which you believe in, deep down, and your bruised little ego and family pride won't let you admit to.'

'For God's sake, Holly, she can paint. Okay, I admit she was a great painter. Now, let's walk along the beach.' He let her go and she was almost embarrassed that she had stayed in his arms so long. What must he be thinking?

'You won't think much of this beach; there's very little sand.'

'This is neat,' he said ten minutes or so later. 'Shall I pick up a stone and write Taylor, 1999, or wouldn't your John like that?'

'It's not his business any more.' She avoided his eyes and walked quickly. She wanted to tell him that she was free and she could not get the words out. 'There was a painting the world will never see. *Les Bébés qui Chantent.*'

He looked down at her, puzzled. 'Singing babies?'

'She painted their babies waiting on clouds to be born. They were all singing and painting but we can't find it.'

'Maybe she painted over it. Maybe Otto will be able to tell, but look, they're not dead; they just haven't been born yet. Look, see that cloud.'

She looked up. There were clouds in the sky, not the puffy white clouds of Tony's paintings but pale grey just kissed by the pale pink light from the evening summer sun.

There were no seraphim.

'See,' he said, pointing. 'There, on the pink cloud, that sassy little one is painting streaks on her brother's ass.'

This was an unexpected side to Taylor Fougère Hartman and his silliness allowed Holly to pull herself together. 'Do you usually go crazy on Scottish beaches?'

'Only when there's no sand.'

They walked on quietly for a few minutes.

'Holly, my mother says Blaise lost his voice completely in 1957. He only regained it when I was born in 1959. Maybe it was the abortion; maybe he was ashamed of leaving Tony, if he did leave her. There's that painting *Grief*. That's 1957. If he was gone, how could she have painted him?'

'Memory. She saw him sitting in the rowboat.'

'He was planning to row to the States?'

'I don't know what he was doing in the blasted boat. He was in it, that's all I know. You're trying to make me say *Grief* wasn't painted from life so the other paintings are made up.' She turned away from him and began to hurry back down the beach towards the point. Shit. Every time she thought he was human he said or did something to prove her wrong.

His legs were so long he didn't even need to break into a trot to catch up with her. 'Holly. Pax, please. Let's eat and then we'll sleep on it and talk again in the morning.'

'Eat. Sleep. You're unreal, Taylor. Go away.'

She walked on and could hear him, almost feel him, following on behind. They arrived at the cottage together.

'You should put geraniums in those window boxes. Look great all summer.'

'Doesn't start here till about July.'

'Heck, that should give you two whole months of flowers.'

'Pax, Taylor. We'll eat and then I am going to bed and when I wake up, you will be gone.'

'Fine. White wine or red?'

'I don't care.' Her voice was shriller than she meant it to be.

'Then we'll have red. The white will be hot, sitting in the car for hours.'

The food looked delicious. Holly thanked Taylor. He cut into his quiche. 'Hot food is great, don't you think?'

She laughed. 'Do you hate cold quiche?'

'Hate's too strong a word. Detest is good.'

'I have an oven, you know,' said Holly, picking up their plates.

He followed her into the tiny kitchen. 'I was scared to suggest it.'

'I bet.'

Once again the atmosphere had changed. If she could forget Tony and her sorrow she could like Taylor.

Hollyberry.

You stay out of it.

They ate warm quiche washed down by a delicious claret, followed by pastry that stayed like a snowflake on the lips for a second and then dissolved and was gone, leaving only a lovely memory. They talked only about Holly's plans for the cottage but stayed at the table long after the light had faded. Neither seemed to want to shatter the dusk with the garishness of electric light. Taylor talked about his years at Oxford University where, he said seriously, his heart had been well and truly broken, but if that was true, he seemed now to remember only fun and laughter. He moved to pour more wine into their glasses and then changed his mind and put the bottle behind him on the sideboard.

'Better not, I think.'

Holly stood up. 'I'll wash up.'

'You heated the quiche.'

She laughed and looked at him.

Big mistake, Holly.

She felt herself swaying. No, impossible. Two glasses of wine. What else could intoxicate?

His fingers very lightly stroked her cheek. 'I'll clear up.'

Still she stood unable to move and his hand slipped from her cheek and she was in his arms. His lips, warm, soft, were on hers, and his arms were around her. She responded to him and the demands of his mouth grew stronger, bolder. She was drowning and she had to hold on to him. She felt flames that she had thought dead spring into life and she crushed herself closer to him, for only he could quench the flames. His tongue parted her lips; she felt her whole body melt.

He let her go so abruptly that she almost stumbled. 'Forgive me, Holly.'

She tried to be nonchalant as the blood that was hurling itself around her body began to slow down and behave itself. She could not speak.

'You go up first. I'll wash up.' And so that she was left in no doubt that he did not intend to join her he said, 'Goodnight, Holly.'

She stumbled up the stairs and hurried into the bathroom and as quickly as possible got out again and hid herself in her virginal little room.

Had she thrown herself at him?

No, we were in that together, weren't we?

Tony.

I'm here, darling girl.

Comforted, Holly undressed and crept into bed. She lay there and listened to the sounds Taylor was making in the kitchen. He was, she was pleased to note, not laughing. At last the sounds she had dreaded. He was coming up the stairs.

'Holly.'

What should she do, say?

'I want you very much, Holly. Downstairs I was so ready to seduce you.' He laughed a little. 'There's no place big enough in that room for seduction. I even thought of carrying you upstairs. The blasted staircase is too small: had I bent over I would have banged your head against the damned wall: stand up straight and I hit my own head off the roof. The thing is, Holly . . . if you were any of the other women I have ever wanted it would be over by now but I find myself thinking, Love? Lust? It's this damned cottage; there's some strange kind of atmosphere. Probably damp. I don't know whether you're sweetly asleep but I'm taking a rain-check. *Le coeur a ses raisons que la raison ne connaît pas.* That's Blaise, but Blaise Pascal this time. Whatever is between us is not over. Remember what I said: "It's not over till the fat lady sings." Goodnight.'

He was gone and she sat up, her heart pounding, and looked at the door. The French had been too fast for her to understand; something about the heart having its own reasons – whatever that meant.

She heard him walk across the landing and again stand for a long time in his room. At last she heard the creaking of the old springs and then nothing until the early summer sun played on her eyelids and forced her awake.

She would pretend it had never happened. 'I hope my plumbers turn up today,' she said. 'Plumbers never come when you're waiting for them.'

'Serves you right for hiding yourself in the boonies.

But, boy, do you need a good plumber.' Maybe he was remembering his scalding hot bath.

The exhibition? There had to be an exhibition, no matter what happened or did not happen between her and Taylor, because Tony mattered, Tony who was dead and who had asked her, from the grave, to show her work.

'Taylor? The exhibition?'

'Sell me the paintings. I'll double my offer. You can build a house someplace with big enough walls for the ones you want to keep.'

'They want them exhibited now.'

'God, you're talking to those ghosts again.'

How could she ever have imagined that she might . . . yes, admit it, Holly, love him. Holly, the genius, has done it again. Backed a loser and this time with eyes wide open so there was no excuse.

'You'd better go.'

He got up immediately. 'Don't throw out the bath with the painted toes. I have plans for that bath.'

She looked up at him tremulously but he was smiling, an open friendly smile.

'Remember that fat soprano.'

He bent swiftly and kissed her fiercely on the lips and then he turned and walked out of the cottage.

24

———◆———

Torry Bay, 1965
CLOVER

'Come on, Blaise, just a little farther.'

'What do you want me to see?' He was laughing. Always she wanted just a little more exercise. The view from the next hill was just that bit better. He wanted to sit down in the grass and look at Toinette. So soon he would be in Vienna, then Buenos Aires, then . . . no, better not to think, better to go and see what there was to see from the top of the next hill. Water, of course, more hills, strawberry clover and common clover, some of its heads already turning pinkish, and rose bay willow herb. That was a new one; she did not remember it from her childhood. Blaise had seen it in Europe.

'It came here in the bombs, I think.'

'Don't be silly. Nothing nice ever came out of a bomb.'

'Then, Mam'selle so clever, tell me why it is all over ruined streets?'

She had no answer and so ignored the question and

walked on, and he smiled quietly and followed. 'My favourite role,' he said to himself, 'to follow my Toinette wherever she leads.'

They had been together for two glorious days and still he found his heart contracting at the sound and sight and smell of her. Why? She was not beautiful. Eleanor was beautiful, but Tony had . . . something. A *je ne sais quoi* . . .

Already she was over the top of the next hill, standing in the midst of a sea of flowers. 'Stand here,' she ordered, and she was the painter again. 'If I can capture the blues . . . look around you, Blaise. It's so beautiful, it hurts.'

So it is, he agreed silently but he was looking at Tony.

He did as he was told and stood half turned to the sea. Does she even realise I am me? he wondered as he watched her work. Am I just her subject, the right height, weight, colouring?

Then she smiled at him slowly, the smile creeping down from her eyes to her mouth and he knew the answer. Her mouth. He would concentrate on her mouth.

She forgot him again as she swiftly sketched the lines that would later become one of her most sought-after paintings and Blaise stood and enjoyed the picture of concentration.

She is so like me in the way she works, he decided. The concentration is total; she is aware of nothing but her art.

He was having trouble holding his pose because he

could feel something crawling up his right leg. He did not dare look down but squirmed inwardly as some little creature reached the back of his knee.

'Toinette, *s'il te plaît*,' he begged. 'There is an ant crawling up my leg and it's drive me crazy.'

'In a second,' she began. 'For heaven's sake, Blaise. Oh, you have ruined it.'

'*Merde*,' swore Blaise and he began to claw at his trouser leg. 'I'm sorry, Toinette, but it's bitten me.' He hauled his trouser leg up as far as he could but was unable to get it past his knee.

Tony was laughing. 'Poor little boy,' she teased. 'Bitten by a little creepy-crawly. Will I kiss it better for you? Try to get back into that position, sweetheart.'

He tried but he was uneasy. He had the feeling that the field around him was crawling with hungry insects all heading for his bare legs. Was he a baby as she teased? How dare she say such things? He would stand and be the subject and he would be very cool all evening and she would have to win her way back into his, what did she call them, good books.

'*Je regrette*,' he began formally and then switched to English. She said she would learn French as she had said she would learn to drive, but she forgot everything when she was painting. 'I feel strange, Tony. I'm sorry about the picture and the light and your blues but I want to go home.'

To go home. He was calling the cottage *home*. It was his home and she would keep it like that, the place where he could be safe and sound and bad-tempered over nothing as he was being now. She looked at him. She did not like what she saw.

'Blaise.' She did not finish but dropped her pad and her charcoal and ran to him across the clover. 'What is it? Let's look at the bite.'

Blaise began to hop around trying to take off his trousers. 'I feel strange,' he whispered. 'I need to see.'

'Blaise, Blaise, my darling, let me help.' She eased his jeans down over his hips. 'It's just a little sting, darling. Look, can you see? It's on the back of your knee and it is a little red, maybe an inch, not much, nothing to worry about.'

'*Bien.*' He tried to smile. 'A little bite and I am a baby but I can't pose more.'

'No, we'll go home, Blaise, and it will be fine.' She put her slim arm around his waist and he leaned on her as they began to walk back to the cottage. She could see that the sweet-smelling clover was alive with bees. It was a beautiful picture. Such beauty to hold such terror. A bee must have stung him. She did not dare ask if he knew whether or not he was allergic; surely if he was there would be a much more livid swelling of the entry wound. Of course there would be. It was nothing. He was a singer and singers were all paranoid about their health. He would be fine.

They walked on. Why had she demanded just one more view?

He was leaning on her more and more heavily. 'I feel dizzy, Toinette and with nerve, like before I sing.'

'With nerve.' He was panicking. She had to keep him calm. 'We are almost there. Everything will be fine.'

He clutched at his chest and then he let go of her and began to scratch his arms, his chest, his face. 'It's so itchy and my chest. It's tight, and my neck . . .'

Tony turned to him and she suppressed a gasp as she saw that his face and neck were beginning to swell. 'Can't breathe,' he gasped. 'Can't breathe.'

What on earth was she to do? They were miles from the village. She put her arms round him and held him as if her puny strength could defeat whatever it was that was attacking him. She had to keep him quiet. He must not be allowed to panic. 'Blaise, try to keep calm.' Dear God, he was sweating and he was beginning to tremble as if he were cold. How could he be hot and cold at the same time? 'We are almost there. You'll be safe at the cottage while I go for Simon. Look, look, *ma mie*, hold on, *ma mie*, we are home.'

They stumbled together across the shore and into the cottage and he half fell onto the settee. She pulled a chair up to take the weight of his long legs that hung over the side. Shock. Tea. Should she make him a cup of tea? Better to go for Simon. She ran upstairs and pulled the bedcover off and carried it downstairs. 'Sing *Fidelio*,' she ordered as she wrapped him up. 'All the parts. Go through it all very calmly. I will be back with Simon long before you get to Florestan's aria. I promise. You'll sing it for me, my darling.'

He tried to smile but she could see the terror in his eyes and she knew its cause. 'There's no poison in your throat, believe me.'

She kissed him quickly and then ran outside. There

389

was Blaise's car. This year I'll learn to drive. She stumbled back into the cottage and took the keys from the nail at the door. She did not look at Blaise and he did not seem to hear her. She had never driven before. Two or three times a year she thought about learning to drive and buying a car but there was Will the taxi, and Chrissie's shop that had everything she needed between visits from the mobile shops and so she forgot about driving until the next time she needed a car. But it had to be easy, hadn't it? She turned on the engine. So far, so good. The brake . . . that was the next thing. She released the brake but still the car did not move. It's this knob thing. I have to move the knob thing . . .

She wanted to scream and cry with vexation. He would die, she knew he would die and all because she had never followed through with lessons. How many times had Blaise said that a car was a necessity?

She pushed the knob and the car lurched forward and then stalled. 'Shit, shit, shit. St Blaise help me. St Cecilia help me.'

She turned the key again and then somehow found the clutch pedal which she rammed into the floor and held down as the expensive car, which had never been so badly treated before, jumped, with the most alarming sounds of grinding and squealing and affronted protest, up the path to the road. As she lurched drunkenly onwards she prayed. 'Dear God, don't let him die. I'll do anything. Let Simon be there and let him have the right medicine. Please, God, I'll give him up if you don't let him die. I promise. I'll give him up.'

Never had such a short journey seemed to take so long but at last she was in the village. She parked the car by the simple expedient of stalling in the middle of the road directly in front of Simon's surgery and she threw herself out of the car and into the house.

Simon had seen the erratic approach of the car, which had been watched by all the villagers who were anywhere near the street. They were accustomed to expensive cars slicing through the town like a knife through butter and so this one's demented approach was observed with great interest.

'It's the artist lady from the bay,' a customer informed Chrissie who was weighing cheese and Chrissie pulled off her apron and ran out into the street. She was just in time to see Tony running into the surgery and she followed.

She and Simon reached Tony together.

'Simon, it's Blaise. Help me, help me,' Tony sobbed as she collapsed into Chrissie's strong old arms.

They had no idea what she was talking about and despite her exhaustion she realised this and pulled herself up. Blaise was dying, perhaps dead, and she was babbling.

'A friend, Simon, he's at the cottage. A bee sting, I think. An allergic reaction.'

'I'll get my bag. Chrissie, get someone to move that car off the road. Are you able to come with me, Tony?'

A weight seemed to have lifted itself from her shoulders. Simon was here, so capable, and Chrissie, dear Chrissie.

'Of course.'

'You'd better ring the cottage hospital for me, Chrissie. We'll take him straight there.'

Her energy had returned. She could have run every step back to him. 'It was the meadow beside the stream. I was sketching. Oh, Simon, his throat is swelling.'

'We'll be in time, Tony.' He did not ask anything. His heart was telling him that a man, the man whom Tony had always loved was in her cottage dying by the sound of it if not already dead. He forced his old car faster.

Idiot, he chastised himself. You should have taken his fancy car. Goes three times as fast as this old heap.

Too late to think of that now.

Tony turned to him. 'He's terrified, Simon. He can't breathe. His throat has swollen. His throat, that's what's terrifying him. I felt so helpless. I didn't know what to do. He's in shock. Should I have made tea?'

Simon almost snorted. The British and their tea. 'No, Tony, not if he's experiencing an allergic attack.'

'I put a blanket on him.'

'That was wise,' said Simon and sensed her relax.

Oh, what a burden my profession sometimes is, he thought. Whatever I said she would believe.

They had reached the cottage. Even from outside they could hear the horrid choking sounds and the threshing of a large thing caught in a small space. Tony threw open the door and Simon saw a tall man. His face was turned almost black and his eyes, which looked, not at him but at something they could not see, were popping from his skull. He gave another gasp and fell from the sofa and chair that had tried to contain his long body to the floor.

Tony screamed. It was a sound that Simon prayed he would never hear again. She reached the patient before him. 'He's dead, Simon. He's dead.'

He pushed her out of the way and kneeled down. The patient's lips were horribly swollen in the contorted face that was grotesquely discoloured and the grossly swollen tongue had blocked the airways. Part of Simon recognised his patient but the important part of him worked quickly, efficiently. He pushed the head back and the chin down and then he put two fingers of each strong hand under the jawbone just below the ears and he thrust the jaw forward. Blaise gave a cough, a little like the sound a disturbed pheasant makes and then lay still.

'It worked,' Simon told Tony. 'The mandible thrust, we call that.' He reached for his bag and prepared a syringe. 'Adrenalin, and then I'll give him epinephrene.' He smiled up at her. 'You can make your tea now, Tony – for me.'

Tony burst into tears. 'His chest, Simon,' she whispered. 'It's moving.'

'We medical men call that breathing.'

She was half laughing, half crying. 'I will honour you all my life,' she said, and he fussed with his recovering patient because he could not say thank you. He could not say, That's more than I want and less, much less.

Tony did not move and together they looked at Blaise. Already the face was almost back to normal, the swelling was going down, and the breathing was regular.

'You know who he is,' said Tony.

He nodded. He could not look at her. 'I heard him sing at the Edinburgh Festival. You will have to help me get him to the car, Tony. He's a big man. Can you manage?'

It was a rhetorical question. He felt that, had she needed to do so, she would have attempted to carry him herself.

'Hospital? Oh, Simon, must he? Can't I nurse him here?'

'He was within seconds of death, Tony. He should be checked out thoroughly, watched overnight at least.'

'You could tell me what to do. I'll watch him. Please, Simon. His world must never know about us.'

He was not there to judge. For years he had hoped but now, here in the cottage with Tony and this man for whom she was sacrificing everything, Simon saw that she would never love him. Oh, she loved him, but not the way he loved her and she never would. He wanted to say, 'I don't give a damn about his world,' but Tony did.

'Tony, I'm a doctor. Everything I have ever learned tells me this man should go to hospital but I can't force him. He's over the crisis. I'll do everything I can to help but he should be in the cottage hospital.'

'Doctor.' The famous voice was very low. 'You are a good man and I owe you my life but I cannot go. There are others to consider. Please.'

'Newspapers,' said Tony.

'Please, Doctor, for Tony's sake also.'

They propped him up between them and half carried, half supported him back to the settee.

'Blaise, I can stand it, if you can,' said Tony. 'You must go to the hospital. It's such a small place. Perhaps no one will know who you are.'

There was a sound that could have been an attempt at laughter. 'No hospital, Toinette. I am better.'

'Please.'

'You'll need help, Tony.'

'Chrissie will help if I need it,' and as she sensed a stiffening in Blaise, 'She won't tell, *ma mie*.'

Simon looked down at his patient who now, thanks to the miracle of modern medicine, was easily recognisable as the treasure of countless opera houses. 'I can't force you to accept hospital treatment but I have to say you are unwise.'

'Simon, please,' begged Tony. 'You will treat him?'

'I'm a doctor, Tony. I just want it on record that he should be in hospital.'

'Recorded, *Monsieur le Médecin*.'

Simon closed his bag. 'You must tell your own doctor. No doubt he'll arrange for you to have a syringe with you.' His tone was curt, professional. Then he relented and smiled. 'Keep out of fields of clover no matter what the inducement.'

Blaise shook his hand and Tony held her breath for a moment but all he said was, 'Thank you.'

'That tea?'

Simon was making for the door. 'I have a surgery in a few minutes and I must ring the hospital. Will I send Chrissie down?'

Tony walked with him to the car. 'I'll manage. Don't tell her his name. Tell her I'll come up to see her tomorrow.' She did not wait to see his old car climb the hill.

Blaise had pushed himself up and was more comfortable. He held out his arms and she ran to him. They did not speak. They did not kiss. He held her and she lay against his chest and listened to his heart beat. Most precious of sounds. How close. How close. At last she pushed herself away.

'For a second I thought you would offer to pay him.'

'I almost did. I will think of something.'

'Can you manage the stairs, darling? The bed is more comfortable.'

'This is nice for now.' He kissed the top of her head. 'You saved my life, Toinette.'

'Simon did.' She tightened her arms around him. 'I will learn to drive and I will see about a telephone. Oh, my God, I left your car in the middle of the road. I drove it, Blaise, hop, hop, hop.'

'*La pauvre voiture*. Will the company ever give me another car? Never mind. My Toinette will learn to drive. Now I could drink some tea, *ma mie*. I am thirsty.'

'Simon said you had to have something light to eat. You will direct the making of an omelette.'

'And she will learn to cook.'

Simon drove Blaise's car down to the cottage and

Tony persuaded him to stay for supper. 'I came really to get another look at my patient. Heartbeat, pulse, everything is normal.'

'I am very healthy.'

'You'd be dead if you were not so healthy. You will see your doctor?'

He had no chance to answer, for they heard a car and looked out to see an old black Hillman coasting down the hill. Tony ran to the door.

'It's the canon, saving petrol again. I hope he stops before he reaches the sea . . .' Tony had not seen Canon Gemmell for some weeks. She knew that occasionally he stopped at the top of the brae but, respecting her privacy, never came down if there was a strange car. Now she was torn. He would recognise Blaise and would be bound to disapprove. She would lose her friend. All these thoughts rushed through her head as she went down to the sand where the car had finally stopped.

'Hello, my dear, a party?'

'Canon, how lovely to see you.'

'I got back from retreat yesterday and thought I would stop but you had some visitors. I won't intrude now. They said Simon was here and I wanted a word.'

'You could never intrude, Canon,' she lied. Of course he was intruding. He was a Catholic priest and he lived and breathed his vows. She did not want to lose his respect, his friendship, and surely she must. 'Simon's here – in a professional capacity, I suppose, seeing a friend who was staying with me. We're having omelettes and salad. You are welcome to join us.'

They had reached the door.

'Simon, the canon,' began Tony but the old man had walked past the local doctor, his eyes on the man who sat wrapped in blankets on the settee.

'Monsieur Fougère, this is a great honour, sir.' He pushed Blaise, who was trying to rise, back on to the seat. 'Now I understand *Lohengrin*. I will take a little supper, Tony, if I may.' He turned back to Blaise. 'I trust you are not ill, Mr Fougère.'

'Bee sting,' filled in Simon.

'Canon, Blaise has been staying with me here,' said Tony and Blaise and the priest smiled at one another. She was so honest. She could not bear it that the canon might not understand.

'What a lovely place to escape to, Tony my dear.'

Later, after they had eaten, Simon helped Blaise upstairs and Tony walked with the priest out to his car. 'Tony, whatever did you do with *Sea Sprite?*'

She started. 'You could not have known then.'

'No, I had never seen him nor heard him sing. I remember the painting sometimes. Now I know why.'

'It's upstairs in the attic.'

'What a waste. It should be in a gallery.' He eased his old body into the driver's seat. 'The first time we met I told you I was always here, Tony. I'm always here.'

'Thank you,' she whispered as he waved and drove away, and then she turned as Simon joined her.

'I was sure he would disapprove.'

'I'm sure he does. It doesn't change his affection for you.'

He kissed her lightly on the cheek as he had done once or twice a year for over twenty years.

'He's fine, Tony,' and he was not talking about the canon. 'The constitution of an ox. He will be well enough to travel.' He started off towards the road into the village. 'I'm here if you need me.'

She said nothing but stood watching him until he reached the brow of the hill. He was 'here' and the canon was 'here' and for one more day so was the man she loved more than life itself. She would go in and she would not talk about his leaving and she would not remind herself that he had nearly died.

'*Ma mie?*' The voice was questioning.

'I'm here, my darling, here.'

25

---◆◆◆---

Torry Bay, 1999. New York, 1999

Every morning Holly made coffee, real coffee, and every morning, except when it was raining heavily, she took a mug out to the point where she stood and watched the sea. Sometimes Lohengrin was there; at any rate swans tended to gather in the shelter of the bay and Holly watched them, for, from where she stood, they were very graceful. She reflected on the little she knew about swans. They mated for life, were supposed to sing a beautiful song just as they were about to die, were elegant in water and amazingly ungainly on land, and their apparent serenity was a front for furious activity. Perhaps elegant serene women were more like swans than she thought; mainly surface show.

She felt close to Tony on the point. Tony had painted from here often.

She thought about Tony a lot too when she was painting the living room. After the living room she planned to paint her own small bedroom. It had not been redecorated since she had left school but she knew that she would be unable to sleep there until the smell of paint had gone: she would have to use the main bedroom and somehow that still seemed like an affront. Childish, but that was the way it was. She hoped her redecorating would not progress from the living room to the tiny kitchen as a way of staving off the evil moment.

Twice a week she phoned Otto or was contacted by him, but Taylor had returned, as she had known he would, to his world of high finance and corporate deals. His lawyers and Otto's lawyers argued with each other and by doing so added to their already healthy bank balances and still Tony's magnificent portraits hung with no one to admire them but Otto, his staff and the cleaners.

Holly sighed. Everything was drifting like the swans in the bay.

She had had enough. She would bend her stiff neck and ring Taylor.

As usual, 'Mr Hartman is unavailable.'

'Chandler, tell Mr Hartman that if he does not ring me back within the next two hours I am personally going to stand in Otto's gallery and sell the paintings to the first person who comes in off the street.'

'You would be breaking the law, Miss Noble.'

'Then he can visit me in jail,' she said with rather too much false bravado and hung up.

Taylor rang four hours later. 'The thought of visiting you in Wormwood Scrubs or wherever hardened criminals are sent, Holly, is unbelievably appealing but I'll do a deal with you. I'm not in the States at the moment. Could you please meet me in New York and we'll talk?'

'New York? Taylor, that is three thousand miles away from here.'

'So sell a diamond.'

'Very funny.'

'At this moment, oh so exasperating Miss Noble, I am a good twelve thousand miles from New York. It's important that we talk and New York is as good a place as any.'

Holly had never visited the United States. It was always one of the things she was going to do when . . . when . . . 'About what? Why can't you talk now?'

'Trust me. We need to meet in New York.'

This is stupid. New York? She would think twice about agreeing to meet someone in Glasgow. 'Fine. I'll meet you in New York.' The plumbers would certainly be finished by the time she got back.

'I'll make you a reservation,' he began.

'No, thank you. I'll let Chandler know where I am. Goodbye, Taylor.'

When the call was finished she poured herself some wine with very shaky hands and then sat down in the big chair for a minute. What had she done? New York?

I am out of my tiny mind.

Through the open window she could hear the sea and gulls calling and far overhead an aeroplane. She was as excited as she used to be as a child when she knew that soon a plane would take her to Aunt Tony and the freedom of Torry Bay.

'Am I crazy?' she asked the empty room.

Darling girl. Hollyberry.

Why am I doing this? Why? she asked herself as, still almost feverish with excitement, she rang airlines and travel agents and packed a few clothes into a weekend bag. She had to drive to Glasgow but first there were calls to be made to the Reids and keys to be left at the village shop.

'Don't worry about a thing, Missus.'

She wouldn't. She would live for the moment.

Two days later, sitting in a hotel in New York waiting for Taylor, her excitement had gone to be replaced by nausea.

What does he want? What do I want?

'Coffee, please, and . . . a toasted muffin.'

That was why she was sick. She was starving and the smell of the melting butter on hot toast at the next table was activating all her glands. Hot coffee, hot toast and melted butter. Was there a more comforting smell anywhere?

Expensive cologne is not comforting. Taylor had somehow materialised before her.

'I'll wait,' he said by way of greeting. Breakfast arrived. 'Another cup, please.' He smiled at the waitress, who almost ran to fetch a cup, and then he sat down across from Holly and waited patiently while she poured.

'I've been doing a lot of thinking, Holly, and I have never been absolutely straight with you.'

'Good heavens,' said Holly, and she was not talking about the quality of her coffee, delicious though it was.

'Come on; don't make it harder. I have never actually lied to you. No, that's not true. I did deliberately lie about one point and if I have allowed you to believe something I knew to be untrue, I honestly thought that it was the best way to handle it, for everyone concerned.'

'I hate riddles.'

'I want you to come with me to visit my aunt.'

She dropped her toast and ignored it as it lay butter side down on the white cloth. She could not believe this. It was some kind of sick joke. 'Your aunt is dead.'

'To the world, yes. Will you come with me? I will bring you back here.'

With shaking hands she reached for her cup. 'Taylor . . .' she began.

'Have your breakfast. Don't fuss, Holly,' he added as she moved to stand up. He smiled, bent over and lifted the toast from the tablecloth, and said, 'Good thing there wasn't jelly on this piece,' and walked away.

She watched him go. Other people were looking at him too. He was just that kind of man but he walked as if he were unaware of the attention. Hands still shaking, Holly gulped coffee, poured another cup and swallowed that down too. She ignored the toast. Once she had finished her coffee, she went upstairs to fetch a jacket, and when she reached the foyer, Taylor was there.

'You are the fastest girl at getting ready I ever met,' he

said with a smile, but it did not register because the words, 'I want you to visit my aunt,' kept chasing one another round and round in her head.

It was a sick joke but Taylor was not into sick jokes so it had to be true, but he had said Eleanor was dead, hadn't he? That then was the lie to which he admitted. Tony had believed that Eleanor was dead, or had she merely assumed that by the time Holly read the note Blaise's wife would have died?

What were the words? *No one is alive now who cares one way or the other.*

Oh, Tony, dearest aunt, how wrong you were.

As usual a car was waiting outside. Holly was too upset to be even vaguely impressed.

'Take a look at the Hartford papers,' said Taylor curtly.

Holly leaned back against the soft white leather and took the newspaper he handed her. EXCLUSIVE: ELEANOR RIDGEWAY FOUGÈRE IN A SANITARIUM.

It could not be so. An 'intrepid reporter' had tracked Eleanor Fougère to a sanitarium in Connecticut.

'Last night our reporter uncovered the mystery that has baffled the gossip columns of America for nearly fifty years. Eleanor Ridgeway Fougère, wife of the tenor Blaise Fougère who died in an air crash – some say on the way to his paramour Antonia Noble, the British painter – is alive and living in an exclusive sanitarium in Connecticut.'

'Satisfied?'

'Taylor.'

'She trusted me, and I promised her, and him, his memory, but you had to show the paintings. The money wasn't enough, was it?'

'If you even think that I sanctioned any salacious gossip, Taylor, there is no point in us going any farther.'

He did not look at her but kept his eyes on the road and his hands firmly on the steering wheel.

'Isn't this fun, Holly? I really love this part, sneaking around avoiding the press. Great fun.'

'I don't understand.'

'This is not one of my cars. Chandler is in my car heading for Madison. We are going in the opposite direction.' For some time as he drove he was quiet, concentrating on the road. Occasionally he would look in the rear-view mirror and at last he began to relax.

Holly sat and said nothing as Taylor drove. She watched Connecticut, its trees, its beeches, its lovely towns and villages sweep by but did not see them, for she was seeing the end of her newly born hopes and dreams. The reporter, who had found a woman she had believed to be dead, had destroyed whatever there might have been between Tony's niece and Blaise's nephew. At last they came to great iron gates set in a tall, stone wall. They waited for a moment, no more, and were admitted.

The house was beautiful, an English country house of great charm, transported to the Connecticut countryside.

'The Fougère Foundation pays for this,' said Taylor tersely as they waited for admittance at the beautiful carved oak doors, and Holly stood beside him and dreaded what was to come.

The door opened. 'How bad is it?' he asked.

'We are so sorry, Mr Hartman. I don't know what more we could have done.'

He brushed everything aside. 'How is she?'

The doctor, if it was a doctor, smiled. 'The same.'

Holly went, with Taylor, along a corridor to a suite of rooms. Taylor did not knock but opened the main door softly and walked in, almost dragging Holly behind him.

The room was beautiful. The furniture was French provincial, and the upholstery of the armchairs was yellow and full of the promise of spring. Huge vases of specially grown spring flowers stood on every table, and even in the fireplace that had been cleaned out for the summer.

A young girl sat in a chair by the window. Her hair was as pale as the gold of the fabric that covered her chair and her peignoir was a masterpiece of the dressmaker's art.

She turned as the door opened. 'Blaise, my dearest one, I knew you would come. I have been waiting; I knew you would come.'

'Of course I'm here, Eleanor.'

He stepped forward and Holly started almost with horror. The hair and the clothes were those of a young girl but it was no child who held Taylor's hands, babbling away in words that made no sense at all.

Taylor continued to hold her hands, making soothing noises and Holly stood transfixed and watched him. An attendant was there and she stood for a few minutes and then stepped forward. 'Now, now, Madame Fougère, there's a performance in five minutes. We wouldn't want to hold him up now, would we.'

'No, oh no,' said the ghost of Eleanor. 'My Blaise must sing; he sings for me. Don't you, my dearest.'

'*Pour sûr, mon ange.* I sing for you.'

The attendant led the girl-woman out of the room and Taylor almost fell into a chair.

'I thought she was dead,' Holly whispered.

'Her body lives. She's eighty-two years old and has been diagnosed as legally insane for almost sixty years.'

Tragedy upon tragedy. 'Oh, Taylor, but I thought she didn't recognise Blaise.'

He lifted his head from his hands. 'She didn't and then, one day maybe eight years ago when I visited, for some reason – maybe my age at the time – she thought I was Blaise. We, the family, had promised that we would care for her always, protect her as he protected her.'

He got up and moved across to her so quickly that she was startled. 'I blew it, Holly, because of you, because of this damned mixed-up love-hate thing we have going. I knew the right thing was to close the exhibition, not to let those damned sewer rats in to poke their sleek, cold little noses into my family but I was too late.'

He grabbed her and pulled her over to a window. 'Look out there. Look.'

He was hurting her, pushing her face almost against the glass. 'Taylor.'

He let her go. 'See those cars,' he said, but he was looking down at his hands as if he were surprised at their violence, as if he were not in control. 'That's gutter press, Miss Noble. I thought I had hidden the trail, but nasty old world, isn't it? Your best friend will sell you, if the price is right.'

She hated the cynicism; it wasn't true, was it? 'They'll get tired of sitting out there.'

He laughed harshly. 'They thrive on sitting "out there". They'll wait and take photographs if she appears at a window, walks in the grounds. They'll talk to gardeners, boot boys, deliverymen. They'll find out what she eats, what she wears. God damn you, Holly, why didn't you just take the money?'

'Love-hate thing. Love-hate thing.' So he felt something too or had felt something. Damn, damn, damn.

'It wasn't a question of money, ever,' she began desperately. 'You could have told me, Taylor. Tony thought everyone was dead.'

'We allowed the world to believe that.'

'What are you going to do? Move her . . .'

'Blaise built this house for her. I can't take it away from her too. We'll see if Hannah can keep her away from the windows and out of the gardens for a while.' His great frame seemed to sag. 'Soon we will be yesterday's news. A sort of Connecticut Miss Havisham, in a peignoir, not a wedding gown.' He got up and walked to the door. 'They'll bring you coffee. I'm going to sit with her for a while.'

He left the room and Holly sat for a while looking out at the line of cars outside the gates.

What have I done? If I hadn't given Otto the right to exhibit the paintings maybe no one would have found out.

But they have found out so what difference will showing the paintings make now?

The prurient will come to gape. The prices will go sky-high because they will outbid one another to be part of this soap opera.

But it's not a soap opera; it's a tragedy . . . for everyone including me.

A cheery-faced woman brought her a tray. She had no idea what time it was. She felt exhausted but did not know whether it was because of the time or the trauma. The fresh fruit salad on this tray looked appetising and Holly ate some of it gratefully.

Tea. He had had tea sent to her. A spark of hope lit in her belly and she felt tears start in her eyes. Oh, Taylor.

'We'll go now.' She had not heard him enter. 'When we get in the car put your scarf over your face if you don't want to be famous tomorrow.'

She had never experienced anything like it.

Taylor drove like a maniac straight for the group of photographers waiting at the gates and they jumped out of the way, flashes exploding all over the place.

'Fun, Holly?' he asked angrily as they screeched out of the gates. 'That was what life was like for my uncle who wanted only to sing, to bring joy, peace, to look after his poor sad wife.'

She dared not mention Tony.

'They waited for him outside opera houses, restaurants. Sometimes he wore disguises. One of the most sublime talents the world has ever known. Why wasn't the world content just to hear his voice? They wanted everything. He never gave interviews. We would laugh and make up answers to silly questions.

'"Oh, I start the day with three peacock's eggs."'

'"Three?"'

'"No, so stupid of me, only two."'

'He used to ask me, "What good does it do them to know that I like raspberries more than strawberries?" He could not understand their interest in him. He would look so puzzled. "I'm a singer, Taylor," he would say. I had no idea how to comfort him.' He turned and looked at her. 'Do you know his voice, Holly?'

Hollyberry.

'I've heard him once or twice.'

'That's not enough. You have been abducted, Miss Noble.'

For a second she panicked and sat up straight in the seat and then she relaxed. 'Seriously, you are taking me back to New York.'

'No. I'm taking you to the opera.'

'Don't be ridiculous.'

'There's something else I want you to see; something you need to see.'

He looked across at her again but could read nothing in her expression. 'I thought you might like to see my beach house.'

She looked at him, trying to work out what was going on inside that beautifully sculpted head.

'It's near here. We can walk on the beach and talk, grill a couple of steaks, listen to a CD. You could stay over; there's a guest room, but if you prefer to go back to the city, just say so.'

Holly looked at him, at his profile, his firm chin, his beautifully shaped nose. She saw his hands correctly positioned on the steering wheel; fingers long, slim, strong. 'Why should I see this particular house, Taylor?'

'When you see it, you'll know.'

She said nothing and he took this for assent and drove surely towards his destination. 'Freeway system is great here. It's like a bedroom community for New York. Loads of bankers, lawyers commute from here to New York by road but usually by rail. There's one called the Connecticut Commuter. An hour and a half maybe from Grand Central and you're at the beach. Look.'

And there was the sea, really the Atlantic Ocean, rolling up on sighing waves on to sandy shores. Taylor's house stood on a point and was, she was surprised to see, a moderately sized wooden building, white, with blue doors and shutters. It was built on a little promontory and the rhododendron-lined driveway that led to the front door also meandered on down to a private beach. There was a sign on the gates. TORRY BAY.

Holly gasped.

Taylor stopped the car at the front door and switched

off the engine. 'My uncle bought it thirty years ago,' he said at last. 'He came quite often when he was at the Met. We could never understand why he had rhododendrons, although they were kept well cut back.' He looked at her white, still face. 'You must have noticed in Scotland: they're alive with bees in the summer and Blaise was allergic to bee stings.'

Holly could say nothing. Taylor had known all the time that there was truth in her story and yet he had pretended. She remembered his stunned comment when he had first seen Torry Bay. She had thought it was the location when all the time it was the name.

'Take me to New York; no, the nearest railway station.'

'Holly, please. He was my white knight. I was his page. Your paintings ruined my memories. I didn't want to believe he'd loved someone else, loved another child. I wanted to be special. Childish, I know, but I'm not perfect.'

'You knew all the time.' The realisation hurt like a slap.

'No, of course I didn't. He said the bay reminded him of a friend's house. That's why he called it Torry Bay. He didn't say, "I'm calling the beach house after the place where I am happiest, where my heart is." I never lied to you about that. The lie was saying she was dead, *pauvre petite*. I promised, Holly. "I'll never let anyone hurt her," I said.'

There was silence in the car for some time, as they sat deliberately not looking at one another. The silence hung heavy, tense. 'No harm in taking a look,' Holly said at last, but she avoided his helping hand as she got out of the car.

It was at the same time like and unlike Torry Bay. It was bigger, more luxurious, and where Tony had had a window that looked out on to the bay, Blaise had had a wall of glass that slid away at the touch of a button. There were stones on a table to the right of the window. Taylor 1970, Taylor 1973. Above the mantel was a small painting that Holly recognised at once.

'She must have painted that for him.'

'I don't think so. There's an ancient sales receipt signed by Otto. Blaise took it everywhere with him. I'm surprised it wasn't on his plane the night they crashed. I hung it here after his funeral. Would you like to walk down to the bay? No swans, I'm afraid.'

She went with him out on to the terrace. Pots full of rioting flowers greeted her with their perfume. They were geraniums. 'Is there a lot of rain?'

At first he did not understand. 'Oh, the flowers. I grow tomatoes too. The people who look after the house water them. Blaise never left anything to die.'

No, he left nothing to die, except Tony. Holly began to cry and it seemed so right that Taylor should hold her in his arms and mutter incomprehensible nothings.

'It's so sad,' sobbed Holly when she could speak.

'Yes, but wonderful too. They loved one another for nearly sixty years, Holly. Isn't that something? I'd like that, wouldn't you?' His voice was intense and so were his eyes, those eyes so like Blaise's that stared into hers, forcing her to admit to feelings that she had tried not to acknowledge. 'Took me for ever to understand why you got under my skin so much, Holly. You're so unlike any woman I ever loved, even dated.'

She laughed shakily. 'I'm no oil painting, as the saying goes.'

He looked surprised. 'Everything's in the right place but there's something more important than surface beauty. Anyone can look good if they work at it. No, it's you, Holly, just you. The Holly who went to Africa for a year and stayed for two; that Holly who's ready to take on the world and Taylor Hartman if she feels he's wrong. She shines right out of your lovely blue eyes.'

He tilted up her chin and bent down to kiss her lips and at his touch the pent-up fires exploded, consuming her.

How did they return to the house? She did not know; neither did she care.

They were in the bedroom and he was kissing her mouth while his hands found buttons, fastenings, and she was his equal. She stroked his shoulders, the muscles on his back. She unbuttoned his shirt as he removed her blouse and his lips found her breasts. She gave herself up completely to sensation. She heard a voice begging, please, please, and was not ashamed that it was her own.

He pushed her down on the white cover and then his body was on hers. He slid into her as easily as if their knowledge of one another was primeval and she gasped as her body matched and responded to his rhythm.

Never had she experienced such a flood of sensations. Even her throat burned and tingled as feelings long banked down exploded into awareness of his body, her own, and she gloried in her femininity, in her power to receive such a gift and at the same time to give so abundantly. They climaxed together and lay silent, entwined, exhausted and satisfied.

'Your mother told me everyone spoils you, Taylor.'

He laughed and she loved the feeling of the deep rumble from beneath her head.

'I want you to spoil me atrociously every day for the rest of my life.'

Every day. She sat up and looked down at him. 'I didn't mean this to happen.'

'Now me, it's all I have been able to think about for months.'

'Taylor.'

He sat up at once. 'See how I mind you. You just have to say, Taylor, the way you used to say *Mr Hartman*, to make me tremble in my shoes. See.'

'You're not wearing any shoes.'

'But I'm trembling,' he whispered as he lay down again and pulled her down beside him. 'Trembling.'

With his hands on her willing body she could do nothing. Ineffectually she tried to stop him.

'I want to make love to you again, Holly.' He took her hand. 'Feel how much I want you. Say, stop it, and I will stop.'

She wanted to say it. Her mouth desperately tried to form the syllables, but his hands. Oh, where had he learned how to work such magic? She had never experienced being loved like that; she had never dreamed that the act could be like that, so much giving, taking, and no false modesty. She felt beautiful, voluptuous, a woman.

At last they fell asleep and hours later she woke in the dark with his legs and his arms wrapped around her and her head pillowed on his chest.

She was cold and she was embarrassed. How was she to get out of his arms, his bedroom and his house? She was insane. He had said he wanted to make love to her. Well, he had. Indeed he had, but why? Because of whatever he thought he saw in her eyes? This had been a horrible, horrible day. They should never have allowed themselves to get into this situation. How could they evaluate their feelings after a day in which their emotions had been beaten and battered? Eleanor, poor Eleanor. How many miles away was her gilded sanitarium, her cushioned cage?

How quickly we forgot her in our passion, Holly admitted as she looked down at him. He was her Lohengrin, her knight and she loved him and would willingly wait for ever. But what was she to him? And had Tony's glorious portraits anything to do with what had just so beautifully, wonderfully happened? He was just like John: not one single word of love.

Shit, how embarrassing.

He stirred. 'Dinner now, sweetheart, or is it breakfast?'

'Taylor, this is very awkward but I'm afraid this

417

should never have happened. I'm not . . . looking for a relationship.'

He sat up and she was glad it was dark, only pale moonlight showing them as dark shapes in the pastel room. 'You sure as hell found one.'

'I'm sorry. I never meant . . .'

'Lie to me if you like, Holly, but don't lie to yourself. You could have stopped me at any time and you didn't. Well, I hope I was a good lay. You were great. In fact, you were so good, I thought we might even have been made for one another.'

What was he saying? What had she done? Another Noble mistake? A real humdinger this time.

'We don't even like one another.'

He pulled her round and for a moment she stiffened with fear. He was so strong, but no, it was Taylor, and she did not fear him. There was no reason to fear. She relaxed but it was too late.

'I never rape, Holly. I get it for nothing whenever I want it. Usually I send a little gift, just like my uncle. What will it be . . . diamonds, rubies; no – sapphires, I think, to match your innocent blue eyes.'

She slapped him as hard as she could and he got off the bed, stalked into the bathroom and slammed the door. She slid from the bed and searched frantically for her clothing. She could not find her panties but pulled on her tights and her skirt and saw the pants, a wisp of silk and lace, on the floor at her feet. She snatched them up and tucked them inside her skirt. No time to put them on properly.

He was dressed when he came out of the bathroom; the clothes she had helped pull off him were still lying on the floor and he wore a tracksuit.

'The bathroom's all yours. I'll get the car.'

'Thank you,' she managed stiffly.

They said nothing on the way to the city and at the door of the hotel he leaned across her to open the door. She was conscious of his body, as she had never been conscious of a man's body before. She felt like a streetwalker.

The doorman came and held the hotel door, his face expressionless. Holly kept her head as high as she could and walked bravely past the great gilt reception area to the elevators and was whisked up to the fifteenth floor. She looked down at her feet. 'Have a good Wednesday,' was written on the carpet. She thought she would never have a good Wednesday again.

She was weeping when she managed to get the little card to work so that she could enter her room.

The bathtub was as big as the one with the painted toes and she filled it and lay in the hot scented water, meaning to wash Taylor away. As she lay looking at her body every nerve ending seemed to ask for Taylor's hands and she relived the whole evening.

'Oh, God, what have I done,' she sobbed and took her nailbrush and tried to scrub the memories away.

26

Torry Bay, 1999. Torry Bay, 1967–1972
UNCLE FIRE

Holly kneeled in front of the fire looking at the photographs. Everything you have ever learned is buried in your subconscious, a lecturer had informed her during her university years. She dug deep. Of course, of course. She remembered now, Uncle Fire. She had met him twice, maybe three times. Tony must have taken great pains to see that they never met when she was older, when she was capable of recognising one of the world's most famous men, and, worse, telling her strait-laced parents all about him.

Holly sat back on her heels and looked at the picture. Blaise Fougère in a fur coat was walking out into the sea and he was holding by the hand a little girl dressed in nothing more than a minuscule bikini. The child was dancing beside him and it was obvious that she was ecstatically happy and not at all cold. Blaise, his feet bare and his trousers rolled up around his calves under the folds of the fur coat, was looking back at the artist and laughing. He looked young, carefree, and incredibly happy.

'And as sexy as all get out,' decided Holly as she stared at the picture of her four-year-old self.

He had not been expected. She had been staying with Tony while her parents were away on yet one more evangelical crusade and together aunt and niece were lining a path with lovely white shells that they had collected on the beach. Neither of them had heard the car but, all of a sudden, something big had blotted out the sun and Holly looked up to see him standing there.

Tony had, to a four-year-old mind, behaved very strangely. She had jumped up and thrown herself into the man's arms and they had kissed, a kiss that was very different from the chaste salutes exchanged by Holly's parents and that had gone on for a very long time; so long that she had lost patience and pulled at Tony's legs.

'The path,' she had demanded imperiously, and to her surprise the big man had squatted down beside her.

'Hello, Holly, I am your Uncle Blaise. Permit me to help.'

Immediately she had handed him a shell that he had arranged with gratifying care on the path; she had awarded him a smile.

In the morning she had not remembered his name and when he did not appear at the breakfast table she had cast around in her memory bank for his name so that she could question Tony. At last, when she was

almost ready to explode with frustration she had remembered. 'Where is he?' she had demanded. 'Uncle
Fire.'

Uncle Fire he had remained. Funny how she had
forgotten all about him and had never once found
anything familiar about Blaise Fougère. She had heard
his recordings: she had seen occasional broadcasts from
Covent Garden or the Metropolitan Opera House in
New York, but she doubted if she had ever heard his
speaking voice. Surely she would have recognised
Uncle Fire's voice, but Blaise Fougère was notorious
for avoiding interviews and he appeared on no talk-
shows. Perhaps if she had seen him in a live performance, some chord of memory would have been
plucked, but tickets to his performances were prohibi-
tively expensive.

Holly looked at the painting with eyes bright with
unshed tears. The child Holly had loved her Uncle Fire.
It was obvious in the way she danced confidently beside
him, her little toes barely touching the sand: the tall
figure in the ridiculous fur coat was making no concession to the child's size.

How the child, now grown up, wished she could
remember more.

Tony had looked up when his bulk had blotted out the
sun and her heart had danced. She had forgotten Holly,
the path, everything but her overwhelming love and she
had thrown herself into his strong, reaching, waiting,
demanding arms.

Eventually little Holly had pulled on her legs with her small but equally demanding fingers. 'The path.'

Blaise had stooped down with his inexhaustible courtesy and begun to help and Tony had said nothing. Ineffable thoughts and feelings had swirled around in her head but she was unable to speak. He was here. Holly was here. The two people she loved most in the entire world, in her heart, and now here in her home. She watched them. Soon she would leave him with the child and she would run down to see what there was that could be turned into a meal and later, later . . . She thought her heart would choke her and he knew what she was thinking because he looked up from the shells and smiled.

'Now we are a family, *ma mie*,' he said. 'Does she sing, this little one?'

'No, but she makes lovely red paintings.'

'I will teach her to sing. All children should sing. It is as easy as to breathe.' He began. '*Sur le pont d'Avignon, l'on y chante, l'on y danse* . . .'

When Tony stood up to go into the cottage Holly was lisping along in recognisable French and curtseying to the tall man who bowed to her in their song as if she were the greatest diva in the world.

'Don't fret, *ma mie*. I have our meal in the car.'

She blushed because she intended to change the sheets and he knew that too and smiled at her wickedly. 'But there are other things you have to do while Mam'selle and I complete our task.' He bent again to the little girl. 'Tell me, Hollyberry, do you prefer white chocolate or brown?'

'Bof,' she said and smiled at him with a smile that stole his heart away.

'You have a rival,' he told Tony later. They lay wrapped in one another's arms and scents. 'The parents must be better than you say.'

Tony sighed and twisted her fingers more tightly into the curling hairs on his broad chest. 'She likes you.'

'*Bien sûr*,' he agreed complacently. 'All women love me. I don't even have to work at it.'

She pulled the hair to punish him and much later they again lay bathed in sweat and moonlight.

'When?' she whispered softly.

'I have tomorrow and the next day I must go. London for three weeks. You will come?'

'I can't.'

'Bring her. During the day you can show her all our favourite places, the park, the bandstand; and in the evenings . . . what can we do in the evenings, Toinette?'

'We can do nothing, my heart, because they love you too much in London. On the nights when you are not singing there will be parties and I cannot go to them.'

She did not mean to sound aggrieved. She tried so hard not to let her status rankle.

He sat up and propped himself up with pillows. He had no idea how flattering was the moonlight. He looked like a creature not quite of this earth, of air and water perhaps. His annoyance, however, was most assuredly worldly. 'I will not parade you before the world as a trophy, Tony.'

'I would hate that,' she mumbled into her pillow.

'Or even as a friend. The world would talk.'

His world, the world of the opera, and that other world, Eleanor's world. Tony's world was Chrissie, Simon, the canon and Holly.

'If you exhibited more, came to London more . . . New York . . .'

'I could not hide how I feel, Blaise. Could you?'

He rolled over onto his elbow and looked down at her. Her face was hidden and he traced her spine with one finger and felt her tremble. She looked, he thought, like a little boy. His finger continued its voyage of discovery and when he reached her ankle he turned her over and began the journey up, up, until neither of them could bear more and he gathered her trembling to him. 'No, *ma mie*, I could not hide my love.'

When she climaxed she screamed his name and only when they were calm did they remember the child.

'I'll check her,' Tony said and slipped off the bed.

He made to accompany her and she pushed him back towards the bed. 'You might frighten her.'

Holly was lying on top of her bed, one little leg bent. Her arms cradled her parents' sole concession to childhood, a toy cat. 'Tomorrow we will buy you a doll, Holly,' she whispered as she straightened the child's limbs and covered her up. 'I loathe cats.'

Blaise was sound asleep and she sat looking down at him for a long time, memorising him before she slipped into the bed beside him. Immediately his arms reached out for her. 'Toinette,' he murmured and she lay held

425

uncomfortably against his chest feeling his heart beat until she too fell asleep.

The morning brought another perfect day and after breakfast Tony took Holly down to the beach.

'Uncle Fire?'

'He'll come. He works very hard, Holly, and so he was very tired last night. He came all the way from Australia to see you.'

The little girl looked up from her digging. 'Mummy and Daddy too?' she asked hopefully.

Instantly Tony wished she had said nothing. 'No, darling. They're very busy.'

'Like Uncle Fire?'

'Sort of.'

'He singed me a new song. Does he sing hymns like Daddy?'

She was not comparing the voices but Tony smiled at the thought. 'I don't think so.'

'Good.'

She went on with her digging, singing to herself. '*Sur le pont . . .*'

Tony leaned back against a boulder and dozed.

'*Café*, Mam'selle?' Blaise was bending over her with a mug of fragrant coffee. 'You have been snoring with your mouth open, *ma mie*. Hollyberry and I have been laughing.'

Tony squinted up at him. 'That's rather unkind,' she said as she took the mug. 'I got very little sleep last night.'

He reached down and touched her cheek. 'I will watch the child.'

No, she could not bear to leave him. There would be plenty of time to sleep when he had gone. He sat on the sand beside her and she transferred her weight from the stone to his broad chest. They sat quietly drinking their coffee and watching the little girl.

This was how it should have been. If only, if only. No, she must not remember that.

'You are cold, *ma mie*?' he whispered against her hair.

'No. I was just thinking . . .' She could not go on.

His arms tightened around her. 'I too, but we have this time, this child. We must be grateful, Toinette. Hollyberry,' he called. 'Aunt Tony wishes to buy you a doll. What shall it be?'

The little girl put down her spade very carefully. She stood up and brushed the sand from her plump little knees and then she came and stood in front of him, looking straight into his eyes. 'A really truly doll?'

'*Ça va sans dire.* Whatever Hollyberry wishes.'

'A fairy princess with a beautiful frock and a magic wand.'

Tony was distressed. 'Blaise, Chrissie won't have a doll that looks anything like that.'

He pulled the little girl down on to his knees and she sat looking at him solemnly. 'Holly, Aunt Tony will take you to Chrissie's shop to see the dolls and if your princess is not there I know exactly where she will be.'

'Where?'

'In London.'

London meant nothing to Holly. Her eyes, however, were full of expectation.

'Tomorrow I go to London, Hollyberry, and I will go to this wonderful store which is full of dolls of all kinds and I will find the most beautiful princess for you.'

'A fairy princess,' she reiterated anxiously, 'with a wand.'

Again the child examined his face and, as if she liked what she saw, she smiled. 'All right,' she said and clambered off his lap. 'Swimming now?'

He groaned – he found even the Pacific chilly – but he stood up. 'Swimming now.'

'Blaise, the water is freezing. You will catch cold.' Tony knew he hated being fussed over but he was due to start rehearsals for *Tristan and Isolde*; he would need to be in the best of health.

'Let's get changed. Mam'selle Holly will swim and I will, what you call, paddle.'

When Tony had changed Holly into her little swim-suit they found Blaise in the living room. He was wearing the heavy fur coat he had left in the cottage at the end of his last winter visit. Holly saw nothing strange in his attire but Tony laughed. 'God, if your fans could see you now. You look so ridiculous; a fur coat and bare feet.'

He leaned over and kissed her. 'The sun is hot but the water is cold. Is that not so, Holly?'

Holly shrugged. She was four years old and accepted everything that adults did. Her touching innocence affected Blaise deeply and he tightened his grip on the little hand that pulled him towards the door. 'I have a nephew called Taylor, Holly. I love him as much as

428

Aunt Tony loves you. You must meet him one day and play with him. You will be good friends.'

'Is he a little boy or a big boy? I don't like big boys.'

'One day you will.'

'How very French you are, Blaise Fougère, French and silly. Now, if you are going to walk into the sea in a fur coat I must get my sketchbook.'

'Another chef-d'oeuvre. What is it to be called, *ma mie*? The fur coat . . . *Siegmund in the Sea?*'

She looked up at him as he grinned down at her. He was so happy with the child and his silly coat. Her stomach tightened with love. 'No,' she said slowly. 'It will be called *Uncle Fire.*'

Uncle Fire.

Holly stood up and jumped around to relieve the pins and needles in her legs. How long had she been sitting there lost in thought? The fire had gone out and the cottage felt cold and damp. *Uncle Fire*. Blaise Fougère was Uncle Fire. She remembered the doll. He had sent it but it had stayed at Torry Bay in its box for two years before she had been able to play with it. Her parents had returned to a church in Glasgow and so there were no visits to Torry Bay for a while. Tony had come though, that first Christmas, and she had tucked the little girl up in bed on Christmas Eve.

'Holly, do you remember the fairy princess, the one you wanted?'

Holly had looked at her and had remembered. 'He forgot,' she said.

'No, darling. She arrived the day you left and she's the most beautiful princess in the world.'

'With golden hair?'

'Of course, and blue eyes, and a white dress sparkled with stars.'

'And a wand.'

'*Bien sûr*,' Tony had said and buried her head in the pillow so that Holly would not see how close she was to crying.

'*Bien sûr*,' Holly had repeated. 'Tell her I'm coming as soon as I can.'

'She'll wait. We are very good at waiting in our family.'

The princess had waited for two years and Holly had played with her every holiday. Where is she now? the grown-up Holly wondered. I remember playing with her until . . .

Until what? She had absolutely no idea what had happened to the beautiful doll. Had her memory of Blaise Fougère and of the doll disappeared together? No point in trying. The memories would come back when they were ready. She looked at the painting again, saw the expression of mischievous delight on Blaise's face, and saw Tony so clearly, although her body was not in the painting. Her heart was.

How they loved each other. That's what I want: love that can withstand anything that life throws at it.

'I will keep this painting, Taylor,' she said and would have felt a great deal better if she had thought for one second that Taylor even cared.

27

Torry Bay, 1999. London, 1999

The next few days remained for ever a blur. She got to the airport, how she could not remember. Did she take the shuttle bus or was she so dejected that she forgot her usual caution – after all, there was no real reason to economise – and took a taxi all the way to the airport? On the long flight she ate nothing, drank nothing, read nothing, and, when she arrived, found Scotland echoing her misery. It was raining in Glasgow.

The voice of the man beside her in the line for the shuttle bus did penetrate the pall of misery. 'Wouldn't you know it – bucketing?'

Sure. Somebody up there was chucking buckets of the stuff. He continued to pitch, bung and heave buckets of cold rain down on the beleaguered little island all the way from Glasgow to Torry Bay. Cascading rain and her own tears hid the scenery that Tony had delighted in exploring and painting from her.

'Please, God; don't let me meet a lorry.'

She did reach Achahoish safely and drove slowly

down to the cottage beside a sea angrier than she had ever seen it. Holly sat in the car looking through the driving rain at the cottage. Inside there was her nice warm bed and, oh joy, a cup of hot sweet tea, but first she had to venture out into that deluge. She buttoned up her coat, took the key out of her handbag and ran, buffeted by the wind, her face stung from drops of rain sharp as needles, to the cottage door but it was not shelter from the storm she was seeking, or was it? Tony had come back here bruised and beaten to seek shelter from the storm of life. She had found it too if the beautiful painting *Shelter from the Storm* was true. She opened the door.

Darling girl. Hollyberry.

She sat down in the chair by the window and wept but she was comforted. The cottage was warm, too warm, and delightedly Holly ran from room to room exclaiming over her brand-new radiators and opening windows.

'Oh, Reids, loud and quiet, I love you both.'

There was no mess left, only things that could not be helped like little holes where pipes or wires had had to be threaded through walls or floorboards.

'My newfound painting skills will fix that. Central heating and telephones.'

She swooped down on her little green telephone, lifted the receiver and held it to her ear. But there was no one to ring to tell about the dizzy heights of modernisation. 'Yes, there is,' she said defiantly. 'There's Otto and Mr Gilbert and the Reids, old friends in Glasgow who'll be wondering what I'm doing, and I may well ring painters and decorators.'

Anything to stop herself thinking of those magical hours with Taylor.

She felt tired, lethargic and, for two days, stayed closeted in the cottage hiding from the raging wind and making her telephone calls as if the implement were a brand-new discovery. The Reids were delighted and promised that their bill would 'be with you shortly. Are you sure you want to leave the big bath there?'

Holly avoided looking at the bath with its bright green toenails, but she could face no more upheaval for a while.

She rang Mr Gilbert and promised to make an appointment with a financial adviser and then she dialled Otto's number. 'You will never guess where I have been.'

She was beginning to read the tone of his voice. 'How intriguing, do tell,' he said, but she was almost sure that he already knew.

'New York,' she said and she let herself remember. For just a moment her body felt as if it were wrapped in the finest silk. Oh, God, why did I leave? What demon possessed me to take the gift I had been given and throw it back?

Back to reality.

'Otto, Taylor took me to a sanitarium in Connecticut. Eleanor is still alive.'

She heard him gasp. There was a heartbeat pause. 'I know; I rang you when the story broke but, of course, you didn't answer. Holly, every paper had something, even the better papers, but you were not mentioned. I had no idea that you were there.'

Sweet relief. He had not known. She was glad of that. He was Tony's friend and was selling her paintings: too cruel if he had known. Again she pictured the look on the old young face. 'I can see why Taylor is so protective. The poor woman thinks he's Blaise. She is in good health, although she was expected to die years ago, but she's eighty-two years old. Don't you see, Otto, it wasn't his mother he was thinking about when he asked me to hide the paintings for twenty years, it was his aunt.'

'Holly,' he began again and for once his voice sounded as old as his years. 'I, we, everyone thought her dead years ago; you must believe that.'

Holly felt cold. 'Of course I believe it, Otto. What are you trying to say?'

'I knew.' It was her turn to gasp but he hurried on. 'Taylor's lawyers told me, or at least they told my lawyers. That was the only reason he got the temporary order; it was a sympathetic temporary or some legal jargon.'

'You knew – and you didn't tell me.' She was fighting nausea now. Was there any man in the world she could trust?

'I thought the Hartmans would prefer—' he began but a furious Holly interrupted.

'The Hartmans? How could you lie to me, Otto?'

'I never lied. Look Holly, Miss Noble, I'm a businessman. I want to sell these wonderful paintings but I'm like the lawyers: I wanted an equitable remedy, the right to sell them, but I need the business of the Hartmans and all the clients they send and so do you.'

She was crying now. 'You should have told me; it would have made everything different. I would have . . .' She stopped and blew her nose. What would she have done? Not fought so much with Taylor, for a start, but the paintings? Tony and her paintings; that was all that mattered. *No one is alive now who cares one way or the other*. But there was something else in the letters, something she had overlooked. *I never wanted to sell in my lifetime. I made a pact*. A pact? Who with, Tony?

Darling girl.

Oh, God, Tony promised Blaise not to exhibit in Eleanor's lifetime. Shit, shit, shit.

Hollyberry.

'You should have told me. It was your duty to tell me.'

'I'm sorry; I didn't take the decision lightly, my dear, and if you hadn't stormed off and said you were taking them off the market we could have discussed it rationally.'

She wanted to hang up on him, never see him or speak to him again, hide away at Torry Bay from them all. No, she was through running.

'I'll have to think, Otto.'

'Madame Fougère doesn't understand anything, does she?'

'No.'

Dracula had drunk human blood and was rejuvenated, invigorated. 'Then what does it matter when you found out? Now that the story has broken every city where there's a major opera house will run a story, and most will be perfectly sympathetic.' He was quiet for a moment and Holly could picture him gathering himself together to say something he knew she would not want to hear. 'I know you dislike any talk of filthy lucre but the telephone and Internet bids on the paintings will go through the proverbial roof.'

'This is unbelievably distasteful.'

'This is human nature.'

'Otto, I really have no energy at the moment and I have to think. I don't know what to do for the best. Besides, Taylor and I . . . we had a blazing row,' seemed like the best way of explaining.

'Oh, dear, I actually thought I saw a *tendresse* developing.'

A *tendresse*, tenderness. Oh, shit. 'Pigs might fly as my old Granny never said.'

She remembered to give him her brand-new telephone's number before hanging up, only to sit down and gaze into space. Her mind kept reliving the events of the past week, the sanitarium with its sole sad occupant, Otto's dénouement, and Taylor, Taylor, Taylor. She stood up.

'Get a grip, Holly. You blew it again – three strikes and you're out – so get on with life and stop feeling so damned sorry for yourself.'

She would look at the pictures of the paintings again

and compare them with her memories of the real masterpieces. She picked up one of Otto's expensive professional photographs of the paintings; it was the clover picture. Blaise stood in a meadow and his feet were buried in a drift of white clover flowers. He smiled, such a tender loving smile, obviously directed at the artist. She noticed that the clover was alive with bees. Now, after what she had learned she wondered. Had he known he was allergic to bee stings? Had he found their droning musical or frightening?

A photograph of Lohengrin. She tossed it aside. She would not think of Paris, for remembering Paris made her remember Taylor who had loved her but had not said that he even liked her. Oh, shit, I am getting really maudlin. What is wrong with me? Weepy, weepy. She picked up another of the photographs and stared at it, at the absurdity of it, the tall elegant man, the skinny little girl. He had taken Tony's lovely tradition of a stone kept and dated at each visit of a beloved child and transported it to his house and his nephew. Had that made him feel closer to Tony? She wished she could remember more but it seemed as though much effort had been put into erasing her memories of . . . Uncle Fire. There was a doll, a fairy doll with a wand and golden hair. He must have brought it, for Holly's parents did not believe in spoiling children and it had been a very expensive doll. She heard an echo of a childish voice.

'A really truly princess with golden hair and a wand?'
'If that's what my Hollyberry wants . . .'

The doll, if there had been a doll, was no longer in the cottage.

Let it go, Holly. Remember only that I love you . . .

Uncle Fire.

The outside with its constant drizzle was now more appealing than the cottage where Taylor had intruded. Perhaps she would find Fougère or at least some memory of him up at the point. The world looked sorry for itself. She walked on. The sheep in the field huddled together miserably and the sea was almost hidden by a cloud of grey rain. She had forgotten how mild Scottish rain can be and took off her scarf to allow it to bathe her hair and her face with its soft gentleness. She reached the point and stood looking out at the sea but no voices called her; no murmurs told her of times past. There were no swans on the water; one or two ducks bobbed along at the whim of the tide. Incongruous sight: two beer bottles bobbed along beside the ducks. Holly clambered down and fished them out of the water.

Did you deal with beer bottles in your refuge, Tony? It's so lovely here but it won't be enough for me. I'm not you. I can't paint and there is no one I love who will rush to me whenever he is free and I will not stand here day after day looking for a swan and finding a bloody empty beer bottle.

Her eyes filled with those so ready tears and she sighed and turned back with the bottles to the cottage that seemed to hold out its arms to her, welcoming her. She threw them in a carton she had labelled *Recycling*

– *glass* and then sat in the window until the storm passed, the rain stopped. Even the bay was quiet. She curled in Tony's scruffy old chair and looked out. No wonder Tony had been happy to stay here and to paint. If I wanted to tell anyone how unbelievably beautiful this is, Holly thought, I would fail. I don't have a gift for choosing the one word that is right. What could I say? The water is now calm and tiny ripples on the top are caressed by moonbeams so that it looks like, looks like a . . . a silk scarf nonchalantly tossed down. The sky is grey-blue or is it blue-grey and there's pink there, and there, just there where the clouds almost touch the water, I can see the merest sliver of pure molten gold.

Tony had not needed words. She had taken her palette and her brushes and transferred the picture to her canvas; no need for inadequate words. The cottage was so cosy and the moonlight played on the walls and Holly sat in Tony's old nightgown and dozed. The strident ringing of her new telephone wakened her.

'We've done it, Holly. Taylor has given in.'

Otto was jubilant. After months of expensive litigation, Taylor Hartman had capitulated. No reason given. 'Miss Noble may sell her paintings. Mr Hartman sees no reason to continue the action and has withdrawn his suit.'

Holly did not feel the exhilaration that she had expected. In fact she felt even more bereft. She roused herself to pretend normality. 'Why, Otto?' Because the secret was a secret no longer or because he . . . Shut up, Holly.

She almost heard the shrug of expensive tailoring. 'Obviously it doesn't matter now; the secret is out. He has given in. We've won. I shall ring all my friends in the media immediately.'

'Wait, Otto. Let me speak to Taylor first. I have to know why he gave in. The paintings have waited; they can wait a little longer.'

'Very unwise, Holly; the timing is perfect.'

Her mind was made up. 'Otto, make no plans until I have spoken to him.'

'Well, I certainly won't put any plans into action, my dear, but plan I will.'

With that she had to be content.

She was sick with tension. She nerved herself to dial Taylor's office number.

'Mr Hartman has just left Switzerland for Japan, Miss Noble. May I ask him to call you?'

At least the throngs of secretaries no longer evaded her.

'Give me his number.'

'I have no authority, Miss Noble. Let me call you after Mr Hartman contacts us.'

Holly had no choice but to wait.

She telephoned Otto again when it was obvious that she was not going to hear from Taylor that day. 'It's time zone, I think, Otto, but I won't authorise the sale until I hear from him.'

Suddenly she felt ravenously hungry and she went into the kitchen and scrambled some eggs, made some toast and tea. She put it all on a tray and went back to the window.

Why had Taylor resigned from the fray?

Is this my pay for services rendered? I can't bear it. Don't make me a whore, Taylor.

Much better than sapphires, but it was such an empty victory.

Oh, Tony, what's the right thing to do? Maybe he won't phone because he won't speak to me, because he hates me.

She had eaten too much too quickly. She felt absolutely dreadful and had to run for the bathroom where she was violently sick. The last time she was sick was when Nicole told her about the abortion so this, obviously, was a delayed reaction to her visit to the sanitarium. Her horror at the picture of poor Eleanor had been buried for a while by her passion for Taylor.

She felt much better in the morning. Then the postman cycled down the hill and brought her a packet. It was from the Hartman Corporation. Her hands were trembling as she held the square packet. She could not bring herself to open it. Obviously he had carried out his threat and had sent sapphires.

Pain grabbed at her insides. 'No, Taylor, please no,' she howled like a mad woman.

She stood with the parcel in her hands. She wanted to open it and, at the same time, she wanted to dispose of it. Thoughts went whirling around and around in her head and her fingers itched to tear open the brown paper. There was no reason for Taylor to send anything to her and this was square and hard. It was, therefore, not a letter. She stared at the label while something inside sighed and died. She had hoped and prayed and now she knew it had been futile. She could not bear to see what value he put on their glorious abandonment.

What was I worth, Taylor? A thousand pounds, ten thousand, surely not a hundred thousand?

She held the packet up once to the light as if she mght see through the wrapping. I can't handle this now. I just can't handle it.

She dropped the package on the floor and almost recoiled from it as it lay there. She had to get away from it, to get out, to breathe deeply in the clean air.

A few minutes later she was standing on the headland and tears of the most abject despair were rolling, unchecked, down her cheeks.

If my tears fell into the sea would they make a difference? Oh, God, to whom, to what? I care only for Taylor and he has paid me what he thinks I'm worth.

Holly stood there for some time, aware of the swans at anchor, like ghostly galleons, on the waves.

Sweat beaded on her forehead. She felt hot and clammy and colder than she had ever felt in her life.

She sniffed loudly and drew her fingers across her face. 'Stuff you, Taylor,' she said, turned, and almost ran back to the cottage. At the table in the living room she punched the button on the telephone that would give her Otto's number.

'I have changed my mind. Never mind Mr Hartman. Sell the paintings and to the highest bidder.'

'But Holly, what—' he began.

'Just do it.' She almost slammed the new receiver

back on its rest, and then, calmly, but with the same violence she kicked the offending package and watched it slide out of sight under the chest of drawers.

Two weeks later Holly, in a designer suit and an almost as expensive designer haircut, stood again in Otto's newly decorated salon nervously awaiting the hordes of socialites, international critics and buyers, and representatives of the world's media who had promised/threatened to attend. Many, unfortunately, were interested in more than the worth of the paintings. The painter, the subject and the subject's wife were all favourite topics of conjecture.

'How many years did the affair between artist and subject last?'

'All their lives.'

'Oh, how sad.'

'Oh, how sordid.'

'No, how stupid. What a waste.'

'His wife was in a loony bin, for God's sake. I think it's lovely.'

Holly sighed and looked round. Already there was barely room to move among the paintings, so great had been the interest. Several carried NFS stickers; they were not for sale and were the ones that she and Nicole had decided to keep. Nicole's cheque, her donation to the Tony Noble Foundation for artistically talented but disadvantaged children, seemed a heavy weight in Holly's ridiculous evening purse. What was a woman supposed to keep in such a tiny receptacle? She had a lipstick, a handkerchief and the cheque, and she could see the bulge of the lipstick.

There was a stir among the great and the good, in other words, the wealthy. Holly's stomach fluttered as she sensed the reason for that stirring. Taylor stood at the door, surely aware of his amazing looks, and the effect they were having on Otto's guests. So must his uncle have stood, allowing the masses to admire, while only the special few could get close enough to touch. Holly looked across and saw Nicole Fougère Hartman eye her son, a smile hovering around her mouth before she deliberately turned away to look again at her favourite painting.

Taylor took his time looking around and then pretended that he had just seen Holly. She was at the door of the office – he knew that that was where she would be, and was not at all surprised – and she stared back at him. What she thought of his sapphires, still lying under her furniture, she would never tell him – unless he asked. She would hold up her head and, what was the expression, 'tough it out'.

He did not ask.

Followed by his satellites, both male and female, he ploughed his way through the crowds towards her. 'Miss Noble,' he began politely, coldly as he reached her. Then he smiled thinly. 'I like the suit, and the new haircut. A new image?'

She ignored that. 'Why did you come?'

'My dear Miss Noble, I have every right to be here. Besides, have you been reading London's finest news-

444

papers?' The words seemed to spit themselves out from between the oddly smiling lips. 'You don't think they're done with us, do you? Believe it or not' – for a moment his eyes softened and his face relaxed – 'I am here to protect you, even though you have shown me that you don't give a damn what I do.'

She flushed. She was the one who had been paid in stones. What had she done to him but limp away from him, a moth with badly singed wings? 'The speculation was bound to be renewed; if you had only told me the truth.'

'I spent a great deal of money and an unbelievable amount of time hiding the truth that the scavengers wanted. I failed. My aunt's misery is fodder for gossip columnists. I will brave it out and watch you become rich and I truly hope that you are strong enough to bear discovering that money can't buy happiness.'

'I'm giving it away.'

He looked down at her and smiled, that smile that turned her very bones to thistledown.

'Well done, *ma mie*.'

He turned and was gone.

Holly stood, will-o'-the-wisp turned back to stone. *Ma mie*. It was, surely, a French endearment and she knew that she had heard it before. Not from Taylor. A few days ago she had been reflecting that his accent was so American but there was something, something in the way he had said *ma mie*. She was shaking from her confrontation with him and wished she was anywhere else. No, not anywhere. Torry Bay. The peace of Torry

Bay. She felt so tired and dissatisfied. She took a glass of champagne from a passing waiter and wandered off among the crowds and at last found a small space in front of *Shelter from the Storm*. She tried to turn away because the painting made her want to weep but there was a mass behind her and she was compelled to stay and overhear the remarks, some inane, some profound, some speculative, most flattering.

Then there was Nicole.

Holly had had some difficulty speaking to Taylor's mother. She definitely had lied or at least had not told the truth. She had known about Eleanor. When Holly had taxed her with deception she had said, as she had said once about Taylor, 'But, my dear, it was none of your business.'

The French. So practical.

'Sometimes I wish Tony had painted some smaller canvasses,' Holly said now, trying to smile. She put the glass down; she had no taste for champagne. She could not bear for Nicole to know that she was upset.

'You must buy an apartment with lots of wall space.'

Holly shook her head. 'No, I've decided to stay at Torry Bay for the foreseeable future and the walls are really too small for such work.'

'I saw that your Mr Robertson was elected to his local council. A rising politician might have wall space for good art.'

Too intimate, Nicole. 'He doesn't understand art.' Flippancy was as good an answer as any.

Nicole looked at her. 'What's that got to do with

marriage? For instance my husband loathed opera. "I love opera," he told me once when we were at the Met. "It's all the singing I can't stand," and Blaise Fougère was his brother-in-law. Bless him, he put earplugs in his ears and we stayed married happily for fifty years.'

'Nicole. Darling.'

'Amy, how nice. Miss Noble, have you met Amy Rosenthal?'

Holly had so far managed to avoid the celebrity journalist but knew from the gleam in her eyes that she would not get away easily.

'Miss Noble, how wonderful. I did see you chatting with darling Taylor but his body language said, "Not even you, Amy," so I waited.'

'There was no need. Mindless chatter, Miss Rosenthal, as is usual at parties like this.'

'Nicole, darling, you'll let me steal our little celebrity, won't you?'

'*Je vous en prie.*' Nicole smiled and slipped away.

Amy looked after her. 'There's something about the French language, don't you think. I could listen all day.' The eyes stopped smiling and all at once the predator appeared. 'Now, Holly, I want you to know whatever anyone else has offered, we will beat it.'

'The paintings are priced, Miss Rosenthal; no negotiation.'

'You deliberately misunderstand me. Taylor, why don't you go away for a while.'

Taylor, alone for once, had returned to Holly's side. 'Your wish is my command, Amy dear, but . . .

forgive me, I must take Holly with me. We have an interview with a Japanese station. How's your Japanese, Holly darling?' He smiled into her eyes as he tucked his hand into her arm. 'What are you thinking of?' he hissed as he propelled her through the crowd, which parted like the Dead Sea before the wrath of God. 'That woman could make mischief if she was locked in an empty room.'

'Mrs Hartman left me with her.'

He stopped in mid stride. 'Mother? Now what's her agenda?'

The next hour was a blur for Holly. She and Taylor smiled and posed for countless photographs and were asked innumerable questions in several languages. They answered the polite ones that were mainly about the discovery of the paintings and became adept at avoiding or deflecting those that probed too closely. Holly was grateful that Taylor made no attempt to deny the relationship that had existed between the artist and her subject.

'Miss Noble, when did you discover that there had been an affair between Blaise Fougère and Tony Noble?'

'All is speculation.'

'What documentation exists?'

Holly swept her hand around the vast room and said nothing.

'Mr Hartman, your aunt—'

'Has suffered enough in her life. Like Mr Fougère and Miss Noble she must be left in peace.'

'Since the evidence suggests a love affair, Miss

Noble, can you tell us why Tony and Blaise never married? Did they make a pact to wait until Mrs Hartman passed away?'

'They are dead and their tragedies and sorrows should be allowed to die with them,' Holly managed bravely while her fists curled, willing themselves to punch the journalist right between her beady little eyes.

'Is it true, Mr Hartman, that the Ridgeway family refused to countenance divorce?'

'That's it.' Taylor was still smiling but he seemed a full foot taller and Holly could feel the tension. 'My uncle loved my aunt until the day he died. No more questions, gentlemen, I'm sorry, and ladies. Go look at the paintings. They should be enjoyed as great works. The critics, the connoisseurs, are buying them up. See them while you can.'

He turned Holly around and pushed his way through the crowds into Otto's office. Nicole was there.

'Was that dreadful, darling?'

'You were clever to hide, Maman,' said Taylor, ignoring her question. 'Did you buy the ones I wanted, with your permission of course, Miss Noble?'

'*Clover* and *Dents de Lion, mon ange.* Is that permissible, Holly?'

'Of course.' Holly was exhausted. She wanted to leave, to steal away somewhere very quiet, like a wounded animal to lick her wounds. Her arm hurt from the grip of his fingers and she did not want to remember the last time he had grasped her firmly. 'When will this be over?'

'It has been over for some time; they have all sold.'

Holly, feeling both drained and exhilarated, looked at him. 'How do you know?'

Taylor pointed to the gallery. 'You can see red dots from here, of course, but my secretaries are there; I am informed.'

Holly sat back and closed her eyes. Tony Noble had arrived in the world where she had always belonged. 'The buyers, Taylor?'

'Just as you wanted,' he said flatly and without emotion. 'Galleries all over the world as well as to private collectors. You have made millions. That should make you happy.'

She ignored him.

He walked over and kissed his mother. 'Goodnight, Maman. I have a dinner engagement.'

He said nothing to Holly but walked out and they sat and watched his progress through the room, attendants running along to keep up.

'He works too hard,' said his mother.

'Coming to an opening night with several beautiful women hanging on his every word doesn't seem like hard work to me,' said Holly tartly and was immediately angry with herself.

Again that amazing laugh. 'Holly, be fair. Those girls are his secretaries and assistants. They like parties; they're working too.' She stood up. 'Will you dine with me?'

Holly shook her head. 'I have an unbearable headache, Madame.'

'Tension, my dear, but look at darling Otto. He's almost jumping up and down. We have a foundation too, you know, and all the money from the sales of Blaise's re-releases goes into it. I did tell you I authorised re-releases, didn't I? So sensible. Both our foundations have done well and, for you, the best thing, *ma belle*, Tony is acknowledged, *n'est-ce pas?*'

'I will wait to see what the papers have to say.'

Holly stood up, the world swam around her, and she knew no more.

28

---◆---

Torry Bay, 1978
RAINBOWS

'It is extraordinary, Tony, you have no education.'

She turned round and laughed at him and the breath caught in his throat at the love and laughter in her eyes. 'I know wot I likes,' she teased.

He determined not to smile. 'I am serious, Antoinette. Do they teach nothing in these English schools for girls? You can read and write, and you can paint, but that you did not learn at this St Agnes.'

'I learned to love beauty there. Rainbows for instance. I learned some poetry. "My heart leaps up when I behold a rainbow in the sky." And it does, Blaise. There were rainbows in the sky when I saw you walking down the hill that wonderful day, do you remember? Every time I see a rainbow now, my heart fills with joy. Just think, Blaise, all the flowers that wither are gathered up together to form rainbows.'

She was teasing him. He knew it, but his practical French soul would not allow him a way out. 'Wait a moment. I have to translate that.' He closed his eyes and thought for a moment, conscious that she was looking at him. He could feel the heat from her. Then he lifted his head, just as he did on the concert stage after he had managed to think himself into a role, so difficult, one minute Manrico, the next Nadir, and then Lohengrin. 'A rainbow is an . . . arc, an arch with prismatic colours in order, the seven colours, you know, and it is cause by the reflection and –' he hesitated; what was the word in English? – '*disperser* . . . the dispersion of the sun's rays in the drops of the falling rain.'

'Darling Blaise,' she said. 'How dull. I much prefer the withered roses theory and so we shall use that.'

He shook his head. 'It is not good to pretend to be without knowledge.'

She caught his hand and kissed the palm. 'How very French of you.'

He had to laugh. '*Bien sûr*, I am French.'

They had reached the top of the hill and the sea disported itself wantonly in front of them, rushing in wildly and then drawing itself shyly back.

'It's so beautiful.'

'*C'est vrai*,' he agreed, but he was not looking at the sea.

Much later they brushed the grass from their clothes and wandered back down the hill, hand in hand.

'Sometimes I think I am human only when I am with you,' he said.

'You are always human, my darling, but when you are with me you are not on guard.'

453

'You will still love me when I lose my voice?' The eternal ever-present fear of every singer.

'Even more, if that is possible.'

He cooked dinner while she painted. Months later when he saw the finished work and examined it closely he saw that the rainbow over his head was composed of tiny flowers.

29

---◆◆---

London, 1999. Torry Bay, 1999

When she came to she was lying on one of Otto's white sofas. It was so comfortable; she would stay there for ever. There was no sound. Holly sighed.

'Well, you did take centre stage for a moment there, *ma chérie*,' said a voice she vaguely remembered. She looked up, trying to get the face into focus. Nicole Hartman.

She sighed again and lay back. Then she remembered where she was. Oh, my God, the exhibition. She started up, but a firm cool hand held her down.

'Only Otto and the catering staff are left, and me, of course. How professional of you to wait until the party was almost over.'

She sat up. 'I don't know what came over me; the heat and the crowd, I suppose.'

Older, wiser eyes smiled gently into hers. 'I think you know very well what came over you, Holly. It is the whites of the eyes, *mon enfant*; one can always tell.'

Holly eased her legs onto the floor and sat up properly. 'It honestly never occurred to me. My age,

I suppose. When I did think . . . I was afraid to hope.'

'*Et maintenant*, like Tony, you will—'

Holly put out her hand to stop the words. 'Oh, no, I won't.'

'Dear child, I meant like Tony you will go back to Torry Bay to wait. *Pauvre* Otto, I shall let him in? He was quite terrified.'

Holly nodded and watched Nicole walk across the seemingly miles of white carpeting to the glass door.

When she returned Holly was on her feet tidying her hair. 'I'm so sorry, the heat and all those people.'

'My dear girl, you quite frightened me but Taylor was so good.'

She felt that telltale flush stealing up her neck. 'Taylor? But he was gone.'

'Luckily he had turned to say something to Chandler when you fell, Holly,' said Nicole in a deliberately matter-of-fact voice. 'Otto was literally wringing his hands and so Taylor reached you first, picked you up and put you on the sofa.'

Taylor had carried her in his arms. My God, did he know?

Nicole seemed to read her mind. 'He would have stayed, Holly, but I explained about stress and heat, and possibly alcohol on an empty stomach.'

She was light-headed again but with relief this time.

'I had planned a lovely celebration but perhaps a light meal and early to bed,' suggested Otto.

'You have been so kind, Otto, but I think I'll go back to my hotel.'

456

'But I insist you come with me, Holly.' It was Nicole.

Holly shook her head. Never, that she could not possibly bear. 'You are all so kind but I'm quite well now and so embarrassed. I have caused enough commotion. Otto, thank you again for all your hard work.' He would make a healthy commission but he had worked hard and had been shut down for such a long time. 'I can't talk any more tonight but tomorrow . . . I'll talk to everyone tomorrow.'

She had to get away; she had to be alone to digest this wonderful but rather terrifying news. She wanted to laugh, to cry, to jump, to sing and she could do none of these things while these pairs of caring eyes were looking at her.

'Very well,' said Nicole, taking charge. 'I shall drop you at your club, Holly, and you, Otto, perhaps you would dine with me? We have so much to talk about.'

Less than thirty minutes later, Holly was alone in her room. She had promised to meet Otto next morning to read the reviews in the papers but she had no intention of keeping her promise. He'll forgive me. She smiled to herself. And anyway, they'll be wonderful. We have done it, Tony. You are taking your rightful place in art history and there hasn't been too much damage done to anyone.

She put a hand gently on her stomach, frighteningly, breathlessly aware of the miracle. This isn't damage. At least I don't think it is, but I'll think better at Torry Bay.

She ordered the prescribed light meal from room

457

service, rang the desk to reserve all the recommended newspapers, bathed and got ready for bed. She felt wonderful. Now she understood the mood swings, the depression, the elation and the fatigue of the last few weeks.

'I should have remembered that I never refilled my prescription.' She smiled to herself. She would not think about Taylor tonight. She wanted to be alone communing with her unborn child. Will you be a singing baby or a painting baby? Both? Well, genes would have to do an awful lot of jumping. Neither? I don't care, little treasure, little gift from God. I don't care.

Next day she stuffed the newspapers into the front pocket of her weekend bag and took the train to Scotland. How different from her last journey when everything had been a dark mess. Even the sun echoed her happiness. When she reached Glasgow she got her car out of the long-term parking lot, stopped at the first supermarket and filled the car with healthy foods before driving north to Torry Bay. She bought the latest issue of the *Big Issue* magazine although she had bought the same one in London. She felt generous.

No car sat in her driveway but she had not expected one. There was no sense of disappointment, just security and overwhelming peace.

The ghostly voices drifted out on sunbeams to meet her, to welcome her home.

Darling girl. Hollyberry.

She would not look under the chest of drawers.

'Works of a master discovered, Tony. The papers are full of your ability to paint light, to paint emotion, to suggest with a flick of your paintbrush. *Uncle Fire* and *Flowers in the Stream* are coming back here. I've changed my mind about *Sea Sprite* and let Nicole have it, especially as she bought *Grief* to donate to a Scottish gallery. She also has *Refuge from the Storm* and Taylor has *Clover* and *Dents de Lion*. Boy, did he have to pay for them. A ghastly woman kept begging some Marvin to get the dandelions for her.'

Suddenly she laughed out loud. 'I'm talking to myself but I don't care. From now on I can blame my wonderful, magnificent condition.' She sat down abruptly. Her wonderful condition? Was it wonderful? She had always wanted a child – but not like this. She had wanted to create a family – but not like this.

The telephone disturbed her. Don't let it be Taylor. Let it be Taylor.

It was Otto. 'Do you know that Taylor did say that you had an odd habit of running away. We had a date, remember?'

'Forgive me, Otto. I saw the papers and the reviews were good so I came home to tell—'

'Say hello to them for me,' he said dryly. 'Holly, you mustn't lock yourself away up there. It's not healthy. Are you well this morning?'

'Never better.'

'And never richer. Even when I take off my modest expenses—'

She interrupted him. He would not cheat. 'It's all going to the foundation, Otto. You may be on the board.'

'Honoured, but how are you going to live?'

'Tony left me a substantial legacy, Otto, so much so that I need to see a financial adviser. Isn't that a scary thought? I'll ring you in a few days. Bye.'

She felt more at ease in the kitchen and was singing as she unpacked her groceries. '*Sur le pont d'Avignon, l'on y chante, l'on y danse . . .*' From what layer of memory had that song come? She remembered a beach, a tall man in a fur coat bowing to a little girl in a bikini . . .

'All children can sing, *ma mie*. Sing, Hollyberry.'

Ma mie. Of course. Nicole had told her. Blaise called Tony *ma mie* and Taylor . . . Why Taylor?

The light went out of the day. Taylor. She could not ignore him, could not ignore that he was the father of her unborn child. Did he have rights? Did the child have rights . . . to Taylor's love, to Nicole's? A family; but we're never going to be a family because he sent me sapphires to show me that he thinks no more of me than he does of a highly paid call-girl.

Darling girl.

'Oh, you don't understand. He sent me sapphires to pay me. I kicked them under the chest in the living room. God, how stupid and childish that sounds.'

She went into the living room, got down on her knees and peered under the chest. There it lay, an innocuous-looking little package.

'Damn, damn, double damn. I should have taken them to the exhibition and thrown them at him.'

She left the package where it was, got up off her knees, and went to sit down in the big chair by the window.

Did you look out from here and wonder about your baby, Tony? I'll keep mine. It's a different time. No one that I care about will be shocked. One or two might wonder what on earth possessed me and I know it won't be easy on my own even though I have enough money to live on.

The packet drew her as the North Pole draws magnets. She could not avoid having to deal with the sapphires any longer. I'll go up to the village, buy a padded envelope and send them back; no need to explain.

But to send them back she first had to fish them out from a dusty corner of her living room.

Why didn't he ask me about them?

She answered herself. It would have been cruel, ungentlemanly. Oh, don't be so wet, Holly Noble.

Hollyberry.

She retrieved the package, blew off the accumulated dust, and sat down again, looking at it, at the computer-generated label.

'Oh, Tony, why did I let myself love him?'

There was no answer. Of course there was no answer. She was alone, always alone.

She tore open the packet. Taylor had written a letter to accompany the gift. His writing was black and bold and very legible.

There was no excuse for the things I said. Forgive me but I hated you so much. I thought at last I had found someone . . . yes, maybe someone who would be like Tony, a woman who would love me unconditionally; who wasn't impressed by my money, and you threw it in my face. Then I went to Switzerland because Mother asked me to check all the original recordings in Blaise's bank vault. She's quite a businesswoman, my mother. She decided to make the publicity work for us. 'It's coming anyway,' she said, 'so milk it.'

We plan to re-release all of Blaise's recordings for the Fougère Mental Health Foundation. Blaise never recorded cross-overs although he could sing almost anything and so I was surprised to find this; he must have been working on it when he was killed. I admit it, Holly, and will no longer fight: Blaise loved Tony and these must have been letters to her. I send them to you. Please accept them, and with them – your Taylor.

The box did not contain sapphires. Inside was a compact disc. There was no company label. Instead there was a label bearing a few words: '*Pour ma mie.*'

Ma mie, my little crumb, *ma mie*, the breath in my body.

Holly sat looking down at the note and the box. Stand up, genius of the month. If she had not been so quick to judge she would have opened the packet, found the letter, realised why Taylor had lifted his court order, greeted him with a warm smile instead of coldness. No wonder he had at first been frosty.

Please, God, don't let it be too late.

But first, what was on the disc? Tony? Tony? Tony was in love with a tenor. There had to be some way of playing compact discs in this cottage. A cupboard under the stairs revealed a gramophone and boxes of records. *Tosca, Otello, Lohengrin, Carmen.* Oh, God, where is there a disc player? Tony had held technology at bay. She had conceded and put in electricity, but no telephone and she could never have understood disc players.

Will I have to drive all the way to Glasgow to buy one?

The car. She rushed out. Thank God for yet another miracle of modern science. She sat in the driver's seat, turned on the engine and inserted the disc. In a few moments the most flawless sound that Holly had ever heard enveloped her. The voice was at the same time beautiful and heroic, small in some passages and then robust and round in others. Everything was sung with exquisite style and outstanding musicianship and was of a highly individual timbre.

With tears running down her cheeks, as Holly listened to the great tenor sing love songs in faintly accented English, she could think of nothing but melting honey on hot buttery toast.

He sang songs from musicals and he sang folk songs. Had they ever been sung more beautifully?

From *Brigadoon* he sang 'Come to Me, Bend to Me'.

Who could have resisted?

There were others, some successful, others not quite so. It was as if he were playing, singing new things, snatches of this and that, a line here, a few words, occasionally a complete verse. The glorious voice sang accompanied at times only by a piano. At other times he sang *a capella* as if he were merely trying words out. They were, after all, in a foreign language.

'You would have loved it, Tony.'

With shaking hands Holly took the CD out of the car player and put it back into its box. Then she went back to the cottage. A peerless voice was singing . . . Holly smiled. Pregnancy does funny things. She sat down at the table and picked up the telephone receiver.

'Mr Hartman is in Paris, Miss Noble.'

Where was his home? Where would it be?

'Would you give Mr Hartman a message, please. Tell him I didn't open it; I thought it was sapphires.'

If his secretary's secretary was surprised she gave nothing away. She repeated the message carefully and Holly thanked her and hung up. Now there was nothing to do but to wait.

He came when she was sitting up at the point looking out to the bay where some swans floated serenely on the water.

She heard the car, turned and smiled. Taylor was having trouble levering his frame out of the salmon-pink mini car. Her heart swelled with happiness. It must have been the only car left at the airport. Only a man very much in love . . .

He managed eventually, turned and saw her.

'*La raison ne connaît pas.*' Even reason doesn't understand.

He began to run.

30

Connecticut 1990. Torry Bay, 1990

Blaise sat down beside the woman who had been his lawfully wedded wife for forty-three years, and who had been a wife to him, in every accepted sense of the word, for only three of those years. He felt deep sorrow and that overwhelming guilt. It had to have been his fault. He had never loved her as he had loved Tony but had she been with him, he would have been faithful. Even when apart from Tony for months he had resisted all temptation, and, of course, in the early days, there had been so many temptations.

'I'm tired, Eleanor. I'm almost seventy. I can't sing, not in the way I used to and you know that when I was singing I could be oblivious of all the problems in my life, all the worries, big and small. I could forget you and even Toinette. Sometimes I used to go almost mad with guilt about you and about her. Two women loved me and I ruined both their lives. I'm leaving, Eleanor. I want some peace and I know where to find it.'

His heart filled with an intense joy. 'Toinette, my darling Toinette.' She was his wife, except in the eyes of God, or was God kinder than man?

He decided not to contact her immediately. First he would take care of all the legal business in New York; he had not sung for years but there were so many teaching colleges, so many boards, and opera houses and he was leaving them all. His stomach churned and he felt like a boy on his first date, scared, full of anticipation. Fifty-two years. Over half a century of love and pain, sorrow and great joy, and soon, please God, if Tony agreed, he would be able to tell the world.

The milk boy brought a message. 'There's going to be a phone call – near to nine in the morning as he can get it.'

Tony as usual, rose early to meet the demands of the light but her heart was full as she hurried up to the village.

In the shop she sat quietly for a minute or two but at last the telephone rang.

'Hello.' His voice was dark with exhaustion.

'Blaise, why aren't you in bed at this time?'

Impatiently he brushed away the question. Fuss, fuss. '*Ma mie, ma mie*, will you marry me?'

'Marry you?'

'I looked in the mirror a few days ago and saw the world's greatest—'

'Tenor.'

'*Imbécile*, the ass,' he said and there was laughter in his voice but then he added desperately, 'I did all I could, Toinette, didn't I?'

'You've been wonderful, my darling.'

467

She knew that he was smiling.

'Tony, you haven't answered me.'

Tony sighed. What difference would a few words and a piece of paper matter at this stage in their lives? They could be together though; that was something. 'I have been your wife all my life.'

'Will you marry me? I am on my knees.'

She laughed. 'Like Lohengrin?' she asked. 'Eyes raised to heaven, sword clasped between your beautiful, beautiful hands?'

'*Bien sûr*,' he said, 'but I am, as they say, fresh out of swords.'

'I will marry you.'

She heard his sigh of relief.

'There is much to do here, the divorce and cutting all the ties, legal affairs, lawyers, wills, that kind of thing, and then, Toinette, we will marry before the eyes of God and man and we will never be apart again. I can't believe how stupid I have been. Forgive me, Toinette.'

'You have been the most decent man, Blaise.'

'For decency's sake I have wasted your life, and mine too. As soon as I sign the last damn piece of paper I am coming to you.'

'I shall watch for you sailing across the bay on the wings of your swan.'

He laughed. 'I am too old for swans,' he said, 'but not for love.'

Stefan died with him, of course, and so Tony read it in the papers like everyone else: BLAISE FOUGÈRE KILLED

IN AIR CRASH. 'Blaise Fougère, arguably the finest tenor of his generation, and certainly the greatest singer ever produced by France, was killed this morning when his private plane exploded on take-off . . .'

She did not need to read further. He had been coming to her and he was dead. There was nothing else to know.

'Except, perhaps, why can't I die too?'

He had never changed his London lawyers. She could contact them to see if it was possible to attend his funeral, but no. What was the point? He was dead and she could mourn him better here. She went up to the headland and sat watching Lohengrin. Surely he would sail away now, abandoning her as Blaise had abandoned her. It was final this time. There would be no loving letters, and no sudden visits. How would she bear it? There was Holly, of course, but she could not write to her, not yet, because Holly would know that all was not well and the time was not right to reveal her secret. She would reveal it though – after poor Eleanor . . . one day.

She began to make her preparations. She took Blaise's clothes and wrapped a few old favourites in garment bags and hung them in the wardrobe. Holly would recognise them in the paintings. She opened all the boxes of jewels. She hoped Holly would wear them. Jewels would suit the girl as they had never suited her aunt. She sat for hours remembering each occasion on which he had given her a gift.

'Don't say no, *ma mie*. You let me do so little for you.'

469

'I saw this in Winstons. It was made for you, Toinette. It called me as I passed the window.'

'Let me buy you a ring, Toinette. You have only my old signet ring.'

She had persuaded him to take the ring back to give his beloved nephew; of course she had wanted to keep it, but Taylor was like the son she had stolen from him and the ring should be his.

'I feel that you are my husband, Blaise. I no longer need a ring to prove it to myself or to the world. See, I will wear my rubies.'

He had laughed at her. Oh, his laugh. It was like life-giving water tumbling down from the burn behind the house.

'Rubies with jeans, *ma mie*. You have set the trend.'

Now Holly should wear them and enjoy them, not with that rather stuffy young lawyer she was dating, but that was not for her aunt to say. That was for Holly's heart to decide. Can I write, 'Never settle for second best, Holly', or is she sensible enough? Shall I write and explain my relationship? No, Holly will understand. She will have memories, buried by that worthy mother of hers, but they will surface and she will know he never ever meant to hurt me. Carefully and methodically, and very slowly, because the weight of a broken heart was dragging her down, Tony wrapped her jewels, and went upstairs to look at her paintings for the last time.

I cannot stand up in here, ma mie.

Had she known he would be there? She smiled at

him. 'I was wondering whether to write Holly a long letter.'

Your life's work is a long letter. My Hollyberry will understand, and she will make Taylor understand too.

'Can you stay?'

I will always be with you, ma mie, *while I wait as you waited.*